The New Camelot

Also by Robyn Schneider

The Other Merlin
The Future King

The New Camelot

ROBYN SCHNEIDER

VIKING

VIKING
An imprint of Penguin Random House LLC
1745 Broadway, New York, New York 10019

First published in the United States of America by Viking,
an imprint of Penguin Random House LLC, 2024

Copyright © 2024 by Robyn Schneider

Visit us online at PenguinRandomHouse.com.

Library of Congress Cataloging-in-Publication Data is available.

ISBN 9780593623015

1st Printing

Printed in the United States of America

LSCH

Design by Opal Roengchai
Text set in Garamond MT Std

For everyone who has loved and lost and kept going

—R. S.

The New Camelot

PROLOGUE

Morgana le Fay stood at the edge of the tallest turret, her dark hair whipping across her face in the icy wind. Below, the jagged cliffs were cloaked in darkness. And above, the full moon looked as frozen as she felt. Mountains and stars rose in the distance, and the best part was, she was queen of it all.

The view would have been spectacular, if not for one thing: she had no memory of how she'd gotten here.

Yet here she was, on the roof of Lothian Keep, wearing only her silk slippers and nightdress. She shivered, the soft sole of her slipper sliding on the icy ledge. Pebbles cascaded over the edge of the roof as she grabbed desperately for the nearest crenellation. Her heart pounded, and her legs kicked out into nothing as she held on to the frozen stone.

She wasn't going to die. Not here, like this. So she gripped the stone harder and began to draw herself back up onto the roof. One of her slippers dropped onto the cliff below. She bit back a curse.

Enjoying your stroll? a woman's voice crooned inside her head.

Bellicent. Of course.

"I should ask you the same thing," Morgana said through gritted teeth.

Slowly, painfully, she drew herself back up onto the roof. She refused to let Bellicent get the best of her. Although she suspected the sorceress already had. Her normally polished nails were torn, her knuckles scraped and bloody. Worst of all was her nightgown, streaked with grime.

I only wanted to see more of your world, Bellicent said, sounding hurt.

Beautiful and deadly things have always intrigued me. And this tower reeks of death.

So she was on the western tower. That's why the view was not one she recognized, and why the drop onto the cliffs was steeper. She never came to this part of the castle. Its empty rooms still stank of fire, their ceilings and floors streaked with soot from the accident that had claimed the lives of the former royal family.

Not that it had been an accident. Yurien had always been a man to take what he wanted, and he would never change.

Her teeth chattered as the frigid wind ripped through her thin linen nightdress. Her bare foot was numb, and her fingers were fast following suit. "*Calor,*" she commanded. Conjured warmth settled over her like a thick cloak, and she sighed with relief. That was much better.

"*Arcesso,*" she insisted, holding out her hand for her lost slipper. Yet the shoe did not come. She reached impatiently for her magic, but when she tried for a handful, she found only shreds. She yanked at them anyway, snarling out the spell once again.

It didn't work. She swayed dizzily and scrambled for something to hold on to.

Careful, Bellicent purred. *Your magic isn't what it used to be.*

Of course it wasn't. In her hurry to escape Bellicent's grasp, she had given back all the power she'd taken from the Isle of the Blessed. The magical isle had refused to let her go otherwise. She'd believed the sacrifice was worth it. That she was free.

Until she'd fallen from her horse at the castle gates, having curiously lost her grip on the reins, with Bellicent's voice in her head. The sorceress had followed her back from the Otherworld, coiled quietly in her mind, waiting to take control. Instead of a grand homecoming, the royal guards had found her in a daze, bleeding and filthy from weeks on the road.

Her courtiers now treated her like a madwoman. Like an invalid, instead of a queen. She had been gone for four months. Her husband, Yurien Vortigen, King of Lothia, Regent of Northumbria, and Lord of the North, had thought her dead.

She nearly *had* died in that frozen, cursed world. Her magic hadn't worked, and so she'd made a deal with the high sorceress of Anwen. A deal that had gone horribly wrong.

Below, in the castle forecourt, two guards marched past on patrol, and Morgana ducked down. She knew what they'd think if they saw her—that she was planning on hurling herself off the castle's gloomiest tower. A crowd would gather, like they did for the hangings, taking pleasure in witnessing her literal downfall. Already, rumors nipped viciously at her heels whenever she walked amongst what had once been her adoring court.

No, no one could know she was up here, just as no one could know of the hold Bellicent had over her, and how time sometimes slipped through her fingers like sand.

Bells rang out, marking the hour as nine o'clock. Across the courtyard, she could see the flickers of candlelight in the fogged windows of the fortress's southern wing, and smoke twisting from narrow chimneys in a futile attempt to warm the perpetually drafty castle.

It was peaceful. Cozy. A quiet night in the last days before war. For it was clear what her husband was planning. He chafed at the idea that Arthur, a boy of nineteen, could be considered the rightful heir to all of England. If anyone should be named the High King, it would be him.

Morgana had fallen in love with his ambition. She'd recognized the rage that steered him as a twin of her own. She couldn't remember the day when his bloodthirst had outpaced hers, just the slow realization that motherhood had tempered her taste for violence. War wasn't for sorceresses. It was for men with something to prove, who hungered to take what didn't belong to them at the tip of a blade.

She didn't crave war. Or to rule over strangers from kingdoms that weren't her own. She wanted revenge against King Uther, who had taken her mother for himself and thrown Morgana away, exiling her in a convent when she was just a child. She wanted power she could use for herself, magic that would sing through her veins with promise.

Carefully, she lowered herself down the side of the tower until she was standing on a narrow corbel. From here, she could almost reach the iron shutter bar of the tower window. Almost, but not quite. She was going to have to jump. She gathered her nerve, barely daring to breathe. For a terrible moment, she was holding on to nothing, and then her fingers closed around the cold iron bar and her toes scraped the window ledge.

She'd made it. She let out an incredulous laugh as she climbed through the window and back into the castle. She felt dizzy, and her stomach ached from emptiness as she descended the stone steps from the charred tower. She tried to remember eating, or getting ready for bed, but there was nothing. Just a curious blankness. Dimly, she could hear music and frivolity. She hoped that night's feast was still on the table.

In her rooms she threw on a billowing black dress and matching silk slippers, and went down to the Great Hall. When she stepped through the large doors, the entire court paused to stare, then started to whisper. She caught her reflection in a serving platter and winced at the wild tangle of her hair, the fresh scratches on her cheek, the crust of blood on her knuckles. Still, such things shouldn't matter. She was a sorceress. A queen.

Their queen.

So she held her head high, marching toward the table at the front of the hall where her husband sipped from a jeweled goblet as he surveyed his courtiers. The main course was picked over, platters of wild game sat cold and congealing, the best pieces taken. Still, she reached for a glistening drumstick and took a bite, dropping into the first vacated seat she could find, which happened to be across from her husband's mistress.

"Did no one think to save a plate of supper for me?" she said haughtily, knowing she hadn't been expected at all.

Her husband regarded her with annoyance. He lounged across an ornately carved seat that was more throne than chair, draped with soft furs. His current mistress, Lady Mara, sat at his side in the seat that should have been Morgana's. The girl couldn't have been more than nineteen, with her breasts on display, her lips painted red. She glared at Morgana, then turned to the king and whispered, "Darling, get rid of her."

Funny, since that was what Morgana wished her husband would do with his young, status-seeking prize.

"You should be in bed, my sweet," urged the king. "You're not well."

"I'm fine," Morgana snapped, reaching for a goblet of wine.

Are you? Bellicent's voice teased.

Morgana's hand felt heavy and clumsy, as though it wasn't her own. *No*, she thought as the cup tipped. A blood-red stain bloomed across the crisp table linen, and Morgana hissed in annoyance.

"My dress!" Lady Mara gasped, pushing back her chair. Wine was splattered across her skirts, and she glared at Morgana. Then her eyes lit with cunning. "But surely you'll buy me a new one," she purred, tracing a finger along the king's jaw.

"Whatever you wish, my love," he said, biting playfully at her finger.

Morgana rose to her feet, her fists clenched at her sides. How dare her husband carry on like this? In front of the entire court, no less. She'd always known that he strayed, but he was discreet, and he always returned to her bed. After all, she'd given him a son. He was hers.

But ever since she'd returned from Anwen, he had flaunted his affairs—dining and caressing the girls where the whole court could see.

And he hadn't visited her chambers once for his pleasure.

Belatedly, Morgana realized she was standing there, trancelike, staring at him and the girl.

"My queen, please. Let's get you back into bed," said a maid.

"We'll warm a water bottle for you. So you don't catch cold," said another, as though she was speaking to a feverish child.

She hated to be seen like this. Like someone to be pitied, instead of feared.

"I'll visit you in the morning," promised her husband.

No, he won't, Bellicent sang cruelly inside her head. *He's repulsed by you.*

"You mean he's repulsed by *you*," Morgana snarled.

"What was that, my queen?" one of the maids asked hesitantly.

Morgana realized she'd spoken aloud without thinking. "Nothing," she snapped.

In her head, Bellicent laughed. *There's no use resisting. Let go. You are mine.*

Not yet, Morgana replied.

She could feel Bellicent trying to push her down and lock her away deep within herself. But she knew all too well what it was to be made small and tossed away, and so she fought back with every ounce of strength she had.

She would not surrender.

Oh, but you will, Bellicent promised, her voice as soft as silk. *I'll wait.*

CHAPTER 1

Arthur Pendragon kept his head down and his hood up as he crossed the bustling market square. The mouthwatering scents of roasted chestnuts and meat pies filled the cold night air as a street busker sawed merrily at his fiddle. Crowds pressed in from all directions, eager to warm their hands with a mug of spiced cider, or to trade a coin for a prediction of their future.

In his plain wool cloak, scuffed boots, and leather jerkin, Arthur did not earn a second glance from anyone, which was exactly what he was going for. It was a chilly evening in late January, and that alone was enough of an excuse to bundle inside a hooded cloak.

When he'd traded his royal finery for more suitable garb and announced he was going out, his guards had sighed but had stood aside without protest. All except for Tristan, who had insisted on coming with him, for protection.

And, Arthur suspected, for a night out. His friends had left for the tavern directly after supper, and he'd promised to join them when he could. Which had taken longer than he'd hoped, since nearly half the court wanted a word with their king. Thankfully, some quick subterfuge was all it had taken to slip away. Well, that and an outright lie about a guest waiting in his chambers, which would have everyone speculating for days. But that was Future Arthur's problem.

Current Arthur's problem was Tristan, who'd promptly forgotten about their destination in favor of buying snacks from the market stalls. Arthur pressed back a sigh. They were late enough as it was.

"I never get leave on a market day," Tristan enthused, his mouth full. "Want some?" he asked, proffering a cone of spiced, roasted nuts. Arthur felt a stab of guilt for his impatience. He forgot sometimes that he wasn't the only one for whom the castle was both home and prison. He plucked up a roasted chestnut, popping it into his mouth.

Sard, it was good. Perhaps Tristan was onto something. Lightening his purse here would disguise his true destination. He'd learned that if he headed out with his friends after supper, any nobles who desired a word trailed them to the tavern. No doubt a few enterprising courtiers were already waiting at the Gilded Lion, which he was avoiding for that precise reason.

He drifted toward a bookseller's stall, sifting through the worn copies of romance and adventure stories until he found a few that looked interesting.

Tristan joined him, wiping crumbs from the front of his cloak. "Aren't there enough books in the castle library?"

"I've read all of those," Arthur deadpanned, and for a moment, the young guard believed him.

He picked up a thick novel, catching a glimpse of the book beneath it, entitled *Cornwall: A History*. He winced at the unexpected reminder of the last thing he wanted to think about. It had been two months since his disastrous wedding, or lack thereof, when the Duke of Cornwall had used the cover of the festivities to lay siege to the unsuspecting castle. The losses had been staggering. And it was only through Emry's quick thinking and imaginative magic that they hadn't been worse. Arthur still had nightmares of his father dying in his arms. Of picking up a sword and doing what King Uther couldn't—killing the Duke of Cornwall and putting an end to his deadly grab for the throne.

But with the duke out of the way, Arthur's worries focused constantly on an even bigger threat—King Yurien. The worry ate away at him as paperwork piled on his desk, and council meetings had him terrified that he would make the wrong call.

Not that his advisors afforded him the opportunity to make any decisions at all.

What was it Lord Agravaine had said just that afternoon? *No one expects you to run the kingdom straight out of the gate. Take your time.*

Still, two months felt like enough time that he should be doing more than signing preapproved legislation and doodling in the margins of his parchment during council meetings. Every time he tried to voice a concern to his council, they dismissed it, making it clear he didn't know what he was talking about. And he worried they were right. That he wasn't truly ready to lead the kingdom, and that, if he pushed, he'd only make things worse. So he fretted in silence, and when his friends asked, he pretended he had it all under control.

His friends! Sard, they were still waiting for him at the tavern. He paid for his books and hurried across London, Tristan rushing after him and grumbling about getting indigestion. When the spire of St. Paul's came into view, sticking up above the London rooftops at a slightly crooked angle, Arthur tried to push away the memory of how that had happened. He slipped down the alleyway that separated the churchyard from a tavern, passing the slab of stone that sat in the courtyard between them.

Almost two years ago, on a drunken night out, he'd pulled the sword from the stone. Back then, he'd been convinced that the people of Camelot wouldn't want him as their king. That, no matter what he did, he'd never be able to prove himself.

And he still worried that he wouldn't. Even though he'd recovered Excalibur, made an ally of the King of France, defeated the Duke of Cornwall in combat, and even signed a peace treaty with the King of Cameliard after narrowly avoiding marriage to his daughter, Guinevere.

Despite all these victories, he still felt like the unwanted spare who was never supposed to inherit a kingdom.

London had dozens of taverns far better than the Crooked Spire.

Yet Arthur found himself drawn to this one. In the dim light of the candles that dripped indiscriminately over table and patron from the iron chandelier, the whole place had a cozy glow. Better yet, the barkeep made sure no one bothered him, or his companions, and let them hold on to their weapons instead of leaving them by the door.

When Arthur entered, he spotted his friends playing cards at one of the round tables by the back staircase. Lance was talking animatedly, and Percival was beaming at him. Emry rolled her eyes and said something that twisted her mouth into a smirk.

Arthur's heart squeezed at the sight of her. She wore a black dress that laced up the front, her hair falling in dark waves to her shoulders. Black makeup was smudged around the corners of her eyes. She looked fierce and powerful and entirely magic, even just sitting there laughing.

When she spotted him, she grinned as though he was exactly the person she wanted to see most in the world. And something deep within him fluttered, feeling the same.

"Look who finally showed up," she teased.

"We weren't sure you'd make it," added Lance.

"Then you highly underestimate my ability to sneak around like a castle rat," said Arthur.

"Wait, are those books?" Emry gleefully pointed at the stack under his arm. "Did you bring books to a tavern in case we're poor company?"

Arthur bristled. "Of course not. I bought them on the way here."

"But if we're really boring, I bet he'll read one," Lance said, as though issuing a challenge.

Percival grinned. "Now, what's everyone's favorite type of door? I personally prefer wooden ones."

"The kind with bolts, or the kind with locks?" Lance inquired.

"I suppose it depends on the thickness of the door in question," Perce said thoughtfully. He turned toward Arthur, the picture of innocence. "What's your opinion?"

Arthur rolled his eyes. "You do realize I'm the ki—"

"Kind of person who prefers ones with enormous knockers?" Emry finished brightly as Tristan quietly had a coughing fit.

Arthur glanced toward the bar. "Shall I get the next round?"

"Obviously, since you were late," said Lance.

"Extremely late," Emry added.

"Lance drank your ale," said Percival.

"How was it my ale when I wasn't even here?" Arthur asked.

"It was in the least chipped mug," said Lance.

Fair enough. Arthur headed toward the bar, and when he returned to the table with extra mugs and the pitcher of ale, he slid into the booth next to Emry, leaving no space between them.

"We're in a tavern," he said, smiling, as his leg pressed against hers.

"We are," she replied solemnly.

"Which means no one will mind if I do this," he finished, tilting her face toward his for a kiss that would've made courtiers whisper with envy or disapproval, if only they were there to see. But they weren't. It was only his friends, and Emry, wonderful Emry, whose fingers slid through his hair and whose sigh as their lips brushed made his trousers feel unbearably tight.

He had only meant to kiss her hello, but somehow, he was kissing her far more deeply. He didn't want to stop. Except he knew they had to.

When they pulled apart, Lance's head was resting on Perce's shoulder, and they were both grinning shamelessly.

"Don't mind us," said Perce. "Just pretend we're on a completely separate date."

"Oh." Tristan's cheek turned pink. "I, uh, didn't realize I was crashing a double date. I could wait outside? Keep watch in case anyone unsavory tries to come in?"

"Don't be ridiculous," said Emry. "Everyone trying to come in here is unsavory."

Arthur snorted. She wasn't wrong.

"Stay," Lance insisted. "There's plenty of room. And ale."

"If you insist." Tristan eagerly reached for a mug and swallowed deeply.

"Are you drinking on duty, in front of your guard captain?" Percival asked sternly as Tristan paled in horror.

Perce's frown cracked into a grin as he said, "You should have seen your face."

"It's not funny," Tristan complained while everyone laughed.

This, Arthur thought, was what he'd been terrified he'd lose by gaining a kingdom. Casual nights out with his friends, who were his chosen family. Flirting with his wizard, who was just as likely to make fun of him as she was to make out with him.

He was slowly starting to move past the enormous fog of grief that had enshrouded him since his father's death. Some days were better than others. But no day went by without a dozen painful reminders of what he had lost, and what he had now become.

And he worried that, as king, he was accomplishing nothing of consequence. He knew what his advisors saw: a nineteen-year-old boy who had no idea what he was doing. And they weren't wrong. But he could learn. He would learn. He was going to get this right, because he owed it to Camelot.

But tonight, he owed his friends his company. So he bought the next pitcher of ale, and laughed at their antics, and grumbled as Emry beat them all at cards and swore she wasn't cheating.

When the hour grew late, they stumbled out into the cool night air, their breath clouding in front of them. Arthur reached for Emry's hand, pleased that she let him take it. But then, they weren't at court. Here, on the streets of London, no one watched and gossiped about what he did. Here, they weren't a king and his court wizard. They were simply a girl and a boy holding hands.

A couple of tentative snowflakes drifted down, dusting the shoulders of their cloaks. Candlelight glowed in the passing windows, and even though it was the bleakest, darkest month of the year, for a moment it didn't seem that way.

Emry pressed a kiss against the side of his neck. "We should do this more often."

"What, pretend you weren't cheating at cards?" Arthur teased.

"I wasn't, I just know all your tells," she protested. And then she bit her lip, as if debating whether to say the next part. "I meant spending time together."

"Away from the castle," Arthur finished, knowing she'd left that bit unsaid. And he hated how hard it was to feel normal. How much effort it had taken just to have this one night, this barely-even-a-date.

"If you're not sick of me yet, wizard, you could always come back to my apartments," he offered.

Emry wrinkled her nose. "Better idea, you could come to mine. I hate Lucan barging in on us."

"He promised to knock," Arthur said.

"Knocking isn't the same as leaving us alone. It's just barging in politely," Emry argued.

Lance, who was walking behind them with Perce, snickered.

"Something amusing, squire?" Arthur asked.

"You never knock," Lance accused. "I bet you could describe the birthmark on Perce's butt in detail."

"He doesn't have a birthmark on his butt," Arthur said before he could think better of it.

"Which you know how?" Lance crowed.

Emry laughed. Perce looked furious. Tristan looked as though he wanted to sink into the ground and disappear.

They crossed the empty square where the market had been set up earlier, and Arthur noticed a man outside the castle gates making a fuss.

One of the guards was blocking the man's passage with his halberd. Arthur reached for his own blade, then hesitated. The man didn't seem dangerous so much as indignant. He wore a shabby cloak that was far too thin for the chilly weather, and he carried a traveler's pack over one shoulder.

"Like I told ya, the kitchens stopped handing out leftovers hours ago," Morian said, brandishing his halberd. "Go home, if you have one. At the very least, go have yourself a bath."

"I am no vagrant!" the man retorted imperiously. "And I certainly have no desire for kitchen scraps. If you cannot inform the king that I wish an audience, then have someone fetch the court wizard. Immediately."

"Right," said Morian with a nasty sneer. "I'll just go an' do that." He didn't move.

"You mock me," the man accused.

"With pleasure," Morian returned.

"You'll regret that," the man said, plunging a hand into the folds of his cloak as though to draw a weapon.

"What's going on here?" Arthur called in his most royal tone, striding forward.

"I've got it under control, sir," Morian promised.

Somehow, Arthur doubted that. And then he got a better look at their visitor and went still.

The man was in his forties, with shoulder-length hair just starting to go gray at the temples, a pointed beard, and an unmistakably familiar face.

"It can't be," Arthur muttered.

Emry stepped forward, her voice wavering. *"Father?"*

CHAPTER 2

E mry stared at the weary traveler in disbelief. It couldn't truly be him. Not after all this time. It was impossible.

Yet there her father stood. It was no trick, and no illusion. And she wasn't prepared for it.

He frowned at her. "Emry?"

She nodded, blinking back tears, and flung herself into his arms.

He stank of horses and clothes worn too long on the road, but when he wrapped her in his arms, his hug was warm and familiar, like rediscovering something precious she'd given up for lost. Like a memory coming to life in front of her.

"I don't believe it," she said as they broke apart.

"Neither do I. You're all grown up," said Merlin, taking her in. "You have your mother's smile."

"And my father's magic," she said proudly.

"You're still interested in that?"

"In magic?" Emry frowned. "As opposed to what? Hair ribbons?"

"Finding a husband? Unless you're already married to one of these strapping young gentlemen?" He looked hopefully at the quartet of boys with whom she had returned to the castle.

"Definitely not," she said, hoping Lance wouldn't be tempted to joke that they had five children together.

"Well, Master Merlin," Arthur said crisply, stepping forward. "You must have had a long journey. Why don't you come inside?"

"I was attempting to do so, yet these guards refused to let me pass."

"I can assure you, they won't make that mistake again," Arthur said with the unshakable confidence of a royal who expected the world to rearrange itself at his command.

Morian bowed and stepped aside, with a mumbled "Yes, Your Highness."

"My word," Merlin said, staring at Arthur in astonishment. "Surely you can't be the same Arthur Pendragon who used to hide from his fencing master under the library tables?"

Emry bit her lip to keep from laughing.

"The very same," Arthur said wryly. "You must remember Lance?"

Lance gave an awkward wave, in the process of sheathing his sword. "Long time. Er, well, goodnight." He hurried past them, dragging Percival with him, who was clearly bursting with questions.

So was Emry. Her father was *here*. And it was truly him, not some apparition designed to lure her into a trap, like the one Morgana had conjured all those months ago. She couldn't stop staring at him as Arthur guided him into the castle and asked a maid to ready a chamber for their unexpected guest. There were so many things to say that she didn't know where to begin.

And it was clear her father didn't, either. They stood in awkward silence in the castle's entrance hall, Merlin fiddling with his pack, Emry wishing she'd had fewer glasses of ale.

The castle was far less crowded than it was during the day, but the staff's and residents' footsteps still echoed through the stone corridors. Torches burned low, flickering off the polished suits of armor. The same suits that Emry had mobilized to defend the castle from the duke's attack. She couldn't wait to tell her father of the magic she'd used to bring them to life. He was going to be so proud.

"I'm having some food brought up to my chambers," Arthur said. "I hope you'll join me."

"A kind offer, lad," Merlin said. His stomach let out a hollow growl, and he laughed, not at all embarrassed. "I confess, I did travel through supper to reach the city before the gates closed." He turned to Emry. "Why don't you fetch a strong pot of tea along with those refreshments?"

Emry spluttered. Surely she wasn't meant to fetch the food from the kitchens?

"I—" she began.

"Will be joining us, of course," Arthur said, pushing open a door hidden cleverly in the castle's wooden paneling with an apologetic half smile. "This way, please. Unfortunately, the subterfuge is necessary."

It was for his benefit as much as theirs, Emry realized, taking in Arthur's plain wool cloak and rough-spun tunic. When he didn't unsheathe Excalibur to light the way, Emry pulled her own wand from her sleeve. "φως," she muttered, illuminating the tip so they didn't trip over their own feet.

"Most impressive!" her father enthused, as though she'd performed some complicated magic, instead of a simple spell she'd mastered as a child.

Finally, Arthur pressed a piece of paneling, and a hidden door swung open, depositing them in his apartments. He'd staunchly refused to move into the king's bedchambers, and had remained in his own. He'd claimed the south-facing windows had better light for his plants, but Emry suspected that wasn't the real reason. She didn't blame him for wanting one less thing to change.

Except now, staring at her father, she felt like nothing would be the same again.

"I wasn't expecting company," Arthur said sheepishly, sweeping an armload of scrolls from the dining table, and attempting to move them to his already overflowing desk.

Not expecting company, Emry thought, rolling her eyes. He'd only begged her to come back to his apartments. But she didn't blame him for trying to be a good host for her father.

Merlin glanced around curiously before taking a seat, making no comment at the window ledge that was crammed with potted specimens, or the towers of books upon nearly every surface, including the floor.

Emry waved a discreet hand at the fireplace, which was burning low. The flames roared to life, and Merlin jumped.

"Much better," Arthur said, still relocating his paperwork.

Emry did the candles next with a flick of her finger.

Her father frowned. "I could have gotten those."

"It's no trouble," Emry said, sitting across from him. As she did, she gasped, for in the bright candlelight, now she could see what she hadn't been able to before.

"You haven't aged," she said in disbelief.

He looked as she remembered, without a wrinkle more.

"Time has moved differently for me," he said carefully. "It feels as if I've only been away a few months."

"It's been *nine years*," Emry said, her voice breaking. She blinked back tears as she confessed, "Everyone said you were dead. *I* thought you were dead."

Her father scoffed. "Preposterous. I'm the greatest wizard Camelot has ever known."

There was a knock at the door, and then a scuffle on the other side, with Tristan insisting, "I've got it, Mary. They're not to be disturbed."

"You're no fun, Tris, all I want's a peek," a girl complained.

The young guard barged in with a bottle of wine, three glasses, and a platter of bread, meat, and cheese.

A maid in the corridor giggled, trying to peer inside as Tristan slammed the door in her face.

"Gossiping kitchen maids," he muttered, setting the refreshments down and returning to his post. "Don' know what they expect's happening in here that's so interestin'."

"Sard." Arthur groaned, an embarrassed flush rising to his cheeks. "I—er . . . I claimed I had company in my chambers earlier, so I could slip away."

Emry bit back a laugh. "And now you've requested three wineglasses? No wonder the girl was desperate to see."

"Emry!" her father accused, shocked.

"No, she's right." Arthur sighed ruefully, running a hand through his already tousled hair.

Merlin hungrily snatched up a piece of cheese and bit into it with relish. "Not that I don't appreciate the hospitality, kids," he said, swallowing thickly, "but I really do need to speak with the king or the court wizard as a matter of some urgency."

"Yes, I remember," said Arthur, pouring the wine. "Would you prefer to speak with us together, or separately?"

Merlin frowned and reached for the goblet, drinking deeply. "Separately, of course. Surely your father doesn't summon you to his side for every matter."

"I would think not," Arthur said, taking a careful sip of wine, "seeing as how he passed away some months back."

Merlin looked horrified. "Uther's dead? What happened?"

"A duel with the Duke of Cornwall, about two months ago," Arthur said, his lips going thin, the way they always did when Emry knew he was trying to keep his emotions at bay. "Neither survived."

"And you—" Merlin began.

"I'm his only heir," Arthur confirmed.

Merlin pushed back his chair and sank into a bow at Arthur's side. "Forgive me, I didn't realize I had the honor of visiting with the king.

Your father was a great man, and a great leader. As I know you will be."

Emry had never seen her father behave so formally. It was strange to watch his posture change to one of such deference. Especially to the boy whose bedchambers she'd been sleeping in.

"Thank you, but flattery isn't necessary," said Arthur, gesturing for her father to return to his seat.

"In fact, it's strongly discouraged," Emry added helpfully.

"Emry," her father growled in warning, his voice low, "you're in the presence of the *king*."

"That does tend to happen, since I'm his court wizard," she said, lifting her chin.

Her father gave an incredulous laugh. "Surely not. What's happened to Master Ambrosius?"

"He died in the duke's attack," Emry said quietly, thinking of how her wise, old mentor had sacrificed himself so the wedding guests could get to safety.

Merlin's expression rang with alarm. "And where is my son?"

"Oh, Emmett's fine," Emry assured him. "He's made a charming mess of things, per usual. He's off on his honeymoon."

"Married?" Her father frowned. "At only . . ." He paused, doing the math. "Eighteen?"

"You know Emmett," Emry said sweetly. "Always getting into trouble. Congratulations, by the way, you're going to be a grandfather."

Merlin choked. "Arthur's the king, you're the court wizard, and my son's knocked up some girl and taken her as wife?"

"Exactly," Emry said, glad he understood the general gist of things.

"Although I'd hardly call Guinevere some girl," Arthur put in. "She's the Princess of Cameliard."

Merlin looked impressed. "My son seduced a princess?"

"The seduction was mutual," Emry said. "The two of them weren't at all discreet."

Arthur gave her a meaningful stare, and Emry silently added, *Like us.*

Merlin reached for another piece of cheese, and Arthur said, in his best conversational tone, "Why don't you tell us how you got free of that enchanted cave in Anwen?"

Merlin spluttered, dropping the rind of cheese. "How do you—"

"Long story," Emry interrupted. "Yours first."

Arthur slanted her an approving look. "I couldn't have said it better myself, wizard."

Merlin looked between the two of them, and Emry wondered just how discreet they were being after all. "Hmm" was all he said.

And then he explained how he had gone to Anwen. How he had trapped Bellicent in a mutual sleep. And how, when he woke up, Bellicent's body was gone.

"Gone?" Emry repeated, alarmed. She could feel Arthur tense at her side.

"There's no reason to worry about Bellicent," Merlin promised. "She's still in Anwen. And she has no way to travel through the stones."

Arthur's posture relaxed, and Emry felt relief flood through her. Everything would be fine so long as Bellicent hadn't found a way into their world.

"Wait," Emry said, realizing. "How did you wake up? Weren't you in an enchanted sleep?"

"Well," he said sheepishly. "Fortunately, an old pupil of mine had come to rescue me."

Emry gave Arthur a horrified look and saw that his expression mirrored her own. *Surely not.* She was just about to ask when her father boasted, "But unfortunately her magic didn't work in the Otherworld, so I ended up rescuing *her.*"

No! This was a disaster. Perhaps, Emry thought hopefully, her father meant something different by *rescuing.*

"Morgana came back with you?" Arthur pressed. "When?"

"A few weeks ago," said Merlin, and then he frowned. "That's strange, I don't believe I mentioned her name."

"That would be the long story I mentioned earlier," said Emry, refilling her father's glass of wine. "Now, where to begin?"

CHAPTER 3

"My father sent me to Camelot to marry the crown prince," said Princess Guinevere as the young priestesses leaned forward, eager to hear the story. "But then I met the handsome apprentice court wizard."

The girls sighed. In the weeks that she'd been on Avalon, Guin had told this story many times before, but the girls always begged to hear it again. And Guin couldn't resist an audience.

She made changes each time, refining and adjusting based on the girls' reactions. She was planning how she would write it down, since penning romances was what she hoped to do now that she no longer had to become queen.

"Was it love at first sight?" asked one of the girls.

"It was." Guin smiled indulgently, smoothing a hand over the bodice of her dress, which swelled over her now unmistakable baby bump. "The prince and I were just friends, and we didn't wish to marry. But our fathers wouldn't hear otherwise, so we devised a secret plan. We'd turn each other down at the altar."

The girls gasped.

"Except something unexpected happened, which made that plan impossible," Guin went on. A few of the older girls smiled knowingly.

"What did you do?" one of the younger girls asked, her weaving forgotten in her lap.

Guinevere thought guiltily about how she'd tried to seduce Arthur and convince him the baby was his, but how she hadn't been able to go through with it and had confessed the truth.

That part she'd skip in this telling.

"The handsome apprentice court wizard came up with a new plan," she said. "The prince and I couldn't get married if I was *already* married. So we arranged to run away together the day before the royal wedding."

The girls gasped, their attention rapt. "Did you?" they asked, even though they already knew the answer.

"We did," Guin confirmed.

"And then you lived happily ever after," one of the girls called dreamily.

That's how she wished she could write it. But it wasn't the truth.

"And then we came here," she said.

"To stay forever?" one of the youngest girls asked with a hopeful expression. She couldn't have been older than six, and she worshipped Guinevere.

"To stay for a while," Guin amended.

At that moment, Emmett stuck his head through the doorway, carrying a steaming mug. "I brought your tea," he said.

Guinevere pressed back a sigh. She hated that tea. It tasted like dirt and left a gritty feeling in her mouth. Yet Emmett kept bringing it to her because it was supposed to be good for the baby. She'd asked him to stop, but he wouldn't listen.

Just as he ignored her requests to stop clutching her arm whenever she descended a flight of stairs, or to quit asking if she was dressed warmly enough. He urged her to be careful all the time, and she couldn't stand it.

They were supposed to be on their honeymoon. She wanted passion. Romance. The boy with the pirate's grin who had led her into the hedge maze and trailed kisses down her neck until she went weak in the knees. Instead, he treated her like she was made of glass, and he was terrified she would shatter.

Guinevere made her excuses to the girls and dragged her husband into the hallway.

"After you finish your tea, we should take a walk along the shore," Emmett said. "The Lady of the Lake said fresh air is good for the baby."

"Emmett," she warned.

"What's wrong? Is it the baby?" he asked nervously.

"It's *you*," Guin said, her temper flaring. "All you do is fret and hover!"

Emmett frowned. "I do?"

How could he not see it?

"Oh my god, yes!" Guin snapped. "You're completely smothering me!" It came out harsh, perhaps harsher than she'd meant, and Emmett flinched.

"I—um—sorry," he mumbled, dejected. "I guess I'll see you at supper."

Guin watched him go, both relieved that she'd finally said something and horrified at how it had gone.

She'd thought coming here would be different. She'd imagined an adventure to a magical island full of sorceresses, where they could sneak off into the woods and, well, have a honeymoon. Instead, she was stuck at a convent full of unwanted daughters, telling the same stories to the same audience, drinking the same terrible tea, and having the same fight with her husband.

She thought wistfully of her wedding night, when Emmett had merrily cheated at cards at the tavern with his friends, and Guin had played darts with Marion, a crown of flowers in her hair, and everyone had danced to fiddle music and been merry and young and carefree.

That was the life she wanted. Not this one.

Emmett threw open the doors of the cloister's library, his cheeks burning with embarrassment. He couldn't do anything right. Not back home, not at court, and certainly not here.

He'd only been trying to help. He hadn't meant to make Guin so angry, which couldn't be good for the baby. The last thing he wanted was to lose either one of them. His mother had died in childbirth, and he was terrified the same thing would happen to Guin.

She was the best thing that had ever happened to him, and he knew she couldn't say the same. Sure, the village girls had blushed at his flirtations, but he was nothing to a princess. His father was the legend, and his sister was the hero, and he was . . . the clingy husband. He'd thought Guin would appreciate being looked after. That he was demonstrating his commitment to her and the baby, and proving that he wanted this. Which he did.

You're completely smothering me!

He cringed as the accusation echoed in his head, taunting him. He needed something to concentrate on. Unfortunately, there was nothing to do on this island except practice magic, help out around the convent, and try not to get creeped out by the screaming forest.

For once, a book seemed like his best option. The library was thankfully empty, although unlike at Castle Camelot, it was dusty with disuse.

Emmett poked around miserably for a few minutes before finding his way to the magic section. Maybe he could find some interesting spells here, like the combat one he'd gotten from a book back at the castle.

That was strange. The magic section, unlike the rest of the library, was clear of cobwebs and dust. A few volumes stuck out, as though they'd been returned to the shelf in a hurry. He reached for those, since someone else had clearly found them interesting, tucking the books under his arm and taking them over to one of the overstuffed and underdusted chairs.

The first book was bound in emerald-green leather, with a bumpy texture he'd never felt before. He couldn't stop running his fingers over it. It was almost warm to the touch. And then he noticed the slips of parchment poking out the side of the folio, and his mouth went dry.

His father was the only one who had ever bookmarked the sides rather than the tops of what he was reading. But that didn't mean anything. Perhaps lots of wizards used the same system.

Still, his hands shook as he opened the book to the first slip of parchment and stared down in disbelief at his father's familiar handwriting scrawled in the margin.

Cost v benefit unclear, his father had written, about a long, dense description of some tonic. Emmett could feel the letters rearranging themselves on the page, and his concentration sliding away.

The next tab held a note of his father's as well. And then Emmett realized what was wrong. All these books that had been recently removed from the shelf were filled with the same crabbed, back-slanted writing. Except the ink and the parchment slips looked fresh, as if his father had pored over these books last week, and not ten years ago.

Had his father been here recently?

And if he had, why hadn't the Lady of the Lake mentioned it?

CHAPTER 4

E mry spun in the cool darkness of the castle dungeons, practicing her magic. She'd formed a habit of coming down here in the morning before opening up the wizard's workshop.

When Gorlais's men had laid siege from inside the castle disguised as servants and guards, she hadn't been prepared. And she wouldn't let that happen again.

But now her father was back, and he could teach her everything she'd dreamed of. After all, he was the most powerful wizard who had ever lived. And she was the new court wizard, carrying on the family legacy.

ἐκρηξη, she thought, sending a blast of power smashing into the far wall. She did it again and again, until she was casting the spell with her eyes closed, and hitting the same mark every time.

She needed a bigger challenge. She looked around, spotting the training equipment that belonged to the Knights of the Round Table. That particular boys' club hadn't met for a while, so she doubted they'd miss a few blades.

"*Fleoges,*" she demanded, sending two broadswords sailing from the pile. The blades floated in midair, awaiting her next command.

"*Pugnare,*" she told them. The more ornate sword swung at the plainer one, which parried neatly and then feinted to the right, before making its attack.

Clang! The two blades clashed together, flying up and down the length of the dungeon, and Emry laughed, delighted at the floating sword fight. It was even better than animated suits of armor.

"That's amazing," a voice said admiringly from the doorway.

Arthur stood there, dressed in his sportswear. He was tousle-haired and red-cheeked, and Emry grinned at the sight of his bare forearms and form-fitting trousers. He looked like his old self, like the boy who'd insisted on being her lab partner in the wizard's workshop and tormenting her in the library.

"Excalibur's welcome to join the fray," Emry offered.

"That would hardly be a fair fight," Arthur replied, grinning.

Up close, Emry could see the exhaustion in his face, the dark smudges beneath his eyes despite his cheer. Because he wasn't the boy from the library anymore. He was the king, and she knew how much pressure he was under. Even though he kept pretending like he wasn't. And she wished he'd just admit to it, so she didn't have to pretend, too.

"Figured I'd find you down here smashing up the castle dungeon," Arthur said.

"If I ruin it, I'll fix it," she promised.

"If you ruin it, I'll be impressed."

"Don't tempt me," Emry warned.

"Shut up, wizard, you want me to tempt you." Arthur's smile turned wicked. He slouched back against the wall, his eyes never leaving hers.

They were all alone down here. And judging from Arthur's expression, he knew it, too.

Somehow, she lost her concentration on the swords. They clattered loudly to the ground. "Sard," she swore. "That was your fault."

"What can I say? I'm very distracting." Arthur grinned. "Resume your practicing, wizard. I'm just here to watch."

Emry scowled and raised the swords back into the air with a flick of her wrist.

"Go on, do your worst," she told them. The swords obeyed, swooping and clashing as they sailed across the dungeon.

"Can they fight actual assailants, do you think?"

"That's the plan, eventually," she said.

"Your father will be impressed."

"First time for everything," Emry said, trying not to get her hopes up. He hadn't seemed particularly pleased when he'd found out she was the court wizard. He'd seemed . . . taken aback.

"How could he not be impressed by you?" Arthur said.

Emry waited for the barb, but none came. "Oh," she said. "You actually meant that."

"Course I did," said Arthur. "You're frustrating and arrogant and reckless, and you've blasted literal holes into my castle, but you're the most impressive person I know."

"That sounded suspiciously like a compliment," Emry said, frowning. "Is there a new form of sarcasm popular at court that I don't know about?"

Arthur's shoulders shook as he held back a laugh. And then he winced in pain, clasping a hand to his side.

"I knew it!" Emry crowed. "I knew you didn't come all the way down here just to tell me how amazing I am. Show me."

"It's hardly anything," Arthur protested.

"You said that once about a stab wound," Emry reminded him.

"So did you," Arthur accused. He tugged his shirt from the waistband of his trousers, and Emry swallowed, feeling her heart speed up as he came toward her, lifting his shirt over his head.

Sure enough, a large bruise darkened his left side.

"Please tell me you weren't walking and reading at the same time again," Emry teased, examining it.

"I still maintain someone moved that suit of armor into my path," Arthur said. "Actually, I was training in the armory with Lance. I didn't want him to know how well he landed a hit." Emry prodded the bruise, and Arthur winced in pain.

"He landed a hit against *Excalibur*?" she asked, shocked. She knew Lance was a talented swordsman, but that was next level.

"I wasn't exactly paying attention. I had a lot on my mind," Arthur defended.

Emry knew what he meant. Even after her father had been settled in a guest room, she'd lain awake in her own room for hours, staring up at the ceiling, her thoughts racing with the unexpected turn the night had taken, and everything they had learned.

"We knew Morgana might return," Emry pointed out. She thought of Bellicent, who was thankfully still in the Otherworld.

"And now that she has, and is possibly armed with enchantments and magic from the Otherworld, it's only a matter of time before King Yurien starts a war," Arthur reminded her. "He has an army. He has an enchantment that defeats death. And he's made no secret that he intends to seize Camelot for himself."

"That won't happen," Emry insisted. "You're the one true king of all England. You have Excalibur. And you have me."

Emry pressed her hand over his wound and thought, *Angsumnes.* The spell came as easily as it ever had, flowing from her hand with a surprising warmth. Arthur's injury disappeared beneath her hand, and he sighed with relief. Emry didn't stumble or feel dizzy from using such advanced magic. Sure, her heart was racing, but that wasn't because of the spell.

"Better?" she asked.

"Much," Arthur said, pressing his hand over her own. His gaze dropped to her lips.

It was probably undignified to make out with the King of Camelot in the castle dungeons, but Emry didn't care.

◑ ◑ ◑

Arthur hurried down the corridor, late to that morning's council meeting. The lateness was his fault for losing track of time in the dungeon, but it was worth it.

Very worth it.

When he threw open the double doors to the circular chamber, every head swiveled in his direction. A page, who was no doubt supposed to announce him, stood frozen in place against the wall.

Arthur steeled himself against the scrutiny. "Good morning," he said, taking a seat at the head of the table. "Let's get started."

"We already have," said Lord Agravaine.

He wasn't that late. Yet as Arthur took in the stacks of parchment upon the table and the paragraphs of notes Sir Bors had already penned, he suspected his advisors had purposely plowed through as much as they could without him. He sighed.

You're the king, he reminded himself. *Act like it.*

"Next time I'm delayed, I expect you to wait," he said. "Is that clear?"

Everyone looked visibly upset at his pronouncement. But they muttered their assent.

"Where are we, since we have already begun today's session?" he asked.

"The repairs to the eastern city gate have resumed, after some delays due to weather," Sir Bors read. "And General Timias has received an increase to the military budget."

"Not enough of an increase," complained the general, whom Arthur had been hoping was still away, overseeing the construction of the new Cornish training facilities. No such luck.

Arthur didn't particularly like the general, whom he'd known since he was a boy, and he knew the dislike was mutual. Timias preferred the sound of his own voice to the favor of his new king, and still acted as if Arthur was a schoolboy bothering the adults. The man was deep in his fifties, with thinning gray hair and watery blue eyes. He wore a gaudy waistcoat that strained to button over his sizable paunch and had a foul habit of mopping his brow with a handkerchief, then blowing his nose into it and examining the results.

"When it comes to military spending, there's no such thing as too much," the general insisted, tipping his chair back so the front legs tilted off the floor.

"This is not a tavern, Timias," Lord Agravaine hissed.

The general returned all four legs of his chair to the ground, unperturbed. "That fact is exceedingly obvious," he grumbled. "And very disappointing."

"We have weapons enough for a kingdom currently at peace," said Lord Agravaine, as if Cornwall had been their only threat.

"But if we were to go to war," Arthur said, trying to sound casual. He could feel every one of his advisors staring at him intensely. "Hypothetically speaking," he added hastily, "would we be prepared?"

His advisors burst out laughing, and Arthur felt his face turn red.

"Prepared for war!" Sir Ban repeated, amused.

"There's no such thing, lad," said the general, wagging a finger in Arthur's direction. "And if you say otherwise, you're a fool who tempts fate. But aye, should the horn of battle sound its call, we'll have weapons and men enough to wield them."

Arthur sighed with relief. That was good. He'd never gotten around to telling his council about Morgana and the portal to the Otherworld. At first, he'd kept the truth of it from his father, who wouldn't see reason. But after his father had died, and there had been so much to do, he'd never found the right moment. And now that it had been so long, he didn't know how to broach the subject.

Something that felt increasingly like a problem. Because now that Master Merlin was back . . . sard, he was going to have to tell them about Merlin, too. About all of it. Including the part where he'd almost died after sneaking out of the castle to face his half sister, Morgana.

You're the King of Camelot, he reminded himself. *Your advisors can't lock you in the castle to keep you safe.* Except he wasn't sure about that. They'd certainly made him feel as if he couldn't be seen with Emry. And had retained his father's seating arrangements in the Great Hall, forcing Arthur to dine between Lord Agravaine and Lord Howell, which was pure misery. With great effort, Arthur dragged his attention back to the meeting. It turned out they were once again discussing the festivities surrounding his upcoming coronation.

"We shall accept the Queen of the Isles's offer of her eldest daughter, Princess Fiona, as His Majesty's escort to the coronation," said Lord Agravaine.

Arthur sighed. "We'll do nothing of the sort. Please send my regrets, since I've already asked Miss Merlin."

The table of advisors radiated disapproval.

"I don't believe pursuing a public dalliance with your court wizard is wise," said Sir Bors.

Arthur grimaced. "I don't believe I have ever called it a dalliance. We're dating. Courting. Whatever. The point is, we're just doing what people our age do."

"As you should," said Sir Tor, with a merry wink.

"I disagree," said Lord Howell, shooting the cheerful knight a withering glare. "A king's duty is to take a politically strategic wife who will bear him heirs. Of course, after an heir is secure, there's no harm in sampling the court's offerings."

Arthur grimaced at that unappetizing description of infidelity. "The subject of my marriage exhausts me," he announced. "Am I to have no peace?"

"Are you to have no heir?" Lord Agravaine returned. "You may have stripped young Maddoc of his dukedom and shipped him off to boarding school, but he is still next in line for the throne until you make things otherwise."

"I know." Arthur cringed at the reminder. Maddoc becoming king would be a disaster. But that didn't mean he needed to upend his life to prevent a hypothetical scenario.

"Then I suggest you fix that as soon as possible," Lord Agravaine concluded, as if it were as simple as signing a piece of legislation, and not as hard as giving up his entire future.

It was a depressing topic that Arthur couldn't escape. No matter how hard he tried, his council always came back to it, as though hoping he'd changed his mind. Which he hadn't.

"I will not be forced to take a wife and have her bear children until I—and the woman of my choosing—are both ready to make that commitment," Arthur said evenly. "Nor will I hear anything more on the subject. Is that clear?"

"For the moment," Lord Agravaine said, which was at once an acquiescence and a threat.

"Are there any updates from Cameliard?" Arthur asked, looking to Sir Tor.

"We have soldiers stationed along the northern border at all crossing points, who rotate a constant watch. They should be able to warn us of any impending attack."

"A constant watch? In this weather?" Arthur frowned. "Wouldn't an enchantment work better? Some sort of . . . magical trip wire that would give instant alert of an approaching army?"

He was sure Emry could devise something. Perhaps her father could help.

"Indeed it would," said Sir Tor, "if King Leodegrance approved of such magic."

Arthur sighed. It was a bother the way Cameliard clung to the church and disapproved of, well, *everything.* "I'll write to him personally and try to convince him."

Not that he thought it would work. Because of Camelot's treaty with Cameliard, the moment Yurien attacked, they would be forced to intervene. It was unnerving, waiting for a war to happen in another kingdom, and knowing the inevitable weight of that bloodshed rested squarely on his shoulders.

CHAPTER 5

Emry sipped the dregs of her coffee as she stared out the window of the wizard's workshop, practically vibrating with anticipation.

Her father would be here any moment. And then they'd spend the morning together, in the wizard's workshop. It was something she'd dreamed of since she was a little girl and had begged him to let her visit the castle, promising she'd be on her best behavior.

But he hadn't wanted to be burdened by a pair of unruly twins, and he'd said as much, leaving Emry and her brother behind in Brocelande with their gran, and making an occasional, unannounced visit.

And then an unannounced disappearance.

When she finally heard footsteps on the stairs, her heart raced with excitement.

"Behave," she warned the stone gargoyle, which sat on a rickety wooden stool by the door.

"When have I ever done that?" it retorted.

"Act vaguely civilized, then, please, or I'll use you as a coatrack," she threatened.

"You wouldn't dare," it grumbled.

"Try me," Emry returned, snapping her fingers to smooth the wrinkles from her skirts. She'd worn one of her more impressive dresses, a gray silk that had once belonged to Princess Guinevere.

The footsteps grew louder, and then her father appeared in the doorway, trying to catch his breath.

"Have they always been that steep?" he panted.

"Only on Mondays. It really is the strangest enchantment," Emry joked.

Her father didn't laugh. Instead, he frowned as he took in the space, with its bundles of herbs drying from the ceiling, its untidy stacks of books, and its shelves of glass bottles. "It's just as I remember."

"It most certainly is not!" protested the gargoyle. "Unless you travel backward through time."

Emry sighed. "Don't listen to the gargoyle. It's depressed and French, and it's a dreadful combination."

Her father spotted the creature, and his eyes went wide. "Where did it come from?"

"A gift from the French court wizard," Emry said. "Nicolas Flamel. Do you know him?"

"I know his work, certainly. I've never found alchemy quite as dull as when Flamel writes about it."

Emry snorted. "He's even duller in person."

Her father frowned. "You went to France?"

"Last year, with Arthur."

She couldn't wait to tell her father about her Anwen powers. Or better yet, show him what she could do. She had dreamed of this. Of him finally being proud of her powers, and teaching her all the spells and potions that made people say he was the greatest wizard who had ever lived.

"Father, there's something I have to—" she began.

"Emry, we need to talk," her father said at the same moment.

"Of course," she said, taking a seat on one of the overstuffed arm-chairs by the fireplace.

Her father joined her. In the daylight, up close, he looked as though he had slept badly, or perhaps not at all. And though his clothes were freshly laundered—or, magicked to appear that way—the style was years out of date.

He ran a hand through his damp hair and sighed, as if dreading what he was about to say. Emry frowned, waiting.

"I couldn't help but observe that you were out drinking—at what I presume was a tavern—with four young men last night," said her father, his expression terse and disapproving.

She almost laughed. *That* was the problem?

"Only technically," she said with a dismissive wave of her hand. "And it hardly matters. I could have gone with four court ladies and nothing would have been different."

Not that most of the court ladies, other than Issie and Branjen, would wish to visit such an establishment. Off her father's frown, she realized belatedly that her father didn't know she had no preference for a person's gender, and this wasn't quite how she'd envisioned telling him.

"It matters because it's wholly inappropriate behavior for a young, unmarried woman," her father said, ignoring the important part of her statement entirely. "You're at the royal court, not back in Brocelande."

Emry's good mood evaporated. She could sense a lecture coming on, which was so unfair. If it had been Emmett coming back from a tavern with his friends, or worse, with an amorous girl on each arm, their father would have winked in approval.

"Emry, I worry for your reputation," her father went on, "What will people think?"

"Like you never had a drink with the king after a long week when you were the court wizard?" Emry shot back.

"That's different," protested her father, even though it wasn't.

"Can't you act proud of me for one minute before starting in with the criticism?" she demanded.

"It's hardly criticism to express concern over my unmarried daughter's reputation," he protested. "And it's clear to anyone with eyes that you're—you're"—he paused, looking at a spot on the ceiling—

"warming the king's bed in exchange for your position."

She gaped at him, hoping she'd misheard. "Excuse me?"

"Don't make me repeat it," her father said, massaging his temples, as if the conversation was too much for him.

Emry's jaw felt tight. He didn't seem to be joking. "I saved Castle Camelot from a literal siege! And Master Ambrosius named me his successor. Me! Not Emmett!"

"Then he made a mistake!" her father insisted.

She should have known it would go like this—badly. Her father was as arrogant as he'd always been. And as convinced that he knew everything.

This is who he was. Who he always had been. And there was nothing she could say or do to make him proud of her. She bit her lip and fidgeted with a seam on her dress, her chin trembling as she blinked back tears.

He wasn't proud of her. He wasn't even impressed that she'd been named his successor. He thought she was bedding the king for her place at court, and that it should have been Emmett, who was without fault, no matter how much evidence indicated otherwise.

There were footsteps on the stairs, and one of the first-year squires appeared in the doorway, clutching his arm and looking pale.

"Dryan, what's happened?" Emry asked, rising to her feet. His arrival was a welcome interruption.

"Fergus took a cheap shot and popped my shoulder out of joint. I don't suppose you could help?"

"There's still no healing salve," she warned.

"I know. The physician sent me away. He seemed to be having a panic attack?"

Emry sighed. They really needed a new court physician. The Duke of Cornwall had accidentally poisoned their old one, and his hapless apprentice seemed to do nothing other than administer laxatives and hyperventilate about it.

"I can reset it by hand, but you'll be in a sling for a few weeks," Merlin said, butting in.

"Actually, I—" Emry said.

"I've got this," her father interrupted, shrugging off his jacket. "Go and fetch me some pain tonic from Master Ambrosius's stores."

Emry's hands fisted in frustration. "You mean *my* stores."

"It should be a blue liquid," her father went on, as though he hadn't heard her.

Maybe he hadn't. Emry watched in frustration as her father pushed up his sleeves and led Dryan over to the cot.

"Er, who are you?" Dryan asked nervously.

"Master Willyt Merlin," her father said grandly. "I assume you've heard of me."

"You're Emry's father?" He stared back and forth between them, eyes wide. "Actually, you do look alike."

"The tonic, girl," her father demanded, making a flapping motion with his hand. "Where's your head?"

Emry stepped forward, before she could stop herself. "I'll thank you to stop ordering me around in my workshop. Now, step aside, so I can take care of this." She shoved past her father, taking out her wand. He spluttered, staring as if he hardly recognized her.

"W-what are you going to do?" Dryan asked nervously.

"Healing spell," Emry said. "Takes two seconds, and I'll have you back to your training tomorrow."

"Is that what you always do for Lance?" Dryan sounded eager.

"And Arthur," Emry said. "Stand still and take a deep breath."

"Emry—" her father began.

"Not now!" she scolded.

The spell released with a snap, and Dryan's shoulder gave a sickening pop. He sighed in relief.

Dizziness rolled over Emry from having cast the spell silently, but she pushed it aside.

Her father was staring at her in disbelief.

"How does that feel?" she asked the young squire.

Dryan gingerly rotated his arm. "Perfect!" His face split into a grin. "Sard the infirmary! I should've come straight here."

"Put something cold on it," Emry instructed. "And take the rest of the day off, if Sir Dinadin can spare you."

"I'm sure he can. Thanks, Em."

After the lad had gone, Emry twisted the tension from her neck.

Her father was still staring at her as if he couldn't quite make sense of what he was seeing. "You fixed that boy's arm with Corperus magic," he said. Magic on another person, he meant.

"I did." When he'd taught her and her brother magic, he had warned them never to work those kinds of spells. Unless you knew what you were doing, they could snap back as easily as they could bend forward.

Something her brother knew all too well. After being summoned to the castle to serve as a wizard's apprentice, Emmett had been knocked unconscious by the blowback from his own misfired spell, a memory erasure gone wrong. Desperate to not lose the job and its much-needed wages for their family, Emry had taken up her brother's identity and come to the castle in his place. When her brother had woken, he'd refused to switch back, and had insisted it should have been her who was summoned all along.

"That's extremely delicate spellwork." Her father shook his head. "What if it had gone wrong?"

"Unlikely. Master Ambrosius trained me in it."

"In *theory*, perhaps."

"No, in *practice*," Emry corrected. "I cast the same spell on Arthur earlier this morning." Belatedly, she realized how that sounded but too late to fix it. "I've performed magic far more advanced than resetting a dislocated shoulder. And I can do it all silently, without my wand."

She waited for him to look impressed, but instead, her father wore a pained expression, as if tales of her powers were the last thing he wanted to hear. "This isn't the life I'd have chosen for you," he said.

Yet he'd wanted it for her brother. She burned with resentment.

"Well, you weren't here," Emry snapped, her temper flaring. "So I've had to choose for myself. And take care of myself. And everyone else I care about."

Emry's heart was pounding, and her hands were clenched into fists. But still, she lifted her chin defiantly, staring at her father.

Her father grimaced. "This is all my fault," he said. "But don't worry, I'm going to set it right."

CHAPTER 6

Emry didn't know what she'd expected, having her father back at the castle. It certainly wasn't for him to scold her, undermine her, and disapprove of everything about her. When he'd failed to return to the workshop after lunch, Emry had spent the rest of the afternoon brooding over the fact that their reunion couldn't have gone any worse.

It's only our first day working together, she told herself as she dressed for supper. *Things will get better.*

She twisted her hair back into an elaborate braid the way the maid at Gawain's house in France had done, put on a silk gown with a green velvet bodice, and dabbed rose salve onto her lips.

There. Let her father see she could be the daughter he wanted, and the woman she wanted to be. And it wouldn't hurt if Arthur blushed adorably when he saw her in a low-cut gown, which he seemed to like almost as much as when she wore trousers.

"I hope you didn't go to all of that trouble for me," said an amused voice as she headed down to the Great Hall.

Gawain was slouching against a wall, his lips twisted into a smirk, his smooth brown skin glowing appealingly in the firelight. He wore a damask suit that cut away in the front to draw attention to his obscenely tight trousers.

"Don't flatter yourself," Emry retorted. "And don't move, I'm afraid your trousers will rip."

"Then I shall send your compliments to my tailor, since that's exactly the impression I was going for."

"Uncomfortable?"

"Provocative," he fired back, looking her up and down. "And I see we've dressed to match."

"Hardly." Emry snorted.

She noticed he had paint flecks and charcoal stains on his fingers, and without thinking, she waved a hand. *"Extergio."* The paint and charcoal melted away.

Gawain stared down at his hands, his smirk tipping dangerously into a true smile. "A shame. I'd left them like that to torment my father. Speaking of fathers, I ran into yours at my favorite suit-maker's shop this afternoon."

Emry's eyebrows raised. "You did?"

"He seemed to be buying an entire wardrobe. And charging it all to the royal accounts." Gawain sounded impressed.

"I can't believe it," Emry said. That's where her father had disappeared to all afternoon? *Shopping?*

"His shopping spree is the part you can't believe?" Gawain said carefully. "And not his being in London? Interesting."

Emry shot him a look. "You're a terrible spy."

"And a flawless dresser, to make up for it," Gawain added, offering her his arm. "Shall we enter together?"

"If you insist," she said grandly, resting a hand on his surprisingly hard bicep and letting him escort her into the Great Hall.

No one noticed them come in. The courtiers were too busy gawking at Master Merlin and whispering over the wizard's unexpected return.

Her father wore an expensive-looking new coat, and his hair was freshly cut and slicked back behind his ears. A gold earring glittered in one ear, and his new boots shone with polish. He stood clutching a goblet of wine and holding court to a rapt audience of noblemen. When he spotted her, he waved.

Emry crossed the Great Hall, feeling as if she'd stepped into a scene from a long time ago. Her father was still the age she remembered him, and he looked as he used to, resplendent in the latest fashions.

"I hope you didn't spend the rest of the afternoon in that stuffy workshop," he said a little too loudly, and then laughed as though his comment had been hilarious. He smoothed an invisible wrinkle from his new velvet jacket. The buttons, Emry noticed, looked like real pearls. Her father grinned at his companions. "Gentlemen, have you had the pleasure of meeting my daughter?"

"Of course they have," said Emry. "I *am* the court wizard."

"Surely not anymore, now that you've returned, Willyt," protested a portly, gray-haired man Emry thought might have been called Sir Ban.

Emry hadn't thought of that. But Arthur would never. They'd been through so much together. Yes, her father was the greatest wizard who'd ever lived, but she was *Arthur's* wizard.

Her father was about to say something, but she never found out what, as she was descended upon by the passel of young lords with whom she was assigned to dine. They were silly things, but very earnest in their charms, especially Lionel Griflet, who had attempted to court her and still wasn't over her rejection.

"So the rumors are true," Lionel said, staring at Emry's father. He sank into a bow. "Delighted, Master Merlin, absolutely delighted. You know my father, I believe? Lord Griflet?"

"A fine man," Emry's father said, inclining his head in return.

"Coming, Miss Merlin?" Elian asked. "You can sit between Lionel and Cal and make sure they don't elbow each other out of the way for the last drumstick again."

"He nearly gave me a black eye," Cal complained, glaring at his older brother.

"I should go," Emry said. "Without me, the entire table will fall to chaos."

"Surely you don't dine with these lads," Merlin protested. "Where are the other young ladies?"

"Hiding," Emry suggested as Elian snickered.

She wasn't sure what her father had expected. There was no place for her with the noble daughters and court ladies. And she certainly wasn't sitting at Arthur's side, as he'd once devilishly suggested, in the seat that had been Guinevere's. She didn't need that kind of attention. Or pressure. Besides, it would hardly be pleasant, squeezed in next to Lord Howell, who had tried to have her executed when he'd discovered she was masquerading as her brother. Or worse, next to Lord Agravaine, whose mere presence inspired indigestion.

So she followed the boys to their table and sat through supper in a daze, ignoring the conversation as she spied on the table where her father sat. He drank to excess, laughed so loudly that it turned heads, and flirted boldly with one of the ladies whom Elian had been courting.

Elian's expression turned stormy as Merlin invited the lady to take a seat on his lap, conjuring her a flower with a snap of his fingers. She giggled as he pressed a kiss to the back of her hand.

"Honestly," Emry said, rolling her eyes.

Her father was behaving like a rake. Like Emmett did, whenever she wasn't there to make him feel terrible about it.

But then, she supposed he had been stuck in a cave in an enchanted sleep for a long time. She couldn't blame him for seeking company. She just wished he'd be more subtle about it. And pick someone closer to his own age.

"If he wasn't a wizard, I'd challenge him to a duel," grumbled Elian.

Her father's behavior got progressively worse. The young woman left gratefully with Elian, who gallantly came to her rescue when Merlin's hands strayed to her backside. After that, her father seemed content to flirt with the serving maids tasked with clearing the courses. And worse, his companions did the same, laughing uproariously every time a girl approached the table.

"Perhaps they should try a brothel, if they insist on behaving as though they're in one," a voice observed drolly over her shoulder.

Emry turned and found Gawain smirking down at her. "You're enjoying this," she accused.

"Immensely," he agreed. "My father's been glowering at yours through the entire meal. My mother kicked him under the table, and he spilled wine on his new doublet."

"How thrilling," Emry replied, rising from her seat. She looked for Arthur, and found him surrounded by a dozen desperate courtiers and clearly trying not to hyperventilate.

"Your boyfriend's busy," Gawain reported. "Well, come on. Let's get this over with." He began rolling up his sleeves.

"Er, what are you doing?" Emry asked.

"Helping you get your father back to his room before he embarrasses himself even further," he said, as if it was obvious.

Emry blinked at him. The offer was unexpectedly kind. And Gawain was right—her father was in no state to find his own way around the castle. "Um, thank you?"

"No, thank *you*. I'm going to enjoy having you in my debt," he said with a devilish grin.

That sounded far more like the Gawain she knew. Thankfully, her father was too far gone to protest being lifted from his seat and hauled into the corridor.

"Oof, he's heavy," Gawain complained before they'd even reached the stairwell. "Can't you, you know, lighten him?"

"Magic doesn't work on magic," Emry reminded him.

"I'm magic," Merlin slurred as they coaxed him toward his room. "Greatest wizard that ever lived. Tell your friends. And your daughters."

Gawain snorted. "Now I see where your brother gets it."

Finally, they reached his room and dumped him into bed, where he let out an enormous snore and reached for a pillow to hold as if it might be one of the kitchen maids he'd been lusting after.

"He'd better not do this again tomorrow night," Emry said with a sigh.

"If he does, you'll need to enlist Lance and Percival," Gawain said. "This was a one-time offer."

"Because you were curious if he'd let anything interesting slip in his half-awake state?" Emry guessed.

Gawain scowled. "Spying is an art, Miss Merlin, and one does not mock art."

"I wasn't mocking art, I was mocking the artist," Emry said sweetly as she wiggled her fingers in farewell.

She had just rounded the corner to her bedroom when she noticed a figure hovering in the alcove that led to the servants' stair. This was the last thing she needed. She sighed, marching straight up to the shadowed lurker. "Can I help you?"

Lord Agravaine stepped into the light, looking as haughty as ever. Where Gawain was sarcastic and snobbish, his father was humorless and shrewd. "That is what I'm about to find out," said the man, blocking her way. "A moment, if you don't mind."

Whatever he wanted, this couldn't be good. "Well?" Emry prompted. "What is it?"

"I'll be brief." Lord Agravaine gave a humorless grimace that might have been an attempt at a smile. "Our young king is in a precarious position. He must marry and produce an heir for the good of the kingdom. Yet he refuses, because of you."

"He refuses because of himself," Emry corrected.

Lord Agravaine arched an eyebrow. "He agreed to wed Princess Guinevere. It was only after the two of you grew close that he became so . . . intractable."

That couldn't be true. Could it?

"An unfortunate coincidence," Emry said.

"I don't think it is," Lord Agravaine replied. "He believes he's in love. And that you feel the same."

Emry folded her arms across her chest. "And?"

"It would be better if he thought otherwise," Lord Agravaine said. "You can't harbor any illusions that you'd make a suitable queen."

Emry scoffed. And then she saw that Lord Agravaine meant it. "We're just courting," she told him. "It's not serious."

How could it be, when they barely had time to see each other?

"The consequences of your . . . courtship are very serious. If he believes himself to be in love with a girl he can never marry, he won't be the king that Camelot needs," Lord Agravaine informed her. "It would be in Arthur's best interest—in *Camelot's* best interest—if you ended things."

Emry's mouth went dry. "I can't do that."

"A pity. I thought you wished to be a court wizard, not a courtesan."

Emry was done listening to this. "If you'll excuse me, it's late, and I'm desperate to take my wand out of my bodice."

She stepped around the man, her chin held high. He reached for her shoulder gently, with no malice. His expression was one of concern as he said, "It's noble to let someone who loves you go if you're only going to hurt them."

She jerked her shoulder away and hurried down the corridor and threw open the door to her room, trying to come up with a retort, even though it was far too late to utter one. But no clever remark came. Instead, his words echoed in her head and dug in, taking root.

She loved Arthur. And he loved her back.

But what if love wasn't enough?

What if, by loving him, she was going to drag him down? Prevent him from being a great king.

She was never going to be what Arthur needed. Because what he needed was an heir. And the last thing Emry had any interest in doing was following in her brother's disastrous footsteps and being pressured into having a child before she'd gotten a chance to do, well, anything. She was eighteen. She certainly wasn't bearing some royal heir while the entire kingdom watched and waited, hoping it was a boy, and blaming her if it wasn't. She was a wizard. Not a queen.

But Arthur was a king. No longer a prince who had time to do what he wished, but the leader of a kingdom, with all the responsibility that came with such a title. No matter how much they both wished things were different. Surely they still had time to be young and in love and nothing serious. Surely Camelot didn't need a queen, or a male heir, just yet?

Except she didn't know that. She only wanted it to be true.

It's noble to let someone who loves you go if you're only going to hurt them.

Emry flopped down onto her bed, filled with the most terrible fear that Lord Agravaine was right.

CHAPTER 7

Willyt Merlin crept toward the staircase to the wizard's workshop in the dim glow of his wand light. It was late, and most of the castle was asleep. He didn't remember returning to his bedroom from supper, yet he'd woken up there, with his new clothes rumpled and his boots neatly placed at the foot of his bed. He doubted a flirtatious kitchen maid would have been so tidy.

A flash of memory came back to him: a young man in a gold brocade coat helping him stagger down the hall.

Which meant he must have passed out again. To anyone observing, he would have appeared to be very drunk. But drunk wore off on its own. Too large a dose of Godfrey's root did not.

He tiptoed past his old room—now his daughter's—noting that there was no light shining through the keyhole. But that didn't mean she was inside. Somehow, he suspected she was just as likely to be in the workshop, or in the young king's apartments, a complication he hadn't foreseen. He'd expected Uther to welcome him back with a feast in his honor, not to encounter a merrymaking band of youths stumbling home from the tavern and learn they were in charge.

Uther was gone. Igraine, gone. Ambrosius was dead, and so was crusty old Captain Lam of the castle guard.

The Lady of the Lake hadn't warned him of this. She'd said the castle would not be as he had left it, but she spoke in riddles, and he thought she'd meant they'd added a new wing or changed out the tapestries for oil paintings.

Instead, nothing was the same. The world had jumped forward, and he felt like he could barely keep his balance. A female court wizard. Courtiers of the same gender holding hands in well-lit corridors. When he'd seen an unfamiliar knight wearing eyeliner and braids and had asked Sir Ban his name, the old knight had informed him that he'd used the wrong pronoun.

Uther wouldn't have stood for any of it. And it seemed the members of his graying council were just as uncomfortable as he felt. He had wanted to impress them at supper with his magic and with stories of his adventures. Grumpy old Sir Ban hadn't been on a quest in decades, and Sir Bors seemed content to make sport of flirting with serving maids, when once he had been a fierce contender at the joust. But Merlin had pushed himself too hard since his return, and now he was suffering the aftermath. Or, he was about to. Unless he could fix it.

He staggered exhaustedly up the staircase to the wizard's workshop, then pushed open the door. Empty. A small mercy. The effects of his tonic were starting to wear off, and he didn't know how long before the signs of withdrawal would be obvious, especially to his infernally clever daughter or to sharp-witted Arthur.

They knew about Bellicent. About Anwen. About the cave. They even knew things he did not, making him feel a fool as they'd explained that Morgana had used him and he'd brought a threat against their kingdom back into this world. In hindsight, it was infuriatingly obvious. Morgana didn't have the ability to open a doorway to Anwen. That particular talent lay only in the Merlin bloodline.

Everything had changed while he was away, especially his daughter, who was clearly responsible for opening that doorway. She'd grown up into everything he'd worried she would be, and more. And so had his lazy, irresponsible son, leaving everything to his sister. Including his summons to court. But boys would be boys. Surely he could talk some sense into the lad, which would be his first order of business after the royal council reinstated him as court wizard.

He yanked impatiently on the door that led to the herb storage and hissed in annoyance when he found it locked. No doubt Emry had the key.

"*Reserare*," he muttered.

The magic was painful when it came, another sign his tonic was fast wearing off. He gritted his teeth against the sharp stab of pain, waiting for it to subside. The lock clicked open.

"What are you doing?" a voice asked.

He turned, but no one was there.

"Are you sneaking?" the voice continued. "Is that why you look so guilty?"

The gargoyle, he realized. He almost laughed in relief. "Of course I'm not sneaking," he said imperiously. "I need a headache potion. How was I to know the stores were locked?"

"Oh," the gargoyle said, disappointed. "I was hoping I'd caught a thief."

"I am no thief," Merlin snapped. "This is my workshop! *Was* my workshop. Same difference."

"It isn't, really," mused the gargoyle, but Merlin was done listening to the annoying creature.

He closed himself inside the long, narrow storeroom. Godfrey's root was unpleasant, and the supply he'd brought from Avalon was quickly dwindling. But it was worth it to have his magic back, even with such foul side effects. He ran his fingers along the shelves, which were spotless and alphabetized, no doubt his daughter's work.

Garlic, powdered . . . ginger root, dried . . . there! Godfrey's root. An entire bottle, nearly full. He tucked it into his pocket with shaking hands.

It needed heating, but he didn't dare do that here under the gargoyle's watchful eye. He could manage with his washbasin and the fireplace. He felt dizzy by the time he made it back to his room. He barely got a pinch of the root heating over a flame before he was over-come. The effects began as they always did, with light hurting his eyes, a gut-wrenching nausea, and a clammy sweat breaking out over his entire body. The shivers came next, and he crumpled to the floor, head in his hands, desperate for relief.

But the elixir wasn't ready. *Come on, come on*, he thought, watching the substance turn charred black, and then, mercifully, powder white.

He reached eagerly, with trembling hands, for the small mound of powder in his washbasin, realizing too late that the metal was red-hot from the flame. He hissed, drawing back his hand, but it was already burned.

"*Refrigescant*," he gasped, watching the bowl grow instantly cool.

And then he snorted the powdered root and lay on his back staring up at the coffered ceiling, his heart pounding like a drum as the drug took blessed effect.

CHAPTER 8

Morgana wrapped her fur cloak tighter around her shoulders as she strolled through the castle's grounds, her boots leaving fresh prints in the new snow. Distantly, she could hear her son's delighted laughter as he lobbed snowballs at his nurse. The woman begged him to stop, but Mordred paid her no attention.

Morgana smiled at his determination. She had helped him fashion the snowballs, her maid watching nervously, as though the woman thought her incapable of such a simple task.

"The spell to make them hard as ice is *glacio*," Morgana had whispered, before leaving her son to his games.

Winter was unrelenting this far north. All around her, the castle was dusted with white. Icicles dripped from the towers, and snow capped the bushes and trees that lined the frozen pathways. It was cold and cruel and beautiful, but she couldn't enjoy it, not the way she used to. Not after she'd suffered Anwen's frozen landscapes, stumbling through the forest with nothing, not even a coat. Not even her magic.

But I saved you, Bellicent whispered inside her head.

"I saved myself," Morgana snapped.

Except she hadn't. Not yet. And that was the problem.

She could feel Bellicent prodding at her consciousness, trying to grab hold. The sensation was horrible, like needles jabbing at the inside of her head. She winced, gritting her teeth against the pain. *Stop it!* Morgana thought.

Stop what? Bellicent asked innocently.

And then she *shoved*, and Morgana was falling. Not into the snow, but out of herself entirely.

No. Not this. Not again.

Except this time, it was different.

Everything was cold and dark and faraway, as if she had tumbled into an oubliette and could only look up at a piece of the world she had once inhabited. If she concentrated, she could make out the dim shapes of the trees in the castle grounds, the faint shrieks of her son playing in the snow. Bellicent may have taken control, but Morgana wasn't gone. She was just . . . elsewhere.

So she held on to her elsewhere, treading through shadows thick as water, until she found out what Bellicent did when she took control.

The sorceress held out a hand—*Morgana's* hand—and let a snowflake fall onto her palm. Morgana shivered—she could feel the sting of the cold snowflake melting on her skin—but the feeling was curiously distant.

"Let go of me!" Morgana demanded.

Bellicent grinned with stolen lips. "When I'm ready," she promised, speaking the words aloud with Morgana's mouth.

Yet her voice betrayed her. It was Bellicent's sickly sweet drawl, not Morgana's deeper tone.

And then King Yurien rode into the clearing atop his fine black destrier. Her husband was returning from a hunt, Morgana knew, and she could see the blood splatters on his fur coat. He slowed his horse, frowning at Bellicent.

"Sire?" called one of his attendants.

"Go ahead without me," he said impatiently as a dozen men rode past, their horses' hooves thundering.

Her husband had killed a stag. Morgana didn't know how she knew that. She watched as he slid from his mount, frowning at his wife's body. "What are you doing out here?" he asked.

"That isn't me!" Morgana shouted. But of course he couldn't hear her. She was a phantom, as Bellicent had been.

"Enjoying my freedom," Bellicent said with a sharp smile.

Yurien frowned. "You are not my wife," he accused.

He knew. Morgana felt relief wash over her, pleased that he would not mistake a witch wearing her skin for his queen.

"I'm someone better," Bellicent promised.

Yurien's expression grew thoughtful, calculating. "What have you done with her?"

"Only borrowed her body for a while. She made a foolish promise to me in the Otherworld, and now I may control her as I wish."

"You must have great power, to control someone from another world," said Yurien. He sounded impressed. Intrigued. And not at all angry, or afraid.

"Of course I do, you dim-witted mortal king!" Bellicent snapped, and he shifted uncomfortably at the insult. "I am descended from Queen Maeve herself! Royal fairy blood runs through my veins. I have been worshipped as a goddess by magicless men such as yourself. And now you have the privilege of speaking with me."

He gave a bow. Yurien Vortigen, who bowed to no one, bowed to the high sorceress of Anwen. "I am honored, my lady."

Morgana screamed. Or perhaps she only imagined that she could scream as the truth of his betrayal hit her. He would not save her. He wasn't even concerned to learn what had happened to her. Did he care for her so little?

No, she realized. He cared for himself so much.

"You should be honored," Bellicent went on. " For I can give you what you truly desire."

Yurien looked triumphant. "You could make me High King of England?"

"Why stop at England?"

He grinned. Preened. And then he frowned.

Yes! Morgana thought. *He's realized he ought not to bargain with the sorceress. He knows what happened to me. How everyone thinks I'm mad.*

"And in return?" he asked. "What would I give you?"

"That remains to be seen. I shall let you know what I desire, *when* I desire it. Do we have a deal?"

No! Morgana tried to shout. *Don't promise her anything!*

"Indeed." He smiled.

And so did Bellicent.

CHAPTER 9

The council meeting had been going on for hours, and Arthur couldn't wait to escape back to his apartments for some peace. Or to the library for some books. Or to the wizard's workshop to surprise Emry. Honestly, he was down to be anywhere his council wasn't discussing his upcoming coronation and the royal tournament to select his new knight champion. Apparently, he was required to host said tournament in the hours between being officially crowned king and attending the coronation ball.

"As for the champion's prize, I suggest a small estate and a yearly sum of gold enough to run it," said Lord Agravaine, looking to Arthur for approval but receiving only a frown in return.

"It's a handsome prize," the general added. "I know many will be eager to compete for such a holding."

"Shouldn't they be eager to compete for the honor and glory of being named champion?" Arthur asked.

The men around the table laughed, and Arthur realized he'd called attention to his inexperience once again.

"Hardly," admonished Sir Bors. "Knights look forward to competing for the honor, and for the prize awarded to the winner. They will come from every corner of the kingdom, not just to show their skill, but to swear fealty to their new king."

How tedious. They had to swear fealty, too? Arthur held back a sigh.

"And fewer knights will come to publicly swear their allegiance if the prize does not entice them," Lord Agravaine added.

Ah. So that was the important part he'd been missing. The political angle to offering a large prize.

"Well, if it's tradition, then that's fine," he said, trying to make light of his miscalculation. "We'll award an estate to whomever wins the joust. Er . . . do we have an estate?"

Sir Ban consulted a scroll. "Joyous Gard has sat unoccupied for a while and is in need of some repairs."

"Some repairs." Sir Tor chortled. "I know Joyous Gard. It sits in the Forest of Camlann, just across the border from Cameliard. To call it anything more than a pile of old stones would be generous."

"Then it's high time someone moved in and began renovating the place," Lord Howell said.

And then a knock sounded at the door, interrupting.

The page darted out, then promptly reentered, his eyes wide. "It's, er—the wizard."

"Send her in," Arthur commanded, wondering what Emry was doing here.

But the wizard who entered wasn't Emry. It was her father.

"Ah, Willyt," said Lord Agravaine, pushing to his feet and extending a hand. "Welcome back, old friend."

"It's good to be back," replied the beaming wizard, exchanging handshakes and enduring slaps on the back from most members of the council. Only Sir Tor, who had just recently begun serving as ambassador from Cameliard, frowned in confusion over their visitor's warm arrival.

Not a moment too soon, Arthur realized that Master Merlin had sat on his father's council, and likely assumed Arthur expected him to do the same.

The wizard looked around, clearly noting that there weren't any empty chairs.

"Our guest will need a seat," Arthur said to the page, who raced off to procure one.

By the time the page returned, red faced and dragging an antique spindly thing embroidered with roses that must have come from some lady's dressing table, half the members of his council were clustered around Master Merlin, eager to hear of his adventures.

Arthur couldn't believe it. This room was filled with the most powerful nobles and knights from the most powerful families, whose loyalty and respect were not lightly given. Yet they deferred to the wizard, with his boastful tales and booming laugh.

"Easy, gentlemen," Merlin said, holding out his hands. "Now is not the time for the tale of how I traveled to a different world and imprisoned the most powerful sorceress to ever live, to keep Camelot safe."

Arthur snorted. That was one way to describe what had happened. A *ridiculous* way.

"Then we shall have to steal away to a tavern to hear these sordid tales," proclaimed the general. "Drinks are on me."

As the men eagerly made plans for the following evening, Arthur realized that he wasn't invited. Of course not. He caught Sir Tor's eye, and the knight shrugged, as if to say, *Same.*

"Well, Master Merlin," said Arthur, trying to regain a sense of order. "Are you here to advise, or to petition?"

Merlin frowned, considering. He took a seat, stretching an arm over the back of the chair. "Both, I suppose. You do wish me to rejoin the royal council, do you not?"

The wizard grinned, and his expression reminded Arthur strongly of Emry whenever she was acting a menace and enjoying every moment of it.

Arthur hadn't expected Master Merlin to put him on the spot. But he couldn't very well refuse. The man was an important ally. And then there was the small matter that Arthur was dating his daughter.

"I believe you already have," Arthur said, raising an eyebrow.

The council banged their fists against the table in approval.

"Naturally, Master Merlin should be reinstated as court wizard, as well," said Sir Bors, who rarely spoke up in their meetings.

"A wonderful idea," General Timias said.

Arthur choked.

"I agree," said Lord Agravaine.

Others voiced their assent. Merlin said nothing, just flashed that cocky grin and waited for the position to be handed to him. It was almost as if the wizard had *planned* this.

"But I have a court wizard," Arthur protested.

At that, the mood soured significantly.

"Ah yes, my teenage daughter." Merlin's tone made it clear he found the situation ridiculous. A couple of council members snickered in agreement. "But surely an eighteen-year-old girl isn't suited for this level of responsibility."

The others agreed.

"You don't know her," Arthur protested.

"I should hope that a father knows his daughter better than the king." The wizard lifted a brow.

Arthur knew a trap when he saw one, so he didn't dare to refute the wizard's statement.

"Your Grace, it seems natural that Willyt should retake his previous position," said Lord Agravaine.

"I concur," added the general. "We can't have some young lass swooning at the sight of a battlefield."

"Emry would never do that," Arthur interjected, but no one was listening. And why would they? He had never felt so small, or so useless.

"Camelot needs a good, experienced wizard like Willyt," the general went on. "Anything else is poor strategy."

"Hear, hear!" the members of Arthur's council agreed. Only Sir Tor remained silent.

Arthur's stomach twisted. His council had him backed into a corner. No defense he gave of why he'd chosen Emry would be enough. But she'd understand. Perhaps she'd even be relieved.

After all, he wasn't ready to be king, but he was making the best of it, because he didn't have a choice. Was Emry truly ready to be the court wizard? He'd never asked. Now that her father had returned, surely she'd step aside, eager to learn all he had to teach.

Perhaps Master Merlin is the better choice, a small traitorous voice whispered in Arthur's head. *He's the greatest wizard Camelot has ever known. Look how the most powerful men in the kingdom defer to him. How they respect him. And more than that, he knows Morgana. He'll be useful. And with Emry as his apprentice, Camelot would be unstoppable.*

"The position is yours," Arthur said grandly. "Upon demonstration of your magic."

Master Merlin laughed. "Well, lad, I'd expect nothing less. What would you have me do?"

That was a very good question. One that could almost make Arthur ignore the fact that Merlin had called him "lad" in front of his entire council.

"I could drink poison, and you could produce a magical antidote?" Arthur suggested, not entirely joking.

The council laughed uneasily, and Sir Tor shot him an inquisitive look.

"What a wonderful sense of humor our king has," said Lord Agravaine.

"Whenever you're ready, wizard," Arthur said, trying to summon a semblance of his father's stern command. "Any demonstration will suffice."

Merlin reached for his wand and pushed to his feet. He looked every inch the powerful court wizard, from his expensive new coat buttoned with pearls to his trim beard and polished wand. He smirked, raising a single eyebrow. The room hushed.

"*Nox!*" the wizard cried.

All the candles in the room extinguished at once, along with the fireplace and the torch by the door. The room plunged into total darkness.

"*Elevo omnia!*" Merlin intoned in the darkness. Arthur had the strangest sensation that his chair was lifting off the floor. From the murmurs of his council members, they also felt something.

"*Ignium!*" Merlin insisted.

The candles flickered back to life, the torch flared, and the fireplace crackled. Arthur's mouth fell open at what the wizard had done. Every object in the room floated in midair. Including the chairs they sat on, and the carpet beneath their long, rectangular table.

Only Merlin himself remained on the ground, staring up at them with a triumphant smile. "*Chalo omnia,*" he said, with a flick of his wand, and everything clattered noisily back into its usual place.

Arthur's chair touched down a tad harder than he would have wanted, but he was barely paying attention. He watched as his council members rose to their feet applauding. And he didn't blame them. Master Merlin had truly put on a show. Arthur saw where Emry got it from.

"Do you still wish to be poisoned?" the wizard asked, quirking an eyebrow. "Or will that suffice?"

"I suppose I ought to put that question to my council," Arthur deadpanned. The men looked suitably horrified.

Sir Tor snorted, then hastily tried to turn it into a cough.

"Ah, another joke," guessed Lord Agravaine.

Merlin's eyes danced with amusement. "Another time, perhaps," he said with a wink in Arthur's direction.

This was what he needed, Arthur thought gratefully. A powerful ally on his council. One who hadn't witnessed the past decade of Uther's disapproval.

Reinstating Master Merlin as Camelot's court wizard was a good idea. Sure, Emry's magic was extraordinary, but she'd only truly begun her studies when she'd arrived at the castle barely eight months ago. And everyone knew Willyt Merlin was the most powerful wizard who had ever lived.

Arthur beamed back at his new court wizard, thinking that, perhaps, his impending confrontation with King Yurien and Queen Morgana of Lothia might not be so ill fated after all.

CHAPTER 10

E mmett steeled his nerves as he approached the Lady of the Lake. She was locking the gates of the convent, her lantern floating by her side in the moonlight.

"So, child of Merlin," she said without turning around. "You have a question to ask of me." The key scraped in the lock, and she folded it away in her gown before turning to face him.

She knew that he knew. He could sense it. He could feel her daring him to ask the right question—only he didn't know what that was.

"Has my father been here?" he finally asked.

"He has been to Avalon many times over the years," said the Lady, motioning for him to walk back with her through the courtyard. The bone-white arches rose up around them on all sides, like the bars of a cage. He felt trapped here. Imprisoned.

He was restless. And bored. And while he was glad Guin was enjoying her time away from court, he missed his friends. His life. And he worried that it was gone forever.

The Lady of the Lake didn't speak, merely waited in silence as he walked at her side. Which meant he was going to have to ask again.

"I suspect there's something you're not telling me, my Lady," he said nervously.

The Lady of the Lake nodded gravely. "There are many things I'm not telling you, some of no consequence, and others of great import."

"If there was one thing in particular," he pressed, "one thing that might make a difference if I knew . . ."

The Lady looked at him with her strange gray eyes, which seemed to swirl with mist. "Your father was here just before you arrived," she said.

So that had been his handwriting in the library. But that wasn't possible.

"I thought my father was dead," he said.

The Lady tilted her head, staring at him as though he was a curious thing. "He was no longer in this world, but that has changed."

"You mean he never died?" Emmett asked.

"I'm surprised your sister has not told you," she said.

Emry knew something that he didn't, and hadn't bothered to say anything. Because of course she hadn't. "Told me what?" Emmett asked in frustration.

"Your father slumbered in an enchantment in another world. He was not meant to return." The Lady of the Lake paused, staring up at the night sky. Her tone was dreamy, as though she was speaking half to herself. "The fact that he has returned portends bad fortune. A shift in the fabric of our very world itself. This is not how I wished things to come to pass. But he is very much alive."

Emmett's head spun to make sense of it all, and eventually concluded that he wasn't meant to. So he asked gravely, "Where is my father right now?"

Her eyes fluttered closed. She muttered something under her breath. Emmett felt the magic of the forest draw near. Tree branches rustled in a whispering rhythm, and a cloud passed over the waxing moon, blocking its light. Just as quickly as it had come, it drifted away, moonlight spilling back over the cloister courtyard.

Emmett shivered.

When the Lady opened her eyes, they were thick with mist. "Castle Camelot."

"Why didn't you tell me this before?" he demanded.

Nimue merely smiled, the mist fading from her eyes. "You did not ask. You said you wished to stay here for what would be three months' time in Camelot. It has only been two."

Emmett knew that. Still, he felt the Lady should have told him. After all, it was his father. He bit back his frustration as he made his excuses and left the Lady's side.

He pounded on Guinevere's door, and it wasn't until she answered it, frowning, that he remembered they were fighting. "What?" she snapped, looking magnificently annoyed with him. And then she saw his expression. "Emmett, what's wrong?"

Emmett wrapped her in a hug, pressing his face against the side of her neck and breathing in the scent of rose salve and orange blossom perfume. "She wasn't ever going to tell me." He wasn't sure if he meant Emry or Nimue, but it didn't matter. He was furious with them both.

Guin ran her fingers through his hair, and he realized his breathing was ragged. "It's okay," she soothed. "Whatever's happened, we'll get through it."

He hadn't realized how much he needed her to say that until she did. He took her hand in his, grateful that he wasn't alone right now. "It's my father. He was here just before us."

"Your father's alive?" Guin looked shocked.

"Apparently so," he said, overwhelmed. "Nimue says he's returned to Castle Camelot."

She gave her husband a long look. "Then that's where we're going."

"We? But what about—"

Guin lifted her chin. "I'm not leaving your side, and you're clearly not staying here."

"But you're—"

"Let the courtiers say what they wish about me. I don't care."

"If you're sure," Emmett said.

"I am," said Guin, and he'd never loved her more than he did in that moment. She was fierce. And wonderful. And his wife. "Now, pack your things. We leave tomorrow at first light."

CHAPTER 11

E mry was in a foul mood when she arrived at supper that evening. Her father hadn't shown up to the wizard's workshop at all. She'd waited the whole day, trying to keep busy, and had told herself he'd turn up eventually.

But the only person who climbed the stairs was a pimply-faced page asking for a dose of pregnancy-prevention potion with such embarrassment that he hadn't even looked her in the eye. She'd felt so bad for the lad that she hadn't even tormented him. Especially after the gargoyle had advised him to try and last past the count of three.

Emry half expected her father to be missing from supper as well, having vanished as suddenly as he'd arrived. But there he was, laughing heartily with some graying, goateed lord who wore a dangling pearl earring and a feather in his cap. He didn't even notice her come in.

Unfortunately, the same couldn't be said for Lionel Griflet, who rushed to her side with an expression of adoration.

"You look lovely this evening, Miss Merlin," Lionel said, offering his arm. "Shall I escort you to our table?"

She couldn't very well refuse. So she smiled politely as Lionel told a long and boring story about ordering a new saddle for his horse. A story that showed no sign of ending as the first course arrived.

Suddenly, the music stopped, and the murmur of chatter quieted. Everyone looked to the royal table, where Arthur had pushed back his chair and stood with goblet in hand.

"Before we dine, I'd like to make some important announcements for the court," Arthur said, his voice echoing throughout the Great Hall.

Emry frowned, wondering what was so important.

"As you know, my coronation is to take place in three weeks' time," he continued, and Emry relaxed, realizing it was just court nonsense. "And there is to be a royal tournament that day, to decide my knight champion."

The Great Hall descended into excited whispers. *A new champion!* Emry caught sight of Sir Kay, whose expression was livid.

"And what good is a tournament without a prize?" Arthur continued. The speech sounded memorized, the sort of thing he was required to do in front of the court, and which he made faces about behind closed doors. "I have decided to award the estate of Joyous Gard to the competitor who wins the honor of becoming my champion."

The court buzzed at this news. Many noblemen who hadn't seemed interested before certainly seemed interested now. An entire castle for the winner of a joust. It was a rare and worthy prize.

Arthur waited for the murmurs to settle down. "There is one last announcement," he said. "As many of you know, a valued member of my father's court has returned and joined us after many years away. Please welcome Master Willyt Merlin."

Applause mingled with curious whispers as Willyt rose to his feet, grinning. Emry beamed at Arthur, pleased he was giving her father a royal welcome. Knowing her father, he'd probably insisted on it.

"Master Merlin will be resuming his duties as court wizard," Arthur went on. "Effective immediately."

Emry stared at him in disbelief, her cheeks burning. She couldn't have heard him correctly.

He lifted his glass and drank deeply, and the rest of the court did the same.

"To Master Merlin," the court cried.

Her father basked in the attention. At his table, a few royal councillors were slapping him on the back in congratulations.

"What the hell?" said Cal with a frown.

"I'm confused," Lionel said, turning to Emry. "Do we have two court wizards now?"

"It certainly seems that way," Emry said crisply, lifting her skirts and rushing over to her father's table for answers.

Arthur couldn't have made a bigger mess of this if he'd tried. Emry didn't understand it. If he meant for her to share the position with her father, he should have said something to her in advance.

"Well," her father said with a broad grin. "What do you think?"

"So we're both the court wizard?" Emry demanded.

"Of course not," he said, as if it was obvious. "Arthur doesn't need you now that he has *me*."

The words landed like a blow. This wasn't happening. Suddenly, Emry couldn't breathe.

"You're to serve as my apprentice," her father said grandly, as if it was a great honor.

His apprentice. Once, she would have given anything for the chance. But now, it wasn't enough. Not by half.

"How generous," Emry seethed. This had to be a mistake. Surely Arthur wouldn't have decided this without her. Surely it was all a big misunderstanding. Her throat felt tight, and her hands clenched into fists. She looked to the royal table, but Arthur wasn't there. He was hurrying toward her, a corner of his mouth lifted hopefully, as if he hadn't completely shattered her life.

A misunderstanding, she told herself again, with the smallest flicker of hope. That's all that was happening. "Well, Merlins," Arthur said, looking back and forth between them. "What do you think?"

"I need you to clarify something," said Emry slowly. "When you said you were reinstating my father as court wizard, did you mean for us to share the position?"

Arthur winced. And somehow, before he spoke, Emry knew.

"Your father was my father's court wizard," he said. "Naturally, you'll serve as his apprentice."

No.

Emry's heart felt as if it was breaking in half.

"That's what the two of you were doing today?" she accused. "Deciding this? Without me?"

Neither of them denied it.

It wasn't fair. And the worst part was, it made sense. Who would choose a teenage girl over the most powerful practitioner of magic who had ever lived?

She'd assumed that Arthur would. But then, he'd never been in that position.

"I—" Emry said, blinking back tears. She thought of all the nobles she had worked so hard to deceive into believing she was her brother, and then had worked so hard again to befriend once they knew the truth. It had taken months, but they finally respected her. Accepted her. And she could feel it melting away. She could feel herself becoming smaller. Lesser. Arthur's girlfriend. Merlin's daughter. The negative space in relation to powerful men, rather than her own person.

She wanted to scream. There, in the crowded Great Hall, which was filled with courtiers delighting in each other's company, she had never felt so alone. She would never fit into this world in the way she wanted.

"I can't believe this," Emry said tightly, then fled out into the corridor. She stomped down to the dungeons, where she took out some of her aggression with a game of magical target practice.

She'd *earned* her title. She'd spent the last eight months working harder than she ever had in her life studying and improving her magic. She had fought bandits and saved Arthur's life, she had mastered her unpredictable Anwen powers, and she had mobilized dozens of suits of armor to defend the castle.

She knew she had more to learn. Maybe six months ago, she would have jumped at the chance to have her father teach her magic in the royal court. But she was more than just an apprentice now. She could handle being Camelot's court wizard. She'd *been* handling it.

Her father didn't want her as his apprentice. He just wanted his old job back.

He wouldn't have done this if Emmett was court wizard, she thought traitorously.

Her father had never believed in her, but Arthur had.

Or so she'd thought.

Now she didn't know what to believe. They'd decided this without her. Announced it to the entire court without considering how she'd feel. They were the two people who were supposed to care about her the most, and it turned out they were only thinking of themselves.

She heard footsteps on the stairs and sighed, hoping it wasn't him.

But of course it was.

Arthur appeared, still dressed from supper in his royal finery, a golden crown glinting on his brow. He looked so different from the boy she'd met in the library. He'd come so far. And she'd mistakenly believed they'd traveled that distance together.

Emry wasted no time. "How dare you do that to me?"

Arthur frowned. "I thought you'd be pleased."

She didn't think she'd heard him correctly. "*Pleased?* I'm humiliated! You said I'd earned my position as your court wizard. But that was just the empty flattery of a prince who could promise the world and deliver nothing. When it really counted, you betrayed me."

He bristled at this. "I put Camelot first! It's what a king does!"

"And what does a boyfriend do?" Emry demanded.

"You haven't given me a chance to explain."

"Explain what? That you'd rather impress your advisors than treat me with respect?"

"That's not what happened!"

"That's exactly what happened!" Emry snapped. "First you demoted Sir Kay from being your champion, and then me from being your court wizard. Is this the kind of king you want to be? One who discharges members of his court at his whim, publicly, to rounds of applause?"

Arthur's jaw grew tight. "Stop telling me how to run my kingdom!"

The tension turned thick and awful, and the silence stretched on.

She waited for him to take it back. But he didn't.

Emry glared at him. "Gladly, Your Majesty," she said, dipping into a curtsey. "After all, I'm just an apprentice. Why should the king care about anything I have to say?"

"Emry, don't," Arthur said wearily. "Nothing between us has to change."

"It already has," Emry retorted. "You changed it!"

He'd taken away everything she'd worked for. And he'd announced it in front of everyone with a toast, like it was something to be celebrated. She wished he'd apologize. That he'd save this somehow. Save *them*.

Instead, he stubbornly lifted his chin. "My council is in agreement over Master Merlin's reinstatement. And I stand by the decision," Arthur insisted.

Emry couldn't believe he was behaving like this. "Fine."

"Fine," Arthur snapped.

Emry fled up the stairs with her heart lodged in her throat and tears pricking the corners of her eyes.

A small traitorous part of her hoped he'd rush after her and apologize and fix things, but he didn't. And somehow, that made it even worse.

CHAPTER 12

Arthur lowered his broadsword with a grimace, wondering if he'd ever get used to the weight of the thing.

"Can't I switch to Excalibur?" he asked, wiping sweat from his brow.

"Not until you disarm me one more time," said Lance.

Arthur groaned. They were in the armory before dawn, just like old times. And, just like old times, Lance was trouncing him while they sparred, and being annoyingly smug about it.

Tristan poked his head in. "Are you sparring? Can I watch?"

"Sure, why not?" Lance said.

Tristan beamed. "Epic."

"Don't look so pleased. You have to fight whichever of us wins."

Tristan paled and muttered that, on second thought, he'd just wait outside. Arthur pressed back a grin. He hadn't realized the young guard was so gullible.

He adjusted his helmet and hefted his broadsword, swinging it with a move that had his muscles shaking from the effort. Yet Lance blocked his blow effortlessly. Arthur pressed forward again, and again, Lance's blade swung up to meet his own. He stumbled back, letting the tip of his weapon drag against the ground with a sigh.

There was no amount of practice that could make him a decent broadswordsman, and he didn't know who he was kidding by continuing to try.

"What's going on?" Lance asked, lowering the tip of his weapon. "You're all mopey."

"I'm not mopey. I'm preoccupied. I screwed everything up with Emry. You know, the thing at supper."

Lance frowned. "I had supper with Percival in the guards' mess. Wait, what happened? You didn't ask if she'd magicked her face again, did you?"

"Worse." Arthur sighed. "I reappointed Master Merlin as my court wizard."

"And demoted Emry back to apprentice? Oof." Lance grimaced. "She must have been pissed when you told her you were planning to do that."

"I didn't exactly warn her," Arthur admitted. "I didn't realize it would be a thing." He felt enormously stupid now for having let everything play out the way he had, and convincing himself it would be fine.

Lance shook his head. "No wonder she's upset."

Arthur slid down against a wall, his feet out in front of him, unbuckling his bracers. "What else could I have done? My council was pushing me to do it. He technically never left the position. And she's barely had any training."

"She saved your life a dozen times," Lance pointed out.

"Four at the most," Arthur corrected crisply.

"Well. If that's all." Lance rolled his eyes. "She magicked suits of armor to defend the castle in a siege. Half your court owes her our lives."

"I know." Arthur sighed. "And I've made a mess of it. I disappoint everyone I mean to impress."

"That's not true," said Lance.

"Yes, it is." Arthur's shoulders slumped. "I'm drowning under all of this responsibility. If I could give it back, I would. I thought she'd understand. I meant to do her a favor, relieving her of this burden. But she took it as an insult."

"Have you told her that?"

Arthur raised an eyebrow. "Bold of you to assume she's talking to me."

"You're the king. She can't give you the silent treatment."

"Oh yes, she can. Help me out here. What am I to do?"

Lance thought about it a moment. "You could start with considering her feelings when you make your choices."

When Lance said it, it sounded laughably simple. And like the exact opposite of what he'd done. Besides, it was a fine idea in theory, but it wouldn't work in practice. Not for him, anyway.

"Well, that's impossible," he scoffed. "I can't put my girlfriend ahead of the kingdom. My duties as king have to come first."

"Have you two discussed that? Or did you just assume she understood that's how it would be?"

Arthur started to reply but closed his mouth. Upon reflection, he *had* assumed. She had literally told him she couldn't believe how he'd behaved. Sard, he hadn't just shown her how little he cared, he'd told her.

And the worst part was, it wasn't true. Because he cared for her more than anything. Except it didn't matter. His duties were more important than his happiness. And he'd made them more important than her happiness as well.

Arthur looked stricken. "Sard, I'm never going to be able to get her back. I'm doomed. I'll never have a girlfriend."

Just a wife he didn't want, selected by his royal council. He suppressed a shudder at the thought.

"If you're looking for a boyfriend, I hate to tell you this, but I'm taken," said Lance.

Arthur barked a laugh. "If that were going to happen, it would have years ago."

"That's what I told Perce."

"Jealous, was he?" Arthur was slightly cheered at the thought.

"Hey, we're not talking about my perfectly functional and adorable relationship. We're talking about your disastrous former one."

Arthur groaned. "Don't remind me."

"Fine," Lance said, pushing to his feet. "If it will make you feel better, you can spar with Excalibur."

Arthur grinned and reached for his unbeatable magic sword.

◑ ◑ ◑

Lance was surprised to find Sir Kay waiting for him outside his bedroom when he returned from the armory.

Sard, was he late? He hoped he hadn't lost track of time sparring with Arthur. But no, it was still dark outside, and the torches hadn't yet been lit in the corridor.

The knight scowled, holding up a lantern. "Where have you been?"

"Training with Arthur." Lance frowned at Sir Kay's obvious impatience. "Is something wrong?"

"I wish to be on the tilting field early today. Hurry and saddle my horse. I ride in half an hour."

That was impossible. Cerberus was still in his stall, and Sir Kay wore no padding or armor. "But—" Lance started.

"Is there a problem, squire?" his uncle barked.

"No, Sir Kay. Half an hour." As the knight left in a huff, Lance jammed on his tunic and scraped his hair back into a knot, wondering what had inspired such an early start.

When he arrived at the knights' stables, a dozen squires were already there, many of them frantic. How strange. It seemed everyone had decided to start training early today.

"What's going on?" Lance asked as Dryan darted around him with an armload of equipment.

"Can't stop now!" Dryan called over his shoulder.

Lance frowned.

"You really don't know?" drawled Fergus, blocking Lance's way to Cerberus's stall.

"Clearly not," Lance snapped, losing patience. He was sorely regretting having dined in the guards' mess last night.

"They've announced the royal tournament." Fergus grinned nastily, leaning against the door. "Winner is the new king's champion. It seems Sir Kay is about to lose his title."

No wonder Sir Kay was in a state. The knight was vain about being the king's champion, a position he'd held for, well, decades. But after injuring his shoulder, he'd taken a step back from fighting. It seemed that with Arthur's coronation looming, the title was up for grabs. Lance hadn't realized it would work like that. That certainly explained why Sir Kay had been pacing outside his room before dawn.

"That's not the best part," said Fergus. "The winner gets Joyous Gard, and funds enough to run the estate."

"The prize is a castle?" Lance frowned. "Shouldn't it be the glory of being named king's champion?"

Fergus laughed. "What use is glory? The king's favorites should be rewarded. It's the way things have always been done."

Lance shouldn't have been surprised by the prize, yet somehow he was. It felt like a bribe, and he could sense the royal council's hands all over it. Most knights were second or third sons, those who weren't going to inherit their father's estate and needed to make their own fortunes and fame.

They'd do anything for lands of their own. Even fight to be named champion of a king whom they didn't fully support. But then, it wasn't as if Sir Kay was a better choice. He detested Arthur's vision for a new Camelot, and made no secret of his disapproval.

I wish I could be Arthur's champion, Lance thought wistfully. *Sard the castle. Arthur needs a knight who will fight for Camelot, not just for himself.*

But that was an impossible dream. He was barely a squire. And there was no hope Sir Kay would train him.

Ask him anyway, a small voice in the back of his head urged. *You never know.*

The mood was tense as he saddled Sir Kay's horse, and when he finally led Cerberus out of the stables, the knight was pacing impatiently.

"Finally," snapped Sir Kay. "Now hasten to the armory for as many practice lances as you can carry." The knight swung into the saddle and galloped off toward the tilting fields.

Lance sighed and hurried off to the armory. It was going to be a long day. He didn't even have an opportunity to broach the subject of entering the tournament himself until it was nearly time for supper, when he was repairing a tear in Sir Kay's mail.

The knight had been too impatient to remove his chainmail, for fear he would lose his favored tilting field to another knight should he abandon it, so he'd stuck out his arm and insisted Lance mend it on the spot.

"I was thinking," Lance began, frowning as he worked to pry open the loose link, "that I want to enter the tournament and try for the title."

Sir Kay laughed. "Surely you jest. As if *you're* going to be the next king's champion!"

"I might be, if you helped me train," Lance said. "Please, uncle. I know you want to defend your title, but isn't passing it down to your squire honorable as well?"

"Don't speak nonsense," Sir Kay scolded. "You're a first-year squire."

Lance winced. He knew that. "But I'm good. You've said so yourself. And I know Arthur would want me to try."

"What about me?" Sir Kay demanded. "I aim to defend my title. Did you even think how arrogant it would look to publicly challenge your own knight?"

Lance bit his lip. "I'm not challenging you. Not any more than every other knight in the realm."

"Then you don't expect to advance in the lists?" Sir Kay asked coolly.

Lance's mouth hardened into a thin line. Of course he hoped to advance.

"It's a handsome prize for the winner," taunted the knight.

"I don't want a castle!" Lance insisted.

"But you'll compete against those who do." Sir Kay raised an eyebrow. "And they won't show mercy. Not with such a prize at stake."

Lance hated that Sir Kay had a point. Jousting was dangerous. There was a risk of injury even for the most seasoned knight, and Lance was only a first-year squire, who had never tilted off the practice field.

"I'm not afraid to fight," Lance insisted. "Either in the joust, or at court, for what I want to be mine."

"Then you're a fool," declared Sir Kay. "At the last royal tournament, two fine knights died—one lost an eye, and another lost use of his legs after being trampled by his horse."

Lance winced. He hadn't known it was so bad. He'd seen tournament injuries before, mostly dislocated shoulders and broken ribs. If what Sir Kay said was true . . .

No, the knight was only trying to scare him off. To make certain that Lance helped him in a futile bid to retain his title, instead of graciously stepping aside. It was so entirely selfish, so entirely Sir Kay, that Lance nearly broke the link he was mending in frustration.

"So you won't help me train?" he asked.

"I'm not having my squire lose a limb or an eye for some foolish glory. Some use you'd be to me like that. Or to anyone. Now, hurry up with my mail. I have a title to defend."

Well, if Sir Kay wouldn't help him train, he'd just have to find a way to prepare for the tournament on his own.

CHAPTER 13

"Never heard of it and never stocked it!" the apothecary pronounced with a frown, before turning his back on Emry.

"Thanks anyway," Emry grumbled. *For nothing*, she nearly added. Somehow, she wasn't surprised that the final item on her father's list was impossible.

As she exited the shop, she glared down at the scrap of parchment in her hand. Instead of training her as his assistant, her father had provided her with a list of errands out in the city.

Never mind that it was freezing, and any sensible person would be inside by a roaring fire wearing thick woolen socks. Apparently it was vital that she pick up his new tunics, his custom parchment adorned with his initials in real gold, and a silver quill nib from a shop so exclusive that it didn't even have a sign, just a discreet bell.

As if that wasn't bad enough, she was also meant to acquire eight ounces of a plant she'd never even heard of called Godfrey's root, which she was starting to think didn't exist.

The first apothecary she'd visited had laughed at the request, the second had been closed, the third had quoted her an absurd sum, then told her to come back in three months, and the fourth had just been rude.

And now it was starting to snow. She brushed at the melting flakes that dampened the shoulders of her cloak. *Well, if I can't find it, I can't find it*, she decided, shivering.

She put up her hood and made her way back to the castle, taking her favorite shortcut past a hat shop that usually had an adorable cat snoozing in the window. The cat opened its eyes, regarded her solemnly for a moment, then yawned and went back to its nap. Emry pressed back a grin. Once, London had seemed large and intimidating, but now it felt like home.

When she reached the castle gates, Gawain walked past, whistling a merry tune and carrying a sketchpad and charcoals under his arm. He wore a plain black cloak, which wasn't his style in the slightest, and Emry noticed a dagger at his waist, its sheath functional rather than fashionable.

"You look like a storybook villain," she accused.

"From you, I take that as a compliment," he replied with a smirk. He nodded at her armload of parcels. "Shopping, I see?"

"I'm running errands for my father."

"Same here." Gawain made a face. "And I plan to do them terribly, so mine doesn't ask me again."

That was a good idea. Emry sighed. "If only I'd run into you earlier."

"You could still make a mess of it," Gawain suggested. "Join me for a drink at the Fortune and Favor?"

"Tempting, but no."

"Alas, keep turning me down, Miss Merlin, and one day you might wound my feelings."

Emry raised an eyebrow. "You have feelings?"

Safir, who was on guard at the gate, snickered beneath his helmet, then tried unsuccessfully to turn his laughter into a coughing fit.

"Only when it comes to you," Gawain said with a smirk. He gave a brief bow, and then stepped out into the city.

"I believe he meant that," said Saf. "The part about having feelings for you."

"Oh, shut up, Saf," Emry snapped, pushing past him with her armload of parcels.

Gawain didn't have feelings for anyone but himself. Unless they were feelings of disdain, judgment, or lust. It was why they were friends; because she had declared him uncourtable, and he had declared her the same.

Halfway up the stairs to the wizard's workshop, Emry was enveloped in a thick cloud of foul-scented steam. She frowned, coughing. And then she lifted her skirts and took the rest of the stairs two at a time, wondering what had gone wrong.

"Father?" she called.

The door to the workshop was open, and the steam was even thicker and more noxious. She couldn't even see through it. But she could hear arguing.

"—really done it now," crowed the gargoyle.

"I don't need your help, you meddlesome block of granite," her father retorted.

Emry stepped inside. "What's going on in here?"

Her father emerged from the billowing cloud of steam, his eyes cold and hard. "I'm brewing a temperamental potion, and I cannot tolerate unnecessary interruptions," he snapped. "What do you want?"

"I've run your errands," she said sourly, gesturing at the parcels.

"Good. Did you find the Godfrey's root?" her father asked.

"Well, no, but—" Emry began.

"Why not?" her father demanded.

"No one had it!" Emry fumed. "I went to four different apothecaries!"

Merlin shook his head in disappointment. "Then you hardly tried. There are at least a dozen apothecaries between here and Blackfriars."

"What's it even for?" she asked.

"It enhances magic," the gargoyle called.

"Really?" Emry frowned, wondering why Master Ambrosius had never mentioned it. "Would it work in a healing salve?"

"Enough questions," her father snapped, gesturing impatiently for her to hand over his packages.

"Fine," Emry muttered mutinously, and peered around her father at the potion he was brewing. "Can I help with that?"

"No, you cannot," he said stiffly.

"I'm supposed to be your apprentice," Emry reminded him.

"Then find me some sarding Godfrey's root!" her father growled, practically shoving her out the door.

He slammed it in her face, and she heard the muffled sound of a locking spell being cast.

Emry glared at the locked door in frustration, tempted to use her Anwen powers to erase his spell and barge back inside and yell at him until the tightness in her chest went away and she could breathe again.

She should have expected this. For her father to treat her like an errand girl, instead of a proper assistant. And the one person she wished she could talk to about it was the last person in the world she wanted to see right now, because this was all his smug, royal fault.

She wished she'd gone for that drink with Gawain after all.

Well, fine. If her father insisted on commandeering the workshop, then he could have it. She'd rather spend the afternoon in bed reading salacious novels and eating too many biscuits.

Which she did, with great enjoyment.

She was just getting to a good part when there was a knock at her door.

"Guin!" Emry squealed, embracing the girl. The last person she expected to find calling on her was Princess Guinevere. Yet there she stood, looking tired and travel worn in a crimson cloak trimmed with white fur. "What are you doing here? You're not supposed to be back for weeks."

"Change of plans," Guin said, sweeping past her with a sigh. "The

Lady of the Lake was keeping the fact that your father had returned to herself. Emmett only found out by accident."

"Oh," Emry said, understanding. "Oh dear."

"He is still here, isn't he? Emmett will be inconsolable if he already left."

"He's definitely still here," Emry said, unable to keep the bitterness from her voice. She cleared a stack of books from her desk and gestured toward her poor excuse for a sitting area. "So, where is my brother?"

"Shaving." Guin rolled her eyes. "Wanted to clean up his scraggly excuse for a beard before seeing his father."

Emry giggled. "Sounds like Emmett."

Guin stared longingly at Emry's half-empty plate of biscuits. "Er, do you mind if I have some?"

"Finish them, please," Emry said, offering her the plate.

She watched, amused, as Guin took a seat at her desk and shoved an entire biscuit into her mouth. Emry much preferred this version of Guin to the proper, perfect princess she'd been when she'd arrived.

"I can't believe you came back with him," Emry said, since even the flowing fabric of Guin's cloak couldn't disguise her growing baby bump.

"He wouldn't have left otherwise. And I could never forgive myself if he felt so trapped in our relationship that he sacrificed what was truly important to him," said Guin. "Speaking of relationships, how are you and Arthur?"

Emry winced. "Over?"

"Oh no." Guin made a face. "What did I miss?"

"Just Arthur reinstating my father as court wizard in front of everyone, without warning me he was going to do it," Emry said sourly. "And he didn't even apologize! He was like, 'I have to put Camelot first,

I'm the king, and you should be grateful to be such a powerful wizard's apprentice.'"

"He did not!" Guin said, shocked.

"Well, I'm paraphrasing," Emry admitted. "But that's basically what happened. And he's avoided me ever since."

Guin shook her head. "For someone so smart, he can be so stupid."

"Tell me about it," Emry said glumly. "The problem is his council. They don't let him decide anything. And instead of putting them in their place when he disagrees, he just goes along with what they say. I don't understand what he's so afraid will happen if he stands up to them."

Guin thought about it for a moment. "It can't be easy, being in his position, with no one helping him figure out what he's supposed to do."

"I don't care," Emry declared, even though Guin made a good point. "He's being awful, and I have zero sympathy for anyone but myself, currently."

Guin pressed back a smile. "You two really are the same."

"We are not!" Emry said. "That's it, give those back. You've lost your biscuit privileges."

She lunged for the plate of biscuits, but Guin was faster. She dumped every last treat into her lap, leaving Emry holding an empty plate.

"Impressive," Emry commented.

"Learned it from my brother." Guin serenely selected a biscuit from her lap and took a bite. "Boys always try to keep the best things to themselves, and sometimes they don't even realize they're doing it, because it's so ingrained in them that the world works to their advantage." Guin sighed, a faraway look on her heart-shaped face.

"I was supposed to change that, being the first female court wizard," Emry said, propping her chin miserably in her hands.

"And you did," Guin insisted. "You know, I doubt my father would want to train me as his replacement, either. Not that my brother is at all enthusiastic to take on the role."

Emry frowned, seeing Guin in a new light. She hadn't realized Guin had ever thought about being queen.

"So how is it, being your father's apprentice?" Guin asked.

"Awful," Emry said. "I'm more of a valet, or a serving maid. He has me running personal errands like picking up his new shirts." She was gratified when Guin rolled her eyes. "And he has no interest in instructing me in magic. He literally kicked me out of the workshop today when he was brewing a potion, instead of letting me assist him."

"I'm sorry," Guin said.

Emry sighed. "It's infuriating. I can't stand men. I think I'm done with them."

"Same," Guin said.

"Oh no, what's Emmett done now?" Emry wondered if she even wanted to know.

"We were supposed to be on our honeymoon, but he won't even kiss me," Guin complained. "Not like he used to. He acts as if I'm made of glass."

Emry frowned. "That doesn't sound like Emmett." Or did it? Now that she thought about it . . . "Our mother died in childbirth. Perhaps he's afraid of losing you?" she suggested.

Guin gave her a skeptical look. "Emmett? Afraid?" She shook her head dismissively. "It's easier to believe I've simply lost my appeal now that I'm the size of an armoire." She stared down at the swell of her stomach and gently brushed away some stray biscuit crumbs.

"Hardly!" Emry protested. She hated to see Guin down on herself like this, and she was furious that her brother had caused it. And then she had an idea. "Come on, I have those cosmetics you gave me. We're going to make you look so alluring that when you arrive at supper, half the lords in the castle will go tight in their trousers at the sight of you."

Guin grinned. "Emry Merlin, are you giving me a makeover?"

Emry scowled. "Don't tell anyone, or I'll curse your unborn child with permanent hiccups."

Half an hour later, Guin was freshly bathed, her dark curls swept enticingly to one side of her neck, and her lips freshly slicked with a rosy salve. Her tan skin glowed, and a ruby pendant rested just between the swell of her breasts, drawing attention to her curves. Emry had enlarged one of Guin's silk gowns that had grown too tight, and the crimson fabric swirled around her ankles, showing off matching slippers.

Guin beamed at her reflection in Emry's wardrobe. "The gown is perfect! I can't believe you added pockets!" she enthused.

"Magic pockets. They hold twice as much as you'd think."

"Even better." Guin patted a piece of stray hair back into place. "Well, even if Emmett doesn't take notice, I'm feeling myself, and that's what really matters."

Emry laughed at Guin's informal speech. "I'm so glad you're back."

Guin smiled. "So am I."

"And trust me, Emmett will notice," Emry said. Guin was magnificent. She looked every inch a confident, beautiful royal.

Something Emry would never be.

If you love him, let him go.

A frantic knock sounded on Emry's door. That would be Emmett.

"It's not magicked," she called, waving a hand. The door cracked open.

Her brother goggled at them. "What are you two doing in here?"

"It's my room," Emry reminded him.

"Right, but it used to be Father's," he said, his shoulders deflating. "I—I thought he'd be here."

"He's probably still in the workshop," Emry said sourly. "Nice to see you, too, by the way."

Shaving wasn't all her brother had gotten up to, Emry saw, taking in his freshly polished boots and his silver-buttoned jacket. His hair had grown long, and the carefully mussed way he wore it swooped over one eye made him look like a rogue.

"Right, the workshop," he said. "Thanks." He turned on his heel and hurried down the hall.

Emry looked at Guin, who shook her head in shared disappointment.

"He's been in a state all day," Guin reported. "I think he's nervous, though he'd never admit it."

Nervous? That wasn't like her brother. But Emry suspected Guin was right. After all, Emmett might be their father's favorite, but he had screwed up his legacy pretty spectacularly. And he shouldn't have to face their father's disappointment alone.

"I'm going after him," Emry said, hurrying after her brother. "Emmett, wait!"

When she caught up with him at the bottom of the workshop stairwell, he fixed her with a glare. "I can't believe you!" he accused. "You should have told me Father was alive!"

Emry winced. She couldn't even begin to explain. But she owed her brother an apology—that much was clear. "He was trapped in an enchanted sleep in another world. The Lady of the Lake said his return was impossible."

"Clearly not," Emmett said.

"I know that *now*," Emry said. "Look, I'm sorry. Truly. You know how the Lady of the Lake is. She misled me. Told me his life had been taken, used all of these Lady of the Lake–ish phrases that sounded like he was really gone. But that's no excuse. I should have told you."

"Yeah, you should have," Emmett said fiercely. And then he sighed, the fight gone out of him. "Well, how is he?"

Infuriating. Close-minded. Arrogant.

"The same," Emry said. Bitterly, she added, "Arthur reappointed him as court wizard."

"He *is* the greatest wizard who ever lived," Emmett reminded her, sounding proud.

Emry didn't want to hear it. "You should have seen him when he found out I'd been given the position. He wished it had been you."

She'd been trying to make her brother feel better, but his expression darkened. "Then he's the only one," Emmett muttered.

They climbed the stairs to the workshop in silence. Halfway up, they were enveloped in the same thick cloud of foul-scented steam. So he was still at it. Why was she not surprised?

The door, naturally, was still locked. Emry took a tiny dagger from her pocket and pricked her finger, feeling her Anwen powers surge to the surface. "*Isaz*," she muttered, directing the spell at the lock's mechanism. It clicked open. One of the first rules of spellcasting was that magic didn't work on magic, but Emry's Anwen powers defied that law.

Emmett wiped his palms on his jacket. He really was nervous.

"You okay?" she asked.

He nodded, and she pushed open the door of the workshop.

"Father?" she called. Inside, the steam was even thicker and more noxious. "Is everything all right?"

Her father looked up from behind a thickly bubbling cauldron, which was billowing steam, annoyed. "Go away!"

"But—"

"Must I repeat myself? I'm not to be disturbed," her father replied tersely.

"Father!" Emmett called, pushing past Emry. "I came as soon as I heard you were back!"

Of course Merlin abandoned his precious potion instantly, clasping Emmett by the shoulders and beaming. "Look at you! A man now! And married, I'm told."

"It's not every day you convince a princess to fall in love with you," Emmett bragged, his grin wide.

"I always knew you were destined for greatness."

Emry rolled her eyes. *Greatness.* Honestly. Her brother had neglected to use a protective potion. That was the *opposite* of greatness.

"Runs in the family," Emmett said, looking pleased.

Emry slouched on a stool at the table, forgotten and ignored as her father and brother chatted excitedly. She knew she shouldn't be so annoyed. Still, she could have done without being shown just how much happier the great wizard Merlin was to see his son, who could do no wrong.

They were so alike, Emry realized. It was uncanny, seeing them together. They both held themselves arrogantly, like men who had the kind of power that couldn't be taken away. Like men who expected the whole world to respect them, and bend to their will.

The worst part was, it too often did.

"Hello?" Guin called from the doorway. "Is everyone up here?"

"Guin! You didn't have to climb all those steps!" Emmett said, looking panicked.

So that was what Guinevere had meant about Emmett treating her like she was made of glass.

"I've spent the entire day in a cramped carriage." Guin rolled her eyes. But Emry could see she was out of breath. The girl's bosom was heaving.

And ugh, her father had definitely taken notice. How could he not, when Guin stood there in that low-necked gown, her glossy curls swept over one shoulder? Emmett was staring, too. "Come in, my dear," Merlin said. "You must be the ravishing Princess Guinevere."

Guin bobbed a curtsey. "My apologies for interrupting your family reunion," she said prettily, "but I was so eager to meet you."

And there it was. The thing that Emry would never be. Even five months pregnant, Guin was the perfect princess. Lovely, demure, well-spoken. Who wouldn't be enchanted?

"A beautiful woman is a welcome interruption." Merlin pressed a kiss to the back of her hand. "Welcome to the family, princess."

Guin blushed. "Thank you." She hesitated before pressing on. "You must be so proud that your daughter was made Arthur's court wizard. I know I was! What a new world it is, having women be recognized not just for their talents, but also for their innate power."

"Indeed," Merlin said politely.

Emry pressed back a smile. Oh, she adored Guin.

Merlin looked between his twins. "I'll expect to see both of you in the workshop tomorrow morning for lessons. Naturally you'll both serve as my apprentices."

But of course—only now that his son was back would the great and powerful Merlin deign to instruct his daughter in magic. Emry fought back a growl of frustration.

"Emmett's not interested in—" Emry started to explain.

"Shut up, yes I am," Emmett finished, glaring at Emry.

"Tell him you have no interest in becoming court wizard," Emry hissed at her brother.

Emmett shrugged. "Now that Father's back, things have changed."

That was exactly the problem.

CHAPTER 14

No. Not now.

Morgana was being pushed down deep within herself. Again. She gritted her teeth and pushed back, refusing to give Bellicent total control.

Miraculously, it worked.

She was trapped a long way down in the dark, but she was still there. If she concentrated, she could see and hear what was going on.

And she was pretty sure Bellicent had no idea. She could feel the woman's emotions, her unbridled glee over being given access to Morgana's world.

The sorceress's first stop was the valley below Lothian Keep, where Yurien's soldiers were arriving and making camp. She approached the king's tent, its flaps trimmed in gold, and pushed her way inside before the guards could protest. There stood Yurien, flanked by two of his best commanders, bent over maps of the terrain they intended to travel. He was dressed for war, with plate armor over his mail, and black leather bracers covering his forearms. A heavy fur cloak hung from his shoulders, making him look wider and more intimidating than his short stature did.

"What now?" he snapped at the interruption.

"Come with me," Bellicent ordered. "It is time."

Yurien grinned as he recognized his visitor.

"Finally." He reached for his goblet and drained it in a gulp, a trickle of wine running down his chin and into his ginger beard. He didn't wipe it away. "Let's see if you can deliver what you've promised." He looked to one of his commanders. "Assemble the troops."

"But, sire—" the man began, a bit hesitant. "They're eating breakfast."

"Assemble them anyway," Yurien growled. "This is more important."

"Do you have the trinket?" Bellicent asked.

Yurien fiddled protectively with the ruby stone around his neck. "I do." Bellicent reached for it greedily, but Yurien snatched it back. "Not yet," he said.

"Fetch your son as well," Bellicent suggested. "A boy should know his father's greatness. And his source of power."

No, Morgana thought. Mordred was too young to see any of this.

"But—" Yurien began.

"You think he will mistake me for his mother?" Bellicent gave a scathing laugh.

"Of course not," promised Yurien.

They crossed the field, and Morgana saw what had to be hundreds of tents, and thousands of men. *My son will not ride with them to battle*, she vowed. He would remain at the castle, where it was safe.

When they reached the edge of the tents, lines of soldiers waited for them at attention, ignoring the fat snowflakes that drifted down onto their helmets and shoulders.

"My men," Yurien said with pride. "Five thousand of them."

"The stone," said Bellicent, sounding bored. Dimly, Morgana was aware of her own hand rising, palm outstretched. Of the weight and pulse of power of what was placed in it. The enchantment that had once belonged to Excalibur's scabbard, which made its wearer unkillable in battle, pulsed from where Morgana had trapped it in the simple gemstone pendant.

Yurien licked his lips, nervous.

Morgana felt Bellicent reach for her magic. Gasped as the power flowed out of her and wrapped around the enchantment. The stone glowed, and then cracked.

Anwen's magic rushed forward, cold and bright. Morgana yearned for it, to take it for her own. To send Bellicent back to her own world, and reclaim her body, her life, her power.

The high sorceress held out her hand, and the icy magic settled over her arm like a glove.

Bellicent cast no spell. Instead, she molded the magic through sheer will. "Make them bleed," she demanded.

Yurien turned to one of his commanders. "You heard her."

"Soldiers, cut yourselves!" the commander called out.

The men reached for their daggers and plunged them into their palms. Their blood dripped onto the ground, and Bellicent smiled in her borrowed body, then flung her hands wide.

"Make them bow to me," she demanded.

Yurien looked taken aback.

Refuse her! Morgana wanted to say, but her words were stuck, silent, just as trapped as she was.

"Have them do it," he told his commander.

The man shouted for the soldiers to bow, and they did, kneeling in their own blood.

Bellicent's grin stretched wide. The icy wind rippled through her hair, tangling its wild lengths.

"You are in my service, bound by your blood, and your fealty, freely given!" Bellicent cried. "And for that, I give you a reward: Any wound you receive in battle will heal instantly. You will be able to cheat death!"

The magic was pulsing over her skin, giving it an undeniable glow. A bright white light enveloped the field, and when it cleared, Morgana saw a faint, unearthly glow over her husband's soldiers. It faded within seconds.

"It is done," Bellicent announced. "Here, this stone is worthless now."

She tossed the cracked gem to Yurien, who caught it with a frown. "Worthless? What about my enchantment?"

"I transferred it to your soldiers."

Yurien's face clouded with anger. "That wasn't our bargain!"

"Of course it was," said Bellicent. "You asked for your soldiers to be unbeatable. Not their king."

Yurien let out a foul curse. "You deceived me."

"I have given you what was promised," said Bellicent. "Test it, if you doubt me."

"Rise!" called the commander, and the ranks of soldiers climbed to their feet.

A soldier in the front line sneezed.

"You," said Yurien. "Step forward." He tightened his grip on his sword.

"Wait!" cried a voice, high and young. Mordred sprinted toward them, followed by an out-of-breath servant. "What are you going to do?"

"Stab this soldier through the heart," Yurien said grimly.

"For what purpose? I thought hanging was the usual punishment?"

"He is not being punished. I am testing an enchantment."

Mordred's eyes blazed with intensity as he made the imperious demand, "I want to do it!"

No. Morgana twisted, fighting to reach the surface. To prevent it. Her boy was too young. Too innocent. She didn't want blood on his hands.

Yet she watched in horror as Yurien lowered his blade with a laugh. "You wish to do it?"

"Yes, Father," said Mordred.

"Say please," prompted Yurien.

"Yes, please, Father!" Mordred said eagerly, holding out his hand.

Yurien beamed with pride as he removed a sharp dagger from his belt and offered the boy his weapon.

Morgana couldn't watch. But she couldn't look away. Not as Bellicent thrummed with excitement over what was taking place. Morgana squirmed as her precious child—her little boy who still begged for stories at bedtime and carried a carved wooden snake in his pocket—raised his father's dagger and plunged it into the chest of the kneeling, trembling soldier.

The man gasped and fell to the ground, the blade sticking out of his tunic. A dark stain spread at the wound. Mordred stared down at the man with round, frightened eyes, his hand shaking.

"I did it!" he said, looking to his father for approval.

"You did," said Bellicent, her voice an indulgent croon.

"Mama, did you see?" Mordred asked excitedly.

Morgana wanted to scream. Her son didn't know the difference. He didn't recognize the monster wearing his mother's skin.

"I'm impressed," Bellicent said coolly.

The stabbed soldier went still. Then he let out a great shuddering gasp, and the knife embedded in his chest popped out, as though he were being stabbed in reverse.

He sat up, his eyes wild and haunted, his chest heaving.

The spell had worked.

CHAPTER 15

Lance squinted against the freezing rain, focused on the distant tilting target. Raindrops pelted down on his helmet, drumming against his armor so loudly that he could barely concentrate. He shivered from the cold, despite the warming spell he'd begged off Emry that morning.

"Come on, girl," he urged his horse.

But it was no use. The animal shook her head with a snort, her breath clouding the air. Her mane was soaked and the field was mud, but if he didn't practice now, he didn't know when else he'd get the chance. Sir Kay had him squiring from sunup to sundown. It was only that day's grim weather that had kept the knights away from the field. So Lance had seized the opportunity.

"Please, girl," he begged, tightening his hold on his soaked weapon.

"Your grip is too low on the lance, squire," said a voice.

Lance turned and saw Sir Tor leaning against the fence to the tilting yard, one hand shielding their eyes from the rain. A turquoise scarf was wound thrice around their neck, contrasting merrily against a tan oiled cloak.

"But this is how Sir Kay showed me," Lance protested.

"Oh, I don't doubt the grip will serve you, but humor me a moment."

"What would you have me do?"

"Toss the weapon upward and catch it," Sir Tor advised. "Mark where your hands land on the grip. That's the spot you want."

Lance did. And saw his natural grip settled a finger's width higher than what he'd been using. He gave the weapon a practice thrust, and his eyes widened in surprise. "It's easier to aim like this."

Sir Tor nodded. "There's science to it. I can show you, if you'd like. Preferably inside, and over a mug of hot cider."

"Truly?" Lance couldn't believe his luck. "That would be—well. Thank you."

"Stable your horse, and meet me at the Fortune and Favor," said Sir Tor.

Lance didn't have to be told twice.

Later, when he pried open the door of the nearby tavern, drenched but intrigued, Sir Tor waved at him from a booth along the side. The knight had two mugs of cider on the table, along with a stack of books, a quill, and some curious-looking metal instruments that seemed like they belonged in the wizard's workshop.

Lance peeled off his cloak, half-frozen. He'd forgotten to ask Emry how long her warming spell would last, but he suspected it had worn off ages ago.

"This'll help, lad," said Sir Tor, shoving one of the mugs across the table toward Lance.

Lance nodded his thanks and took a sip. "Speaking of . . . why are you helping me?"

Sir Tor raised an eyebrow. "Why were you out there in the rain when no one else was training?"

"It was the only chance I had," Lance confessed.

"I figured as much. Winning the tournament does come with a desirable prize."

Lance made a face. "What would I do with a castle? Leave it to my heirs?"

Sir Tor chuckled at that. "He's very handsome, your captain."

"He's not my captain," Lance protested, feeling color rise to his cheeks. He and Perce were—well, he didn't know what they were, other than happy. And for now, that was enough.

"My mistake," Sir Tor said, pressing back a smile. "If not for the prize, then for why else were you out there, practicing in the rain?"

Lance took another sip of his cider and stared into the crackling hearth, suspecting the knight already knew far more than they were saying. "Sir Kay won't let me train. He says it's too dangerous for me to compete, and I could get injured, or worse."

"You could," Sir Tor agreed.

"But it's the only chance I'll have," said Lance.

"There will be other tournaments in the spring, lad," said Sir Tor. "And in the summer, and for years to come."

"Not to be named Arthur's champion." Lance bit his lip at the confession. And then he plunged on. "I don't care about the glory, or the honor. And I don't care about unseating Sir Kay as champion or winning some stupid castle that's probably in ruins. I want to ride into battle at Arthur's side. I want to be his best knight."

Sir Tor nodded slowly, taking another sip of cider. "You told me once to pledge to Camelot when Arthur became king."

Lance stared at the knight in surprise. Sir Tor was a knight of Cameliard, and an undisputed champion in the joust. They had even beat Sir Kay, jousting a perfect tournament where no knight could land a hit against them.

"Are you entering the tournament?" Lance asked with a sinking feeling.

"I also have no use for a castle," said Sir Tor, with a wry smile. "But you were right, telling me to believe in Arthur. The kingdom he's trying to build is one I should like to see. And help build."

"Then the title will be yours," said Lance. He had never met a knight who was Sir Tor's equal.

"Not necessarily, lad. A knight needs luck as well as skill, and nothing is guaranteed. But if you're going to try for it, I'd like to help."

"How?" Lance asked.

"Did your tutors happen to teach you much in the way of geometry or physics?" Sir Tor inquired, opening a book.

"I suppose," Lance said, frowning. "But what does that have to do with jousting?"

Sir Tor smiled. "Everything."

CHAPTER 16

Emry pushed open the door of the wizard's workshop, expecting the tower to be empty, but her father had arrived ahead of her. He was bent over a thick, dusty book, muttering to himself. He didn't even look up as she entered.

"Morning," she called.

Her father startled, as though he hadn't been expecting anyone. "A bit early, isn't it?"

"Not really." Master Ambrosius had always demanded a crack-of-dawn start when she was his apprentice. And Emmett had always been unforgivably late. She assumed today would be no exception, especially after all the wine he'd drunk at supper the night before.

The lads at their table had welcomed him back with glee. And of course had been delighted to have Guinevere join them, raising their table's status considerably.

Emry looked around the workshop, feeling as though something was missing. And then she realized what. "Hey, what's happened to the gargoyle?"

Her father grimaced. "I had it relocated to the royal vault."

"Oh, poor thing, it'll hate that," Emry said.

"It was driving me mad. Why don't you nip down to the kitchens for a pot of tea and some toast?" Her father suggested. "And I wouldn't say no to some jam."

Emry shook her head, trying not to lose her temper. "There are servants to do that. Why don't we get started without Emmett? I've outpaced him in my training, anyway."

"I'll be the judge of that," her father said crisply, marching off to the storeroom and banging around. Emry tapped her foot and waited for him to emerge. Which he didn't. "The tea, sweetheart?" he called.

"Of course," Emry grumbled, stomping down to the kitchens to fetch it.

At least Master Ambrosius had treated her as an apprentice. Her father was ordering her around like she was a serving maid. Sending her gargoyle down to the vaults. Making her fetch him tea. She had half a mind to cast a heating spell on it, so every sip was scalding, no matter how long he waited for it to cool.

She briefly considered it, but the heating spell would need to renew itself once the temperature dropped below a certain point, and she couldn't quite figure out how to manage it. So she sulked while her father ate his breakfast and ignored her, then while he read his book and ignored her, until Emmett finally poked his head through the doorway.

He was dressed in his courtier's finest and eating a piece of toast smeared with an absurd amount of marmalade.

"Wasn't sure what time you wanted to get started," he said.

"We were waiting for you," said their father.

Emry rolled her eyes. Emmett was an hour late. Yet the world had stopped to wait for him. Or, at least, their father had.

"Finish your breakfast, son," Merlin said indulgently. "There's strawberry jam and toast here, too."

Emmett raised an eyebrow. "You found maids who weren't terrified to bring food to the tower?"

"He didn't," Emry said sourly. "He sent *me*."

Emmett frowned, knowing as well as Emry that the only time Master Ambrosius had sent them to the kitchens was as punishment.

"Er, I actually am thirsty," he said, with a longing glance at the breakfast spread.

Emry waved a hand at the cold teapot, heating it. A ribbon of steam curled from the lid.

"Might as well," Emmett said, helping himself to the toast. As he ate, he boasted of his magic, his talent for gambling, and his snagging a princess for a wife while their father listened raptly. He laughed at the parts that made Emry wince, as though he approved of every foolish mistake and risk.

"You truly are my son," he said so many times that Emry lost count. She slouched forgotten and ignored at the table, glaring down at the leaves at the bottom of her teacup in annoyance.

Her father and brother were being insufferable, and the worst part was, she'd known they would be like this. She'd just convinced herself that things had changed.

And they had—but not as much as she'd hoped.

"Well then," said their father. "Now that you've eaten, I'd like to try a little levitation work."

Finally! Emry had been waiting all week to actually learn something. In different circumstances, she would have given anything for this. So she tried to muster some enthusiasm.

"What will you have us do?" she asked.

Their father gestured at a chamber pot he'd placed beneath the window, which Master Ambrosius had kept for the infirmary.

And then he tipped a coin purse onto the table. Gold and silver spilled out. It was a fortune. Income enough to run their household back in Brocelande for years. Yet he treated it as though it was nothing. Emry wondered where he'd gotten it all. Gambling, no doubt.

"I'm going to have you float these coins into the pot, to work on your precision," he explained. "Who knows what spell to use for that?"

For a moment, Emry thought he was joking. Floating coins across the room? They weren't eleven years old.

"Emmett?" their father prompted.

"Er . . . ἵπταμαι," Emmett managed.

"Why wouldn't you use the Latin?"

"Master Ambrosius preferred that I use Greek," said Emmett.

"And I prefer the Latin. Which is?" their father asked.

"*Volito*," Emry said.

"Well, go on, let's see you both try it."

Try it. Honestly. Emry could cast this spell with her eyes closed. In silence. While brewing a potion.

Yet her father stood there waiting for her to do it aloud, with her wand. Did he think so little of her skill?

"*Volito*," Emmett said, with a wave of his wand. A silver coin rose out of the pile. He was sweating visibly as he maneuvered it above the chamber pot and let it drop in with a clink.

"Good," said their father. "Now, give it a try, sweetheart."

Emry rolled her eyes. Flicked her wrist. A coin lifted and floated into the pot.

"You'll tire yourself out doing it like that," he warned.

"It's a simple floating spell," Emry returned. "I'm way past this."

"I'll determine that for myself."

Emry raised an eyebrow. Twitched a finger. A dozen coins lifted into the air and sailed into the chamber pot in rapid succession.

Their father sighed. "Perhaps a smaller target, to make it more challenging." He reached for a metal bowl the size of his palm and placed it on the windowsill.

"Let's see if you can land a coin in that," he said. "Come on, Emmett, lad. Show me you have the chops to be the next court wizard."

Emmett blanched.

Emry glared at him. "Er, right. Well." Emmett pushed up his sleeves and gritted his teeth, and managed to land a coin in the bowl.

"That's my boy!" Merlin cried. "Go on, sweetheart, let's see if you can manage it."

"If I can manage it?" Emry repeated, temper flaring. "I've already told you, I'm past this. *Elevo metallicum!*" she cried.

Every metal object in the room levitated a foot into the air. Including the thick-bottomed cauldron in the fireplace. They floated there, suspended by her magic, and her wand was still on the table.

She folded her arms across her chest and waited for their father's response.

Emmett was staring at her in disbelief. "Sarding hell, Em. That's incredible."

"I don't believe that's what I asked for," said her father.

"You can't ever praise me, can you?" she snapped, gesturing for the objects to come back down to the ground. They landed a little more roughly than she'd intended, and some of the coins rolled onto the floor.

"Your spell was impressive, but your execution was arrogant and unfocused," her father accused. "Overall, sloppy."

"*Sloppy?*" Emry didn't think she'd heard him correctly. "I made a hundred objects fly at once!"

"And your focus was on none of them," Merlin returned, pushing up his sleeves and taking out his wand. "*Elevo omnia!*" he cried, and every object in the room lifted off the ground in unison. "*Tergo,*" he murmured, and the dust cleared instantly, leaving the tower gleaming. "This is the part you got wrong," he said calmly, and, his eyes narrowed in concentration, he flicked his wand, muttering the spell that gently lowered everything back into place.

Emry's stomach twisted as she watched how precisely and perfectly he had done it. Because as much as she hated to admit it, he was right. In comparison, she *had* been sloppy. Emmett's mouth was hanging open as he surveyed the tower. "Wow," he said.

"How did you do that?" Emry demanded, desperate to learn. He'd maintained two different spells at once, on multiple objects, in tandem.

She'd never seen magic performed like that before. With such power, and such control.

"A lesson for another time," said her father. He dug out a handkerchief and mopped at his brow.

"That isn't fair," Emry complained.

"Did you even consider how Emmett would feel about you skipping ahead?"

"Oh, I'm used to it," Emmett said with a shrug, putting his feet up on the table and crossing his ankles. "Show her, Father. I want to see if she can do it."

Merlin shook his head. "Another time," he said more firmly. "Now, why don't you work on lifting heavier objects? See how much you can handle."

"Sure," Emmett said, as their father selected some sizable tomes from a shelf of old folios.

"And, Emry," their father said as she looked up hopefully, "since, as you've said, you're past this, I have a list of errands I'd like you to run."

◐ ◐ ◐

Emry staggered up the stairs to the wizard's workshop with her arms full of parcels, snow melting into damp splotches on the shoulders of her cloak. It was nearly dark outside, but finally, she'd found an apothecary with that sarding Godfrey's root. The man had been using it as part of a glass terrarium display and hadn't wanted to sell it, so she'd had to purchase the full display. The entire afternoon felt like a punishment. Like her father had wanted an excuse to be rid of her, so he could spend time with Emmett instead.

She hoped her brother had driven him crazy. Yet as she climbed the stairs to the workshop and heard a burst of laughter, she knew she hadn't been so lucky.

"I found everything," she announced, wrestling the door open with her elbow.

Her father looked up from the battered wooden table, where he and Emmett weren't alone. Instead, three of her father's friends had joined them, feet kicked up on the table, goblets of drink at their elbows, and cards in their hands. Coins sat in fat piles, the largest in front of her father.

"Ah, that's great, sweetheart," he said.

"Working hard, I see," she said dryly, surveying the scene.

This was what they'd been doing while she was trampling through the cold and snow? Drinking and gambling? And they'd clearly been at it for some time. General Timias definitely wasn't on his first goblet of wine.

As if he sensed her thoughts, he raised his glass. "Pour us another round, lass?"

Emry waited for a beat, hoping her father would tell the general where he could shove it.

"Go on, then," Merlin urged, and Emry fought down a growl of frustration.

She snapped her fingers, and the wine bottle floated into the air and tipped a heavy pour into the general's goblet. Everyone goggled at the quiet but impressive display of magic.

Emry smiled sweetly. "Anyone else?" she inquired. "Emmett, surely you could use some more wine."

Her brother had the good sense to look embarrassed. "I'm fine," he mumbled.

"Nonsense, lad, with your first child on the way, you need a drink more than any of us," insisted Sir Ban.

It was so incredibly unfair. Emry glared at the men who had taken over the workshop, and at Emmett, who had been invited to join them while she was sent off to run errands and then expected to pour wine like . . . well, like she wasn't a wizard at all, but merely a wizard's unmarried daughter.

"Emry, sweetheart, there's no need for you to hang around here," said her father. "Why don't you see what the other young ladies are doing?"

"I should think embroidery," Emry replied coldly.

"That sounds like a treat," said the general. "Run along, lass. And leave us men to our cards."

She hoped her brother might stand up for her. But instead he averted his eyes, remaining silent. Complicit. Following their father's example. So this was how it was going to be from now on?

This workshop had been *hers*. Now she wasn't even welcome here as a guest, much less an apprentice. Emry's hands clenched into fists as the glassware on a nearby shelf rattled.

No. She needed to calm down. She forced herself to take a deep breath, and then another. She'd come so close to losing control of her magic.

And if she had, she doubted anyone would trust her in the workshop at all. She wasn't wanted? Fine. Then she'd go.

She let her packages drop to the ground. Then she turned and raced down the stairs, burning with resentment.

CHAPTER 17

"I can't believe there's another installment!" Emry beamed, clutching the book that Guin had just handed her. "I was so worried the pirate captains wouldn't stay together after they lost the buried treasure."

"Spoilers," Issie warned, tossing a silk cushion at Emry.

Emry flicked a finger, and the cushion swerved out of the way, smacking Branjen in the face instead.

Bran shrieked, then giggled.

The four girls were having tea and cakes in Guinevere and Emmett's apartments, and, until Emry had arrived, had all been plugging away at their embroidery. She couldn't believe she'd guessed right about what they were doing.

But anywhere was better than the workshop at the moment.

"When I've finished, we can discuss it," Emry promised Guin.

Guin looked confused. "I would have thought you'd do that with Arthur?"

Emry frowned. "Why on earth would you think that?"

Guinevere snorted into her tea. It was entirely unladylike, and Emry adored her for it. "He's the one who bought those for the castle library," the princess said. "He nearly died of embarrassment when he discovered I'd found them. I thought you knew?"

"Nope." Emry grinned. She should have guessed a salacious romance about two pirate captains in the castle library had come from Arthur.

"We'll have to loudly discuss the plot in front of him," Emry decided. "On the chance he hasn't yet read it."

"Oh," Branjen said knowingly, "so you're still tormenting each other."

"We're not tormenting each other," Emry snapped. "He demoted me from court wizard! And then he acted confused about why I was upset. And instead of apologizing, he's decided to completely ignore me."

Branjen tsked. "You need a girlfriend," she said, with an indulgent smile in Issie's direction. "A woman would never."

Actually, a girlfriend wasn't a terrible idea. Neither was the thought of Arthur seething with jealousy to see her happy with someone else.

"If you find someone who would suit, let me know," Emry said.

Branjen looked delighted, but Issie's brows knit together in thought. "Is Lady Viola attending the coronation ball?" she asked.

Branjen grinned. "I hope so! She'd be perfect!"

"Ooh, are we matchmaking?" Guin asked, clapping her hands together. "This is so much better than the convent. Even if everyone keeps staring at me."

"They're just jealous that your gown has pockets," Emry lied.

"They're not," Guin said softly. "I'm a scandal. This morning, when I tried to visit the women's sitting room, everyone looked up when I entered, and went silent."

Guin's shoulders slumped, and Emry didn't think she'd ever seen the princess look so dejected.

"They shouldn't have behaved so rudely!" Issie protested. "That's why we left with you, out of solidarity."

"You're my best friends, so you don't count," Guin said. "All three of you."

Emry blushed, surprised to be included. "I'm so glad you came for tea," Guin went on.

"Mostly for sympathy," Emry said. "All of the men in my life are being positively awful, and I don't think I'm overreacting."

"You're not," Guin insisted. "I'm going to have a word with

Emmett. He shouldn't let your father treat you like that."

"Thanks," Emry said. "But I doubt it will help."

"Fathers never pay attention to their daughters unless it's to criticize," Issie added.

"Yet they take pride in their sons for just existing," Branjen finished wryly. Guin nodded in agreement.

"Without learning magic, I don't know what I'm meant to do at court," Emry confessed.

"My suggestion is that you start with cake, and figure out the rest later," said Branjen, offering up the plate.

Emry took a small sugared confection and popped it into her mouth. She felt like she was breaking the rules, entirely indulgent, sitting around eating cake in the afternoon and doing nothing of consequence. But then, it wasn't as if her father was up in the workshop brewing batches of healing salve. She supposed it was better sitting here with her friends, rather than with those awful friends of her father's at their game of cards. At least she could enjoy herself.

There was a reason women at court sought out each other's company, and she wished she'd spoken with Issie and Bran sooner. Their fathers had sent them here to become the future queen's attendants and secure wealthy husbands, and instead they had marched their own path with each other, in quiet defiance of their families' wishes.

Arthur wouldn't understand what she was going through. Neither would Lance. Emmett was impossible, and she knew far better than to talk to Gawain about anything of import.

It was nice, having a group of girls. But that didn't take away the injustice of her father's behavior.

◐ ◐ ◐

Arthur pushed away his stack of scrolls, exhausted. It was late, and somehow the library felt even lonelier than his apartments. He should have gone to bed hours ago, but he was afraid that he'd be alone with his thoughts, with nothing to distract him. Which was the last thing he wanted.

That afternoon's council meeting had been brutal. He hadn't known the old Lord Bedivere had passed away and that his councillors were speaking of the *new* Lord Bedivere. So he'd hopelessly embarrassed himself by declaring that he refused to recommend any eligible young courtier to become Lady Bedivere. Then he'd butchered the pronunciation of a forest *in his own kingdom* purported to be rife with bandits, and had spilled coffee all over the grain ledgers. That was before Lord Agravaine had pulled him aside to go over the astonishing bills that Master Merlin had expensed to the royal accounts for the running of the wizard's workshop.

When he'd finally had a spare moment to go up to the tower for an explanation, he'd found the wizard hosting a card game full of day-drunk nobles, as though the man had no duties at all other than to drain the castle wine cellar and kick his feet onto the worktable. Emmett, at least, had looked embarrassed about the situation. And Emry, Master Merlin had informed him, was off doing embroidery with her ladies. The mental image was so confusing that Arthur had stood there with his mouth open for a moment too long. Finally, he'd mumbled a flimsy excuse about putting in a request for more healing salve and had fled with no further clarity on the expenses.

He knew his advisors preferred having Master Merlin as court wizard. But he couldn't help thinking that perhaps Emry had been right, and he was making a mistake. He *missed* her. And he missed who he was with her—someone who wasn't afraid to go against the status quo. Someone who dreamed of a new Camelot, and actually did something about it.

She challenged him to be better. And when she was around, he actually liked himself, instead of feeling like an embarrassment to the kingdom. But she wanted nothing to do with him now. And the more he tried to think of an apology, the more he realized that there wasn't anything he could say to fix what he had ruined.

He'd screwed up. Badly. And he had to live with it somehow.

He leaned back in his chair, stretching the tension from his neck and shoulders. He couldn't remember the last time he'd been so . . . lonely. Barely a week ago, he'd felt as if the castle was filled with his friends, but now he couldn't think of a single person he might invite for a drink, or a laugh, or even a few hours of companionable silence in the library.

Lance was busy training for the tournament, Percival was still slightly terrified of him, Emmett wasn't really his friend, and Gawain was a last resort.

Arthur groaned. Perhaps Lord Agravaine was right that he needed a wife. But when he pictured someone by his side or in his bed, it wasn't a politically advantageous princess. It was—

The door of the library creaked open, and Arthur startled at the sound.

"Oh," a voice said. "It's you."

Emry stood in the doorway, her arms folded across her chest, a lantern hovering by her side. Her hair was in a braid over one shoulder, and she wore her brother's old clothes. The tension between them was thick and awkward. He could feel her anger, and he tried and failed to think of anything he could say to dispel it.

"I was just leaving," he promised, gathering his scrolls.

That had clearly been the wrong thing, judging from Emry's tense expression.

"Don't rush out on my account."

"I wasn't," he lied. "I—um—"

"Irritable bowel, or guest waiting in your chambers," Emry supplied. "Which lie were you going to use?"

Arthur winced. "Forgot my quill?"

Emry wrinkled her nose. "Terrible choice," she pronounced. "Well, carry on, I'm just here to look something up."

She brushed past him, disappearing into the stacks. He could hear her moving around and muttering to herself, and he knew he wasn't going to get any work done. This was the most she'd spoken to him in days, and he'd do anything to keep her talking.

"Er, I could help you, if you'd like?" he offered, excited at the prospect. Finally, he could be useful. And perhaps Emry's cold demeanor would thaw the more time she spent around him.

He thought she wasn't going to answer, but finally she called, "Ugh, fine."

Arthur held back a smile and joined her in the magic section. It was in the oldest part of the library, and the shelves were closer together here. There was hardly room for one person in the narrow alcove, never mind two.

Once again, Arthur admired Emry's floating lantern. He wished she'd make him one. Then he could use both hands for carrying books.

"What are you looking for?" he asked.

"Magical uses for Godfrey's root," she said.

"Is that even a real thing?" Arthur frowned. He'd never heard of it, and he'd heard of most herbs.

"I hope so, or else an apothecary scammed me out of a gold coin."

Arthur choked. A gold coin for some *root*? That couldn't be right.

"What were you buying it for, if you're not even sure what it is?" he asked.

Emry looked at him as if he'd just said something impossibly stupid. "*I* wasn't buying it. My father was. I was merely running his errands."

Arthur remembered the wizard's expenses and sighed. He studied the spines of the books, wishing he knew what to say to fix this tension. "Er, what about this one?" he asked, plucking a tome labeled *Liber Herbalis* in fading gilt letters from the shelf.

"Thanks, actually," Emry said, tucking it under her arm and continuing to scan the shelves. "The spine was so worn I might have missed it."

"Happy to help," Arthur said. Emry glared at him, arching an incredulous eyebrow. "Er, how is everything going in the workshop?"

Emry's face clouded with anger. "How should I know?" she snapped. "I'm too busy picking up my father's new wardrobe and fetching tea from the kitchens."

Arthur frowned. Surely Emry was exaggerating. "That can't be right," he said.

"I can assure you that it is." The bitterness in her voice was unmistakable. "My father has no interest in having me anywhere near his precious workshop. Which is why I'm here, trying to teach myself about the potion he's working on."

So it's all my fault, Arthur thought glumly.

"You didn't want to check the books in the wizard's workshop?" Arthur asked.

"He's locked the door," Emry returned. "With magic. So if I let myself in, he'll know."

"Sard, he's locked you out?" Arthur couldn't believe it.

He'd thought making Merlin the court wizard was the right thing to do. That Emry could continue her training, and Arthur would benefit from having someone experienced and respected in the position.

But Emry was acting as if he'd *known* it would be like this. As if he'd done it on purpose. This was a disaster.

"I think I've got enough books," Emry said, gesturing to her stack.

"I could help you go through them?" Arthur offered, not wanting her to go back to her room just yet. "I mean, you're only looking for one thing, right? I should be capable of helping with that."

"It's fine," Emry said. "You've already done enough." It came out harsh, accusatory, and she winced. "Sorry, I didn't mean it like that."

Arthur nodded. "I know."

"It's really late, and I'm having a terrible day."

"Same," Arthur offered.

"How terrible?" Emry asked, unable to hold back her glee at the news.

"There is nobody on my council who doesn't think me an incompetent fool," Arthur admitted.

"What did you do now?" Emry asked suspiciously.

"Nothing on purpose! Apparently every question I ask and every suggestion I make is a disaster." Arthur ran his hand through his hair in anguish.

"You do know they're acting like that on purpose, as some sort of power play," Emry said.

"What do you mean?" Arthur stared at her in surprise. The thought had never even occurred to him.

"Men do it to women all the time. They give nothing but negative feedback, to make us feel inferior and embarrassed. Then we're forced to gain their approval for every little thing. It's infuriating."

Could that truly be the case? That he wasn't incompetent at all, but merely the target of an elaborate political game by his father's former advisors, designed to tear him down?

Sard, the more he thought about it, the more convinced he was that it was exactly what they were doing.

After all, Sir Tor, whom he had personally appointed, never acted as though he was incapable. *Sir Tor isn't from Camelot*, he reminded himself. *And has never sat on a royal council before.* The knight was just as inexperienced and lost as he was.

Emry had no idea how badly everything was going. It was far more likely that he really was the disaster his advisors thought he was.

"But what if they're right about me?" Arthur asked. He hadn't meant to say that out loud.

Emry gave him a long look, and Arthur ached to reach for her, yet knew he couldn't.

"They're not," Emry told him. "You're a good king. A terrible boy-friend, but a good king."

With that, she marched from the library, leaving him to his misery alone.

CHAPTER 18

Emry slouched at the battered wooden table in the wizard's workshop, watching her brother make a mess of his healing salve.

"You're going to give someone boils with that," she warned as he continued to chop his ginger root into large uneven chunks.

"You do it, then, if you're such an expert," Emmett snapped, pushing the ingredients across the table.

Emry sighed, wishing she'd kept her mouth shut.

Their father was slumped in an armchair by the fire, his face ashen, nursing some sort of drink that clearly did nothing to lessen his hangover.

He deserved it, Emry thought savagely.

He let out a low moan, clutching his head.

"Why don't you take a pain tonic?" Emry asked.

"Maybe later," he said dismissively.

"What if you put some Godfrey's root in it?" she suggested. Her father's head whipped up in surprise, as though shocked by the idea. "You said it increases magical potency, right?"

"Not like that." He groaned, rubbing a hand over his face.

"Like what, then?" she pressed.

Under the table, Emmett kicked her. She kicked him back.

"Owww!" he complained loudly. "You'll scuff my suede boots!"

"Quiet!" their father boomed. "The both of you! The court physician wants those potions, and I want silence. Is that understood?"

"Yes, Father," Emry and her brother mumbled in unison.

Emmett rolled his eyes, and Emry rolled hers in agreement. Honestly, their father was treating them like children.

Emry passed the properly cut ginger back to her brother, and he arranged the pieces on the table into the shape of a frowny face. She snorted. At least Emmett wasn't getting any special treatment today. Although she would have preferred another afternoon spent trudging through the icy London streets to fetch packages over this strained silence.

Her thoughts drifted back to her conversation with Arthur the night before. How genuinely shocked he'd seemed at the suggestion that his advisors were tearing down his confidence on purpose. Did he truly think so little of himself? She hoped not.

He didn't trust himself to fight for you to remain court wizard, a voice in the back of her head whispered. His advisors trampled him. And he was too mortified to admit reinstating her father wasn't his idea, because admitting he was bad at his job was worse.

Emry stirred her potion, her lips pressed into a thin line. *You're furious with him,* she reminded herself. *With him, and with your father.*

The moment she and Emmett were dismissed, she went back to her room and started going through the stack of books from the library. Because whatever was going on with her father, she had the distinct impression that he didn't want to tell her about it. Which made her even more determined to find out.

Perhaps once I tell him I know, he'll realize I'm a talented wizard and actually teach me something, she thought. Or perhaps she'd learn something she was better off not knowing. Except she didn't find anything in the books on herb lore, or in the encyclopedia of herbs. She picked up a thin pamphlet labeled *Magical Herbs, Fungi, Roots, and Berries: A Catalogue,* which seemed to have been written by a court wizard decades before Master Ambrosius's time, penned carefully by hand.

When she got to the third page, she clapped a hand over her mouth in delight. The same artist who had defaced the magic textbook she'd needed from the library on her very first day at Castle Camelot had struck again. Graphic depictions of a lusty shepherd chasing his flock decorated the margins. And when she turned the page, she cackled. The artist had added *dialogue*. It seemed the sheep had been a very *baaaad* girl.

Emry flipped through, giggling. And then she stopped, staring down at an entry:

> Godfrey's root, a magical mithridate formed by filling an
> onion with a concoction of *Theriaca Andromachi*, poppy
> flower, rue, yarrow, and vervain, then harvesting the
> onion's roots. When taken as an electuary, Godfrey's root
> is purported to increase one's ability to perform magic,
> but at great risk.

She frowned, reading the entry again, more slowly this time. She still only understood half of it, but what she did understand was that it wasn't like adding salt to a stew, as her father had led her to believe. It sounded dangerous.

A knock sounded on her door, and Emry jumped, her heart pounding. "Guin?" she called, setting down her book. "That you?"

The door opened. It wasn't Princess Guinevere. It was Arthur. He was wearing just his tunic and trousers, and he was carrying an enormous box, and he appeared to be covered in cobwebs.

"Not Guinevere," he said. "May I come in?"

"Is the castle under siege by spiders?" Emry asked.

Arthur looked down and grimaced. "Ugh," he said. "I took the passage out of my room."

Emry waved a hand, vanishing the offending cobwebs from his clothing.

"I was hoping you might do that," he admitted with a tentative smile.

She hated that it made her flutter just a little bit, seeing him look at her like that, wearing just his tunic. So she pretended that it didn't, pushing to her feet and putting her hands on her hips.

"Well, what brings you to my bedchamber?" she asked grandly.

He raised the box a little higher. "This, actually," he said. "I took the liberty of ordering you a gown for the coronation ball a while back. It arrived today." He set the box down on her bed.

"Oh." Emry tilted her head, staring at him. "Thank you."

"You could open it," he said shyly.

And as much as Emry wanted to tell him to go away and leave her alone, she had never felt as lonely as she did right then, staring at the one person she wanted to tell everything, and knowing that, even if she did, it still wouldn't fix anything.

Arthur was the king. No longer the boy from the library, whose hopes and fears he'd shared with her in stolen moments in the wizard's workshop, or during their travels to France. He belonged to Camelot. Not to her. Letting him go had been the right thing to do. But it was easier to tell herself that when he wasn't standing in her bedroom in his shirtsleeves.

"So this dress," Emry said, running a hand over the box. "I assume it's very pink and very ruffly."

"Naturally," Arthur confirmed. "Since yours was made to match mine."

Emry lifted the lid. A beautiful silk ball gown tumbled out. The bodice was a rich, shimmering midnight blue, with delicate silver clasps down the front. The skirts were paler blue, and studded with pearls.

"Oh," she said, staring at it. It was so beautiful, but more than that, it was exactly what she would have wanted to wear, if only things were different.

"I had them add a secret pocket for your wand."

"It's wonderful. Thank you." Emry held up the dress in the mirror.

Behind her, she could see Arthur watching. In the glass, their eyes met. And neither looked away. Emry ached for things to be set right between them. For this awkward weirdness to go away, and for them to be Arthur and Emry once again.

That's never going to happen, she reminded herself. *He's the king, and I'm just an apprentice.* "I'll admit, I had an ulterior motive in delivering the dress in person," he confessed.

"I figured," Emry said.

Arthur cleared his throat, looking horribly nervous. This was it. He was finally going to admit he'd been wrong. To say he was sorry, and he'd made a mistake, and to reappoint her as his court wizard alongside her father. "I was hoping you'd still be my date to the coronation ball," he said grandly. When she didn't respond, he pressed on, "I didn't say anything to my advisors about us not going together. So the seating's already been arranged, and it's going to be a headache unless we go together. But I wasn't sure you still wanted to, so I came to ask and make sure that, um, well, that you did. Even though you're mad at me." Arthur looked to her hopefully.

Emry waited for the rest, and when it was clear there wasn't any more, she folded her arms across her chest and arched an eyebrow.

"That's it?" she said, unimpressed. "That's everything you came here to say?"

"What else would I say?" Arthur asked with a frown.

"'I'm sorry, and I was wrong, and here's how I'm going to fix it'?" she suggested sourly.

"I can't." Arthur sighed. "If you'd just let me explain—"

"Pass," Emry interrupted. "You demoted me without a word, went behind my back about it, and assumed I wouldn't mind. And now you're asking for favors? Arthur Pendragon, you're impossible!"

He blanched. "I'm asking you to be my date to a ball!"

"Because it's too much of a bother to change the seating chart," she snapped.

"That's not the only reason," he protested.

"Right, I forgot. You already ordered me a dress," she said, her voice dripping with disdain. She knew she was only making things worse between them, but she didn't care. He couldn't do this to her. She was his court wizard so long as it was convenient, and his girlfriend so long as it allowed him to dodge marriageable young princesses his council threw at him.

Wait.

"This isn't really about the seating chart, is it?" Emry asked.

Arthur fidgeted. "Um" was all he said.

"If we don't go together, your council is going to pick some adoring princess to stand at your side," she went on.

Arthur opened his mouth, and then closed it again. Finally, he pinched the bridge of his nose and said, sounding exhausted, "Yes, and I'd rather they didn't. Come on, Em. Help me out. Please."

Emry bit her lip. It would be so easy to say yes. To put on that beautiful gown and loop her arm through Arthur's and dance with him at his coronation, tormenting an audience who thought her entirely unsuitable.

She'd pictured how it would feel to finally be on display as Arthur's girlfriend after months of discretion. But this wasn't that. He was asking her to be a shield. A weapon he could wield to protect himself from his advisors. And she hated that.

She wanted to be more. She wanted him to *want* her to be more.

But if he did, he certainly wasn't acting that way.

"I'm never your first choice," she said, "just your most convenient one. And I hate that. You never, ever pick me."

The silence after her accusation was deafening. The room felt too small, too warm, too intimate. "I wish I could," Arthur said plainly.

"Then do it," Emry goaded. "Make me your court wizard. Tell your council you gave my father a chance, and it didn't work out. And announce it in the Great Hall without giving him any warning."

Arthur swallowed nervously. Shook his head. "Emry," he began.

"You can't," she finished for him. "But you wish you could."

He winced. Fidgeted with the hem of his tunic.

"I can't be your date to the coronation ball anyway," she went on, "since I've already said yes to someone else."

Arthur scoffed. "You're joking. Who?"

Sard. That was a good question.

"Gawain," Emry lied.

"You're really going with him?" Arthur asked, seeming defeated.

"Yes!" Emry insisted. "So you can take back your dress."

"Keep it," Arthur said dully. He opened his mouth to say something else, but then he changed his mind and hurried from her room.

Sard, Emry thought. Somehow, that visit had made things between her and Arthur even worse. And now she was going to have to ask Gawain to his stupid coronation ball.

She summoned her nerve as she banged on the door to Gawain's chambers. He answered in a dressing gown, his hands streaked with charcoal. There were suggestive giggles coming from inside, and someone was playing a bawdy tune on a fiddle.

"Well, hello," he said, grinning. He had a light dusting of stubble on his cheeks, and his eyes were bright with drink. "Have you come to join the fun?"

"I've come to ask a favor," Emry replied. "I need you to be my date to the coronation ball."

"But what am I supposed to tell the fetching prostitute I've already engaged to scandalize my father?" he asked, pouting.

"That she can hold my wand?" Emry offered.

Gawain considered this. "Perhaps I'll turn her loose on the unsuspecting courtiers, and tell her to choose whom she wishes, on me."

"Perhaps I'll enchant my boots to be red-hot, then accidentally step on your toes."

Gawain grinned. "It's a date."

CHAPTER 19

A rthur couldn't remember the last time he'd been so nervous. Yet as his valet brushed invisible wrinkles from his coronation suit, Arthur felt as though he couldn't stand still another moment.

"Enough, Luc," he said. The valet backed off. "Sorry," Arthur said with a sigh. "Nerves."

"Indeed, sire?" Luc replied politely, fussing with some documents laid upon a table, and Arthur wished he had someone here whom he could truly talk to.

Instead, he was alone, as he always was these days. And he was about to feel lonelier than he ever had in his life. His coronation was moments away. And even though he was already king, this would make it official. He could already hear the music echoing through the cathedral, the murmurs of guards in the hallway, the cheers of the crowd gathered outside.

And even though it wasn't nearly as traumatizing as the thought of marrying what Emry had helpfully suggested was going to be a horse waiting in Guinevere's stead, this felt more momentous. More permanent.

He would swear his service to Camelot as its king. Have the crown jewels placed on his head and in his hand while everyone watched. He'd take a seat on the throne in front of all the nobles who had gathered for the occasion, and who, one by one, would step forward and swear their fealty to him as their sovereign.

He studied his reflection in the mirror, straightening his jacket. He didn't know how to steer Camelot into the future. Not with so many of his father's advisors giving conflicting instructions on where to turn, and what needed to be done.

Dark thoughts crept in, ones he'd been trying for weeks to push away. Being king was a job. One he'd never asked for, and hadn't been trained to do. And everyone knew it. They were just too polite to say.

What if he couldn't do it? What if he failed, publicly?

No. That wouldn't happen. Camelot and its people were too important to him. So he didn't know how to be king. He'd just have to learn. He was good at learning. Besides, no one was born knowing how to do a job they'd never had.

He remembered what Lance had said to him that night at the Crooked Spire, right before he'd pulled the sword from the stone.

How will we learn from our mistakes if we don't make any?

He wished his friends were here with him. That they'd pushed their way into this antechamber and were standing around smirking and making jokes about his ceremonial cloak. Perhaps someone would have brought a flask, because he could definitely use a drink about now.

"If you have a moment, sire, we should review the day's schedule?" Lucan said tentatively, breaking his reverie.

Arthur's cheeks flushed at the thought that he'd looked as if he'd been admiring his reflection, rather than giving himself a silent pep talk. He gestured for the man to go ahead.

First was the coronation, and after that would be the champion's tournament, where he was expected to clap and cheer as his knights competed for the honor. And then there was the coronation ball. The day felt unbearably long. And everyone would be looking at him the entire time. Not just looking at him—looking *to* him. Judging him as their new king. Waiting for the new Camelot he would build.

It was too much. His chest clenched, and his hands balled into fists, and he could barely breathe.

"Sire?" Lucan asked.

"I'm fine," Arthur said. "I just—give me a moment."

The valet bowed and left. And Arthur was alone in the gilded chamber deep within St. Paul's Cathedral, a room that felt suffocatingly holy, and that he wished desperately had a window.

Sard, he was going to sweat through his suit. He was no longer in black mourning, but in pale blue silk embroidered over with gold and pearls. The cloak he was meant to wear hung over the top of a trifold wardrobe screen. It was heavy crimson velvet trimmed with ermine, the Pendragon rampant embroidered in gold upon its back.

The cloak was ridiculous. As heavy as a chest of coins, with a train that would drag six feet behind him. It reminded him of playing knights with Lance when they were children and wrapping bedsheets around their shoulders as makeshift cloaks.

Except this wasn't pretend.

It was real.

A knock sounded at the door, and Lord Agravaine poked his head in.

"It's time."

CHAPTER 20

Lance paced the competitor's tent, terrified that he'd made a mistake putting his name on the lists. But it was too late now to turn back. The tournament would start any minute. He pulled back the tent flap, peering out at the crowded stands. There were so many people. And all of them would witness his failure.

"Oh god," he muttered, feeling ill.

"Deep breaths," Emry suggested.

"Does that actually work?" Gawain asked. He frowned at a piece of armor. "What's this supposed to be? It looks like a groin plate, but surely not."

"Thigh," Lance told him.

"You're putting that on yourself." Gawain reached for the decanter of wine and poured himself a glass. "Any chance this is poisoned?"

"Try it and find out?" Emry suggested sweetly.

Gawain did and made a face. "Cheap swill," he pronounced.

"Are you going to help me into my armor or not?" Lance asked, biting back his annoyance.

"Of course I am," Gawain said. "I was only joking about the plates. I have worn armor before."

"But never fastened it on yourself, or anyone else," Lance accused.

Gawain shrugged. "I can't help being royal."

Lance calmed slightly as Gawain buckled him into his armor with expert precision. Despite Gawain's jokes, he clearly knew what he was doing. Lance honestly couldn't believe Gawain had agreed to squire for him, but then, Gawain was likely to do anything if it would annoy his father. And Lord Agravaine was certainly irritated to have his eldest son—and the second in line for the throne—buckling a formerly disgraced squire into his armor to compete in the king's tournament.

The flap to the tent opened, and a terrified-looking page stuck his head in. "They're ready for the competitors to take the field," he reported.

"I'll be right there," Lance called. And then he turned to Gawain with a grin. "Squire? My lance."

"Sard off." Gawain scowled, shoving it at him.

The procession of knights felt endless. And the stands were filled. Lance hadn't realized Camelot had so many knights eager to compete for the honor of being named king's champion, or so many nobles who wished to watch.

A few of the lads with whom he would have been a first-year squire had entered, and they shot him curious looks as he rode Lionheart along the edge of the tournament field, displaying his house's banner— a stag leaping over a fleur-de-lis.

His elder half brother was watching, calm and aloof as always. And Percival had arranged to guard the medical tent, which had a perfect view of the competition. Lance swallowed nervously, staring out through his raised visor as he paraded.

His first tournament. There was a time when he thought he'd never have the chance. And now here he was.

It seemed surreal to look up at the royal box and see not King Uther, but his childhood companion upon the throne, a crimson velvet cloak flowing from his shoulders, and a true crown on his head.

Sitting stiffly and prettily at Arthur's side was a blond princess with a cascade of curls, wearing a pink dress with a matching pink cloak. She clearly had no interest in the spectacle, but a lot of interest in Arthur. Well, not Arthur precisely, but in his title.

Arthur rose from his throne, and the heralds trumpeted their fanfare, signaling for the audience to settle down and shut up. "Lords and ladies, competitors and spectators, it is my great honor to welcome you all to Camelot's royal tournament." Arthur paused for applause. "Today, I will name my champion from amongst these brave knights—and bold squires."

The crowd stamped their feet and yelled in approval.

"The competition will take the form of a joust, where all must display their skill and their fearlessness with a lance and shield in order to be named champion. May luck find those who deserve it. And let the tournament begin!"

The crowd applauded once again, and the competitors began their final circle of the jousting ring.

Lance felt both proud and terrified as he rode behind Sir Kay, who was ignoring him. The stands called out the names of their favorites, and noble ladies stepped forward to offer their favors to the knights they wished to champion. The handsome Sir Evan caused a fight between three red-headed sisters, who shoved each other out of the way for the honor. Gawain's mother gave her silk scarf to Sir Kay, no doubt as a political strategy devised by her husband.

"Stop," a voice commanded as Lance rode past the royal box. "I want to wish you luck."

Lance slowed his horse as Arthur rose from his throne, and the entire royal box jumped to their feet as well.

"I'm told the custom is to offer a favor to one's favorite competitor," Arthur said, leaning over the edge of the stand and pressing back a smile.

Lance grinned helplessly. "You absolutely cannot do that," he pleaded. It would cause an uproar. Only ladies offered knights their favors.

"Someone has to, since Percival's on duty," said Arthur. He reached into his pocket and showily withdrew a grubby, ink-stained cloth as Lance laughed.

"Your weapon, competitor," Arthur demanded.

Lancelot tipped his weapon forward, and Arthur tied on the scarf, just as dozens of court ladies had done for their own favored knights. The crowd murmured at the unconventional gesture.

"Your Majesty—" Lord Agravaine protested, stepping forward.

Arthur gave his advisor an innocent frown, and held up a hand, signaling for him to wait. "I'll be finished in a moment, if you need a word."

Lance smothered a laugh. "I think we're holding up the procession," he said, looking behind him.

"Probably, but this is the most fun I've had all day. By the way, who'd you ask to serve as your squire?"

"Gawain," Lance said, spurring his horse to ride on.

He could still hear Arthur's delighted laughter from halfway across the field.

◐ ◐ ◐

Lance rode into the jousting ring, his armor heavy and shining in the thin winter sunlight.

The wooden lance felt heavy in his grip, and his horse seemed to sense he didn't quite know what he was doing.

"It's all right, Lionheart," Lance soothed. "We've got this."

The enormous destrier remained unconvinced.

Sir Pellinore saluted from the other end of the field.

The trumpets blared, signaling the start of the match, and Lance took a deep breath, the whole world narrowing to the tiny slip of the jousting ring he could see through the slit in his visor.

He urged his horse forward, the crowd cheering so loudly that he could hardly hear himself think. As he jolted down the field, the other knight a burning spot in his vision, he brought his lance forward, slotting it down into the cradle at the side of his armor for leverage.

Sard, it was happening fast. He barely had time to aim before the tip of Sir Pellinore's lance crashed into his arm plate.

Wood splintered everywhere. Lance felt as if he'd been struck with a battering ram, but he gritted his teeth and pressed his heels down and kept to the saddle. As the destrier swung around, he glanced at the tip of his lance—broken. A point, then.

He'd scored a point! The same as Sir Pellinore. He could barely keep from cheering.

Gawain swaggered forward, in no hurry to replace the lance. "Great job not dying," he drawled.

Lance rolled his eyes. And then he focused on the match and on Sir Pellinore, whose weakness he now knew—the knight cradled his weapon early. If Lance waited until the last moment, the way Sir Kay had shown him, before twisting his weight and aiming his own weapon, it was possible his hit would land, and the other knight would miss.

Which would win him the match.

Dimly, Lance was aware of the trumpet, of urging his horse forward. He waited until Sir Pellinore's weapon was set, even though everything within him was screaming at him to lower the tip of his weapon, to aim at the target riding toward him.

But he resisted.

Not yet . . . not yet . . . *now*!

Lance aimed on a slight diagonal, rolling one shoulder back and adjusting his weight in the saddle for maximum impact, as Sir Tor had shown him. He gasped as his weapon slammed into the other knight's breastplate, his aim true. And though he braced for the impact of Sir Pellinore's lance, there was none.

The older knight tipped sideways, falling from his saddle in a metallic crash of armor. The stands watched, stunned.

He'd done it! He'd unseated his opponent and won the match!

Lance took in the cheers and applause and huzzahs in disbelief.

Then he employed the same strategy in the next round, and the round after that. He didn't unseat any more knights, but none could break a lance on his armor, and none scored a single point against him.

When Lance ducked back into the tent, dripping sweat and out of breath, Perce flung his arms around him.

"You're doing incredibly!" he said.

"You're in my tent," Lance said, pleased.

"If anyone asks, no I'm not." Perce looked embarrassed. "I'm very convincing about faking an urgent need for the jakes."

Lance laughed.

"I'll give you two a moment," Emry said, lifting the flap and letting herself out. "Unchaperoned."

"You're not our chaperone," Lance called, annoyed.

"Thank god!" Emry called back.

Lance beamed at his suitor. "Arthur gave me a favor," he said.

"I saw. If it had been any other lad, I would have challenged them to a duel."

"He said it was on your behalf," Lance protested.

Perce arched an eyebrow. "A likely story. And he didn't need to go to the trouble. I've brought my own favor."

"Let's have it, then," Lance said.

Instead of a token, Percival removed Lance's helmet, took his face in his hands, and pressed a searing kiss to his lips. "Win this for everyone who's had to fight for what they deserve," Perce murmured.

"I'll try," Lance said doubtfully. He pushed aside the flap of his tent. The stands were louder than he'd ever heard. It was the last match before the final face-off of the joust. The winner would advance, and Lance would fight them.

"Come on, do you want to watch?"

"I have to get back," Perce said unhappily. "But I'm cheering for you. All of the guards are."

"But mostly you."

"Obviously." Perce gave him a clap on the arm, and Lance wished he wasn't wearing plate armor.

He went out to watch Sir Kay face Sir Tor, but before he reached the stands, the herald trumpeted and the announcer called, "Match goes to Sir Tor."

Which meant Sir Kay had been defeated once again by the young knight from Cameliard. And had failed to defend his title.

And that Lance would be facing Sir Tor for the honor of being named the king's champion.

◖ ◖ ◖

Lance saluted Sir Tor, adrenaline coursing through him despite his exhaustion. He didn't expect to beat the knight, who had ridden a perfect tournament to defeat Sir Kay barely three months ago. But Lance had held his own thus far, outlasting the knight for whom he had squired, and every other knight born of Camelot. There was no shame in going out now.

Perhaps Sir Tor would name him squire now that they were relinquishing their place on the royal council as Cameliard's ambassador.

The trumpets blared, the stands stomped, and Lance reached for his weapon, which Gawain handed to him without snark.

For Camelot, Lance thought. *For Arthur.*

He urged his horse forward, trying to guess what strategy Sir Tor might use. Lance watched through the thin slit in his visor as Sir Tor's weapon began to lower.

Not yet, he thought.

Not until he could see the angle he needed.

The seconds passed with agonizing slowness. He wasn't going to have time. He had to—*now!*

Lance lowered his weapon and sent up a quick prayer as—*slam!*

His lance shattered against Sir Tor's shield, and Sir Tor's weapon hit his breastplate.

Lance gasped at the sheer force of the impact, digging in his heels harder than he ever had before in a fight to remain on his horse.

The crowd cheered. Lance rode back to his end of the tilting field as the flags were fitted. One to one.

With his next tilt, he aimed not for Sir Tor's shield, but for their breastplate. He was guaranteed to hit, but he would guarantee Sir Tor's lance would hit him as well.

He gritted his teeth, anticipating the brute force of Sir Tor's weapon. It hit in the same spot, where he was already bruised, and he cried out. His own lance broke against the knight's chest plate.

Another flag was added to each banner. They were tied. The next tilt determined everything.

And then Sir Tor held up a hand for a pause. The knight rode to Lance's side of the field.

"Sir Tor," Lance frowned. "Is everything all right?"

Sir Tor raised their visor and grinned. "Perfect. You've done your training proud."

"You mean *your* training," Lance said.

Sir Tor shook their head. "I never taught you to cradle late. That takes fearlessness."

Lance blushed. "I hope you will consider me as your squire," he said.

"I'll do more than that," said Sir Tor. "You've earned your knighthood. And you already have the king's favor."

"He was just messing around," Lance said.

"From the little I know of our new king, I don't believe he would ever publicly bestow his support on any who did not deserve it," said Sir Tor. "I would see you become champion of this tournament."

"If fate wishes, so would I. But we both know your skill at the joust far surpasses mine."

"Ride true, Squire Lancelot."

"And you, Sir Tor," Lance said, lowering his visor.

Sir Tor rode back to the far end of the field and signaled they were ready to continue.

Lance's shoulder ached. His thighs were numb. Sweat trickled down his back beneath his padding, despite the chilly weather. His body felt as if it was made of jelly, meant to be displayed as a fine dessert on the royal table at a feast, not fit to joust a knight as noble and talented as Sir Tor.

Yet he raised his lance with a grimace and waited for the signal. When it came, he rode with more focus than he ever had before. Sir Tor thundered closer, and closer still, yet the knight's weapon remained raised to the sky.

What was he doing?

If Lance didn't aim now, he would miss the chance to secure his weapon.

He lowered his weapon, knowing that to do so first gave him the disadvantage, and he was already disadvantaged jousting against such an accomplished knight. Why wasn't Sir Tor aiming his lance?

Lancelot's vision narrowed to the tip of his blade, aimed at Sir Tor's shoulder plate. The knight rode closer. Lance closed his eyes—he couldn't watch—and he felt his weapon shatter. Yet no hit landed on his armor in return. The crowd gasped and went silent.

When he opened his eyes, he saw that Sir Tor's weapon had not lowered. Instead, the knight had ridden with their lance aimed high, in a gesture of respect and a sign of surrender.

Lance watched incredulously as the third flag was added beneath his banner. As the crowd surged to their feet.

He had won.

Sir Tor removed their helmet, waving to the crowd.

"Cheer for your new champion," the knight called, gesturing to Lance.

And it hit him all at once: *He had won.*

He felt as if he was in a dream as he approached the royal pavilion. Arthur made his way down the steps to the tilting field. The crowd's cheers quieted, and they watched in silence, wondering what their new king would do.

"Good people of Camelot, honored guests, and competitors in to-day's event," said Arthur, "I present to you not just my champion, but a champion for all of Camelot. His heart is as true as his aim, and his friendship is the greatest gift I have ever received. And so, it is my privilege to do the honors of this small and rather unconventional ceremony, given the circumstances."

Arthur beamed at Lance. Lance's mouth was dry, his heart racing, his hands shaking.

"My champion must be made a knight," Arthur declared. "And all of you will bear witness."

Made a knight? *Now?* Lance couldn't believe this was truly happening. But it wasn't just his victory. It belonged to his friends for helping him train after supper. To Sir Tor, who had stood aside and paved the path for Lance's knighthood. To everyone who had been told their dreams were impossible for someone like them.

"Kneel, Lancelot, second son of Sir Ector," said Arthur, Excalibur in hand.

Lance took a knee on the field, the stands rising up around them. He stared up at his best friend, his king, and the glowing blade that they had used to cure hangovers and practice broadsword. And he thought, *I will be worthy of this. I will be the best knight Camelot has ever known.*

He nodded, and Arthur lowered his sword, touching first one of Lance's shoulders with the side of his blade, then the other. Arthur's voice echoed through the field as he proclaimed, "And arise, Sir Lancelot, king's champion, the truest knight of Camelot."

Lance stood, surveying the stands, which were cheering his name.

Sir Lancelot.

CHAPTER 21

"$\mathbf{D}$are I ask what you've done with your wand?" Gawain whispered as they entered the Great Hall.

Emry rolled her eyes at him. She knew he was only baiting her. And anyway, it was none of his business what she had strapped to her thigh or shoved down her bodice.

"Ask me that again and I'll mobilize a suit of armor to challenge you to a duel," Emry replied sweetly as they stepped into the lavishly decorated room.

The space had been transformed for the coronation ball. The aforementioned suits of armor were polished to a high shine, and crimson banners bearing the Pendragon crest hung from the ceiling. Hundreds of candles lit the space with a warm glow, and a troupe of musicians dressed all in white, with even their faces powdered to a ghostlike pallor, played a courtly tune on their instruments.

Serving staff wove through the lavishly dressed crowd, offering wine and small bites from golden trays. It was Emry's second ball, but the first one she was attending as herself.

She smoothed the wrinkles from her skirts as Gawain gave their names to the heralds.

"Lord Gawain d'Orkney, and Miss Emry Merlin," the herald announced.

Everyone was dressed even more lavishly than Emry had ever seen. At her side, Gawain certainly looked handsome in a dark green velvet jacket embroidered with seed pearls, and a pearl earring to match. He'd begun to cultivate the beginnings of a beard, and the stubble suited him, making his jawline look even sharper, and his lips even fuller. He wore at least three gold rings on each hand.

He looked like an expensive, glittering lord who knew his worth, and who enjoyed baiting everyone by having Emry at his side. She had no doubt he truly would have shown up with Madeleine from Madame Becou's brothel on his arm, had Emry not insisted on the privilege.

But he was her friend. And they both got something out of this little arrangement.

"You look wonderful, by the way," Gawain said, nodding at her gown.

It was the one Arthur had given her, since she hated to see such a beautiful thing go to waste. Naturally, she'd altered it, so she and Arthur wouldn't match. She'd changed the color to green and the clasps to brass.

"Flattery won't make me disclose the location of my wand," Emry told him, looking for Arthur. He was easy to spot, resplendent in a suit of blue velvet, embroidered the length over with golden vines. His boots were brown leather, tooled handsomely, and heeled with gold. He wore a midnight blue cape tied around one shoulder at a stylish diagonal, and his hair was scraped back beneath a heavy crown, a dark lock dangling over one eye. She hated that she knew his crown must be giving him a headache. Wished she didn't ache to brush his stray lock of hair back into place. Though no one else save for the guards were armed, Arthur wore Excalibur at his belt in a jeweled scabbard. He looked exactly like what he was—a young, handsome, and clever king.

And she was merely a common girl on the arm of a royal who had no real feelings for her, staring yearningly at a boy who was no good for her.

She sighed miserably.

"I thought you'd be pleased," Gawain said, "now that Lance is the king's champion."

"You mean Sir Lancelot," Emry corrected smugly. "And I'm assuming you're thrilled as well. Or is your father not horrified?"

Gawain laughed. "He definitely is."

"But not as much as Sir Kay," Emry observed, nodding toward the disgraced knight, who had piled at least three slices of cake onto a single plate and was standing in the corner glowering as he ate.

Gawain snorted. "I pity his next squire."

"My lord," Emry said, shocked. "I wasn't aware you were capable of empathy."

Gawain threw his head back and laughed. More than a few curious glances cut in their direction. "It was the most regrettable day of my life when you turned down my marriage proposal."

Emry grimaced, wishing he hadn't brought it up. He hadn't been serious then, and he clearly wasn't being so now. Besides, she didn't feel that way about him. No matter how much easier things would be if she did.

Heralds raised their horns, blaring royal fanfare, and the Great Hall shushed. Arthur made his way onto the dais, where his throne waited for him. Yet he did not sit.

"Guests. Friends. And castle staff who are so wonderfully serving us all on this momentous night of celebration," he said, which earned a couple incredulous gasps from the crowd. "I wish to thank you for being here. To those of you who have bent the knee and declared your fealty, I did ask for a plush carpet to be set down in the cathedral, but I was told it wasn't tradition." Arthur paused, as if for laughter, but the crowd remained silent.

"Oh my god, tell me he's not doing jokes," Gawain whispered in horror.

"He's doing jokes," Emry whispered back. "He's screwed."

"Right," Arthur said, trying to recover. "Anyway, as we usher in this new era for Camelot, I hope it is one of peace and prosperity, and I will do everything in my power to ensure it. And now, let the revelry begin. Master Merlin, our court wizard, will start us off."

Before anyone could applaud or huzzah, the hall plunged into darkness. The courtiers gasped and whispered.

"What's going on?" Gawain asked.

Emry shrugged. And then she realized. Her father was creating a magical display.

A single light flickered from the tip of Master Merlin's wand. The wizard stepped forward and gave a flick of his wrist. Shooting stars arced their way overhead. Fireworks burst in brilliant colors, raining glittering dust down upon the festivities. The floor beneath their feet turned an inky black, and a dark fog rolled across the room. When the fog cleared, all of Camelot's banners had been transformed from crimson to gold.

Emry's frown deepened as she watched her father, who was sweating in concentration. With another wave of his wand, all the candles in the Great Hall flickered back to life.

Her father took a sweeping bow as the crowd burst into enthusiastic applause. And then he hurried from the ballroom, looking ill, his expression panicked.

Something was wrong.

"Be right back," Emry told Gawain, and then she followed her father. She kept her distance, watching with increasing concern as he staggered into the corridor, bent over in pain. He grimaced as he reached with shaking hands for a flask in his pocket, struggling to unscrew the cap. He took a swig, and then another, and then tilted back the flask, draining it.

He sighed with relief, sagging back against the wood paneling, eyes closed.

She ached to call out to him. To make sure he was all right. But somehow that seemed like a terrible idea. She'd definitely seen something she shouldn't have, and she didn't know what to do, other than pretend she hadn't. Before he could spot her, she ducked back inside the ballroom.

Immediately, Gawain stepped into her path. "Did you seriously run out on me?"

"Sorry," Emry said brightly. "My wand slipped."

Gawain raised an eyebrow at that unlikely story. "Dance with me? I won't make fun of you when you step on my toes."

"Later," Emry promised.

The one person she wanted to talk to about what she'd just seen was Arthur. Yet when she caught sight of him across the ballroom, she hesitated.

First, she needed courage. Perhaps of the liquid variety. And thankfully, there were many such liquids on offer.

Emry stared at the lavish assortment of refreshments, wondering which to choose.

"I've heard whispers you're a wizard," said a girl at Emry's side.

Emry turned and found herself face-to-face with the most exquisite woman she'd ever seen. She was pale, with a long cascade of bright red hair that fell in soft waves halfway down her back. Her green eyes glittered with amusement, and her heart-shaped lips were painted a deep, surprising shade of burgundy. She looked like the best kind of trouble. And she was smiling at Emry as if her assessment had given her the same impression.

"A shame it's only whispers," said Emry. "I should like to be gossiped about at full volume."

The girl's grin widened. "An admirable ambition, and one I'd be happy to help with." She offered a short curtsey. "Lady Viola."

Emry curtseyed back. "Apprentice wizard Merlin," she said, with only a hint of bitterness at having to say the apprentice part. "But since you intend to spread vicious rumors about me, I suppose you'd better call me Emry."

"Salacious rumors," the girl corrected. "Of the flattering persuasion. But of course, I would need to make my ability to know such things believable."

Emry glanced back toward Gawain, who was flirting with a darkhaired beauty in ivory silk, who was leading him onto the dance floor with his hand clasped in her own.

"We should be seen dancing," Emry suggested.

"Would such a thing not cause a stir?" The girl frowned. "I believe you came on the arm of a royal."

Emry rolled her eyes. "Trust me, I'd prefer your company."

Lady Viola's cheeks went pink at the compliment, and Emry blushed as well. She held out a hand and led the girl to the dance floor. Gawain would, of course, be delighted. And Arthur could—whatever. She refused to think about Arthur. After all, she doubted he was thinking about her.

Arthur had never hated being the center of attention more. He smiled and made polite conversation with his well-wishers, trying not to look mortified whenever someone bowed low and referred to him as "Your Majesty."

The title sounded ancient and stuffy, as if it belonged to someone else. This entire court felt as if it belonged to someone else, and he couldn't help but think this party was for everyone but him.

Here they were, celebrating their new king. And here he was, thinking of how his father had died so he could be here, in a thoroughly uncomfortable outfit, with a total stranger of a princess at his side.

He would have rather celebrated with a night crammed into a booth at the Crooked Spire, laughing and playing cards and drinking ale with his friends. At least his friends seemed to be enjoying themselves. He watched as Lance danced with Percival, whom Arthur had relieved of duty for the occasion. The two couldn't stop grinning, and Arthur didn't blame them. He couldn't believe Lance had won the tournament. That his best friend was his knight champion. And—sard—the new owner of a complete money pit of a castle.

Arthur glowered as he watched Emry spin around the ballroom in a beautiful woman's arms. The two girls were smiling and blushing, and Arthur was certain that Emry wasn't faking just to torture him. She truly seemed enamored of this red-haired beauty in the golden gown. He didn't blame her. He sighed miserably, wondering what he'd do if they actually became a thing. So much for her coming to the ball with Gawain, whom he knew for a fact she saw as nothing more than a friend.

"Don't look so upset, cousin, it's not as if she was *your* date," Gawain said, joining him.

She should have been, Arthur thought.

Emry laughed as her dance partner leaned forward to whisper something in her ear.

"Just look at them," Arthur complained. "You'd think they'd been courting for months."

"What's happened to your date, then?" Gawain asked.

Arthur felt a flush rise to his cheeks. "I might have asked a servant to refill her drink after every sip, in hopes she might need the privy and grant me a small reprieve."

Gawain laughed. "You could always show her the library. That usually scares princesses off."

"Not this one." Arthur's lips pressed into a thin line. "I believe she has already planned the particulars of her wedding gown down to the diamond-encrusted trim."

Gawain winced. "Pink, I take it?"

"Pink," Arthur confirmed. "And apparently I shall be dressed to match. As well as all the guests. It's to be a theme."

"How can a color be a theme?" Gawain wondered.

"I don't intend to find out."

Gawain laughed. And then he said exactly what Arthur was thinking. "Emry would never."

Arthur sighed wistfully. "I know."

Of course he would fall for the one girl who had no wish to be queen. He knew how little she desired such things, and how unwillingly he seemed to be on a collision course with them. But his traitorous heart didn't care. He wanted Emry, on whatever terms she'd agree to have him. And currently, it seemed that she wanted him about as much as he wanted a pink-themed wedding.

"She only came as my date to make you jealous," Gawain said. "There's nothing between us, as much as I wish otherwise. The two of you are magic. The two of us are, well, trouble."

"And the two of *them* are blushing," Arthur said glumly, watching Emry and the young woman twirl around the dance floor.

He realized Emry was wearing the dress he'd ordered for her. She'd magicked it to change the color and the fabric, but a small spark of hope ignited in him. She couldn't hate him so much if she'd worn the dress. Perhaps there was a chance to fix things between them.

"Go cut in," Gawain suggested.

Arthur considered it. "Maybe I will," he said.

The crowd parted for him as he stepped onto the dance floor. He was about to tap the red-haired girl on the shoulder when the doors to the Great Hall burst open, and a cloaked figure hurried in.

"Please!" he cried. "I must speak to the king!"

Guards raced forward to apprehend the intruder, pinning back his arms.

"Let go of me!" the uninvited guest shouted. "I require the king's ear!"

His voice was familiar, but Arthur couldn't place it. Morian and Safir got hold of the man and looked to Arthur for guidance.

"Bring him to me, where I may see him and have him speak," instructed Arthur.

The guards brought the man forward, forcing him to his knees at Arthur's feet. The man's cloak was mud splattered but of fine wool, the clasp made of intricate silver. Safir pushed back the man's hood.

Prince Gottegrim of Cameliard stared up at him, wide-eyed and frantic. His dark hair was flattened to his forehead with sweat, and there were bruises beneath his eyes, as though he hadn't slept. His cheeks were shadowed with stubble, and he seemed gaunt.

"Prince Gott," said Arthur, surprised to find himself staring at Guinevere's elder brother in such a state of distress. He waved off his guards. "Please get up, you're always a welcome guest. What's the trouble?"

"I rode here as fast as I could." Prince Gott grimaced, climbing to his feet. In a low voice, he said, "King Yurien's army is camped in a pass in Northumbria, near our border. They're preparing to attack!"

CHAPTER 22

This couldn't be happening.

Arthur slammed the door of the library behind him, his heart hammering. His breath came in gasps, and he felt dizzy, as though he might pass out. He sank to the floor in the stacks, his back against the spines of the books.

It was the night of his coronation. A celebration that was continuing on without him, so as not to alarm his guests.

He'd known a war was coming, even when he'd offered to sign a treaty of aid and alliance with Cameliard. King Yurien was just as likely to sail south and conquer Cornwall, a duchy of Camelot, as he was to attack Cameliard. And if Cameliard fell, it was only a matter of time until the fight marched its way to Camelot's border.

Yurien was an aggressor. He had claimed Northumbria in a fiendish series of border raids on unsuspecting villages, his attacks growing gradually more brutal. And he wouldn't stop at Cameliard. He hated the whispers of prophesy that claimed King Arthur would rule all of England—and he meant to prove them wrong.

Arthur had never wanted to be High King of all England—he hadn't particularly wanted to be King of Camelot. But after he pulled the sword from the stone, everyone knew of the prophesy that claimed he would be, and so he'd tried to live up to it. Not that hiding in the library and avoiding his council chamber, where he was meant to be, was living up to anything except his father's claims that he was a total disappointment.

His father was right about him. He was no great king, no brave leader, nothing but a scared boy hiding in the library stacks, no matter how hard he'd tried to be more.

His elbows were propped on his knees, and his head was in his hands. His crown sat by his side on the library floor. It was heavier than his circlet. He still hadn't gotten used to the weight of it. Any of it.

Sard, he was a coward. He didn't know how he was going to march into the council room and start directing plans to assist another kingdom in a war. He was so far out of his depth that he couldn't even see the surface, much less have any idea which direction he was meant to go. And he hated that this was how his advisors would see him. Scrambling, unprepared, panicked, the exact opposite of how a king was meant to act.

He was supposed to have more time. Not just before he was king, but before any of this.

He heard the door to the library creak open, and his heart squeezed at the impossibly wonderful thought that Emry had followed him. That she'd be here, at his side, as his wizard, right when he needed her the most.

But the footsteps were too heavy.

"Knew I'd find you here," said Lance, sliding to the floor to sit next to him.

He was still dressed from the ball in his finest suede jacket, a dark bruise high on his cheekbone from that afternoon's tournament.

Arthur gave him a weary smile. "Am I that predictable?"

"I'm your best friend," Lance reminded him. "But yes, you are that predictable."

"Wonderful." Arthur scrubbed a hand through his hair. The pomade that Lucan had combed through it came off, coating his palm with a sticky residue. He grimaced. He was still dressed from the ball, a king meant to impress. But he felt like the spare whom no one had wanted. And he knew that when he went back out there and faced his advisors, he'd see on their faces that they didn't want it to be him entering that room. That they'd give anything to have Uther back.

And he didn't blame them.

"You're freaking out, right?" Lance asked. "Because you look like you're freaking out."

"I can't do this," Arthur admitted.

His brown eyes met Lance's blue, and Arthur was surprised to see that there was no doubt or uncertainty in his friend's gaze. Only trust.

"Sure you can," said Lance. "Every king has to face a battle sooner or later. And most of them don't have unbeatable magic swords."

"That's true," Arthur said cautiously.

"You've got this," Lance insisted. "You've read more about military strategy than anyone I know. And you've got a room full of people who've done this before. All you have to do is ask good questions, listen to their answers, and consider their advice. You don't have to be the only one making the plan."

Arthur felt some tension fall from his shoulders. Lance was right. He wasn't alone in this.

He grinned at his best friend. "I suppose you're one of those clever, worldly advisors I should be listening to?"

Lance shrugged modestly. "Well, I am the king's champion."

Arthur rolled his eyes. "Sir Tor let you win."

"Sir Tor wanted me to win. And so did you."

"Of course I did. You're the best man I know."

"Sir Lancelot and King Arthur," Lance said thoughtfully. "It sounds like something we'd make up as boys, back when we were only allowed wooden training swords. Except it's real. It's happening."

Lance was right. It was real, and it was happening. And sitting there brooding about it would only make things worse. He could get this right. He *had* to get this right.

"Well then," Arthur said, pushing to his feet and offering Lance a hand. "I suppose we should get to that council meeting."

◐ ◐ ◐

Arthur stared down at the map spread across the table in his council chamber in despair. No matter how hard or how long he looked at the little metal figures that represented his forces, Yurien's army, and Cameliard's forces, he couldn't find a solution.

Using Cornwall Keep as a training facility meant that, even if they sent word that night, it would take two days to reach the castle, and another three for his soldiers to reach Cameliard's border.

"Our full forces won't make it in time," he declared, looking up at the handful of advisors sober enough to have been pulled into the war council, whose grim expressions mirrored his own.

"No, sire, they won't," General Timias confirmed. "With this little notice, I'd estimate less than half."

The council exchanged uneasy glances, and Arthur didn't blame them. It was an even grimmer number than he'd thought. "What about our knights?" he asked.

Lord Agravaine coughed delicately. "They've been at a joust all day and a ball all night."

"Most are drunk, injured, or both," explained the general.

"I've got that," Arthur said tightly. "I'll need a report on what resources we'll have available, should we ride for Cameliard tomorrow."

"Sir Tor and I can take care of that," volunteered Lance.

"Thank you," Arthur said gratefully as the two knights hurried from the room. His attention drifted to Prince Gottegrim, who was pacing beneath the window with a rosary in hand, still dressed in his traveling clothes. "I'm sorry about this. I know you expected more aid than what it seems we'll be able to give."

Prince Gott sighed. "It's not your fault. I *told* my father we should have used magic to detect King Yurien's army, like you suggested." He shook his head in anguish. "But he didn't listen. If that scout hadn't seen what he did . . ."

The prince trailed off, unable to finish such a gloomy sentiment.

Arthur thought of the stubborn, haughty king, who had been all too willing to trade his daughter for Camelot's resources but had only wanted those resources he understood and approved of.

There was a commotion outside the door, and a girl's voice insisting she be let in.

"Let her enter," Arthur called, curious what was going on.

Princess Guinevere shoved her way into the war room, chin held high. "Gottie!" she cried, launching herself at her brother and wrapping him in a fierce hug. "The guards wouldn't let me see you! Please, just tell me what's happening."

"Guin!" he said, pulling away with a grimace. "Good lord, you're pregnant."

"You really shouldn't be here," Arthur told his former fiancée.

"Nonsense," Guin replied. "I'm here to help." She reached into the pocket of her dress and impossibly withdrew an entire suit of men's clothing, which she shoved at her brother. "You smell like horse. There's a jar of healing salve as well, should you have sustained any injuries. And since I doubt anyone has offered you a meal, I've brought sandwiches."

At Guin's gesture, a maid entered nervously with a heavy tray laden with sandwiches for the entire council and placed it on top of Arthur's map. The general looked as though he wanted to toss Guin from the room. Her brother looked as though he wished to applaud.

"Thank you," Arthur said.

"Will you be rejoining the festivities?" Guin asked. "Because everyone's still in the ballroom."

"Still?" Arthur could hardly believe it. And then an idea occurred to him. "All of the nobles who traveled here for the coronation can send men from their villages. They can ride back and begin preparing immediately."

Lord Agravaine nodded in approval. "A clever plan."

"Make it so," Arthur told him. "Gather any whose estates lie north of London and tell them their king wishes to have a word."

Lord Agravaine bowed and hurried from the room.

"I'll tell the kitchens to send up coffee," Guin said. "And I'll have my maid prepare a chamber for my brother."

The fact that Prince Gottegrim didn't have anywhere to sleep hadn't even occurred to him. "Guin, you're amazing," Arthur told her, grateful to have someone taking care of the small things.

Guinevere beamed as she sailed from the room.

"Sending men from the northern villages was a good idea," said Prince Gott.

"Men, but not soldiers," Arthur said, understanding the full weight of that decision.

The general looked Arthur directly in the eye as he said, "Sometimes, the good of the many must override the good of the few."

Arthur felt faint. He was sending his people to fight an enemy without training. But then, what other choice did he have?

"Our army is made up of village men," Prince Gott confirmed. "Soldier is a low profession, and not one that many who wish to have a family and a wife would choose. God will protect them. And if God cannot, perhaps Camelot's magic will?"

Camelot's magic. *Of course.* That was a factor Arthur hadn't yet considered. "We have three wizards at our disposal. I'll inform our court wizard and his apprentices to ready themselves for the journey."

"Absolutely not, sire," the general protested. "No women!"

"But Emry has faced Morgana before," Arthur returned. "We'll need all the magic on our side that we can get. Or have you forgotten that King Yurien has an enchantment that makes him unkillable?"

"Master Merlin is all we need," said the general.

"Bringing women to war is a bad idea," said Lord Howell. "Not to mention, bad luck."

"It isn't luck, it's strategy," Arthur argued. "Emry defended the castle from the duke's attack. Er, so did Emmett."

"They fought because there was no one else," Prince Gott said gently. "Women and children should stay behind, the way it's always been done. Unfortunately, I count my brother-in-law among the children."

Under any other circumstance, Arthur would have delighted in Gott's joke. But now he merely sighed at the truth behind the barb.

"I don't like leaving valuable resources behind," Arthur said. "Including wizards."

"It's a bad idea," Sir Ban insisted. "They're young. Untested. Untrained."

"We have the most powerful wizard who ever lived on our side," said the general. "The girl stays at the castle. And that's final. Unless you want to find yourself another general."

The man wasn't bluffing. Arthur could see that much. He couldn't believe General Timias was putting him in this position. And as desperately as he wanted to contradict the man, there wasn't time. Arthur surveyed his council, but none of them spoke up that Emry should come. And he hated that Prince Gott was right about Emmett.

"The apprentices will stay here," Arthur declared.

Besides, Master Merlin could defend them. He'd stood beside King Uther in many battles, had even fought with General Timias on more than one occasion. Emry was a talented wizard, but he couldn't ask this of her. Not if he didn't have to.

Still, as the men around him hurried to make preparations, Arthur felt like it was all happening so fast, and if he only had more time, perhaps he'd be able to think through his decisions, instead of making them on the spot.

He wasn't ready. He was terrified. This was supposed to be a night of dancing and celebration, not a night when he readied his kingdom for war.

CHAPTER 23

Emry burst into Arthur's apartments, despite Tristan's protests that the king wasn't to be disturbed. She didn't care. She needed to talk to him, especially after Prince Gottegrim had arrived at the ball, and everyone important had disappeared immediately.

Arthur jumped as she opened the door, startled by the interruption. Emry took in the table he'd been standing over, which was piled with maps, and the outfit he wore. No longer royal formal wear, but protective padding, the kind that went under mail and armor.

So it was true. He was going to fight King Yurien and Queen Morgana's army.

"Emry," he said, frowning. "How did you—"

"You haven't said when we leave."

Arthur frowned at her. "We?"

"I saw Prince Gottegrim arrive. You're clearly preparing to ride to Cameliard's aid," she said.

"I am," Arthur confirmed. "But you're staying here."

Emry scoffed. "You're not serious."

"I'm entirely serious," Arthur said, more sternly this time. "Your father is coming with me. But you and your brother are staying here."

Emry stared at him incredulously. He couldn't mean that. Yet he looked as if he did. His shoulders were squared, and he lifted his chin, staring at her in that imperious, royal way of his, as though daring her to contradict him.

Her father was hiding something. She was sure of it. But Arthur didn't see it. What if something went wrong?

"No. Arthur, you need me," she insisted, trying to explain. "There's something going on with my father's magic, and I'm worried it's serious! Tonight, after his display, I saw him in the hall looking ill."

Arthur frowned again. "What did he say was wrong?"

"He didn't know I was there," Emry admitted. "But he was clutching his stomach, and he drank something from a flask."

"Half the men his age take some sort of concoction after they eat too richly at supper," Arthur scoffed. "The court physician deals with practically nothing but stomach ailments. And I'm not about to confront the greatest wizard who ever lived about his diarrhea."

Emry glared. "I knew you wouldn't believe me."

"Surely if something was wrong, one of his spells would have failed," Arthur shot back. "Has that happened?"

"Well, no—" Emry began, then saw it wasn't going to work. So she changed tactics. "But that doesn't mean you won't need me by your side even with my father. The Lady of the Lake said—"

"A lot of things that didn't turn out to be true," Arthur finished. "And she certainly never said you needed to be by my side in *battle*."

He made the word sound so fierce that Emry took an involuntary step back. "Surely you're bringing healers. Standard-bearers. I'll stay back with them at the camp."

"No, you won't," Arthur ground out. "Because I'm ordering you to stay here. As your king. Even if I have to have you thrown in the dungeons to ensure it."

"You'd throw me in the dungeons to keep me from helping Camelot at your side," she repeated, to make sure she had it right. "I'd expect that of your father, but not of you."

Arthur winced. "I—it's not my decision."

"Who else is here? Who else is king? This is all you!"

"You don't understand," he pleaded.

"I understand perfectly," Emry snapped. "Now that you have my father, you don't need to work so hard to make Camelot better. You can just leave things as they are so no one gets upset. Everything that you promised was just empty words. Including how you feel about me!"

Emry glared at him, seeing just how stubborn he was being about this. He wasn't going to change his mind. And somehow, she wondered why she'd ever assumed he would.

◑ ◑ ◑

"Tell Arthur I'm coming with you," Emry demanded, bursting through the door of the wizard's workshop.

Her father looked up from packing a trunk full of supplies, his mouth set in a hard line.

"You're staying here," he said. "Both of you."

"But I can help," Emry insisted. "Please, Father." How was she supposed to learn what to do if she couldn't even watch?

Her father shook his head. "Do something useful and pass me that mortar and pestle."

Emry snapped her fingers, the objects flying gently into her father's hands. "Precise, focused, not sloppy," she said.

There were footsteps on the stairs, and Guin and Emmett arrived, out of breath.

"I hope these will do," Guin said, setting down an armload of bandages.

"Perfect, my dear," said Merlin, with an indulgent grin. He turned to his son. "Emmett, have you got that chainmail?"

"Should fit," Emmett confirmed, holding out a shirt made of finely linked mail. "General wants to know if you'll need a sword."

"Something light, in case of an emergency," Merlin said.

Emry stared at them in shock. They were preparing for war—without her. "Why didn't you ask *me* to help?"

Emmett frowned. "Figured Arthur had you busy enough. Aren't you going?"

"No, I'm not!" Emry practically shouted. The bottles on the shelves trembled dangerously, and the windowpanes rattled.

"Emry," her father scolded. "Get ahold of yourself."

With great effort, Emry unclenched her fists and took a deep breath, and then another, stilling the chaos.

"That's exactly why you're not coming," her father said. "Women are far too emotional."

Emry's eyes met Guin's, and the princess made a face, clearly disagreeing with such a ridiculous pronouncement.

"I'll go see about that sword," Emmett said delicately, trying to back out of the tower.

"Oh, no you won't," Guin said, grabbing hold of his arm. Emry wanted to cheer.

"Emmett's in charge of the workshop while I'm gone," Merlin said.

Emmett paled. "I am?" he said at the same moment Emry cried, "He is?"

Guin winced, putting a hand to her belly. "Ow."

"What's wrong?" Emmett asked, panicked.

"Just the baby kicking. But maybe I should lie down," Guin said in a small voice.

"It's very late," Merlin said. "You should rest."

"Emry, will you come with me?" Guin asked, her eyes wide and pleading.

"Of course I will," Emry said, taking Guin's arm and helping the girl down the steep, narrow stairs. "Tell me if you need to stop and rest."

Guin shot her a guilty smile. "I was faking."

"Why?" Emry asked.

"Well, I *am* tired, and the baby does keep kicking me—ugh, right in the ribs. But mostly, I figured someone needed to defuse all that toxic wizard energy before you three started throwing spells at each other's heads."

"You don't throw spells," Emry tried to explain.

"You know what I mean. Tensions are running high right now. Everyone's under a lot of stress."

"Of course they are, with Camelot's army marching off to war," Emry said as they walked down the darkened corridor.

Guin darted a nervous look at Emry and shook her head. "We shouldn't talk here," she said.

Emry frowned. What was it Guin knew that she didn't? She was bursting with questions, but Guin would say nothing more until they'd reached her bedchambers.

"Would you mind helping me out of this gown?" Guin asked, gesturing at the lacings. "It's the most uncomfortable thing, and I don't really want to call for a maid."

"No problem." Emry waved a hand at the dress, but the stubborn lacings didn't budge. She frowned before realizing. Of course. She'd already magicked the dress larger. And magic didn't work on magic. She stepped forward and began undoing the things by hand. "Well, what aren't you telling me?" Emry demanded.

"I pushed my way into the war room," Guin confessed.

"You did? How?" Emry was impressed. She hadn't even made it past the guards at the end of the hallway.

"Princess skills," Guin said. "And a large platter of sandwiches."

It was a good trick. Emry bit back a snort. "And?"

"Half of Camelot's soldiers are stationed in Cornwall," Guin said. "I saw Arthur's map. There isn't a way to get them to the battle in time. Not with Yurien's men already camped in the moors."

Emry's fingers shook as she unlaced Guin's dress. So they only had half an army? That was a disaster. No wonder everyone was so frantic.

"Then what's the plan?"

"Enlisting what villagers they can," Guin said. "I believe the soldiers are to be a second wave, should the battle still be going when they arrive."

"Sarding hell," Emry said. Arthur was sending *villagers*. No wonder he'd been such a wreck.

"I know." Guin sighed. "My brother's barricaded himself inside the chapel."

Guin tugged on the bodice of her dress, the rest of the laces loosening enough for her to step out of it. Standing there in just her linen underdress, she didn't look fierce. She looked seventeen years old, pregnant, exhausted, and scared.

"I don't know how I'm supposed to sit here and wait," Guin said, pacing the richly appointed chamber. "Cameliard is my home. My kingdom. Those are my subjects who are facing King Yurien's army, and they don't even know they won't have proper backup."

When Guin looked up, Emry saw that her eyes were brimming with tears.

"It's going to be all right," Emry said, wrapping Guin in a hug. She didn't know if it was true, but it seemed like the right thing to say.

Guin sniffled into her shoulder. "I feel so powerless. My father and brother are defending our kingdom, and there's nothing I can do except make bandages and hand out sandwiches and wait."

Emry rather agreed with the sentiment. "How are we not absolutely screaming right now?" she wondered aloud.

Guin raised an eyebrow. "I've been screaming silently for hours. I figured by the look on your face, you've been doing the same."

◑ ◑ ◑

Emry stood in the castle courtyard in the gray light of dawn the next morning, blinking back tears as she dully watched Arthur ride for

Cameliard without her, with Prince Gottegrim at his side. Lancelot and her father were at the head of the party, and Emry ached to join them.

She'd known this was coming. She'd just pictured it very differently. With herself in trousers, astride a horse, her wand in her hand.

This was what she'd been in the dungeons practicing her magic for. Why she'd pushed herself to master her Anwen powers. Yet here she was, not part of the story at all, but just a girl left behind while the men rode off to make history.

It wasn't unfair. That was the worst part. It was just unfathomable.

Guin trembled at her side, despite Emmett's arm wrapped protectively around her shoulders. Percival, who stood at the gates, looked crestfallen. The mood was solemn and tense and awful, and Emry hated it.

And the mood only grew worse after they left. Emry spent the rest of the morning pacing the workshop and reorganizing the stores that her father had ransacked, waiting for Emmett to join her. When he didn't, she realized he must be comforting Guin. After all, it was her kingdom at stake. And if Emry knew one thing about Guinevere, it's that she'd been willing to sacrifice her own happiness to help save them.

Which was . . . exactly what Arthur was doing.

It was disgustingly noble, and she hated him for it.

Except she didn't hate him, not truly. He was trying to do the right thing.

When he'd told her she couldn't come, she hadn't known he only had half an army. That he was marching off to war unprepared, with villagers instead of soldiers.

No wonder he hadn't wanted her to come.

But something was going on with her father. Something he was keeping to himself. And Emry had the worst feeling that perhaps the greatest wizard Camelot had ever known wasn't the secret weapon Arthur believed him to be.

She waved a hand at the hearth, banking the fire. And then she closed the door to the wizard's workshop and went down to her bedroom, curling into a ball beneath the covers.

She felt so lost. She wasn't a court wizard anymore. And whatever had once been between her and Arthur felt irreparably broken. She didn't know what she was supposed to do, or be, other than upset.

There was a knock at the door, and Emry frowned. "Guin?" she called, scrambling to her feet and scrubbing at her eyes with the palms of her hands. Certainly Emmett never knocked.

Gawain entered, wearing a thick traveling cloak over a sturdy leather jerkin, with matching riding boots polished to a high shine. He was the last person she'd expected.

"Never been to this part of the castle," he joked. "I half expected it to have dirt floors and leaking thatch."

Emry rolled her eyes. "Can I help you with something?" she asked. "Or are you just here to gloat that you're off to fight Yurien's army without me?"

"I would never gloat about that, first of all," said Gawain, making a face. "Also, as you might have noticed, they left without me."

"That's right," Emry said, realizing. Gawain was an expertly trained swordsman, and at twenty, was certainly old enough to fight. "Wait, why aren't you going?"

"Can't send everyone in line for the throne off to war, or there'd be none of us left to deter a usurper." Gawain's self-deprecating grin didn't quite reach his eyes. He gestured to her mattress. "Is this stuffed with rushes?"

He was such a snob.

"Down feathers, obviously."

Gawain flopped back on her bed, staring up at the ceiling. "Not bad," he said. "I suppose, if you were to invite me to stay, I might consider it."

"Don't worry, you're leaving as soon as you tell me what you want."

"A shame." Gawain rolled onto his stomach, raising an eyebrow. "We'd have fun."

"We'd have regrets," Emry corrected. "So if you're not going to Cameliard, why are you dressed for travel?"

"Because I'm bound for France. Again. My father's dispatching me to persuade King Louis to help."

"He'll never go for it," Emry said, thinking of the imposing French king, who had refused Arthur's request of the same only a few months ago.

"I fear you're right." Gawain propped his chin in his hands. "But there's no convincing my father not to give it a try. And there is a chance, however slight, that King Louis might reconsider. He won't want Yurien as his enemy across the Channel, with a fleet of ships and a thirst for bloodshed and empire. Getting involved now isn't political. It's strategic."

Emry frowned. "Is that why you're here? To give me a last chance to sleep with you before you leave for France?"

Gawain shot her a look. "Of course not. I'm asking you to come with me."

That was the last thing Emry expected him to say. *"Come with you?"*

"I bring nothing for King Louis other than a politician's promises," Gawain went on. "But you have magic. You could be useful. If there's anyone who might persuade France to send aid, it's you."

"Oh." She took an involuntary step back, bumping into the doors of her wardrobe.

Here was this wonderful, handsome royal, who had come to ask her to stand at his side and help save Camelot. This boy who had never made her cry, or rage, or regret her trust in him. Except he wasn't Arthur. And she hated that her traitorous heart wished he was.

"Was this your father's idea?" Emry asked.

"Hardly." Gawain grimaced. "In fact, I may have told him one of my conditions for going was to bring you along."

"He must have hated that."

"Oh, he did," Gawain assured her. "I believe the only thing he hates more than seeing you with Arthur is seeing you with me."

"Is that supposed to be a compliment?" Emry asked, unimpressed.

"It's merely the truth," Gawain said. "But unlike my cousin, I'm not on a clock to marry and produce an heir. I don't care what my father thinks of my choices."

"Choices like asking me to accompany you to France," Emry said, considering his proposition.

She would love to see Pernelle, the sharp-tongued apothecary, again. And there was no way she could stay at the castle, pacing the wizard's workshop while she brewed healing salve and pain tonics and tried to distract herself from thinking the worst.

"Or you could stay here," Gawain said. "And mope."

Emry's mouth tightened at the thought. "When do we leave?"

CHAPTER 24

Arthur watched the sun sink below the hilltops as they left yet another village behind leaner than they had found it. They'd been riding all day, stopping in nearly every town and village to recruit men to join their ranks.

It broke his heart, seeing families hugging each other goodbye, seeing his people march off to fight with whatever weapons they could find, most often tools more suited to plowing the field than fighting a battle.

"It's getting late, sire," said the general, riding up alongside him. "We should make camp in that valley and move out at first light."

Arthur nodded his assent. "How much longer until we reach Cameliard?"

"With so many men on foot? Another two days."

They didn't have two days. Arthur knew that even before seeing the despair on Prince Gott's face.

"We must pray that it will be soon enough," said Gott, looking grim.

"And if it isn't, and we arrive after Cameliard has fallen?" Arthur asked.

The general winced. "Then it does not matter how many men we bring, if the battle is already decided."

Arthur frowned, considering. "Perhaps we should split our forces. Prince Gott and I can take as many men on horses that can move swiftly under the cover of darkness, and ride straight for Cameliard."

The general shook his head. "It's a good idea, but it should be me who takes on such a task. An army should not ride into battle without their general."

Arthur nodded. "Very well. You'll go, then?"

"I'll tell the men."

Arthur sighed, watching his general ride ahead.

"You're good at this," Prince Gott observed.

"Riding?" A corner of Arthur's mouth quirked up. "I've only had lessons my whole life."

"Ruling," said the Prince of Cameliard. "You actually give thought to your decisions. Not just thought of yourself, but of your kingdom."

"I try," Arthur said. "But mostly I'm just muddling through and hoping I don't get it wrong."

"Then it's a good thing kings don't make mistakes. It's always that their advisors have failed to inform them adequately," Prince Gott returned.

Arthur snorted. "Perhaps that's how power is meant to balance, but not in my court."

He hadn't meant to make such a confession, but he supposed if he was telling someone, the heir to Cameliard's throne was his best choice.

"You've kept your father's advisors," Prince Gott observed. "Perhaps that is where the balance tips."

"And you would do differently?" Arthur asked curiously.

Gott stared thoughtfully into the distance, then said, "I should make them name their own successors, so I might add new opinions to the table without challenging those whose seats are indispensable."

Arthur had never thought of that. Making his advisors name their own successors. It would be interesting to see who they put forward, and he might be able to learn by overhearing their instruction. He might even suggest his friends and ensure that they had the proper experience to advise him, so it didn't look like favoritism. His mind practically vibrated with the possibilities.

"That is an excellent idea, Prince Gott," he said. "I believe I might borrow it."

Gottegrim nodded. "I believe you should. I was pleased with the match between you and my sister," he said. "Despite your reputation."

"My reputation? Am I spoken of as a bookworm, a bastard, or a man of questionable appetite?"

"Depends who you ask, I'm sure," said Prince Gott. "What I meant is, you aren't much for religion."

"Not really," Arthur agreed.

"A shame," said Gott. "I turn to God for guidance, and I would turn to him now, to ask that he bless our swords in battle."

"We have a wizard to do that," said Arthur. Noting Gott's disappointment, he added, "But if you wish to lead such a prayer before our evening meal, I'm sure many would find comfort in hearing it."

Prince Gott nodded. "I shall." They fell quiet again and rode a long while through a forest. The sun was sinking fast, and the air had gone even colder, hinting of a frost that would form in the night.

It would be miserable weather to camp. Arthur thought wistfully of his wizard, and how she might cast a warming spell in their tent. Except she wasn't his wizard. And they weren't sharing a tent. She was back at the castle, no doubt cursing his name while brewing healing tonics with her hair tied back in that blobby knot with the shorter pieces escaping, framing her face.

Arthur sighed again.

"I know that look. You're thinking of a woman," Gott observed.

"Emry," Arthur confirmed. "I'm not sure it was right to leave her behind."

"Love makes us fear what we might lose, that we cannot bear to be parted with," said Prince Gott.

"Scripture?" Arthur asked.

"Poetry." The prince gave him a small smile. "We have rather a good poet at court. Guinevere used to beg him to write shockingly inappropriate rhymes when she was little."

"I can picture that," said Arthur, smiling.

Gott looked at him sideways. "I'm not fool enough to miscount the months until my sister will have her child."

"I hadn't assumed you were," Arthur assured him. "But you should know that your sister and I have never—er, that is to say—we were betrothed in name only."

"Guinevere is . . . a handful. Yet you were nearly forced to wed her, unknowing of her condition."

Arthur coughed.

"Ah," said Prince Gott. "So you knew. Yet you did not tell my father, or your own, to escape your arranged marriage."

"There were other ways to regain my future than to tarnish hers," Arthur said diplomatically. "The only thing Guin and I agreed on was that this treaty between our kingdoms is a good alliance. It was anyone's guess upon which kingdom Yurien would make his first attack. This could have easily been Camelot asking for your aid."

"With our kingdoms joined in marriage, it would have felt less like begging for charity," said Gott.

"Charity?" Arthur scoffed. "We'll stomp out the threat of King Yurien once and for all. Or do you forget we have one and a half armies, the great wizard Merlin, *and* Excalibur on our side?"

The prince rode silently a long while. Arthur thought he might not answer. But then Gott said, "I simply worry that may not be enough."

◑ ◑ ◑

Emry hefted her pack over her shoulder as she crept down the dark castle corridor. The castle was just starting to stir, and the scent of fresh-baked bread drifted from the kitchens. Her stomach growled, and she decided a quick detour for a warm roll wouldn't be out of order.

Yet when she pushed open the door to the kitchens, she practically ran into her brother. His hair was a mess, and he was wearing a dressing gown and carrying a tray of cakes and . . . pickles?

"What are you doing here?" she asked, startled.

"Guin was craving pickles and cake, and was too embarrassed to ask a serving maid." Emmett stifled a yawn. "What's your excuse?"

"Same?" Emry tried.

He spotted the pack over her shoulder, and his eyes widened. "Explain. Right now," he demanded, dragging her into the nearest alcove.

Emry sighed. She plucked a cake off Guin's tray and shoved it into her mouth so she wouldn't have to say anything for a moment.

Emmett wasn't impressed. "You better not be going after Arthur and Father," he said sternly.

"I'm not," Emry said, swallowing thickly. "I'm going to France with Gawain."

"You're *what?*"

"I'm accompanying him to Paris to help secure French aid," she explained impatiently. "Lord Agravaine knows all about it."

Emmett shook his head. "Well, I don't. Were you even going to tell me, or were you just going to disappear?"

Emry winced. She knew she'd forgotten something. "I would've sent word," she defended. "It's not like I'm doing anything dangerous."

"No, just selfish," Emmett returned. "I can't believe this. You're as bad as Father."

"I am not!"

"You are! The two of you run away whenever you can, without a thought to those you're leaving behind. You ran away from Brocelande. You ran away from the castle when King Uther ordered you executed."

"That's not fair! I had to leave to fix your mess. And King Uther was going to kill me!"

"I'm not finished," Emmett insisted. "You ran away to France with

Arthur. And now you're doing it again, with Gawain. When things get hard, you run. You've always been like that. Both of you."

Emry's heart squeezed as her brother spoke. This was exactly what she didn't want to hear. "What about you?" she returned. "You run away from responsibility."

"I used to, but I grew up, if you haven't noticed," he replied. "I married Guin. And here I am, taking care of her, because that's what you do when you choose someone. You're the one who can't stand to be around the people who love you, because you're so afraid they'll stop."

Emry gasped at Emmett's words. They were so unfair. Surely that wasn't true, and he didn't see her like that.

"You don't know what you're talking about," she said.

"I know that you took Arthur reappointing Father his court wizard as proof that he doesn't care about you. Even though anyone who's seen that room of fussy old men who call themselves his advisors would know he had no chance of doing otherwise. You pushed him away, Em. And now you're abandoning me and Guin, just because you can't stand it when you can't play the hero."

"Stop it!" Emry snapped, not wanting to hear another word. "This is why I hate goodbyes. Because you make them horrible."

She shoved past him, her heart hammering as she hurried through the castle corridors. Emmett was wrong. She didn't push people away because she was afraid they'd stop loving her. He didn't know what it was like to be a woman with power in a world where men kept it all for themselves, to be chosen last every time, and to get used to what it felt like to never be the one anyone ever loved unconditionally.

She raced toward the royal stables, her throat tight from holding back tears.

"Ready?" Gawain asked impatiently, already in the saddle. "We should have left by now."

"Almost," Emry said. She checked her pack, taking her time, trying to quell her panic and the uncomfortable feeling that Emmett was right, and going with Gawain to the French court really was running away.

She felt like she was forgetting something important. Yet it was all there. Her herbs and potions, gowns to be worn at court, her wand, and even a small bundle of books.

Her horse nickered, and she gave the creature a look. "Don't you start with me, too."

"If you're looking for your brother's trousers, you seem to be wearing them," Gawain said, raising an eyebrow at her choice of clothing.

"I'm not riding a horse in a gown," she snapped. She supposed she was as ready as she'd ever be. "Let's go."

She swung up into the saddle, raising the hood of her heavy velvet cloak. And then she followed Gawain out of the stable yard and toward the gates. Two servants followed behind, their horses heavily laden.

"Did you bring your entire wardrobe?" Emry inquired.

"One should never appear desperate when asking a favor of a king," said Gawain, lifting his chin.

When they rode through the castle gates, Safir waved, and Emry tried to push away the feeling that something had gone wrong. That this wasn't where she was meant to be headed. The feeling only intensified as they made their way down the Strand and toward the harbor.

A great three-mast sailing ship waited, its sailors loading heavy boxes and barrels of cargo. They shouted to one another in French, and when Emry looked closer, she saw the ship wasn't flying Camelot's colors or flag.

"We'll be sailing with a French wine merchant and his crew," Gawain explained. "We can hire a carriage when we disembark in Calais." He swung down from his horse and went toward the ship.

Emry watched as he strode across the wharf, his cloak flowing from his shoulders, his bearing unmistakably royal as he signaled the men loading cargo. He spoke as though he expected to be obeyed, firmly yet gently, in a mixture of French and English.

They'd made it just in time to catch the tide. That much was evident from the flurry of activity on the docks. But they needed to hurry. Packs were removed from their horses at breakneck speed and loaded onto the vessel.

Gawain strode up the gangplank and spoke at length with the captain, a tall, dark-skinned man with close-cropped hair wearing a gray wool jacket that came down to his ankles.

The captain nodded and finished with a bow.

Gawain returned, his eyes bright with the promise of adventure. "So," he said. "You can have the first mate's cabin, but unless you're willing to share, I'll spend the evening bunked with the men."

Emry was surprised Gawain had gone to the trouble of looking out for her, but of course he would. He didn't have the weight of running a kingdom pressing down on his shoulders to distract him.

Which of course made her think of Arthur. Of their journey to France, on a different vessel. Of being attacked by bandits on the road, and of fighting at his side. Of discovering later that night that Arthur had been stabbed but had kept it a secret, preferring to suffer in silence than to ask for her help. He had needed her but hadn't known how to ask.

She went to untie her packs . . . and found she couldn't.

This is wrong, she thought. *I'm not supposed to be here.*

"We'll miss the tide if we don't leave now," Gawain warned.

Emry bit her lip, wondering how to tell him that she'd changed her mind.

Yet somehow, he seemed to guess.

"You're not coming," he said, his expression hurt.

"I need to go after Arthur and Lance."

Gawain nodded tightly, a muscle feathering in his jaw. "Hell of a moment to change your mind."

"Better now than after we're already on board," Emry joked half-heartedly. But it wasn't the time for jokes, and they both seemed to realize that. The silence was full of so many unspoken things.

"I'm really sorry," Emry said. "I wanted to go with you. I was flattered you asked."

"You wanted to go with Arthur, only he *didn't* ask." Gawain sighed. "And he should have."

Emry frowned, wondering if she'd heard him correctly. "But he has my father. He's made it clear he doesn't need me as well."

"Of course he needs you," Gawain said. "I'm not at all confident that our kingdom's forces are a match for Yurien's, but I do know one thing: I have never met anyone who's a match for Emry Merlin."

Emry stepped forward, softly pressing her lips to Gawain's cheek. His skin was smooth and warm, and he smelled of cherries and cloves, and it would have been so easy to slide her mouth over to his, to follow him onto the ship and head for France, hoping her feelings for him would grow, and making a decision she could never undo.

It would be so easy to run away with the boy who no one else ever chose first, either.

And she could sense him waiting, wishing she would. But she would never want him as much as she wanted Arthur. And they both knew it.

She pulled away, trying to ignore the despair in his eyes, and knowing that she was the cause.

"You'll manage perfectly well without me," she said. "You have more to bargain with than you think. And if you're the one who saves Camelot, I won't be in the least bit surprised."

"I could say the same thing," Gawain told her.

"Friends?" Emry asked.

"Always," Gawain promised.

The ship had already raised its anchor. Emry stood on the docks, watching him sail away. Watching the boy she didn't choose and his ship moving farther and farther away.

And then she rode toward Cameliard.

CHAPTER 25

Arthur was sweating under his armor as he made his way through the camp. Down in the mountain pass, the fires of King Yurien's army camp glowed in warning of what was to come at dawn.

He wasn't too late. The fighting hadn't yet begun. He wasn't sure whether that was a gift or a curse. He looked around, trying to catch a familiar face, and was relieved when he saw General Timias hurrying to meet him.

"Sire," said the general, falling into step beside him. "You made it."

"I did," Arthur said. "And it looks like we arrived just in time."

"That you did," agreed the general. "Yurien's forces are more than we had anticipated. You're wanted in King Leodegrance's tent."

"Lead the way," Arthur said, feeling impossibly out of his depth. The last time he had seen King Leodegrance was when he had refused Guinevere's hand in marriage, just before the duke's siege. The wedding had been a disaster, with every guest's life at risk. He swallowed nervously and rested a hand on Excalibur's pommel. The sword pulsed in reassurance.

Two guards standing outside the tent eyed him with confusion.

"Don't just stand there," General Timias snapped. The guards saluted smartly and held aside the tent flap for them to enter. There stood King Leodegrance, with his scowl and thick gray beard and angry tangle of silvering hair. His armor was plated in gold, and jeweled rings adorned his fingers. He didn't look like a man expecting to fight. He looked like an entitled royal who expected his soldiers to offer their own lives to defend his kingdom.

The men in his tent were all at least twice Arthur's age, and dressed for battle, their posture making it clear they held positions of command. They regarded him, in his practical armor and mail, with little interest.

"Well, deliver your message, boy," snapped a man with a thick black beard, holding out his hand impatiently for a scroll.

Arthur would have laughed, if there were anything humorous about the situation.

"King Arthur," King Leodegrance said gruffly. "Took you long enough."

The bearded man went red at the realization of whom he had just called *boy*.

Arthur squared his shoulders and tried to summon his nerve. "There is no need to thank me, if that is what you were going to say next. There was never any doubt that Camelot would come to your aid should you request it. Even on the night of my coronation."

King Leodegrance's expression soured.

A young boy came in to pour wine, and all accepted save for Arthur. He wanted to be sharp for this, not dulled and sleepy. "Can we tell how large Yurien's forces are?" he inquired.

"We are outnumbered," one of Leodegrance's commanders pronounced, as if speaking to a small child.

"Yes, I can see that," Arthur said in irritation. "But it would be valuable to understand to what extent, so we may form a strategy."

"They have magic," King Leodegrance said. "So they will not lead with force, but with trickery."

"Then we shall be ready to meet them with magic of our own," said Arthur. "I have brought Camelot's best wizard."

Leodegrance turned a horrified shade of puce. "You brought that—that *girl* here?"

Arthur blanched at the accusation, suddenly glad that he hadn't brought Emry, if this was the reaction. These men seemed as though they would banish him from their command center if they thought they might get away with it, and he was the sarding King of Camelot.

"Of course not, sire," said General Timias. "We have come with Master Willyt Merlin, who helped King Uther to victory in many battles."

King Leodegrance nodded in approval. "Then bring him here," he commanded, "so my general can determine how he might prove useful."

○ ○ ○

As the battle dawned, Merlin could feel his magic failing. His head spun, and his vision crackled as he struggled to maintain the wards he'd promised would surround their camp, preventing a surprise attack.

He was thankful that was all King Leodegrance had wished for him to contribute.

For now.

Outside his tent, he could hear the preparations for battle. The men shouting, their energy tense and fraught as they sharpened blades and donned their armor. He groaned, dizziness giving way to a dull and stabbing pain inside his head.

He reached for his flask, hands trembling, and took a swig of the foul elixir.

It wasn't enough. If anything, the pain in his head only got more intense. He took another swallow, and another.

His heart sped up, and he felt curiously lightheaded. No, he couldn't lose hold of his power. Not here. Not now. So he upended the flask and drank deeply, imbibing more than he had ever taken before. The elixir made him shudder as he swallowed, and made him drop to his hands and knees, retching.

But he kept it down. In the agonizing minutes that came next, he gritted his teeth and stretched his remaining magic, trying to make it enough to maintain the ward. He felt as if he was climbing uphill with a boulder on his back, and he found himself shaking and sweating from the effort.

If the wards slip, they'll never know.

With a sigh, he let them go. His vision swam, and he gasped for breath. He just needed an hour or two to recover. No one would ever find out. It wasn't as though anyone here could sense magic.

Without the strain of maintaining the protection spell, he could feel the Godfrey's root racing through his veins. A soothing warmth spread from his chest to his limbs, and a wonderful sensation of calm drifted over him. His shaking stopped, and his muscles relaxed. He lay down on his bedroll, and then he closed his eyes and let the elixir overtake him.

◐ ◐ ◐

Emry stared in horror at the battlefield in the valley below. Soldiers clashed in hand-to-hand combat, horses and men lying slain at their feet. The bodies were everywhere. And the noise of it. The clamor of thousands of swords rang out, punctured by shouting and moans of the wounded.

Most of the fallen wore crimson cloaks of Camelot, or the deeper burgundy of Cameliard, or no livery at all, just the rough-spun clothes they had come in. There were none in the black tunic and cloak of Lothia.

That couldn't be right, unless some of the plainly dressed men fought for King Yurien. It was obvious that Yurien's forces outnumbered theirs, badly. The soldiers from the north wore fur and leather over their plate armor, and their black tunics bore the white stamped watchtower of Lothian Keep. They seemed to dominate the battlefield as she watched, slaying even more crimson-cloaked men. Cameliard's and Camelot's forces seemed barely able to defend themselves in combat.

She frowned. Something was wrong. Surely some Lothian soldiers should have fallen in battle.

She pricked a finger and reached out with Anwen's magic, feeling for her father's wards. A deep, unsettling ripple of magic hit her spell, and she gasped.

What *was* that?

The magic was like none she'd felt before. It was cloying, like a perfume used to mask a terrible odor. Beneath the buzzing of the enchantment, the magic stank of men's blood, and rot.

Her heart squeezed with panic at the thought that Morgana had done this. That she had returned from Anwen with unspeakable magic, enough to turn the tide of a battle. Enough to make a graveyard of Camelot's men, with none of her own soldiers joining them.

Emry slid from her horse and paced, trying to think. Her father must have figured out what was going on. Yet she didn't sense any wards around Camelot's camp, or any active traces of his magic at all.

Only *that* magic. That horrible, rotten magic. And something else . . . bright and cold.

It wasn't coming from the battlefield, or from Camelot's camp. It was coming from a small outcropping of woods to the side of the battlefield.

"Smart as spades, foolish as hearts," Emry muttered, trying to give herself courage. She tied up her horse, took out her wand, and continued on foot into the woods.

"Well, well," said a voice. "If it isn't the little witch I was promised."

Emry turned, and found herself face-to-face with Morgana. "You,"

Emry said. But the woman's voice didn't sound like Morgana's. And the sorceress's wolfish smile was nowhere to be found. Something else— *someone* else—peered out through her eyes, lighting them uncannily from within. Emry shivered. Magic radiated off the woman who wasn't Morgana, sweet and cold.

Anwen's magic.

"You're not Morgana," Emry accused.

"No." The sorceress smiled. Waited.

And suddenly, with a terrible flash of clarity, Emry knew.

"I've heard they call you many things," said Emry. "Bellicent."

"Clever girl." The sorceress pulled Morgana's mouth into a smile, and Emry's stomach twisted at how false it felt, like watching a puppet made from a person, with invisible hands pulling the strings. "You have your father's magic."

"I have my own magic," Emry corrected, lifting her chin.

"You have the power to travel between worlds," accused Bellicent, staring hungrily at Emry.

Emry didn't deny it. She could feel something pushing, gently, at the corners of her mind. Tiptoeing, softly, hoping she might not notice.

Stop that, she thought.

Oh, you truly are a clever one, said a musical voice inside her head.

It itched, being spoken to like this, and Emry wrinkled her nose. She'd thought the Lady of the Lake was the only one capable of such tricks.

You forget, I'm her sister, crooned Bellicent.

Get out! Emry thought, more insistently this time. She imagined a wall made of magic going up around her thoughts.

"So quick to figure that out," Bellicent said, aloud this time. "I've been wanting to find you. And now I have."

Bellicent knew about her? This wasn't good.

"What have you done to Yurien's soldiers?" Emry demanded.

Morgana's body shrugged. "I wished to see them win. I was promised great things, if they do. But I wasn't promised the one thing I want. Only you can give me that."

"I'm not letting you control my mind or body," Emry said, folding her arms across her chest.

"I would not control you," Bellicent purred. "I would give you what you desire. If you would give me something in return."

"Such as?" Emry asked.

"Open the doorway between our worlds. Let me pass through in my true form. If you do, I'll give you anything. I'll turn Yurien's soldiers into toads. Or better yet, I'll give your father back the magic he lost. He'll die if he keeps on like this. But I can save him."

Save my father? "What are you talking about?"

"You really don't know?"

Emry frowned, because suddenly, she did know. *Give your father back the magic he lost.* So that's what he was hiding. "What did you do to him?" Emry demanded.

"Me? Oh, child, the question you should be asking is, *What is he doing to himself?* He doesn't have much longer, if he keeps amplifying what little magic he has left. Already, he must be feeling the effects. I'm told the herb is a slow poisoning, when taken in moderation. But I can already smell the sickness within his magic."

Godfrey's root. Emry's heart clenched as she realized what he was using it for, and what that book she'd found had meant by great risks.

Her father's magic was compromised. Yet he'd kept that information to himself, enjoying his reputation as the most powerful wizard who had ever lived. And in order to keep up the pretense, he was killing himself.

How had she missed it?

Oh, she was furious with herself. But even more furious with her father. He'd let Arthur take him to war when his magic could fail. So she'd been right to come. She had known it.

"I'm not letting you through the doorway, for any price," Emry said.

"Not even to save your father? I would find a powerful place for you, once I have conquered all that I desire. I could use a witch with your magic."

"Wizard," Emry corrected. "And for the record, I will never help you."

Morgana's body grinned. "Is that a challenge, little witch? *Strangulo!*"

Vines shot out from the forest floor, wrapping themselves around Emry's neck and squeezing. She couldn't breathe. The vines snaked around her arms, pressing them uselessly to her sides. She choked, gasping for breath, as the vines lifted her off the ground.

She rose higher into the air, coughing and twisting. Her vision started to go dark at the edges, and when she tried to reach for her magic, it slid from her grasp.

"Let me know when you change your mind," Bellicent called.

Emry rose higher, branches scratching at her arms. Blood trickled down her wrist, and suddenly she felt it—a flicker of bright, cold magic. Her Anwen powers.

Dizzily, she traced the rune for *ansuz* in her mind. Power shot out of her, and suddenly, thankfully, the vines wrapped around her loosened. She gasped, sucking in grateful breaths.

Clever air rune. Clever Anwen magic.

"You can't last much longer," Bellicent singsonged, and Emry realized the sorceress didn't know she'd broken free of the enchantment.

"*Uruz*," Emry demanded, concentrating. "*Kenaz!*" She floated down to the ground, vines snapping and curling back onto the forest floor. In their place, purple flames appeared out of nowhere, twisting around her wrists and hovering above her palms. The moment her toes touched the frozen earth, the fire shot out, enveloping Bellicent in an angry inferno.

The sorceress stumbled back, screaming. "How are you doing this?" she shouted, slapping at the flames that licked up her borrowed body.

Emry took that opportunity to run. She didn't want to wait and see what happened when Bellicent got free of the conjured flames. Her throat felt raw, and her chest hurt, and her Anwen magic was coursing through her veins, wanting to be let out.

"Stop it," she scolded the magic. It was making her feel dizzy, carrying on like that. "Chill out."

Gradually, the magic became less frantic, and Emry's breath came more steadily, and it hit her all at once what had happened. The most powerful sorceress who had ever lived had found a way into their world. And no one else knew. They all thought it was Morgana.

She had to tell Arthur.

She hefted her pack over her shoulder and hurried toward the soldiers' camp.

CHAPTER 26

A rthur's heart thundered nearly as loud as the horse's hooves as he rode across the battlefield. Everything was chaos and destruction. So many of his men lay slain, the ground soaked with their blood.

In the unforgiving brightness of the morning sun, all this death seemed grotesque and wrong, as though it belonged to the nighttime. But war didn't choose a time of day.

And so Arthur lifted his shining sword higher.

"For Camelot. For Cameliard. For peace!" he called.

"For peace!" his men echoed.

Lancelot's horse kept pace with his own, and Arthur felt the tiniest bit more reassured by his friend's presence.

Fighting with sword on horseback was different than on foot, and Arthur hadn't trained in it. Still, he knew the basics. Knew to slash rather than thrust, so he wouldn't lose grip on his blade.

Yet as he slashed his way through Yurien's men, something worried at him. The men fell to the ground, yet before Arthur could wipe the blood from his blade, they rose to their feet unharmed. Arthur watched incredulously as one man's shoulder wound closed itself, and he hefted his sword again within seconds.

No. That wasn't possible.

Lance grimaced. "They're not dying! Yurien's soldiers won't die!" he called.

Arthur looked around, hoping that they were wrong. But it was true: Yurien's men instantly stood, ready for battle, after suffering wounds that should be fatal or grievous at best. Some impossible magic was protecting them.

He'd led his men to fight an unbeatable army, and they didn't even know it. Such a battle was a death sentence. A slaughter.

And it was all his fault. He knew Yurien had been biding his time. He should have suspected the man had good reason. Oh, Arthur had been a fool. And now his people would suffer.

He watched as Sir Bors faced a scrawny soldier who couldn't have been older than sixteen. The knight should have had the advantage, yet when his sword plunged through the lad's stomach, the boy didn't even react, just swung his weapon and—

Arthur grimaced as Sir Bors's head rolled onto the battlefield, his body toppling where, moments ago, he had confidently stood.

This was awful. A slaughter of the worst kind. Arthur looked away, bile rising in his throat. Then he fought through the fray, losing his horse to an expertly thrust blade, and continuing on foot. Not too far off, he spotted Lancelot, his friend fighting two soldiers at once.

Lance valiantly sliced one soldier's sword arm off, and the man dropped his weapon and went to his knees, his weapon remaining on the ground, clutched in his severed arm. Lance swung again, taking the soldier's head off. Thankfully, the soldier stayed down, his severed head glaring darkly at Lance.

"You've got to behead them!" Lance called.

"Sarding hell," Arthur swore. Slicing off a man's head was brutal, not at all how he was trained to fight.

And then a soldier rushed right at him, sword extended, his eyes crazed with the frenzy of battle. Arthur tightened his grip on Excalibur, the glowing sword pulsing with power and light, as if it knew what it must do.

The blade took over, and before Arthur knew what had happened, he was staring down at a headless body. His stomach churned in disgust, and he turned away to vomit from the sight of what he'd done.

They had to get the word out to the other men. Yet when Arthur looked around, he saw just how many of the men who had followed him into battle had already fallen. The field was strewn with Camelot's bodies, the soil slick with Camelot's blood. The ground was frozen this time of year, Arthur realized. It would be impossible to bury them.

They had died in a slaughter, and would have no dignity even in death.

His stomach twisted again, and he heaved once more. He didn't even see the soldier coming until the man was on top of him, sword raised above his head. Arthur lifted Excalibur, but he was too late to parry. The soldier's blade slashed his arm, piercing a joint in his armor.

Arthur gasped, stumbling and losing his footing. He landed in the dirt, Excalibur just out of reach, staring up in horror at the soldier looming over him.

Then Lancelot, brave Lance, jumped in front of Arthur.

And the soldier's blade ran him through the stomach.

Lance groaned, slumping to the ground, the blade's tip protruding through his back.

Arthur finally got hold of Excalibur and leapt to his feet, his heart pounding as he slashed and sliced, removing first the soldier's sword arm, and then his head.

When he finished, he was shaking. The wound on his shoulder was leaking blood, and his mouth tasted like curdled metal. He felt like a monster who'd just beheaded two men within the span of minutes. He wiped sweat from his brow with the back of his hand and turned to Lance.

"Well, that was—" he started to say, but the sentence died on his tongue. Arthur stared at his friend, the whole world going slow and still.

Lance was still on the ground, his face contorted in pain as he clutched at the hilt of the sword sunk almost fully into his stomach, its point protruding through his back.

"Lance!" Arthur cried.

"Not—looking good, is—it?" Lance managed, his teeth chattering. He was pale, his brow slick with sweat.

"You have to get up," Arthur begged, extending a hand. He practically pulled his friend to his feet.

"Arthur—" Lance coughed, blood trickling from a corner of his mouth. His tunic was fast soaking through with blood, and he swayed unsteadily, Arthur taking most of his weight.

"Tell me later," Arthur insisted. "After your wound is mended." And then he had an idea. "Switch swords with me."

The moment he handed Excalibur to his friend, Lance nodded tightly. "Better," he said weakly. But he was still unsteady on his feet. He was slick with sweat, and worryingly pale when they reached camp. "I can't go much farther," Lance said weakly, his tunic soaked with blood.

"Wait here," Arthur said, helping Lance to sit propped against a tree. "I'll get help."

And then he ran for Master Merlin.

"Merlin?" Arthur called, lifting the flap of the man's tent. The wizard lay on the ground, curled into a ball. He shivered convulsively, as if racked with fever.

Sard, the wizard's protective wards must be powerful indeed if they were straining his magic this much.

"Master Merlin!" Arthur dropped to his knees beside the wizard.

"Go away!" Merlin insisted, swatting at Arthur. His eyes were dark and shining, his pupils overlarge. Arthur didn't think the man recognized him and wondered what it was that Merlin saw.

"It's me, Arthur," he said. And then, more sternly, "It's your king."

"Leave me—please—" Merlin said, his teeth chattering.

"I can't," Arthur said firmly. "Lance needs your help. He's wounded."

Merlin let out a humorless laugh. "I'm through, lad. Can't you see I've no magic to spare?"

Surely that couldn't be true.

"But you're the most powerful wizard who ever lived," Arthur said.

"Do I—look—powerful—to you—right now?" Merlin choked out.

He didn't. He looked worryingly ill.

"I don't care!" Arthur insisted. "You have to do something! You're his only chance."

Merlin closed his eyes. Rolled over, until his back was facing Arthur, his spine stretched taut against the thin fabric of his shirt. "Go away," he croaked. "I can't help anyone. Go."

Arthur stared at the man in disbelief. He'd chosen the wrong wizard. "Emry could do it."

He'd screwed everything up, because he'd listened to his father's advisors. Because he hadn't trusted what his heart was telling him. And now—and now he might lose his best friend. His bravest knight. The best man he knew.

Emry had begged to come with them. He could have said yes. Insisted her father have an apprentice at his side. But he hadn't. He'd been so desperate to get everything right that he'd gotten the most important thing of all wrong. And now it was too late.

Arthur returned to Lance's side, grimacing as he saw how much his friend had worsened in his short absence. "How are you holding up?" he asked.

Lance's teeth wouldn't stop chattering, and Arthur had never seen him so pale. "Master Merlin can't heal this soon enough."

Arthur bit his lip and sank to the ground. "About that . . ."

Lance studied his expression and blanched. "No," he said, his voice small. "I really thought—"

"Me too," said Arthur, reaching for his friend's hand.

Lance nodded bravely. "You're going to need your sword back."

"Hold on to it for me," Arthur said. "Just a little while longer." He knew too well the effect Excalibur had in a position like Lance's. Once, in the caverns beneath St. Paul's Cathedral, it had blunted the pain of what he'd thought were his last moments.

Sard, he didn't want to lose his best friend. He bit his lip, willing himself not to cry.

Lance had sacrificed himself to save him. Arthur had always known Lance was loyal to a fault, his bravest knight, but facing the truth of what that meant was too much to bear.

"You're a good man," said Lance. "And you're going to be a good king."

"Don't," Arthur said, his heart not so much breaking as already broken.

Lance groaned softly. Blood foamed at the corner of his mouth. "I dreamed of becoming a knight so I could ride into battle at your side. And I got to do that. I got to be—your champion."

"You did," Arthur agreed. He didn't want to say goodbye. Not like this, on a blood-soaked battlefield, facing an unbeatable enemy. Not ever.

Lance's eyes fluttered closed. Faintly, he whispered, "Tell Perce that I love him."

CHAPTER 27

"Tell him yourself," said Emry, stepping into the clearing.

Arthur stared at her, mouth agape, wondering if he was imagining things. But he doubted he'd dreamed up the horrified expression on her face as she stared down at Lance.

"I know you said not to come, but when have I ever listened?" Emry said to Arthur. "Please don't be mad."

Did she truly think he'd be upset about that now?

Belatedly, he realized he hadn't said anything. He'd just been marveling over the impossible good fortune that she had been stubborn enough to defy him and had turned up when she did.

"Emry?" Lance whispered, his eyes fluttering open. "Thank god."

"Can you help him?" Arthur asked, hardly daring to hope. This wasn't just a surface wound, and they all knew that.

Emry's brows knit together, and her teeth sank into her bottom lip. "I've never healed anything this complicated before. But I'll try."

Arthur felt a flicker of hope with the knowledge that Emry was here, and that she was going to help. That he might not lose his best friend after all.

"Tell me—the truth," Lance gasped.

Emry frowned as she examined his injury. "It's bad," she said. "I don't think there's time to fetch a pain tonic."

"I'll manage," Lance said through gritted teeth.

"Arthur, I need you to pull the sword out, straight as you can," Emry said.

They'd done this before, with the arrow that had pierced Brannor's arm during their ambush on the way to Paris. But that had been an arrow, not a *sword*.

"On three," he said. "One, two—" He pulled as Lance let out a string of expletives.

Arthur pressed his hand against the wound on Lance's stomach, which didn't stop the blood from bubbling up through his fingers. He swallowed thickly at the sight of it. Funny how an entire battlefield full of bodies was somehow less horrible than the sight of his best friend stabbed through the stomach.

Emry put her hand on top of his. "Let go," she said. "Trust me."

He did. Because she was his wizard. Because having her by his side was the best thing that had ever happened to him, and he had been a fool to let his advisors convince him otherwise.

Emry pressed her hand against Lance's wound and concentrated. "*Angsumnes*," she murmured, closing her eyes.

She stayed perfectly still, longer than she ever had before. Slowly, the wound began to close. Emry gasped, squeezing her eyes shut even tighter. Her shoulders trembled. She repeated the spell a second time, and a third.

"You've got this," Arthur told her.

She was shaking terribly. Sweat beaded on her brow. Her breath came in ragged gasps. Blood trickled from one nostril, and then the other.

"Emry," Arthur said nervously. "Are you okay?"

She was so pale. Even her lips had no color. Her veins stood out against her skin, a bright silver. She let out a ragged, shallow breath. She looked terrible, as if she was draining her own life force and didn't know how to stop.

"Emry," Arthur said again, urgently.

"*Angsumnes!*" she cried.

And then she collapsed.

CHAPTER 28

Morgana woke with a whimper, underneath a heavy blanket. Her skin felt hot and tight, and the pain was excruciating. *What happened?*

She looked down, and saw her arms were covered with burns, the flesh bubbling and peeling. She felt weak and bleary with fever. And she couldn't remember any of it.

What had Bellicent *done* to her?

Nothing, the sorceress snapped. *Your little witch burned me with magic she shouldn't even have.*

So the Merlin girl had fought back. And it seemed she hadn't agreed to open the doorway between worlds after all. Good for her. Still, Morgana couldn't help but tuck away Bellicent's words to think on another time: *magic she shouldn't even have.*

Keep your miserable body until it's healed, Bellicent snarled. *I don't wish to feel its pain.*

Morgana climbed gingerly to her feet, the tent spinning. Her dress clung to her skin, and when she tried to pry it away, she nearly fainted. She needed a pain tonic, or healing salve. Both complicated potions she hated to brew, and of course she didn't have the ingredients with her.

At least she'd gotten rid of Bellicent for the time being. She couldn't sense the sorceress lurking in her mind, and she had control of herself once again. Though she worried the control would be short lived.

Keep your miserable body until it's healed, Bellicent had said. Morgana gritted her teeth, wondering if she could stand to make that healing take longer than she'd wish.

Her throat was parched. She spotted a carafe of water on the other side of the tent and reached out a hand. *"Arcesso,"* she whispered hoarsely. Her magic came, painful and sluggish. The carafe wobbled through the air toward her but dropped halfway, spilling across the rug that carpeted the tent.

No.

Her magic only acted like this when she'd used too much. But she couldn't remember the last time she'd cast anything more than a simple household spell.

Had Bellicent . . . used her magic?

Morgana frowned, knowing she was missing something important, but unable to piece it together.

"There you are," her husband said, pushing aside the flap to the tent. He was beaming. "Aren't you going to congratulate me on my victory?"

"We won?" Morgana said, surprised.

"Oh, it's you." His satisfied grin faltered as he realized he was speaking to his wife, and not the sorceress who had ensured his win.

"Try to look a little less disappointed," Morgana snapped.

Her husband's brows knit together as he took in the burns on her arms. "What happened to you?"

"Bellicent." Morgana said the woman's name as a curse.

"Whatever she did, it was worth it," he declared. "Cameliard is mine."

"You mean ours," Morgana corrected.

"Yes—of course," her husband said, with a smile that didn't quite reach his eyes

He had forgotten that she was his queen. He had only come to gloat to the sorceress who had assured his victory. Never mind that he'd only won because *Morgana* had stolen that enchantment from Prince Arthur, because *Morgana* had risked her life to go to the Otherworld.

"King Leodegrance has surrendered," Yurien went on gleefully. "His head is on a pike outside my tent."

Morgana grimaced at the thought. "Your whore will enjoy that when she comes to bed you this evening."

"Lady Mara remains in Lothia," said her husband. With a note of pride, he added, "She shouldn't travel in her condition."

So the girl was with child. This day got worse and worse.

"Am I supposed to congratulate you?" Morgana asked. "There's no honor in siring a bastard when you already have a son."

"Jealousy does not become you," he said lightly. "Nor do those hideous burns."

"They will heal," Morgana assured him. "And when they do, if it's more children you desire, perhaps you'll remember you have a *wife*. Who is a queen."

Yurien's face clouded. "She escaped," he said, and Morgana had no idea whom her husband meant. "Both of them did," he went on. "The Queen of Cameliard, and her son and heir. I'm told they fled to the nearest harbor, and boarded a ship bound for Andalusia."

"It hardly matters," said Morgana, annoyed at how deftly he had changed the subject. "The kingdom is ours. Would you have put their heads on pikes, too?"

"To those who stand in my way, there's nothing I wouldn't do," he said.

Morgana knew a warning when she heard one.

CHAPTER 29

Arthur lunged forward, Excalibur in hand.

He was in the castle armory at his usual early hour, the sun's first rays just beginning to stain the morning sky. He wore only his breeches and tunic, the sleeves rolled back. His protective padding still hung on its peg. When he'd gone to put it on, the weight on his shoulders had choked him, reminding him of what it was to get dressed for battle, and he'd found he couldn't breathe.

Besides, what did he need it for, fighting a practice dummy that couldn't strike back?

Everything was a disaster.

Yurien had won the battle. Cameliard was under his control.

King Leodegrance had surrendered, gaining time for his wife and Prince Gott to escape, and for Arthur and General Timias to lead Camelot's men back to their own kingdom.

There had been no hope of victory. Not over soldiers who didn't die. He'd lost two thousand men on that field. What a legacy in his first year as king.

Arthur let his sword fall to his side and squeezed his eyes shut in anguish, haunted by what he had done.

He'd sent his men—his friends—to be killed without a chance. He wanted to be a good king. A fair king. One who made things better for his people. Instead, he had made things worse.

Cameliard had fallen, and Arthur knew Yurien wouldn't stop before he conquered every last kingdom of England. The battle was over, but the war hadn't yet begun.

Excalibur pulsed impatiently in his hand, and he stared down in disgust at the mythical sword.

"I am exactly what you made me," he said softly. "A killer. A man who walks away from a battlefield unhurt, my blade tipped with blood, the road home littered with the bodies of men who didn't have the same advantage."

Yet his advantage hadn't stopped him from getting hurt. He still bore the scar of the enemy soldier's blade on his bicep, refusing to magic it away. There were others who needed the salves and potions more than he did. He deserved a scar. More than a scar. Especially when he thought of what had happened to Lance.

Brave Lancelot, who had come to his defense. Who had offered his life in forfeit for Arthur's own. And Emry, who'd worked so hard to save him that she hadn't known when to stop.

Arthur let his blade clatter to the floor. And then he sank to his knees, burying his face in his hands. His shoulders shook, and his throat went tight, and he wondered if despair could consume him, because he certainly didn't think he would ever feel happy again.

Master Merlin assured him that it was likely she would wake from her enchanted sleep.

Likely, but not certain.

More than a week had passed since she had fainted from using too much magic, and still she had not stirred. According to her father, she should have been awake by now. With every day, he worried that she'd remain asleep forever.

That he had lost her, by trying to keep her safe.

And he didn't think he could bear it. He had done everything wrong. Had listened to the wrong advisors. Had believed in false promises because he wanted so badly for someone else to have the answers he needed to find deep within himself.

But they didn't.

Or perhaps there were no good answers in war.

"I can't do this," he whispered aloud. He felt like he was standing on the edge of a dark place, one that might swallow him whole if he took another step.

And in that moment, he would have welcomed it.

Lance bolted upright in bed at the sound of screaming. He pushed off the covers, grasping for his sword.

"Hey, it's all right," Percival soothed, placing a hand on his shoulder.

Lance winced, realizing he'd been the one making such a racket. He was covered in sweat, his heart pounding. A nightmare. That's all it had been. He was home at Castle Camelot, in bed with Perce. Screaming.

He pressed a hand to his stomach, feeling the perfectly smooth skin where there should have been an ugly scar. "Sorry for waking you," he said sheepishly. "I'm fine. Promise."

After all, he hadn't died on that battlefield. He didn't even have a bruise where the sword had run him clean through. It was as if it had never happened.

But it had. He'd been moments away from death. He felt faint at the memory. How could he forget the stab of blinding pain as the enemy soldier's sword plunged into his gut. The relief when the pain had started to fade—when everything had started to fade. In what he'd thought were his final moments, he'd been filled with regret for everything he was going to miss. But he'd understood: it had been too perfect to be his, so he'd accepted that it was gone.

His future with Percival. His position as king's champion. His knighthood. His friends.

And now he was back, without a mark to show the horror he'd

survived, unable to close his eyes and sleep without reliving the worst parts of it.

His dreams were haunted by his own ghost. By the devastation on Arthur's face, and the agony of not getting to say goodbye to Percival. Death had been right there, reaching for him. And he had reached back.

But Emry had saved him. He'd woken in their camp, in Arthur's arms, Emry cold and unmoving beside him. He hadn't asked her to make that sacrifice. To trade herself for him. The guilt ate away at him, not just in his sleep, but all day, as he wandered the castle corridors like a ghost, or remained in bed to recover from a wound that wasn't there.

He was restless. And the last thing he wanted was to fall asleep again, and torture Percival with his screams. So he slipped on his boots and his sportswear and went for a run through the royal hunting grounds.

His breath came in clouds, then gasps, until he was sweating under his tunic, his heart pounding not from fear, but from the exertion of moving his living, breathing body. It felt good. But it wasn't enough. What he needed was to train. He never felt as much himself as he did with a sword in his hand.

When he pushed open the door to the knights' armory, Dryan startled, nearly dropping the sword he was polishing.

"Morning," Lance called.

"Good morning, Sir Lancelot," Dryan replied with a polite bow. "Would you like your horse saddled for tilting practice this morning?"

Lance laughed at Dryan's impression of a panicked squire speaking to his knight, and then realized his friend was completely serious. "What's going on, Dry?"

"I'm your squire," Dryan said, as if it was obvious.

His squire. Because he was a knight. Of course.

"Right," Lance said, trying to pretend the idea hadn't just occurred to him. "I was actually hoping to get in some sword practice. Do you, er, want to spar?"

"As you wish, Sir Lancelot," Dryan replied.

"You really don't have to do that," Lance said, wondering how Arthur put up with all the scraping and bowing. "Er, did Arthur ask you to squire for me?"

"I volunteered." Dryan gave a sad smile. "After the battle, I was without a knight, and you were without a squire. So I figured . . . but if you'd rather have someone else . . ."

"Of course not," Lance said quickly. "I'm glad to have you."

They'd lost so many men in that battle. Lance hadn't realized that Sir Dinadin was among them. He reached for his padding, his hands shaking.

"Here, let me do that," Dryan protested.

Lance let him. It was a strange feeling, being in charge. He felt entirely like he was making it up as he went along. Or like they were pretending he was a knight for a laugh, and at any minute Sir Kay would burst through the doors and scold him to get back to his duties.

There was still a thin layer of frost on the field, though from the morning sunshine, it seemed destined to melt before noon. Without thinking about it, Lance started the series of stretches and warmups he'd always done when he'd trained with the guard.

Dryan watched, frowning. "Did Sir Kay teach you that?" the squire asked.

Lance laughed. "They're strengthening exercises from the castle guard."

Dryan brightened. "Will they build up my biceps?"

Lance looked at the young squire, realizing that, for a lad of seventeen, Dryan was noticeably slim in stature, his limbs stretched from a recent growth spurt. It would do the squire well to put on some muscle.

"They will, but you should supplement the exercises with lifting weights," Lance said. "I'll show you later."

Dryan grinned. They went through the course of stretches and then switched to broadsword. A few other knights and their squires were out training and shot them curious glances.

Lance felt like any moment, one of the knights would come out and scold them for being where they shouldn't. He settled into a crouch, hefting his weapon and watching Dryan do the same.

"First to three hits on the breastplate or helm," Lance called.

Dryan nodded. It was a typical practice match, one they'd done hundreds of times before.

They lowered their helmets and raised their guard. Dryan's left side was open, and Lance darted forward, swinging his blade around in an attack. But Dryan was quicker than he'd expected and parried the blow.

"Good," Lance said as the lad kept his footing and pressed forward, rather than stumbling back.

Dryan's blade arced high, catching the sunlight, and Lance gasped as a flash of memory overtook him: The unkillable soldier on the battlefield, his blade sinking through Lance's flesh.

Lance froze. Dryan's blade connected with his armor, and Lance cried out, half expecting the weapon to pierce him through.

He stumbled backward, clutching his stomach and gasping for air. He sank to his knees, his weapon dropping to the ground.

His lungs felt like they were going to explode, and his chest was tight, and everything was spinning, wrong, mixed together. He was back on the battlefield, except he wasn't. He was at Castle Camelot, sparring with cheerful, goofy Dryan.

With great effort, he was able to force a shallow breath, and then another. His chest loosened, and the dizziness subsided. When it did, he found Dryan staring down at him in concern. "Are you all right? Sard, it wasn't much of a blow. Unless . . . did I strike an injury?"

"I—" Lance began, and then realized that a lie was the safest cover. "I'm afraid you did. That's enough training for today."

The moment the council meeting ended, Arthur pushed back his chair, desperate to get out of there. Somehow, he'd managed to sit calmly through increasingly grim reports about their losses from the battle against King Yurien.

Two thousand one hundred eighty-three of his people had died following him into battle.

His advisors didn't have to say it was his fault. How could it be anything else?

Someone called after him as he hurried down the corridor, but he ignored them, hoping they wouldn't follow. He just wanted to be alone. And the castle herb garden seemed just the place.

Usually, he found the neat, fragrant patches of herbs comforting. He could walk the rows for hours, recalling their different medicinal properties, and even a few of their magical ones. This early in the year, the plants were small and sparse. But Arthur stopped when he reached a bed of mint that had grown wildly, choking out its border of thyme. This he could fix.

He knelt in the dirt, pinching off an offending spray by the root. He removed another, and another. The task should have served as a distraction, but instead, it only sharpened his thoughts.

Yurien was like mint. Invasive, strong, determined to strangle anything in his path. And Arthur was like thyme, powerless to stop him. He sighed. This distraction wasn't working.

A shadow fell over him, and when he looked up, he found Sir Tor quietly watching him.

"The ancient Greeks believed mint signified hospitality," said the knight. "Once planted, they never got rid of it."

"Maybe they just didn't know how," Arthur suggested.

"That's certainly possible," said Sir Tor.

"Did you need something?" asked Arthur, realizing the knight must have been the one trying to get his attention earlier.

Sir Tor shook their head. "No, but I thought you might. Come, join me."

The knight took a seat on a nearby stone bench. Arthur brushed the soil from his hands and knees and sat down, curious and more than a little apprehensive about what Sir Tor wished to discuss.

"That council meeting was rough to sit through," said Sir Tor with a grimace. The knight was from Cameliard, and Arthur hadn't thought how personal all this was to them, witnessing their kingdom fall to Yurien. "I can't imagine how much worse it was for you," Sir Tor went on.

Arthur gave a ragged sigh. "Because it's all my fault," he said tonelessly, giving voice to his darkest thought.

"You're not the one who started this war," Sir Tor reminded him.

"But my people died because of me," Arthur insisted. "I led them to a slaughter I—"

"Couldn't have known Yurien had unbeatable soldiers," Sir Tor finished. "You came to Cameliard's aid, as you promised. And unlike King Leodegrance, you rode into battle with your men, instead of hiding inside a gilded tent."

Sir Tor looked unspeakably disappointed over their king's cowardice. Arthur didn't blame them. He'd assumed King Leodegrance would fight as well, instead of making others do it for him.

"Of course I did," said Arthur. "I bore Excalibur. But because I fought, Lance got stabbed trying to protect me. And Emry . . ."

He trailed off in anguish, his throat tight, tears prickling at the corners of his eyes. Emry. He hadn't just lost a battle. He had caused harm to the people he wanted most in the world to protect.

"If this is my legacy as king, perhaps I should quit now," he whispered, putting his head in his hands. He didn't mean to be so honest with Sir Tor, but sitting there with the knight in his castle gardens, unable to find peace even here, all his fears were spilling out, and he didn't know how to stop them.

"If you do that, then you're not the king I thought you were," said Sir Tor, placing a reassuring hand on Arthur's shoulder. It had been so long since anyone had done that. Since he'd felt someone was on his side. He closed his eyes and took a deep, shuddering breath.

"Not so long ago, at a tournament, I met a young squire who was being mistreated by his knight," Sir Tor went on. Arthur frowned, wondering why the knight was telling him a story. "He had great potential, so I asked him to squire for me. But he refused, because I did not serve Camelot. Instead, he told me I should pledge to Camelot, because one day Prince Arthur would become a great king, and he would need knights who were loyal and true."

"Lance," Arthur said fondly, shaking his head.

"His passion intrigued me," said Sir Tor. "So I attended the royal wedding that was meant to join our kingdoms. And when that wedding turned into a siege, the King of Cameliard feared only for his safety, as did the King of Camelot. But a young prince defended his people, fighting alongside commoners and nobles, and volunteers of all genders. And I saw for myself that he was everything that squire had promised. He would indeed become a great king. I believed it then, and I still believe it."

"How can you?" Arthur asked in despair.

"You defend those who cannot defend themselves. And you inspire others to do the same. This world you dream of, where anyone can earn their place regardless of gender, or station, or whom they love is one that I would very much like to help you build. And I know that's what you're fighting for. Not glory, or power, or revenge. Yet you sit here doubting yourself, because your advisors have been piling all the blame on your shoulders every chance they get."

Arthur frowned at the knight's accusation. "Why would they do that?"

Sir Tor nodded knowingly. "A king who relies on his advisors is less likely to dismiss them. Your council is plenty capable of leading Camelot. But their vision for this kingdom isn't yours. And unless you stand up to them, that vision will never come to pass."

They are right, Arthur realized. His advisors had experience, but they didn't want change. They wanted everything to continue as it always had been, because it was better for them, not because it was better for the kingdom.

And that was the true reason they never saw eye to eye. Not because Arthur was incapable, or inexperienced. Because he was trying to lead Camelot somewhere they did not wish to follow.

"But how can I trust myself after this?" he wondered aloud.

"Because you must," said Sir Tor, rising to their feet and offering him a hand. "You have a good heart, Arthur Pendragon. You should listen to it."

CHAPTER 30

Where am I?

Emry frowned, taking in the unfamiliar surroundings. She was in a grand, gilded bedchamber, lying in a four-poster bed fit for a queen. The carved mahogany posts were draped with rose-colored silks, the tapestry on the walls was woven with gold thread, and a fire burned in an intricately carved hearth.

She sat up, looking around. A window was thrown open, and from the dim gray slant of light, it looked to be evening, or perhaps early morning.

But she wasn't alone. In a chair by the hearth sat Princess Guinevere, her feet tucked up under her, knitting a fluffy blanket out of cream-colored yarn.

"Guin?" Emry said, trying to figure out what had happened. The last thing she remembered was the battlefield, and Lance lying there with blood trickling from his mouth, a sword through his stomach, and the spell that hadn't been enough, even though she'd tried it four times.

"Oh!" Guin said, startled. "You're awake. We were all so worried!"

"How's Lance?" Emry threw off the coverlet, her heart pounding frantically. She didn't know if it had worked, or—

"Slow down," Guin said sternly. "He's fine."

"He is? But I—"

"You saved his life. And nearly gave your own in the process."

Emry rolled her eyes. "It was just blowback. As you can see, I'm fine. Er, where are we, by the way?"

"Castle Camelot. And you're not fine. You've been out for nearly two weeks."

"Two weeks?" Emry was horrified. She'd figured it had been a few days at most. When Emmett had suffered blowback from that ill-fated memory-wipe spell, he'd been unconscious for a week. It was never more than a week.

Guin bit her lip in concern. "We weren't sure you'd ever wake up. Emmett and I have been taking shifts during the day. And Arthur's slept here every night. He has a pallet on the floor by your bed, like servants use."

"You're making that up," Emry accused.

Guin shot her a look. Emry leaned over, and sure enough, next to her bed was a rumpled velvet quilt and silk pillow on a thin, lumpy mattress, along with a candle stub and a stack of books about military strategy and medicinal herbs.

"Oh." She wasn't sure how to feel that Arthur had done such a thing. "How is he?"

Guin's lips thinned. "It's good that you're awake."

"Before you go telling anyone, would you mind if I freshened up?" Emry asked.

"Bath's through there," Guin gestured toward a door that was mostly hidden in the handsome wooden paneling of the walls.

Emry stumbled through it, and then stopped and stared. Where *was* she?

The bathtub was made of hammered gold and surrounded by clean white marble. The jakes, set into its own little alcove with carved wood paneling, featured a silk padded seat, which was a bit much.

Even for Castle Camelot, these rooms were incredibly grand. Emry turned on the water tap, marveling that she didn't need to conjure water for her bath, or even heat it by magic.

She felt a little wobbly, and a lot starving, but otherwise fine. She snapped her fingers, lighting a candelabra, and was relieved that the magic came easily, and the spell felt as simple as striking a match.

She was okay. She was home. And so was Lance. All those were good things, yet a sense of unmistakable doom hovered over her as she bathed.

She was wringing the water from her hair, dressed in nothing but a linen towel, when Arthur burst through the door.

He looked like he hadn't slept for a week. He was worryingly thin, his skin stretched taut over his cheekbones, dark smudges pressed beneath his eyes. His hair was a mess, his burgundy jacket creased and unbuttoned, his boots a shade of brown that clashed horribly with his sable trousers.

Before Emry could respond, Arthur rushed toward her and wrapped her in a hug.

"Oocamprethe," she said, her face crushed against the front of his jacket.

"What?" Arthur said, letting go.

"I can't breathe," Emry repeated.

"My presence does tend to take a lady's breath away," Arthur joked, one corner of his mouth hitching into a grin. He looked overjoyed to see her. More than overjoyed—elated.

"Are you sure the ladies aren't holding their breath to escape your stench?" Emry inquired sweetly.

"That's probably it," he agreed. "The smell of old books is such a turnoff."

Emry bit her lip to hold back a smile. He was joking, something he did when he was nervous, but not when he was angry.

"Er, where am I?" Emry ventured.

"The queen's bedchambers."

"Ew, why?" Emry wrinkled her nose, hoping she hadn't been convalescing in the late queen's deathbed.

"My guards couldn't secure the corridor with your room for me to stay overnight," Arthur said sheepishly. "So it was either here, or my apartments, and I didn't want to presume."

"Would've preferred yours."

"Would you?" Arthur looked dubious. "Despite the gossip?"

"I'm sure there's plenty, since you've been sleeping at my side like a servant."

"Like a boyfriend," Arthur corrected. "That's what you meant, isn't it? That you needed me to choose you when it really mattered. To put you first without being told that I needed to." Arthur took her hand in his, his eyes a warm, melting brown. "I'm sorry it took me so long to get it right. I wish I had before I thought you might be trapped in some enchanted sleep forever."

"That only happens to maidens in stories," Emry said.

"You're the most storybook maiden I've ever met."

Emry scoffed. "I'd be the evil witch in those books, and you know it."

"You'd be the powerful wizard," Arthur corrected, "who defeated the evil witch and proved the foolish royals wrong."

"Too bad that's only a story," she said.

"Well, I am pretty foolish," Arthur said.

"Oh my god, you know you're brilliant," Emry grumbled.

"At some things," Arthur said. "But I'm truly terrible at others."

"Like boyfriending," Emry replied.

"I'm not sure that's a word."

"Shut up, yes it is," Emry replied, closing the distance between them.

Their kiss was sweet and tentative at first, and then urgent. Emry melted into it, shivering as Arthur's fingers trailed from her neck to her hips. He pressed up against her with a groan, and through the thin linen towel, she could feel the length of him, and how eager he was to prove himself reformed.

"Oops," he said coyly, as he untied the knot in her bath towel.

The towel fell to the floor.

Neither of them retrieved it.

◑ ◑ ◑

"I think you should reconsider," Arthur whispered, pressing his lips to Emry's ear in the castle corridor.

She shivered from the closeness, then whirled around and jabbed him in the chest with her finger. "For the last time, I'm not dining at the royal table. Ask me again and I'll—"

"You'll . . . ?" Arthur asked innocently, raising his eyebrows.

"Do something extremely horrible to your person," she finished.

"Mmmm, is that a promise?" Arthur murmured, tracing a finger down her arm. Her breath hitched at his touch, and he smirked. "Like what?"

"I'll turn all the ink in your library books invisible," she threatened.

Arthur's hand dropped to his side. "Now, that's uncalled for."

She stuck out her tongue at him, and he laughed. He couldn't believe his incredible good fortune that she had finally woken up, and that he hadn't lost her after all. Somehow, he'd gotten it right, and now his wizard was making threats and letting him escort her into the Great Hall at supper.

It was almost enough to push away his dark thoughts of King Yurien and the fallen kingdom of Cameliard entirely, at least for a few hours. Catching Emry up on what had happened had been horrible, even if he didn't quite blame himself as much anymore, after speaking with Sir Tor.

"Last chance for the royal table," Arthur teased.

"And leave Guin with all those horrible boys? I could never."

"It's wildly unfair that Lionel Griflet gets to dine with you and I don't," Arthur said sullenly.

"Look at you, being jealous of Lionel Griflet." Emry leaned over and pressed a kiss to his cheek, and Arthur grinned, realizing that the entire Great Hall was staring and that he didn't care. Let them whisper and gossip and think what they liked about his choices.

Emry had risked everything to do what she believed was right and had saved Lance's life. And she'd done it when no one asked—when she could have very well stayed at the castle.

Arthur watched as she made her way to her table and was waylaid by Lance, who wrapped her in an enormous, bone-crushing hug, swinging her around with her feet in the air, laughing. Percival's hug was even worse. He seemed intent on suffocating her with his breastplate.

Lord Agravaine cleared his throat impatiently and motioned for Arthur to take his seat, so the meal could begin. For him to ignore his friends and his girlfriend, because his role was to sit at the front of the room and formally preside over supper. And something in him snapped. He just felt . . . done. "Oi, Perce! Keep the strangling to the bedroom," he called, teasing.

Everyone in the hall stared at him in surprise. Lance looked as if he wanted to perish on the spot. And then Percival threw his head back and laughed. Arthur's shoulders shook from trying not to follow suit.

"I was holding my breath on purpose, until I was less closely acquainted with his armpits," Emry announced.

Arthur couldn't help it, he laughed. All his friends were laughing. The Great Hall was staring at them as if they'd gone mad, for surely their king, the captain of the guard, and the apprentice wizard had no business speaking to one another so bawdily.

The strange thing was, now that he had done it, Arthur didn't know what he'd been so afraid of. So a few eyebrows were raised, a few incredulous words murmured between courtiers. Watching his friends laugh, he thought that, actually, it had been completely worth it. Yes, he was the king, but he was also nineteen years old, and sick of conducting himself with such rigid decorum.

He took his place at the royal table and held up his goblet. "Well," he said, "since I have everyone's attention, I might as well say a few words."

"What are you doing, sire?" Lord Agravaine whispered disapprovingly.

"Improvising," Arthur said, with his most royal grin. He raised his voice and his goblet. "Please join me in welcoming back Miss Emry Merlin by toasting to her permanent appointment as a royal court wizard."

Emry looked shocked and pleased as the Great Hall rose to their feet, holding their glasses high. Arthur shrugged. It was the least he could do.

"Sire—" Lord Agravaine whispered urgently.

"Not now," Arthur said through clenched teeth. He watched as Emry's cheeks turned red from the attention as the table of annoying young nobles to which she'd been assigned whooped and cheered, as if watching a joust.

Emry mumbled something, and the Great Hall gasped as purple sparks danced across the ceiling, sparkling and fizzing before they turned to lavender smoke. She grinned and took a sweeping bow.

"Are you quite done, sire?" Lord Agravaine hissed.

"For the moment," Arthur said, unable to wipe the grin from his face.

He should have decided sooner that he didn't care what people thought. It wasn't worth exhausting himself trying to live up to everyone else's impossible and exacting expectations.

He cut into his roast pheasant, motioning for the musicians to commence their night's program, and feigning interest, so as to excuse himself from his advisors' heavy glares and waiting questions.

Everything was going to be okay now that Emry had recovered. He didn't see how, but he sensed it. He stared across the Great Hall, watching Lance and Percival flirt and laugh at the table full of squires. And then a thought occurred to him. *If you want things to be different, change them.* He turned to Lord Agravaine, who seemed desperate for his attention.

"My lord," Arthur said. "I assume you wish to discuss some recent changes to castle protocol?"

"Yes, sire." Lord Agravaine practically sagged in relief.

"So do I," Arthur plunged on. "For example, I wonder why my knight champion is dining at a table of first-year squires."

Lord Agravaine choked. "I—"

"Agree completely that something should be done about it?" Arthur finished for him. "Truly, I don't know what I would do without your help. Please excuse me."

He pushed to his feet and headed over to the squires' table. The boys' eyes went wide at his approach. Dryan dropped a half-eaten roll into his lap.

"Sir Lancelot, Captain. Why don't you come with me?" Arthur said pleasantly.

Lance frowned in confusion, and Percival looked terrified.

"Truly, I have bathed this week," Perce assured him. "She was joking about the armpits thing."

"Was she, though?" Lance replied.

Arthur bit back a smile as he led them over to the table where Emry sat between Princess Guinevere and Lionel Griflet.

"Sorry to interrupt," Arthur said.

"You couldn't wait until after the main course to come bother me?" she complained, her mouth full and plate piled high. "I haven't eaten for weeks."

"She means that literally," Emmett said. "I ate an entire loaf of bread the last time I woke from blowback."

"Carry on, then," Arthur said, "but scooch over. We've come to join you."

Emry choked. Guinevere wordlessly passed her a glass of water, and then scooted down, making room for Arthur to squeeze in between them.

When he took a seat, the dining hall rippled in shock.

"Lance, Perce, anywhere there's room," he said.

"What are you doing?" Emry asked helplessly.

"I'm not exactly sure," Arthur replied, "But I'm enjoying it immensely." He reached for a warm roll and bit into it, motioning for a serving maid to bring extra plates.

"All right, then?" Emmett said, nodding his chin at Lance and Percival.

"Confused," Lance admitted, looking to Arthur.

"I couldn't figure out why you were dining at a table of first-year squires, since neither of you falls under that designation," Arthur replied. "So I fixed it."

"Wait, this is permanent?" Emry asked, grinning. "I can keep them?"

"I'm not a stray puppy," Lance told her.

"This is officially the best table in the castle," Elian announced. He nodded at Perce. "Is it true the guards run a secret gambling ring in the north watchtower?"

"I can neither confirm nor deny such rumors," Perce said, darting a nervous look at Arthur. "But what are you doing on Wednesday?"

"Told you!" Cal piped up. Lionel elbowed him.

Guinevere snorted into her drink.

Arthur looked around him, unable to believe this was what he'd been missing by sitting at that stuffy royal table. It was almost as good as being out at a tavern.

"Thank you, by the way," Emry said, scooting closer, until he could feel her leg pressed up against his through the fabric of her skirts. "You didn't have to do that."

"Make it official that you're no longer an apprentice?"

"Make everyone toast to it," she said.

Arthur shrugged. "I quite enjoyed it."

"I just wish my father was here to see it," Emry said with a sigh.

Arthur frowned. Surely Master Merlin was around here somewhere . . . wasn't he? But then, the wizard had been acting strangely ever since their return from battle, keeping to himself and rarely leaving the workshop.

"He really should be back by now," Emmett added, scrunching his nose. The expression was so Emry that for a moment, Arthur felt thrown by their similarities.

"Why?" Emry's eyes narrowed. "Where is he?"

Emmett winced. "You're not going to like this."

CHAPTER 31

Emry followed Madame Becou up the narrow staircase, trying to ignore the passionate noises that drifted from behind closed doors. Of course her father was at a brothel, trying to escape the grim reality of their situation. She didn't know why she'd expected otherwise. Emmett was right: all their father did was run away whenever things got hard.

As she passed a narrow door painted with flowers, a loud, satisfied groan emanated from inside. Behind her, Arthur snorted, trying to keep from laughing. She didn't blame him.

He was being shockingly wonderful. After Emmett had let slip where their father had run off to, Arthur had simply risen to his feet, offered Emry a hand, and said, "Let's go."

And now they were here, his purse lighter by three pieces of silver, which clinked in Madame Becou's pocket as she led them to the third floor of the townhouse.

"This is it," said the proprietress, motioning toward a gilt door painted with constellations.

"Fitting," Emry said. "Thank you."

"After you've finished your business here, we have many pleasures available," said Madame Becou. "And much discretion."

Arthur looked intrigued.

"We'll let you know," Emry said diplomatically.

Once Madame Becou had gone, Emry scowled at Arthur. "Really?"

He shrugged. "Could be fun."

Boys. Honestly. Did they think of nothing else? Emry raised a fist and rapped smartly on the door.

"What is it?" her father snapped.

Emry rolled her eyes and knocked again, more insistently this time. The door flew open. "Good evening, I take it," she said, grimacing.

Her father was wearing his trousers, half-buttoned, and nothing else. Behind him stood Madeleine, in a silk dressing gown, calmly braiding her hair in front of a looking glass.

"Emry!" Her father looked shocked. "You're awake . . . and here."

"Clearly," she agreed. "Hi, Madeleine."

"Hello, Emry," said Madeleine. "I—er—your father?" the girl finished, looking back and forth between them without a frown.

"Yep," Emry confirmed, blushing.

"I'll leave you to your business," said the girl, pressing a flirtatious hand to Emry's back as she slipped past her into the hall. And then gasped. "Your Majesty!"

"Easier if you just pretend I'm not here," Arthur offered.

"Can I do that always?" Emry replied.

Emry's father squeezed his eyes shut for a moment, as if steeling himself. He reached for his tunic. "Better come in," he said. "Both of you."

Once they were settled—Merlin on the edge of the bed, Arthur in the chair, and Emry perched on the windowsill—she wasn't quite sure where to begin.

"Emry, sweetheart, this is a brothel," her father said tensely, as if worried about the propriety.

"Technically, it's a bathhouse with varied offerings," she corrected. "And I don't care. When I woke up, you weren't there. You were just . . . gone. Like always."

Merlin winced at the accusation. "I was coming back," he promised, not entirely convincing.

Arthur coughed. "Er, chilly in here," he commented, when everyone turned to look at him.

Emry waved a hand at the fire in the grate. The flames danced higher.

"Thanks," Arthur said wryly. He turned to Master Merlin. "I've reappointed Emry to the position of royal court wizard. You should congratulate her."

Emry gave her father a hopeful grin.

Yet he frowned. "After following us to battle and knocking herself unconscious from blowback? Are you sure that's wise?"

"Are you questioning my judgment?" Arthur asked, his voice steel.

"No, sire—"

"I should hope not," Arthur replied. "Your daughter has more than proven herself. I regret I can't say the same about you." Merlin blanched, and Arthur pressed on, "I still don't have a satisfactory explanation for what happened in Cameliard. And from your absence at the last few council meetings and tonight's supper, I'm starting to think you don't want to give one."

"My daughter doesn't need to hear this," Merlin said uneasily.

He looks awful, Emry realized, a sheen of sweat on his brow, his skin stretched taut over his cheekbones.

"I already know," she blurted. "About your magic failing."

Her father's eyes went wide. "How cou—"

"Failing?" Arthur interrupted. "Someone explain. *Now.*"

Emry bit her lip and looked to her father, whose expression was furious.

"It's under control," Merlin said tightly.

"For how long?" Emry retorted. "And at what cost?"

Her father sighed. Looked everywhere but at her. He seemed even more tired and fragile than he had before.

"I thought I was making the right choice," he said forlornly, hunching forward until his elbows rested on his knees. He gazed into the grate as if haunted by the flames.

At this, Emry couldn't hold back any longer. "You took away everything I'd worked for," she fired at him. "You lied. And you put everyone who fought against Yurien at risk." Arthur shot Emry a questioning expression, and she elaborated, "When I arrived, there were no wards around your camp."

"No wards?" Arthur repeated, incredulous.

Her father winced. "I had to take them down," he admitted. "They were too much to maintain. I was . . . not at my best."

"Did you do *anything* to help us in battle?" Arthur demanded. Spurred by Merlin's uncomfortable silence, he went on. "Right. Just empty promises. And you said nothing. I trusted you because you were my father's court wizard. I shouldn't have."

"I'm sorry, sire." Merlin's head bowed. "I thought my magic would hold."

"Yet you knew there was a possibility it would not. A possibility with deadly consequences," Arthur finished, shaking his head in disappointment. He looked to Emry. "What do I need to know that I don't already?"

Emry had been expecting him to ask something like that. A moment of tense silence passed between them. "Bellicent is in our world," she said.

"I thought that wasn't possible," said Arthur.

"So did I," said Emry. "But she's not fully here. More like she just has access. When I saw her, she was wearing Morgana's body." She grimaced at the memory. "And I felt her magic . . . it was rotten. Awful. It covered the battlefield."

"That explains the enchantment on the soldiers," Arthur said grimly. "I suspected we were facing magic from another world. But I didn't have proof."

"Now you do," Emry said. "She tried to convince me to open a doorway and let her into this world." She turned to her father. "Bellicent said that if I helped her, she'd restore your magic and health. She said the drugs you're using to amplify your power will kill you."

Merlin put his head in his hands. When he spoke, his voice was strained. "I didn't mean for you to find out like this." Slowly, he pushed up the right sleeve of his tunic.

His veins were a poisoned black.

Emry bit her lip, feeling tears prick at the corners of her eyes.

"You asked me to reinstate you as court wizard while you were in this state?" Arthur said in disbelief.

"It's gotten worse. My magic never fully returned after the enchantment I used to contain Bellicent. Without the elixir, I'm useless."

"And with it, you're killing yourself," Emry said quietly.

"Did it never occur to you to come to us for help?" Arthur asked.

Merlin frowned but said nothing.

Why is it, Emry thought, *that parents never listen?* That they always thought they knew best, even when they clearly didn't.

"The Lady of the Lake would know what to do," Emry said.

Arthur nodded as though he very much agreed. "And she has those healing waters?" Arthur glanced at Emry for confirmation.

Emry's heart squeezed with hope.

"I tried the healing waters already," Merlin admitted. "They did not restore my magic, but it's possible they might reverse the effects of the Godfrey's root. A wise thought, Your Majesty."

Arthur nodded. "I have them occasionally. Fortunately, we're also headed to Avalon."

"We are?" Emry asked. Somehow she'd missed that part.

"Whatever magic Bellicent used on King Yurien's army, I don't understand it, and I don't know how to fight it. I need the Lady of the Lake to point us in the right direction."

"With nonsense riddles," Emry said.

"Better nonsense riddles than nothing," said Arthur. "Bellicent's her sister. If anyone knows how to stop her, it will be Nimue."

Emry fervently hoped that he was right.

CHAPTER 32

Gawain loathed spending time at French court. It was a veritable gauntlet of everything he hated. First, there were all the courtiers he needed to avoid for various reasons: the women he had slept with, their husbands who had suspected or even discovered their liaisons, and the lords whom he had gotten drunk at his infamous house parties and casually blackmailed at the behest of Camelot's spymaster. Then, there was the fact that he'd endeared himself to courtiers whom he couldn't stand for information, and who still thought themselves his close friends. And finally, there was the small matter that he was supposed to be a foreign diplomat, and had neglected to disclose his place in Camelot's royal family. Still, it was a wonderful opportunity to show off his latest suit, made of a fine brocade and trimmed in pearls. He even had the shoes to match.

He stood in the line of courtiers who greeted King Louis as he made his way to the throne, bowing when the king approached.

"Ah, Seigneur Gawain. Quelles sont les nouvelles?" King Louis inquired.

"Much, and such that I should not speak of it where we might be overheard," Gawain replied smoothly, slipping into French with ease.

"Then join me for lunch," replied the king.

Gawain bowed even deeper, the tight waistband of his trousers nearly slicing him in half. Behind him, he heard a giggle. After the king moved on, he turned around, a smirk tipping the corner of his lips toward the young woman who had been so amused by his arse.

"Enchanté, mademoiselle," he said, thinking that he might as well help himself to a diversion before lunch.

◐ ◐ ◐

"Thus, getting involved now isn't political, it's strategic," Gawain said, finishing the speech he'd memorized. He looked to King Louis.

The king lounged upon an ornate chair at the head of a lavish table, with a quartet of musicians playing discreetly in the corner of his private dining chamber. Apart from the quartet, and a guard at the door, the two of them were alone so the king could speak plainly.

"Absolutely not," said King Louis. "I shall tell you what I have already told your young king. France is staying out of this ridiculous conflict. Keep your enchanted soldiers and evil sorceresses away from my kingdom."

"They aren't our enchanted soldiers," Gawain protested.

"Your king has Excalibur," King Louis pointed out. "And that luscious young wizard."

Gawain winced, thinking Emry would probably give the king a pig's tail had she heard him describe her thus. "We do," he allowed.

"Then figure out how to defeat this King Yurien. And if you cannot, it is no blood on my hands." King Louis stood, making it clear their parley was over. "I suppose, since you've come all this way, you may give my well-wishes to your king and to his bride."

Gawain bit his lip. "About that."

King Louis's mouth tipped into an amused smile. "No? They did not go through with that wedding after all? Shocking."

"Attendez! Monsieur!"

Gawain winced, somehow knowing without turning around that the man meant him. He had just posted the letter to Camelot with the wretched news about King Louis's refusal to help and was looking forward to drowning his sorrows in a tavern, or perhaps a brothel.

After all, he had a reputation to maintain.

"Seigneur Gawain!" the man called out.

Gawain quickened his pace. Night had fallen fast, blanketing the streets of Paris in darkness and chill. He flipped up the collar of his jacket, wishing he'd worn a cloak with a hood, but he hadn't wanted to ruin the lines of his ensemble. He turned the corner, into a narrow lane of shops.

"How dare you show your face at court after defiling my wife!" the man called.

Gawain winced. He was pretty sure it was the Marquis de Fontaine-gris, but he didn't want to turn around and find out. And he doubted he could outrun the man. He thought quickly. And that was when he realized how close he was to Madame Flamel's apothecary. Perhaps he could hide in there.

He darted down an even narrower lane, pressing his back into a doorway, and then turning left at a church and looking for the right path. There. He could see the shop with its lights still on. Gawain pushed open the door of the apothecary, throwing himself inside.

"Bonsoir, monsi—oh, it's you," his younger brother, Jereth, said from behind the counter. "What are you doing here?"

"Hiding from a man who thinks I slept with his wife."

"Did you?" Jereth asked.

Gawain shrugged. "Not recently. There should be a statute of limitations on such accusations."

Jereth rolled his eyes. "Why do you look so miserable? And so fancy?"

"Because King Louis is the most stubborn man to ever fart into a throne," Gawain said with a sigh. "And I've just had to write to Father about it."

"I'm sure he already knows," said Jereth.

"Yet he still tasked me with trying to convince the king to ally with Camelot," Gawain complained, fiddling with some of the glass jars on the shelf marked POISONS.

"Put those down, I just dusted them," Jereth snapped.

Gawain reluctantly shoved his hands into his pockets. "How's school?"

"I'm attending my lectures, if that's what you're asking," Jereth said sourly.

Good standing at university and part-time work at Madame Flamel's apothecary were the terms Gawain had laid down for his troublesome younger brother, so long as the lad was staying at the family's Paris townhouse.

"I was just making conversation, not checking on you," Gawain defended.

"We both know you're perfectly capable of doing both."

"Any chance you have wine?" Gawain asked, glancing around hopefully.

"This is an apothecary, not a tavern," Jereth scolded. But he checked his watch. "We close in half an hour. If you wait in the laboratory, we can go somewhere after."

"Might as well," Gawain said. It wasn't as if he had anything else to do. His return to France had been a spectacular waste of time. He couldn't enjoy the company of his friends, silly nobles who reveled in mindless parties, at a time like this. Camelot was at war, and France was not. It seemed wrong to indulge in such shallow vices as his cousin marched off to battle.

He pushed aside the curtain that led into the back room. Madame

Flamel was bent over a glass apparatus, wearing a pair of goggles and some sort of leather coat. At her side, dutifully taking notes, was Jereth's boyfriend, Prince Hugo of Flanders.

The lad looked up with an annoyingly sunshiny smile. "Hullo, Gawain," he said. "Where have you been?"

"Dining with the king," Gawain said, making a face.

Madame Flamel, who was in the process of removing her goggles, choked. "I assume it wasn't a social visit," she said.

"He rejected Camelot's request for aid," Gawain replied.

Madame Flamel shook her head. "King Yurien is giving Lothia a bad name."

Gawain had forgotten that she was originally from that region. "I have to return to Camelot with the news," he said with a sigh. "I told Father this was a fool's errand. And now he's going to accuse me of being the fool for being unable to produce an impossible miracle."

"Not necessarily," Hugo said thoughtfully. The young Flemish royal was looking much improved from the last time Gawain had seen him. His sickly pallor was gone, there was color in his cheeks, and he'd put on a bit of weight. "You seek assistance combating Lothia's forces, correct? Not just alliance from the French?"

"I suppose." Gawain frowned, wondering where Hugo was going with this.

"Perhaps you might persuade my father that Flanders should send aid," said Hugo.

Gawain hadn't even considered that option. "Do you think he'd grant such a request?"

"It is thanks to your help that I have secured my engagement to the French princess," Hugo reminded him. He added shyly, "An engagement I might live to regret."

"Madame Flamel's been helping him with some experimental tonics of hers," Jereth explained, joining them, and making no apology for his blatant eavesdropping

"My stamina is much improved," Hugo said with a grin while Jereth looked as if he wanted to sink through the floor and perish on the spot. "I am hardly out of breath when I exert myself," Hugo went on, unaware. "And I throw away many less handkerchiefs."

Gawain bit his lip. Honestly, the lad had to be doing it on purpose. "You must be pleased."

Hugo beamed. "Very. You have my sincerest thanks. Without Jereth helping here, I never would have met Madame Flamel."

"Technically, it's all thanks to my setting fire to my boarding school," Jereth interjected.

"I think not," Gawain said coldly. He turned to Hugo. "Will you write to your father?"

Hugo sighed. "I fear he won't believe me. I, ah . . . have a history of telling tales." A thought occurred to him. "But perhaps, if we were to visit him together? The truth of my recovery would be undeniable."

"Meet your father?" Jereth said nervously. "Doesn't he think I'm some delinquent who made you burn down a library and run away from home?"

"He does," Hugo confirmed. "And we're going to change his mind."

CHAPTER 33

Morgana gasped as she was shoved roughly aside—inside her own body—as Bellicent took control. She'd hoped it wouldn't happen again. That the pain from her burns was bad enough to scare off the sorceress. Yet as she'd improved, her worries had increased . . . and now her recurring nightmare had returned.

Miss me? Bellicent purred.

Morgana tried to scream. But her mouth wasn't hers anymore. It was Bellicent's.

The sorceress smiled.

"Mama, wait!" Mordred cried, his little footsteps hurrying down the stone path.

Morgana's heart clenched. *No.* She didn't want Bellicent around her son. She huddled within a corner of herself, watching as Bellicent turned toward the boy, and was surprised to sense yearning and jealousy in the sorceress. "I am not your mama," she said harshly.

Mordred considered this a moment, and then he nodded. "Oh. You're the other one. The one who made my father's soldiers unbeatable. Teach me, then. I'm a prince, so you have to do what I say."

"That is not how power works," she told him. "And it is no spell. It is magic, from my world."

"Give it to me," Mordred demanded, holding out a hand. He sounded so very like his father that it chilled Morgana to watch. She had to break free of this corner of her mind where she crouched, caged and waiting. Her son needed his mother.

"Give it to you? Are you sure?" Bellicent asked, her smile sharp.

No! Morgana tried to scream. *No!*

"Will it hurt?" the boy asked, his voice wavering.

"You will feel no pain," promised Bellicent. "But there will be a price."

"I don't care," said Mordred.

"What do you wish, little boy?" Bellicent asked. "What is it you most desire?"

"I wish to have power," declared the boy.

"Give me your knife," Bellicent demanded.

Mordred took the small sharp blade that hung in a jeweled case at his waist and gave it to her, his eyes bright with curiosity.

Morgana couldn't watch. But she couldn't look away. Not as Bellicent thrummed with excitement over what was taking place. The magic rose from her skin and covered the knife. And then she handed him back the blade.

"Injure any man with this blade, and his wound will never heal," she said. "Use this weapon carefully."

Mordred grinned, examining his prize.

◑ ◑ ◑

The world was gone, and then it came back.

Morgana sat at an unfamiliar breakfast table, staring across at her husband. He slouched in a carved wooden chair, eating a slice of winter melon, the juice dribbling down his chin.

"You haven't touched the food," he said. "Are sausages no longer to your liking?"

She didn't know what day it was. How long she'd been gone. She stared down at her plate of food, her head swimming. Her dress itched, and the overskirt was a color she never would have chosen, a bold red. She pushed up a sleeve, checking the scars from her burns. They had faded to a dull pink, as though soon they might disappear completely. She was glad she still had them. They were useful to mark the passage of time.

"Sausages?" Morgana repeated dully. It was only then she noticed the platter of eggs and sausages that sat in the center of the table.

Her stomach rumbled at the sight and smell of the food. How long had it been since she'd eaten? She was famished. She reached forward and speared a sausage, waving away a serving girl who darted nervously forward to help. The serving girl cringed, as though expecting to be hit.

"Leave us," Yurien said, addressing the room. "All of you."

The staff bowed and hurried out, and it was only after they'd gone that he looked to Morgana and frowned.

"You almost gave yourself away," he scolded.

"I wasn't going to say anything in front of them," she replied, taking a bite of sausage. It was heavenly, with just the right amount of snap.

"I can never be sure," said her husband. "Well, what do you think of my new castle?" He gestured expansively at the wood-paneled chamber.

Morgana took in the crenellated ceilings painted with golden flowers, the ornate carved panels on the walls, the large oil painting depicting Christ's suffering on the cross, and the diamond panes in the tall, narrow windows. She had never been in this room before. Not that she remembered.

"Where are we?" she asked.

"Cameliard Keep," Yurien said, lounging back in his chair. "Enjoying the spoils of victory."

And when are we? But she swallowed back the question, not wanting to appear weak. She took another bite of sausage, just as an impatient knock sounded on the door. Her husband's steward entered, darting a nervous glance at Morgana.

"Your Majesties," he said breathlessly. "There has been another incident—"

"I'll handle it after breakfast," Yurien interrupted, raising a hand to silence the man. The steward bowed, placed a scroll upon the table, and backed gingerly from the room.

"An incident?" Morgana inquired.

Her husband flinched. "Nothing to worry about. Just some of my soldiers acting—er—boys will be boys."

"How bad is it?" Morgana pressed, thinking of five thousand strong young men, let loose on a kingdom they'd just conquered, determined to enjoy their spoils. Bellicent had made their soldiers into monsters, and she knew how ordinary soldiers behaved after a victory. She could just imagine the reputation that was spreading before them in this new kingdom, of a conqueror who had beheaded their king, and whose soldiers raped and stole and pillaged as they pleased, and could not be harmed.

This wasn't what she wanted. And she didn't understand how her husband could be so calm that he had caused this. Boys will be boys, indeed.

Yurien reached for his wine goblet and tipped the contents down his throat as he unrolled the scroll. "It's fine," he said peevishly. He read further and winced. "We'll behead them."

Right, because more violence would solve their problems.

CHAPTER 34

A rthur watched as Lord Agravaine tore open the letter, read it with a grim expression, and crumpled the paper into a ball.

"Well?" Arthur asked, even though he already knew.

"France will not offer aid," Lord Agravaine confirmed.

"It was a long shot," Arthur said, holding out his hand for the letter, and smoothing the page so he could read it for himself. Gawain's missive was short and to the point. King Louis was staying out of it, but Gawain would continue to search for potential allies. "Where does this leave us?"

He looked to the general, who had spread a large map across the long wooden table. Small metal tokens sat on top of the designations for England's many kingdoms.

"We have Camelot and Cornwall," said the general, indicating the lion figurines. "And Yurien controls Northumbria, Lothia, and now Cameliard."

"The Isles have pledged for no kingdom. We might still hold our own against Yurien with their aid," Lord Agravaine insisted. "Although I don't know that they will agree to such an alliance without a meaningful tie between our kingdoms."

Arthur knew exactly what Lord Agravaine meant. But he wasn't about to marry one of those pink princesses for an advantage in a fight.

"Not happening," he said. "Besides, we won't need their aid. I intend to travel to Avalon to seek council from the Lady of the Lake."

The general snorted. "A sorceress."

"We were defeated by magic," Arthur reminded him. "We could

have twice as many soldiers as King Yurien, but so long as his are enchanted, the fight is lost, numbers be damned. If we're to have any advantage, we won't find it in alliances with neighboring kingdoms. We'll find it on the Isle of the Blessed."

"You can't intend to travel there alone," Lord Agravaine protested.

"Of course not. I'm bringing my knight champion and both of my court wizards."

"And who is to be in charge in your absence, sire?" asked his advisor.

Arthur had thought long and hard about this. But in the end, there was only one right answer. He put his hand on the man's shoulder. "You are."

◑ ◑ ◑

Emry yawned as she approached the stables, her pack slung over her shoulder. The morning was cold but clear, and with the sun barely over the horizon, the castle was just beginning to stir. On the way there, she had passed guards running drills in the courtyard, and the blacksmith heating his forge.

"Morning," she said, nodding at Arthur. He was far too awake, his eyes bright with excitement as he checked his saddle and packs. A groom, whose job Arthur had no doubt taken, flapped nervously by the stable doors, looking too afraid to say anything.

Arthur glanced over from securing his last pack and grinned. "You wore trousers," he said happily.

Emry stared down at her brother's old trousers, which she'd tucked into riding boots. On top, she wore a tunic and wool jacket, and her best cloak, her hair secured in a braid. "I figured riding a horse was already torture enough without bringing skirts into it."

"And what aren't we going to do?" Arthur prompted.

Emry sighed, hating that he was making her say it. "Magic the horse."

"Good. Come on," Arthur said, swinging up into his saddle as though he'd been born to it. "The others are already waiting."

Emry had expected it would just be Perce, Guin, and Emmett seeing them off, but as she followed Arthur into the castle's forecourt, she was overwhelmed by the turnout. It seemed half the castle was crowded onto the steps.

Arthur sighed, looking uncomfortable with all the attention.

"They're all here for me," Lance joked.

"So they can celebrate your departure," Arthur finished.

Lance rolled his eyes. Emry looked back and forth between the two of them, realizing how long it had been since they'd been on an adventure together. Emry tried not to think about how wan and frail her father looked seated upon his horse. She hoped he was up for this journey.

Arthur raised a hand in farewell, and Emry did the same, catching her brother's eye. She nodded, in silent promise that she'd take care of their father, and then she turned and rode through the castle gates.

CHAPTER 35

"I've been expecting you," said the Lady of the Lake, her mist-filled eyes meeting Emry's as she stepped from the boat and onto the shores of Avalon.

That was a relief. Not that Emry had worried Nimue would turn them away, but it did make things easier if they didn't have to explain everything.

"I'm glad to hear it, my Lady," Arthur said with a courteous bow, reminding Emry of the last time they had traveled here together. She'd still been disguised as her brother and had been trying to deny her feelings for the boy who would one day be king. She just hadn't known he'd been wrestling with the same emotions as well.

So much had happened since then. And so much had changed.

"Then you know why we have come?" Emry asked curiously.

"I know why each of you has chosen to make this journey," said the Lady, looking first at Lancelot, then Merlin with her steady, piercing gaze.

Emry was once again strongly reminded of her first impression of the Lady of the Lake: that she was like talking to living, breathing tea leaves.

The Lady gestured for them to follow her to the cloister. They did, Emry's father trailing behind in obvious pain but attempting to conceal it.

Lance looked around, eyes wide, taking in the magical island. He kept a hand on the pommel of his sword, as though expecting to leap to Arthur's defense at any moment.

Or perhaps, Emry thought, *to his own.* Lance had seemed anxious ever since they'd left London, startling at every snapped branch, or loudly scraped chair in the great rooms of their nightly inns.

She didn't blame him for being on edge. The battle against Yurien's army had not been kind—they had barely escaped with their lives—and it was only the beginning of what was sure to be a terrible fight for Camelot.

Which was why they were here. To give themselves the best chance at victory. Emry only hoped that the Lady would have answers for them, instead of even more questions. And that those answers would be ones she wanted to hear.

The Lady led them to the cloister, where young girls in white robes peered out at them from around corners, whispering and giggling.

"Your journey was long," said the Lady. "Do you wish to ease your troubles and bathe in our sacred waters?"

"I do," Merlin said gravely, stepping forward. "But I know there will be a price. What would you have in exchange?"

The Lady turned to him. "Your daughter is not yours to trade," she said.

"The price is a person?" Lance muttered, horrified.

"The price depends on what you have left that you're willing to lose," the Lady replied. She turned to Merlin again, considering him. And then she nodded. "When the time comes, I would have you defend this island with your life."

Emry bit her lip. It was unclear whether the price was steep, or nothing at all. And she knew the Lady had done that deliberately, as a test.

Merlin did not hesitate. He dropped to one knee, and reached for Nimue's hand. "Gladly, my Lady," he promised.

"Then my priestess will show you the way." The lady motioned for a young girl to step forward. The girl wore loose white robes that fell to the ground, her hair plaited in a style that strongly reminded Emry of Princess Guinevere. The girl shot them a shy smile before leading Merlin away.

"Anyone else wish to partake of the healing waters?" the Lady inquired, her gaze stopping on Lance. "They heal all manner of ailment, not only physical."

"Er, think I'll pass," Lance mumbled.

"Anyone else?" the Lady asked.

"No, thank you," Arthur said firmly, stepping forward. "We came to speak with you about the future of Camelot, not about our own problems. Is there somewhere we might do that, instead?"

The Lady nodded. "Walk with me, Arthur Pendragon, King of Camelot," she said.

Arthur followed the woman across the cloister's courtyard. Emry watched, resenting that she hadn't been invited. Lance, whose hand was still on his scabbard, seemed to feel the same way.

"Is your wizard not coming?" the Lady called.

"Of course I am," Emry replied, hurrying to catch up with them while Lance scowled over being left behind. The Lady led them away from the cloister, and deeper into the forest. They walked silently for a while, the tree trunks increasing in size until they resembled towers.

"Ask me the questions you have brought with you to my shores," said the Lady as they passed a small ring of ancient stones that rose waist high from the mossy forest floor.

It was growing dark, and the forest hummed and buzzed with the sound of insects, and with the vibrations of its strange, wild magic.

Remember my path, please, Emry thought, hoping the forest would hear her. A couple of tree branches rustled overhead, as if nodding. Well, that would have to do. She hadn't expected the forest to answer back. But she wanted to remember where the Lady was taking them, just in case it proved important.

"Is it possible for us to defeat Yurien's army?" Arthur asked, not wasting any time.

Emry slanted him a look of approval.

"That I cannot know," said the Lady.

Arthur's shoulders slumped. They kept walking, the silence thick with disappointment.

That wasn't a true answer, Emry realized. The Lady was being evasive. Which meant Arthur had asked the wrong question. Emry tried to think . . . defeating the army was their goal. But what they needed was a way to do that.

"Wait," said Emry. "Is there a way to break the enchantment, so it's a fair fight?"

The Lady smiled. "There is."

Emry shot Arthur a triumphant look. "Knew it."

"But it will not be easy," the Lady of the Lake warned.

"Please, my Lady," said Arthur. "Tell us what we must do to break the enchantment."

"It is not what you must do, but what you must procure," said the Lady. "There is a magical horn that pours a drink that changes any who sample it into an ordinary mortal, no matter what powers they might have, or what enchantment might be cast upon them."

Emry and Arthur exchanged a glance. Well, at least it wasn't another magic sword.

Arthur's expression sharpened in thought. "If we could get into their camp's water supply," he began.

"Yurien's soldiers would have no idea that they'd lost their abilities," Emry finished, "and Camelot would have not just a fair fight, but an advantage."

Arthur turned to the Lady of the Lake. "Who possesses this horn you speak of?"

"Sir Bran Galed, knight of the Four-Peaked Fortress," said the Lady.

Emry had never heard of either, and judging from his frown, neither had Arthur.

"I'm guessing this Four-Peaked Fortress isn't just down the road," Emry said.

Nimue's silvery eyes flashed in the moonlight as she confirmed, "The object you seek, and its owner, are in the Otherworld."

"Great," Emry muttered. This was what she'd been afraid of. That their quest to Avalon would spawn another, even more dangerous one. She caught Arthur's eye, and he grimaced, as if he'd been suspecting the same thing.

"My Lady, the only two people we know who have traveled to Anwen have returned in significant distress," Arthur said.

Emry realized he was right. Morgana was possessed—or puppeted—by the high witch of Anwen herself. And Emry's father had lost nine years of his life and most of his magic.

"I did not promise the quest would be easy, only that it leads down a path from which you may defeat Yurien's army," the Lady said.

Arthur looked thoughtful, and Emry couldn't believe he was truly considering this.

"No," she said. "No way."

Because if Arthur needed to go to Anwen and back, she was the only one who could make that so. Which meant she'd be responsible if anything happened to him.

"There is one thing that might change your mind," said the Lady, motioning for them to follow her.

They didn't walk long before they came to an ancient stone well, its surface flat as glass, despite the breeze that rustled through the trees.

Emry had been here before, but not with Arthur. She watched as he put a hand to the hilt of Excalibur with a grimace.

"Your sword recognizes this magic," said Nimue. She gestured for them to step forward. "Draw your blade, Arthur Pendragon, King of Camelot, and gaze upon one possible future."

Arthur nodded, reaching for his sword. Excalibur flashed silver-bright.

"And you, child of Merlin, are you waiting for an invitation to stand at his side?"

Emry rolled her eyes. She hadn't realized the Lady of the Lake had a sense of humor.

Together, they peered at the flat surface.

The Lady murmured something too low for them to hear, and Emry felt the hum of magic rise up around them, vibrating through the forest. It rattled her bones, like music that was both high and low at once.

The surface of the well flashed silver, and then faded, revealing the city of London on fire. Flames blazed through the streets, consuming entire buildings. People staggered frantically toward the city gates, cloth over their mouths, coughing through the soot. Women carried crying children. Old men hobbled barefoot. Buildings collapsed, horses reared, glass shattered. People were being trampled, bleeding, screaming.

Yet when they reached the city gates, they found them chained shut, soldiers wearing Lothian black making sure no one escaped.

Emry felt bile rise in her throat.

The scene changed. King Yurien watched from a tower in Castle Camelot, his face impassive as the entire city burned.

"Your Majesty?" a man said from the doorway. Some sort of steward, Emry guessed. "The gates are locked, as you asked."

"Good," said Yurien. "Let Camelot's ruin be a cautionary tale to any who would stand against me."

The scene rippled, and the water stilled once again, flat and empty.

Emry didn't remember taking Arthur's hand, but she found she was gripping it tightly in her own, and he was squeezing back. They couldn't let this happen. The entire city falling, all of Arthur's people dying a painful death at Yurien's hand.

"You said that future can be prevented." Arthur looked to the Lady of the Lake for confirmation. She nodded.

"But only if we go to Anwen and secure this magic horn," Emry finished.

Arthur looked at Emry, a moment of silent understanding passing between the two of them. He needed to do this. And she alone could take him.

"The only hope for saving Camelot lies beyond the stones," the Lady said.

"Then it's a good thing I can open a doorway," said Emry.

◑ ◑ ◑

"Absolutely not," Lance said after Emry and Arthur had explained their plan. The three of them were huddled at the end of a narrow corridor deep within the cloisters, hoping they wouldn't be overheard. "You can't just go off to *another world*. Have you forgotten that you're the king?"

"I already took care of that, just in case," Arthur admitted. "I formally empowered Lord Agravaine to act as regent in my absence. And I've instructed him to send word to King Yurien that if he wishes to fight for control of Camelot, my forces and I will be waiting in the Forest of Camlann on the first of May."

The first of May. That was more than two months away. As much as Emry hated to side with Arthur on this—hated to even entertain the possibility of them stepping through that doorway and into the Otherworld—he seemed set on doing just that.

Despite the fact that no one who had ever gone there had come back the same.

"We don't know what we'll find there, or what might happen to us," Emry said, trying to impress the seriousness of it on Arthur. "Time doesn't run on the same path. And I'm the only one who can get us back."

"I trust you," said Arthur. "With my kingdom, and with my life. If Camelot's only hope is in the Otherworld, then that's where I'm going. With my wizard by my side."

"And with me," Lance insisted.

Arthur rested a hand on his friend's shoulder. "You don't have to come with us."

Lance raised his chin. "I know. But I'm coming anyway. Because that's what friends do."

Arthur nodded gratefully.

"We don't need a chaperone," Emry teased, defusing the seriousness of their conversation.

"Excuse me, am I or am I not Arthur's knight champion?"

"Did he say chaperone again?" Arthur asked with a grin. "He was sort of mumbling."

"I heard knight chaperone," Emry confirmed.

Lance looked as if he wanted to punch them both. "*Knight champion!*" he repeated loudly. "I'm coming with you. Not up for discussion."

◐ ◐ ◐

Merlin floated in the dark pool of water, staring up at the rough stone ceiling. He'd expected the water to be warm, from the steam curling off the surface, but in fact it hadn't been steam at all. It had been mist. And the water was bracingly cold.

But it helped to cool his feverish brow. He'd been rationing his supply of elixir these past few days, taking as little as he could without suffering too badly from withdrawal, and his blood felt sluggish and his mind slow from his dwindling supply of magic.

But now, as he clutched the bar of soap and listened to the water lap at the edges of the pool, he felt invigorated. His heart pounded, but he didn't feel short of breath, or exhausted. The aches had left his muscles, the pain in his back from days in the saddle was gone, and he felt, quite honestly, as if he could swim for miles.

He lifted his wand hand out of the water, examining the once-black veins that had returned to their usual pale blue. And then he reached for his magic.

It was like plunging his fist into a bag he'd thought was full of gold coins, and finding only a few left at the bottom.

His magic was still there, but barely.

The healing waters hadn't healed that part. He'd known they wouldn't. Because magic didn't work on magic. No matter how much he wished it would.

He'd expected to die back in that cave in Anwen. To trade his life for the safety of both worlds. He'd meant to die a hero, because the only other option was to live as a failure—as the wizard who had fallen into a different world, faced a sorceress, and lost.

The fact that he was alive was a wonder. But what did his health matter when his magic was so weak?

A knock sounded at the door.

"Er, yes?" he called.

One of the young priestesses stuck her head in. "The Lady waits for you outside," she said.

Merlin exited the waters and dried himself off, finding someone had taken his clothes and left a long white robe for him to change into. He donned it and went to find the Lady. Her expression was solemn, and the glowing lantern that floated at her side cast shadows across her brow that made her look even more intimidating.

Her gaze swept over him, and she nodded. "Better. Your blood no longer smells of poison. Now, come with me." She turned on her heel, not bothering to wait for him.

He grabbed his cloak and wand, hurrying after her. The gates to the cloister swung open, as if sensing her presence, and he followed her into the moonlit woods.

Merlin always thought that the magic on Avalon tasted different in different seasons. Now it was sweet with a bitter aftertaste, and it blew through him like a cold wind. Breathing in the crisp forest air, he could almost trick himself into believing that the magic he was surrounded by was his own.

But it wasn't. He'd never been able to take it in, the way Morgana could, borrowing what didn't belong to her. And the magic here never listened to him, the way it did to Nimue. But he'd never minded that before. After all, he had magic from two worlds. His father had come from Anwen, and his mother from Avalon. He'd used that dual magic to build his reputation as the most powerful wizard Camelot had ever known.

A reputation he wasn't ready to lose.

"Please, Lady, I need your help," he said as they walked deeper into the forest.

"You do not *need* my help," Nimue corrected. "You desire it. There is a difference, child of two worlds."

Merlin sighed. "Not to me. I don't know how to exist without my magic."

"You still have magic." The Lady stared straight ahead, into the unknowable depths of the forest. Lit in the glow of her floating lantern, she seemed so otherworldly.

"Barely," Merlin said. "But surely there must be a way to restore what I once had. What I lost."

"I know of several." The Lady lifted a branch aside, revealing a narrow footpath, and waited for Merlin to follow. They walked in silence for a few minutes until she stopped without warning. Merlin saw that she had brought him to a cave. "Should you wish it, you could fall into an enchanted sleep here. Over time, your magic would replenish. When you woke, you would be restored to what you were."

Merlin sensed what Nimue wasn't saying. "But when I woke, everyone I know and love would be gone," he finished.

She nodded. "You would wake into a very different world. One of inventions that would appear as magic to your eyes. But yes, if you speak of your children, they would be long gone."

"You said there were several paths?" he asked.

"The magic you lost is not in your world. I cannot help you regain it."

"But you know of someone who can," he finished, familiar with the Lady's evasive games.

She nodded. "My youngest sister, the sorceress Vivienne."

Merlin had not thought of Vivienne in a long time. It was she who had told him how to defeat Bellicent. He didn't know how he could face her again, having failed in his task.

"The choice is yours. Many are not so lucky to have choices," the Lady said.

"But Lady Vivienne is in Anwen." Merlin frowned, wondering if this was a trick.

"How fortunate that our young king, his knight, and his wizard are headed there," said the Lady of the Lake.

"To Anwen?" Merlin frowned. That would be dangerous. And there was no guarantee Emry would be able to control her magic in a different world.

"They will undertake a quest to save Camelot," said Nimue. "But they could use a guide. Someone who has been to the Otherworld before."

"But what good is a guide in a world that's frozen in sleep?" Merlin asked.

"The enchantment no longer holds," said the Lady. "Bellicent's return broke the spell. Anwen is as it was."

"Then, it's only my magic that's lost," Merlin said sadly.

"Spent, of your own choice," the Lady corrected. "You knew the risks."

He did. He just hadn't believed anything could go wrong. That Bellicent could break his enchantment, becoming even more powerful than before, while he became so much less.

"I do not do this for you," said the Lady, her eyes flashing silver. "I do it for the future of Camelot, and the future of magic itself."

"Which is?" Merlin asked.

The Lady gave him a long, hard look. "That remains to be seen."

CHAPTER 36

Emry batted a branch out of her path, hoping it wasn't much longer until they reached the stones. Ahead of her, the Lady of the Lake moved soundlessly, leading the way. Behind her followed Arthur, Lance, and her father, who was coming as their guide. The Lady of the Lake had insisted, and as much as she wanted to do this on her own, a guide would be useful.

Emry glanced back at Arthur, whose eyes were bright with excitement, though his expression was wary. From the dark smudges beneath his eyes, she doubted he'd slept. Lance didn't look much better. And her father's resigned expression made her wonder just what the Lady of the Lake had said to him when she'd taken him into the forest last night. And now he was coming with them to Anwen. Not because he wanted to help them save Camelot, but because he wanted to save his magic. That much was obvious.

When they reached the clearing with the stone arch, Lance let out a low whistle. "You're going to make a doorway to another world out of this pile of old stones?"

"I'm going to unlock one that's already there, using my magic, but essentially, yes," Emry said, pleased that he was impressed.

"Go ahead, child of Merlin," said the Lady. "It is time."

Emry took her dagger from her waist, and her father frowned. "My Lady, I thought you would open the doorway."

She shook her head. "That direction is forbidden to me. I can only close a door someone else has opened. I cannot open one, or step through."

"I can handle this," Emry promised. After all, it wasn't as if she hadn't done it before.

She took a deep breath and sliced a small cut along her palm. She pressed her blood to the altar stone and gasped, still not used to the way Anwen's magic rose to meet the power that flowed through her veins, and the eager way her magic responded.

What do you want? What do you wish? What do you desire? the magic asked, almost slyly.

You'll see, Emry thought. And then she spoke the words that opened the doorway.

For a moment, nothing happened, and then she felt the stone take a slurp of her blood—no, not her blood, her magic.

Her vision crackled with darkness. The stones shuddered, and the air between them shimmered, like a lake caught in the bright afternoon sun. But instead of going still, it rippled faster and faster, until a different world appeared on the other side: twisting trees with black leaves and silver berries. The briny smell of the sea. A cool breeze.

Emry turned to the others and grinned, even though what she truly wanted to do was brace her hands against her knees and breathe slowly until the dizziness subsided.

"Shall we?" Arthur asked bravely, gesturing toward the other world that shimmered through the stones.

"I wish you luck, King Arthur," said the Lady of the Lake, stepping forward. "Even though it is not luck you will need, but your wits."

"Thank you, my Lady," Arthur said, and Emry could tell he was holding back an exasperated sigh.

Her father went first. It was as if he was stepping through a looking glass. One minute he was there, and then next, he was on the other side.

Arthur went second, his hand on the hilt of his sword.

Lance closed his eyes and held his nose, as though jumping into a lake.

And then Emry stepped through the doorway, into Anwen.

◐ ◐ ◐

Emry didn't anticipate that stepping into another world would feel like she'd been taken apart and rearranged elsewhere, piece by piece. She staggered, her head spinning as she tried to make sense of where she was, and what had just happened.

A moment ago she had been in one world, and now she was in a different one.

Her head pounded, and she felt sick, not just from stepping between worlds, but from all of it. In fact, everyone looked a little ill from the journey, and she didn't blame them.

"Fascinating," said Arthur, looking around in excitement.

He was right—it was fascinating. They had come through into a forest. There was a stone archway on this side, as well. And on the other side of it, Emry could see the Lady of the Lake staring back at them, one hand raised in farewell.

No, not farewell. The doorway shimmered and then closed at the Lady's command.

Somehow, the closing of the doorway made it feel more real. They were truly here—in Anwen. Everything was familiar but different, a variation on a familiar tune. And it was warm out. Not winter, as it had been in Camelot, but late spring, judging from the buds and flowers that surrounded the glade

Emry untied her cloak and stuffed it into her pack, watching as her father unbuttoned his jacket and Lance loosened the ties of his tunic.

"I wasn't expecting a different season," Arthur said, rolling back his sleeves.

"Me neither," Emry said. "I guess it's lucky it isn't midnight here as well."

"I think it's morning?" Lance guessed, squinting up at the thin trickle of sunlight.

"Morning is good," said Merlin. "We have far to travel today."

A twig snapped in the forest, and Lance put a hand to the hilt of his sword, his shoulders going tense. He stepped in front of Arthur, as though expecting an ambush to bust through the trees.

Instead of an ambush, they got a bunny. A small white thing that could fit in the palm of Emry's hand. It twitched its pink nose at them, which was adorable, and then hopped away.

Arthur's shoulders shook as he held back laughter. "Terrifying beasts this forest has."

"Shut up, it could've been a dragon," Lance muttered.

Emry looked to her father. "*Are* there dragons here?"

"There are many magical creatures," he said. "But no, I believe the last of the dragons died out along with the fairy kingdoms."

"Fairy kingdoms," Lance scoffed, and then saw Merlin hadn't been joking.

Dragons and fairies. It was a lot to take in.

Arthur, meanwhile, was examining the black leaves and silver berries of a nearby sapling with interest.

"Merlin, do you recognize this species of tree?" he asked. "I've never seen it before."

"Why would I—" Emry began, before realizing Arthur meant her father.

"Silverwood," Merlin said crisply. "I forget the Latin. Be cautious, lad. The berries are a powerful sedative."

"Fascinating," Arthur said again, tucking a few into his jacket pocket.

"Well," Emry said, folding her arms across her chest and raising an eyebrow at her father. "You're our guide. Which direction do we head?"

Merlin knelt and traced a compass in the dirt. "*Norþ,*" he muttered, closing his eyes and pressing his hand to the ground. One of the points on the compass glowed, and he nodded. "That way," he said, indicating the direction the bunny had come from. "We should arrive by nightfall, *if* we don't dawdle." He marched off into the trees, and they had no choice but to follow.

Emry and Arthur exchanged a look. Truly, he didn't have to scold them as if they were children. They weren't dawdling. Well, not much.

"Do you intend to keep our destination even from me?" Arthur demanded, sounding very much like a king.

"We're currently in the Forest of Silverwood," said Merlin. "And Lancelot was correct—it isn't safe here. There are beasts far worse than bunnies. We're headed north, to the kingdom of Argatnell. Castle Pennard lies at the edge of this forest, and we should secure lodging in the town."

"I thought we were going to some four-peaked fortress," said Lance with a frown.

Merlin shook his head. "Not without horses, or a proper map. This world is large, and I know little of it."

"But you know the Castle Pennard, in the kingdom of Argatnell," Arthur said, having already committed the names to memory.

Merlin nodded. "I once performed a favor for King Arawen. It's he who will lend you horses and supplies for your journey to Bran Galed's fortress."

Emry's eyes narrowed. "Aren't you coming with us?"

Her father shook his head. "I'm here to seek Vivienne, the Witch of Silverwood. Nimue said she might help me regain the magic I lost here."

"And I suppose this witch just happens to live near Castle Pennard," Arthur finished, at which Merlin nodded. "Who is this Vivienne?"

"The Lady of the Lake's youngest sister," said Merlin.

Emry groaned. "There are *three* of them?"

"Vivienne is different," said Merlin, and then he refused to say anything else.

So they walked. And walked. The woods felt endless and deep, and Emry yearned for a horse, something she'd never thought possible. Every bramble seemed determined to snag on her cape, every thorn to lash her arms, every spiderweb to lie unseen in her path until it draped horrifyingly across her face.

Her magic felt different here. Excited. As if it felt the magic of the forest and wanted to rise up to meet it. Her Anwen powers pulsed just beneath her skin, longing to be used. When she grew tired of carrying her pack, she tried a lightening spell on it, and had barely thought the word of command before her pack was bobbing after her of its own accord. She had to grab a strap so it didn't float away.

Arthur was delighted, and insisted she do the same to his and Lance's. Her father was less than thrilled.

"It seems your magic is stronger here," he warned. "You'll have to be careful not to overcast a spell."

Emry frowned. "What do you mean?"

"Casting a warming spell that burns your skin. A muffling spell that turns you deaf," he elaborated, pushing aside another silver branch with black leaves. "That sort of thing."

That didn't sound good. It sounded as if her magic might function less as magic and more as a curse. "Is there any way to temper it?" she asked.

"If there is, I haven't found one," he said. "But perhaps Vivienne will know."

Emry tilted her head. "Why do you keep saying her name like that?"

"Like what?" her father asked.

"Like you've got a silverwood at the thought of her," Emry said.

Her father bristled. Arthur and Lance fell over each other laughing, and Lance practically stumbled face first into a tree.

"I've no such thing." Merlin sniffed. "And a lady shouldn't speak so indelicately."

"There goes my reputation," Emry said wryly.

"Oh, well done, I didn't realize it had stuck around this long," Lance said.

"I didn't realize you had one to begin with," said Arthur, with a grin. Off Merlin's glare, he added hastily, "Forgive me, sir, I have great respect for your daughter's impeccable reputation."

"You're lucky you're the king," Merlin grumbled.

"About that," said Arthur. "Perhaps it's best if you don't refer to me as such on this journey. You never know whom we might encounter, and what demands they might make."

"Ooh, can I say you're my squire?" Lance asked.

"Only if you have a death wish," Arthur returned.

Finally, just before nightfall, the woods grew thinner, and they were able to spot the spire of a church in the distance. As they got closer, Emry saw that the church sat in the middle of a small village, which was on the opposite side of a river. Beyond the village, on a hilltop, sat a fortified castle surrounded by a wall.

Though it wasn't as intimidating as the Thames, the river was still a sizable one, with a fast current. Thankfully, there was a bridge across, built of sturdy stone. Torches blazed on the far end, and in the rapidly falling darkness, Emry had never seen a more welcome sight. And she could tell the others felt the same.

"We should find lodging there, across the River Penn," said

Merlin. "Vivienne's cottage is in the valley behind the castle."

"Well then," said Arthur, "I suppose it's time our packs stop floating behind us."

Emry muttered the spell, then staggered under the sudden and surprising weight of her belongings. "Sard, I think it's twice as heavy as it should be," she complained.

"Man up, wizard," Arthur told her. "It can't be that bad."

"*Normalis*," Emry said, doing his pack next. Arthur lost his balance, nearly stumbling into the river. "You were saying?" She arched an eyebrow at him.

"Do Lance's next so he'll stop laughing at us," Arthur demanded.

Lance merely grunted. "The two of you are impossible."

Merlin had wisely set his pack down before Emry could magic it. "You're using the wrong spell, girl. You want *status quo ante*, to return them all to what they once were, at the same time."

Emry frowned. She'd never used that particular command before. "You're certain I won't wind up with a pile of sheep's wool and bread dough?" she asked.

"Only one way to find out," said her father.

Emry tried the spell and was relieved to find that it worked exactly as it was meant to. She grinned at him, and as he picked up his pack, he nodded. "Good. You understand the principle?"

"Negation of a previous spell, cast on multiple enspelled objects at the same time. I'm assuming it works only if they've been affected by the same spell?"

Her father smiled. "You're a quick study."

Emry felt giddy at the praise. She would have given anything to hear him say that when she was a young girl. To have him teach her a spell, instead of letting her overhear his instructions for her brother.

They shouldered their packs and crossed the bridge toward the town. As they got closer, Emry could see guards waiting on the other side, barring their way. From how Lance was holding his shield, and the tension radiating off Arthur, she knew they'd noticed as well.

"Friendly town?" Arthur asked Merlin in a low voice.

"Should be," said Merlin, but he didn't sound too sure, and Emry saw him take his wand from his sleeve.

The guards wore full armor, which was heavy and ill fitted. There were six of them, and not one of them looked pleased. Two held pikes, two held crossbows, and two held halberds.

"Halt, travelers," the tallest guard said, stepping forward from their ranks, his halberd in hand. "State your business."

Emry was relieved that she could understand him, though his accent was flat and unfamiliar.

"We've come a long way, and we're in need of a night's lodging," said Arthur, stepping forward.

The guard frowned at them, taking in their clothing, which was clearly meant for winter, and their light packs without bedrolls. "You traveled here by foot? From which village?"

"That's our business," Merlin said sharply.

The guard's expression darkened. He consulted with another guard in a low whisper. Neither looked pleased.

Emry exchanged a nervous glance with Arthur. This wasn't going well. She couldn't help but overhear snatches of the guards' conversation.

"... Accents are strange ..."

"... Traveled through the forest unharmed."

"Impossible ..."

"... Lying."

The guard turned to face them once again. "You're not from around here," he said.

"Which is why we need lodging," Emry replied smoothly.

"Then prove you can pay for what you seek, travelers," he said.

Arthur dug into his pack and held up a purse of coins. "Does this suffice?" he asked.

The guard snatched the pouch and opened it, tipping the coins into his hand. Gold and silver spilled out, and his eyes widened.

"I 'ent seen coins like this before," he said.

Emry looked to her father, who should have *warned* them that their coins and their clothing and accents were all wrong.

"Silver is silver," said Lance with a shrug. "Keep a coin for yourself, if you've never seen its like."

The guard grinned. "That I will, traveler." He selected a piece of gold, then grudgingly returned the rest to Arthur. "Can't be too careful," he said, stepping aside to let them pass.

Emry breathed a sigh of relief. And then the remaining five guards stepped into their path. "Aren't you forgetting something, travelers?" said the broadest one, who was carrying a crossbow.

"Forgetting what?" Arthur replied with a sigh, clearly suspecting they were about to exact more payment.

"To surrender your blades," said the guard.

CHAPTER 37

Arthur hoped he hadn't heard the man correctly. "Our blades?" he repeated. "Why?"

"Is it not custom where you are from to surrender your weapons at the gates of a peaceful town?" the guard inquired.

They looked to Merlin. He shrugged helplessly.

"You may reclaim them when you leave," the guard said, motioning for his men to step forward.

Emry was relieved of her dagger. Lance held out his sword, wincing as he was divested of quite a few hidden weapons in an expert pat down.

Arthur knew what was coming. He reached for Excalibur, withdrawing the weapon and resting it on his outstretched palms, even though everything in him was screaming that this was a terrible idea. *Chill*, he thought, sensing the sword's anxiety, or maybe just his own.

You'll get it back, he told himself. He had once left the thing in a chamber pot in King Louis's anteroom, after all.

The guard reached for the intricate hilt. And then his eyes went wide. "Commander?" he called, gesturing to a guard whose cape bore a silver brooch at the shoulder.

The commander examined the sword with a frown. Arthur wondered what was going on. Before he could ask, the commander turned to him in astonishment. "You carry Excalibur," he said. He dropped to a knee at Arthur's feet and raised a fist to his heart. "So the legends were true. The great sword-bearer has come to save us."

◑ ◑ ◑

Emry had no idea where the guards were taking them. Just that they were being marched through the city by a dozen guards and causing a spectacle.

"I can't tell if we're prisoners or honored guests," Emry murmured to Arthur.

"I'm worried it might be the same thing," he replied, his expression grim.

The commander still carried Excalibur, and two guards held Arthur roughly by the shoulders. The guard who had charge of Emry let his hand stray a little too low on her back, and she glared at him but held her tongue. The townspeople watched their procession warily, making it clear they weren't welcoming of outsiders.

The town itself was fascinating, at least from what Emry could see of it. The houses were small and made of wattle and daub or stone, with thatched roofs. The streets were packed dirt, the windows unglazed. Clothing was rough-spun wool, in dull dyes. Women wore aprons over their dresses, and most men had beards. Their wooden carts were a bit more rustic than Emry was used to, but it looked like an idyllic small village, one that saw no need to stop doing things the way they always had. They had a church, though it bore no cross, a guildhall, and a tavern that seemed to serve as an inn. She spotted a blacksmith's shop and felt the heat from the forge as they passed. Beyond the smithy was a storefront that smelled enticingly of fresh-baked bread, and from down a narrow lane, she could hear shouts and cheers from what might have been a gambling den.

Rising above the city was a tall stone fortress behind a wall. As they got closer, Emry saw the wall was a palisade made of timber, and around the wall was a deep ditch. They approached a portcullis with an actual drawbridge.

Servants darted cursory looks at them as they scuttled about, the women's hair bound beneath plain cloth caps and kerchiefs.

The guard commander hurried off and left them in a large stone hall decorated with tapestries that depicted fantastical creatures: some with heads of lions and tails of serpents, horned horses, dragons with feet, and others with wings of immeasurably large span. Smaller creatures, with the hindquarters of beasts and the heads of men, frolicking in forests whose trees were heavy with fruit. Creatures at war holding spears, and still more taking pleasure in the woods.

Emry itched to look at them closer up, and she could tell Arthur felt the same.

"Fascinating," he whispered, his eyes bright.

"They think you're the chosen one," Emry whispered back.

"Better that than having Excalibur thrown in a pile of daggers in some storeroom," he said.

"Is it?" Emry wondered aloud as footsteps sounded.

A woman appeared in the doorway, tall and elegant and of middle age. Her dark hair was liberally streaked with gray, her brown skin lined around her eyes, which were sharp but tired. She wore a loose velvet gown of deep green, with sleeves that trailed nearly to the floor, and golden embroidery around the neck. A gold belt fastened low on her hips. Though there was no crown upon her head, there was no doubt she was the one in charge.

"What is this?" she snapped, looking to her guards. "Commander? Is this matter not something the sheriff can handle?"

"No, ma'am," said the commander. "They're not prisoners. They're travelers."

"And you've brought them here under guard to interrupt my supper?"

The commander stepped forward, whispering too low for Emry to make out. The woman's eyes went wide. "Impossible," she scoffed. "Show me this sword."

A guard darted forward, holding Excalibur flat on his palms.

The woman stared down at it, pursing her lips. "Well," she said, looking up at them with unabashed curiosity. "Which of you carries the royal blade Excalibur?"

Arthur wrestled himself free of his guards and dropped to one knee. "I do, my lady."

"Don't bow to me, boy," the woman snapped. "Show me."

Arthur took back his sword, and as he did, the blade lit up the room with a dazzling glow.

"Er, not so much, please," he told it, and the blade dimmed. The guards gasped.

The woman looked him over again, more carefully this time. She shook her head in wonder. "That sword has not been seen since my great-grandfather's time," she said. "You are welcome here, sword-bearer, as my personal guest. You and your companions."

She motioned for the guards to step back, and when they did, Emry had the distinct impression that her father had shuffled behind her, trying to hide. But it was too late.

"Willyt!" the woman exclaimed.

Merlin stepped guiltily forward and bowed with a flourish. "Queen Bronwyn."

The queen—for she was a queen—didn't look pleased. "I thought you were dead."

Not again. Emry nearly groaned. Had her father unintentionally led everyone in his life to believe the same lie?

"Dead?" Merlin frowned. "Why?"

"The curse," said the queen, waving her hand as though her meaning was obvious. "My husband said it was the only explanation."

"There are more things on Anwen and Earth than are dreamt of in his philosophy," Merlin replied smoothly.

"Don't tell him that." The queen shook her head. "The magic man from the world beyond. I did not expect you would come again. And you've brought visitors."

Emry waited for her father to correct the woman, to say that he was one of the visitors that she had brought, but of course he didn't.

"I have," he allowed. "This is my daughter, Emry."

"And I'm Arthur, and this is Lance," Arthur said carefully.

"Then I shall introduce myself as just Bronwyn, if we are to be plainer than we truly are," said the queen with a knowing smile. "I grew up on stories of that sword, and of the heroes who bore it."

"I'm no hero," Arthur promised.

"Then perhaps you have not yet been given the right task," said Queen Bronwyn. "Come, join my family for supper. You are my guests."

Emry looked to her father, who nodded in encouragement.

And then she followed the queen down the corridor and into the main hall.

◑ ◑ ◑

An inn would have been preferable, Arthur thought, as guards threw open the doors to the main hall. Supper was laid out as a feast, platters already upon the table, and candles dripping in front of every place. Thankfully, it seemed the royal family dined in private, for there was just the one table, with fewer than a dozen chairs around it.

"And where is King Arawen?" Merlin asked the queen.

"Away treating with our neighbors to the south," she said with a long-suffering sigh. "I do hope he comes back *himself* this time."

Merlin blanched. "I've only just arrived, Your Majesty, and can promise I haven't interfered."

"Yet," said the queen with a pointed glare.

Arthur looked to Emry, to see if she knew what was going on, but she just shrugged helplessly. Then she looked down with a horrified expression.

"What?" Arthur whispered.

"I'm wearing *trousers*," she whispered back. "To supper. With the *queen*."

Arthur bit his lip. She *was* wearing trousers to supper with the queen. And from the little he'd seen of this world, he didn't think such things were done here, either. "You can tell Guinevere when we get back, she'll love it."

Introductions were made. The old man with the very long white beard tucked into his belt was the queen's father. The young man with bronze skin and a tunic cut to show off his sizable biceps was Prince Tiernen, and the pretty red-haired woman seated next to him was his wife, Princess Rhiannon. On her other side fussed a toddler with golden curls, who was being attended to by an exhausted-looking nurse. There was a short, plump duke with a very large mustache, and his tall, thin wife, who was the king's cousin. They had a pair of unruly twin boys who couldn't have been older than ten, and who looked exactly like their father, except with freckles in place of the mustache. Everyone seemed to know Merlin already, who looked as if he wished to slide down in his seat and disappear under the table.

Before their drinks were poured, the doors burst open, and a tall, handsome man with golden hair rushed in, unfastening his cloak. "Why were city guards leaving the castle?" the newcomer asked.

"We have visitors," the queen said, gesturing to the four of them.

"Willyt!" The man looked surprised. "I thought you were dead."

"A common misconception," Merlin said tightly.

The latecomer was called Sir Hafgan. Introductions were hastily made, and Arthur tried not to notice the way the knight's eyes kept meeting Princess Rhiannon's across the table, or the way her son had exactly his color hair and looked nothing like the bronze-skinned prince.

"Did you escape the curse?" the queen inquired.

Merlin shook his head. "I did not."

"The curse?" Arthur asked, as a servant refilled his cup of spiced wine.

"'Bellicent's Blight,' the people are calling it," said the queen. "The sorceress and her evil brought a plague of enchanted slumber to our land for a year and a day. Beasts ran wild, immune from the spell by their very nature, having been born of magic. Now our land is ravaged by these animals, which have grown bold and large in a world without men. Where once the only manticore were tamed and bred in captivity, now they are wild, and they attack our villages."

"*Real* manticore?" Lance said.

"You can't keep one as a pet," Emry told him.

"Is it . . . common for women to wear trousers where you're from?" Princess Rhiannon asked Emry.

"Oh, definitely," Emry said, and Lance choked on his wine.

"And where is that, exactly?" demanded the prince.

"Tiernen!" his mother scolded.

"We all know they're from another world, Mother," he said. "It's obvious from their speech, and their garb, and the fact that they've arrived with the wizard who gave another man Father's face."

"He what now?" Emry said, looking to her father to explain.

"Er," Merlin began. "No one really needs to hear this story."

"I do," Arthur commanded.

"Yes, Yo—Sir Arthur," Merlin amended.

The old man at the end of the table tutted and muttered to himself, "Wasn't what he was going to say."

"If you must know," Merlin said, "I cast a spell to help King Arawen repay a debt. He traded faces with a commoner who wished to live as a king."

"So you took his face . . . off?" Lance said, looking horrified.

"I enchanted them to look like one another," Merlin clarified.

"The stranger slept in my bed for a year," said the queen stonily. "Looking and sounding just like my Arawen. In all that time, he wouldn't touch me. The night my true husband returned, he confessed what had happened. And the wizard conveniently disappeared."

Merlin shifted uneasily in his seat.

"He does that," Emry said, glaring at her father.

Arthur didn't blame her for being displeased. Her father had made it sound as if he'd been asleep in a cave the whole time, but he'd clearly had adventures in this world before any of that. Adventures he'd neglected to mention.

"I'd like to thank you for the hospitality," said Arthur, "but we really can't stay here much longer, if we're to secure lodgings in town."

"Nonsense," said the queen, "you're to be guests at the castle, where I can keep an eye on the wizard."

Arthur inclined his head, as if the offer was entirely generous, and not at all ominous. "Thank you, Your Majesty. We'd be honored. But I'm afraid we would ask even more of you."

"What is it you seek, young knight?" She raised an eyebrow at the title, as if daring him to contradict it.

"A treasure of Bran Galed," Arthur said simply.

"Good luck." Sir Hafgan laughed, clearly convinced they'd fail.

"We're in need of horses and provisions and directions," Arthur went on. "And we're happy to pay for what we are given in silver and gold, though our coin is not of your world."

"Very few knights return from the Four-Peaked Fortress, who have sought a similar fortune," warned the queen.

"I don't have a choice," said Arthur. "And fortunately, I am no knight."

"And you claim you are no hero as well. Though you bear the sword Excalibur," said the queen. "You ask me for assistance, and I will give it, if you do something for me first."

"Name it, my lady," said Arthur. "And if it is in my power to give, it is yours."

"Spoken like a royal," the woman pronounced. "A prince?"

She peered at Arthur more closely. "No, not a prince. You are too burdened and too laden with grief to still be waiting for your responsibilities to arrive."

"I am just a traveler with a sword," Arthur replied.

"It is easy to deny an accusation of something you are not."

Arthur bowed his head. "You have found me out, Your Majesty."

"A king, seriously?" Prince Tiernen interjected. "He's like seventeen."

"Nineteen," Arthur replied stiffly. Tiernen didn't look older than twenty-two. "You wished a favor of me?" Arthur asked the queen.

She nodded. "I do. There is a fearsome griffin that has been tormenting our village this last month. Do you know the creature?"

"They dated, briefly," Emry joked.

Arthur shot her a look. "I have read of them," he said cautiously. "They have the hindquarters of a lion, but the wingspan of a dragon."

"You truly are from a different world, if you have only read of griffins but never seen one," said Prince Tiernen, indicating his arm that was in a sling with a grimace.

"This beast has grown bold," said the queen. "It attacked the village the other day and carried off two children. That makes five it has taken in a fortnight."

Five children. Everyone looked wan at the thought.

"I tried to fight it off," Prince Tiernen bragged. "Almost succeeded."

"No, you didn't," corrected Sir Hafgan. "We were no match for it. My squire is dead, and the men who tried to fight it off the last time were all killed."

Arthur had a very bad feeling about the way everyone at the table was staring at him with great interest.

"So it is fortunate that a king from another world has arrived bearing Excalibur," said the queen. "Surely that's a sign."

That must have been what the guard commander meant about Arthur coming to save them. Sard, a real griffin. One that had killed or injured nearly every man who had fought it. He tried to tamp down his growing panic at the dangerous task, which he had unknowingly agreed to take on. "I was able to track down the beast's lair," said Sir Hafgan. "It's a cave less than a league from here."

A league. Was that a day's journey, or a week? Arthur looked to Lance in question, and his friend shrugged at the unfamiliar measuring standard.

"Three miles?" Emry suggested.

"About that," said her father.

"The beast must be slain," said the queen. "And perhaps . . . perhaps some of those it has taken are still alive."

"I don't know that I could defeat it, even with Excalibur," said Arthur with a grimace. "I'm no great swordsman. But if this creature is tormenting your people, I offer myself in your service."

"As do I," said Lance.

"Me too," said Emry.

Prince Tiernen snickered. "Surely where you come from, you don't bring women along to fight monsters?"

Emry shot him a murderous look and opened her mouth to say something that would no doubt be shocking. Before she could, Arthur cut in, "It would be foolish not to, since Emry is the most powerful wizard I know."

He tried not to have a sense of satisfaction when the prince was so surprised that he tipped the contents of his wineglass into his lap.

CHAPTER 38

After supper, Arthur climbed up to an unused tower and stared out at the dark silhouette of the Silverwood Forest beyond the wall. Below him lay the town, quiet, torches burning low. He could have been anywhere. Yet he was keenly aware he was in a different world. He felt he had fallen into a storybook and was on the sort of quest he used to read about as a little boy at his mother's bedside, her fingers tracing a path through his tousled hair.

A traveler with a magic sword. A winged beast terrorizing a village. It felt so achingly far away from his own world, and the horrors of war. From the frozen bodies of the dead lying on the hard, blood-soaked ground. From the knowledge that those men had given their lives at his insistence. Because he had believed the fight fair.

He heard footsteps on the stairs, and wasn't surprised when Lance appeared, carrying two mugs. "Kitchen lad took a liking to me," he explained.

Arthur pressed back a grin. Some things never changed.

The drink was spiced and warm, a sort of cider with a kick that Arthur suspected was alcoholic. He took a sip and stared out into the darkness. Lance came to his side and rested his forearms on the crenellations of the tower, doing the same.

They stood there, silently, in perfect understanding. Or so Arthur thought, until Lance blurted, "You don't want my help slaying the griffin."

"Of course I do," said Arthur. "You're my best knight."

"No, I'm not." Lance winced. "That's why I'm here."

Arthur frowned. "What are you talking about?"

Lance stared out into the distance, as if looking through the lights into a memory. "If I stayed at Castle Camelot, everyone would have found out. So I came with you, pretending I was being noble. But the truth is . . . I haven't been the same since I almost died. Surely you've noticed the way my nerves are frayed. I'm no longer qualified to be your champion."

"I think admitting it makes you uniquely qualified," Arthur said.

"Stop joking."

"I'm not," Arthur insisted. "I don't want a champion who's the best warrior, or the most ruthless. I want the knight with the biggest heart. There's no shame in struggling with what happened. You nearly died."

"Sometimes I dream I'm dying," Lance admitted. "I wake up screaming. And when I'm sparring, sometimes I remember being stabbed and it's like I'm reliving it, and I just freeze."

Arthur wasn't surprised. He stared at his friend, whose shoulders were slumped as he looked out at the unfamiliar night sky with its strange constellations. "I wish you'd told me sooner."

"So you could have told me to step down as champion," Lance said ruefully.

"So I could have told you that I went through the same thing after Morgana nearly killed me."

"You did?"

"I wasn't okay for a long time after that happened to me." Arthur thought back to that night in the cave. To Morgana stabbing him. To accepting death. And then to Emry healing him. "I used to be unable to fall asleep, I was so afraid of what I'd dream. I'd spend my nights awake in the library."

"How did it get better?" Lance asked.

Arthur frowned, lost in thought. "It took time. But when we were attacked by bandits, and we were truly in danger, I didn't hesitate. I fought the way I had to, and that was—well . . . that was the first time I ever killed someone."

"So you're saying I should kill someone to get over my fears?"

"I'm saying that whatever is haunting you isn't you. It's just your fears. And you can be fearful and brave at the same time. You don't have to be only one thing."

"Who ever heard of a scared knight?" Lance asked.

"I wish I had," said Arthur. "I never related to stories about brave knights who go out and slay ten men without a thought and take a maiden to bed without even knowing her and ride off the next morning to do it over again."

"Funny thing, neither did I," said Lance, with a ghost of a smile.

"So rewrite the ballad," Arthur suggested. "Be the knight who's scared but fights anyway. The knight who loves his boyfriend back home and needs time to recover emotionally from a terrible battle. You can't blame yourself for what happened or you'll never get over it. You just have to learn from it and keep going."

Lance sighed. "I really should have talked to you about this weeks ago."

There were footsteps on the stairs, and Arthur braced himself for the arrogant prince, or his boastful knight, but it was Emry, carrying a lantern that let out pinpoints of light shaped like stars.

"You better not be strategizing how to kill the griffin without me," she said.

"Actually, we were up here enjoying the view and some fine mead," said Arthur, "but now that you mention it, I really don't know a thing about those creatures."

"Big, scary, flies, kills men, steals children," Emry listed. "That's all I've got."

"If you're trying to suggest that we should visit the library, I absolutely refuse," said Lance, knowing too well where this was going.

Arthur grinned. "As it happens, Sir Lancelot, the library is an excellent idea."

CHAPTER 39

"I can't believe I'm the trap," Emry grumbled, hiking up her silk skirts.

Her borrowed white dress was too low in the bodice, too short, and too fluffy. But Princess Rhiannon had been sweet to lend it to her, and it did fit the part. Even if it made her feel like a courtier on her way to a ball, and not a wizard tramping through the woods to catch a beast. And they'd been tramping through the woods for the better part of an hour, following Sir Hafgan's map, which was a hastily scrawled thing on a piece of parchment.

"They like maidens," Lance said with a shrug. "There's no accounting for taste." He grinned. "Loosen your hair more."

"It's not painting my portrait," Emry complained.

"That part's for Arthur, so he may admire how helpless you look."

"You never look helpless," Arthur promised as Emry glared at Lance. "See? I'm finally getting the hang of this boyfriend thing."

Emry rolled her eyes. "If your plan doesn't work, I vote Lance dresses up as a lady griffin and seduces the creature."

"Bold of you to assume it likes females," Lance returned, unruffled.

"I read the same books you did," said Emry. "The male griffin defends its territory and uses its front talons as weapons but has no peripheral vision and can most easily be killed by being stabbed in the heart. It is drawn to children and to defenseless maidens, for their innocence and purity."

"She literally memorized it," Lance said, turning to Arthur in distress.

"The female griffin rarely leaves its young and can be differentiated by the downy crest of white feathers on its wings," Arthur recited, finishing the paragraph.

Lance rolled his eyes. "You deserve each other."

"Somehow, you make a compliment sound like an insult," Emry informed him. "Come on, we've got to be close."

They were. Within five minutes they reached an outcropping of rocks that Sir Hafgan had indicated on the map, and just beyond that was the dark entrance to a large cave, which Sir Hafgan had marked with an X.

"Let's go over the plan one last time," said Arthur, ducking down behind the rocks.

"I'm the bait," Emry said with a sigh. "I lure it out of the cave so you can Excalibur it."

"And I slip inside the cave while the creature is distracted to save the villagers," said Lance.

"This is going to work," Arthur promised.

"And then we'll be heroes, and that annoying prince and pompous knight can stop smirking at us," said Lance.

"Why does it feel like that's *my* line?" Emry asked sweetly.

Lance shot her a look.

"Well, go on, wizard," Arthur prompted. "Lure it. Act maideny."

"I feel ridiculous," Emry muttered. And then she let out a pretty scream. A screamlet, really. "Oh, help! Oh, woe! Oh, misery!"

"I can't believe you did professional theater," Lance muttered.

"The special effects," she hissed. "Not the girls' parts."

She screamletted again. Arthur snickered and tried to pretend he hadn't.

"Here I am, an innocent maiden, lost and alone in a big, scary forest," Emry called. Arthur was turning red from trying not to laugh.

Then the ground shuddered with heavy footsteps.

"Sarding hell," said Lance, gripping his sword more tightly.

"Go," Arthur told him.

Lance crouched low and made his way toward the cave. Arthur pressed himself behind a tree, out of sight, though Emry could feel the pulse of Excalibur's magic.

She swallowed nervously and then screamed again, slightly more convincing this time.

Leaves rustled and branches snapped as the griffin burst into the clearing. It was larger and far more menacing than Emry had expected it to be. Its scales looked like burnt leather. Its wings were rubbery and coal black, with fluffy white feathers on top. The creature's eyes were narrow and reptilian, its nose two slits, its mouth rows of sharp teeth like rotting knives.

The beast stalked toward her, its head down, its nostrils flaring. Drool dripped from its mouth. Its wings were folded back, as if it had assessed her and didn't anticipate any danger.

"Hey there, nice murderous beastie," Emry crooned, reaching slowly for her wand.

Her brain was screaming for her to run. To fight back. To strike this creature down with conjured lightning or envelop herself in a thick fog so she might escape. It took everything in her to stand her ground and let the creature approach.

"Arthur?" she called nervously.

The creature took another step toward her, and she noticed its claws, like an array of daggers on each paw.

Deadly. Danger. Run! she thought in desperation.

And then Arthur stepped into the clearing, Excalibur flashing bright in the sunlight for a single moment. The creature turned, growling.

The monster's head swung between them, calculating. It was furious, as if it knew it had been betrayed. It roared, shaking the branches on the nearest trees. Emry winced at its rotten breath, and then Arthur darted forward, swinging his blade in a wide arc. The tip hit the creature's scales and slid off. The monster roared, unharmed, and swiped at Arthur with an enormous taloned paw.

Arthur flew backward, slamming into a tree but still holding on to his blade. He groaned, trying to stand as the beast stalked toward him.

"Hey! Over here!" Emry called.

The beast turned toward her while Arthur climbed slowly to his feet. He gripped Excalibur in both hands and, sneaking up on the griffin from behind, lunged at the creature, driving his blade toward its flank.

The beast spun, and Arthur revealed the lunge had been a feint as he slid beneath the creature, thrusting upward. He was impossibly fast and light on his feet, his blade moving with such speed that it was a blur. He was magnificent. Not a warrior, but a hero of legend, worthy of his sword.

The beast roared and snarled, and Arthur withdrew his blade and plunged it in again.

Silvery blood dripped onto the forest floor, smelling of ashes and bile. Arthur was covered in it as he scrambled to retrieve his blade.

The creature raked its claws down the front of Arthur's borrowed mail, shredding it like parchment.

Arthur fell to the ground, and the creature roared, rearing back, Excalibur stuck in its underbelly. It was wounded and furious. The creature stalked toward him, a predator secure in the knowledge that it had the upper hand.

Now Emry let out a very real scream.

This, finally, caught the beast's attention. As it turned, she raised her wand and shouted a spell that engulfed the monster in flames.

It roared, more in annoyance than in pain.

"Great, now it's a monster that's on fire," Arthur said, gingerly climbing to his feet.

He didn't have a sword. And Emry only had her dagger. They watched, horrified as the creature beat its wings, extinguishing the flames.

"Any more great ideas?" Arthur asked nervously, scrambling back.

Emry tried to think. The soft underbelly was the creature's only weak spot. And Arthur had already pierced it. Excalibur was stuck in the creature's stomach. All they needed to do was get hold of the sword and pull.

Suddenly, Emry thought of the floating swords she'd been messing around with in the castle dungeons. "Just one," she said, raising her wand. Her magic was ready and waiting, almost eager for her command. When she gave it, she could feel the weight of Excalibur in her hand. She twisted, and then thrust her hand up.

Embedded in the beast's soft belly, Excalibur moved to match her actions. The griffin screeched as the blade tore through its flesh.

"It's working!" Arthur said.

Emry knew it was working. She was shaking from the effort, sweat beading on her brow from controlling her magic in this world that clearly wanted her not to. She could barely breathe in the tight bodice of her ridiculous dress.

"Just a little more!" Arthur called, encouraging her.

She could do this. She had to do this. She gripped tighter on the phantom blade and tore it through the creature's flesh inch by inch.

Finally, the griffin let out a guttural cry and fell heavily on its side. The trees shook, silver leaves raining down around them, as if in celebration.

The beast twitched once, then let out a moan, and went still.

Emry flicked her wrist, and Excalibur dislodged itself from the creature's flesh, floating in the air in confusion about where it was meant to go.

"Er, over here?" Arthur suggested, raising his arm.

The sword landed in his outstretched hand.

Emry sat down on the rocks, clutching her head in her hands and waiting for the world to stop spinning.

"That was brilliant," Arthur enthused.

"I know you're injured, so don't even pretend you're not," Emry told him.

"A scratch," Arthur promised. "You're not going to swoon on me, are you?"

"Wizards don't swoon," Emry said primly, even though she definitely felt in danger of swooning. She hated how her magic worked here. Perhaps she'd try some Anwen rune magic next time, to see if it fared any better.

And then Lance shouted in the distance, and an animal noise followed, something between a high-pitched growl and a scream.

Emry's head snapped up, her heart pounding.

"Let's go," Arthur said tightly, holding out a hand.

She grabbed it, and ran with him toward the cave, her wand raised. In the glow from Excalibur, they could see to the back of the cave, where Lance had his sword raised, guarding a group of terrified young children from a baby griffin.

The baby griffin was unsteady on its feet, but it was still the size of a deer, with talons as long as knives. It gave a high-pitched growl-scream again, swinging its head toward the visitors.

"All right, then?" Lance asked tightly.

"The griffin's dead," Arthur said. "The—oh no. The white feathers. It was a female."

"And this is the baby. I'm aware," Lance said, waving his sword at it.

"It's cute," Emry offered, "in a murderous sort of way."

The griffin sat down on its hind legs and bleated.

"I think it's hungry," Lance said.

"It drinks milk," the oldest child said shakily. Her hair was in messy braids, and she wore just a tunic, her feet bare. She couldn't have been more then twelve. "It hasn't harmed us. There was another baby, but it died."

"We can't just leave it here," Emry said, looking to Arthur.

"No, we can't," Arthur agreed. He reached into his pocket and took out the bunch of silver berries he'd gathered when they'd arrived. "But maybe we can sedate it and see if it will walk back on a leash."

"It's not a puppy," Emry scolded.

"Hungry, little one?" Arthur asked, taking a careful step forward.

The creature whirled toward him, bleating again.

"Here you are," Arthur said, tossing the berries.

The griffin nosed at them, then swallowed them down. It let out a whine, and then rolled onto its back, its tongue lolling out of its mouth in a way that was disturbingly canine.

"Your belt," Emry told Lance, holding out a hand.

"I better get this back. It makes my outfit," Lance complained, unfastening it.

Emry muttered a spell that lengthened the strip of leather, and the children gasped. There were five of them, she saw, three girls and two boys, all streaked with dirt, and with shallow cuts on their hands and faces, but otherwise fine.

"That was magic, that was!" a boy of about eight with fiery red hair proclaimed.

A younger girl started crying, burying her face in his leg. "No magic!" she sobbed.

"It's—er, good magic," Emry promised, giving Arthur the makeshift leash. "See? I'm not scary at all, am I?"

"They say the high sorceress can look like anyone she wants," the older girl said, making a sign of protection in front of her.

"I'm literally rescuing you," Emry said, exasperated. "Would the high sorceress do that?"

The children didn't answer, but they still looked at her fearfully, which was annoying, and clung to Lance as though he was their savior.

He led them out of the cave and into the forest, with the griffin on its leash. Emry followed, grumbling.

"I'll catch up with you," Arthur promised, turning back.

A few minutes later, he returned with the mother griffin's head, looking disgusted.

"Ew, seriously?" Emry said, wrinkling her nose.

"It's what they always do in the stories to prove the creature is dead," said Arthur.

"*I'm* the one who slayed the beast, so you better not take all the credit," Emry reminded him.

He held back a grin. In the light filtering through the trees, his eyes were a soft brown, like autumn leaves. His hair was a mess, and his mail was slashed, and there was blood on his sleeves. He looked like a hero.

"I wouldn't dream of it," he promised. "It's a better story anyway, the maiden slaying the beast."

"Wizard," Emry corrected. With a glance at the children ahead, she lowered her voice before adding, "I haven't been a maiden for some time."

"Do you truly wish to admit that when we return to Castle Pennard, in front of your father?" Arthur inquired, looking adorably nervous.

Emry went pink. "Being a girl is the worst," she grumbled. "I slay a deadly beast, and you're worried about my dad finding out I'm not a virgin."

"Only because he'd assume I'm the most likely suspect," Arthur said.

Emry shook her head. *Boys.* Or maybe just this one.

When they reached the bridge into town, a crowd was waiting for them, with Queen Bronwyn, Prince Tiernen, and Sir Hafgan at the front. Cheers rose at the sight of them. The baby griffin was prancing along on its leash, and Lance was cooing at it. The children held hands. Emry held up her ruined skirts, and Arthur held the creature's head. The children ran to their joyful families, and Queen Bronwyn nodded, pleased.

"And you said you were no hero," she told Arthur.

"It was a one-off," Arthur promised. He held up the creature's head for all to see. "The beast will no longer torment your town," he told the villagers. "And perhaps the young griffin will defend this place, if it thinks of this town as its home."

Lance handed the leash to Sir Hafgan, relieved to be rid of the creature. "I'll, uh, need my belt back," he said.

"Oh my god, get another one," Emry told him.

Prince Tiernen stepped forward and clapped Arthur on the shoulder. "Our bard will sing of your valor, King Arthur."

Arthur grimaced. "That really isn't necessary."

Emry held up a hand. "Oh, yes it is. I would love a song to torment you with."

"Very well," said Arthur, "but the bard must also sing of my wizard, who made the killing blow."

"And of Sir Lancelot, who saved the children," Emry added.

Prince Tiernen nodded solemnly. "The bard will sing of your brave threesome," he proclaimed in his most royal tone.

At this, it took everything Emry had not to fall over laughing.

CHAPTER 40

Guinevere glared down at the blank parchment on the table in front of her. She'd thought stories would flow effortlessly from the tip of her quill onto the parchment, like paint from a paintbrush, or embroidery from a needle. She couldn't have been more wrong.

She groaned, leaning back in her chair and glancing out the window. It was late morning. Emmett had gone up to the wizard's workshop hours ago, doing his duty to take over in his father's and sister's absence. He'd left her behind in their apartments, with a fresh stack of parchment, a tray of breakfast, and a kiss on the top of her head.

And it had all been downhill from there. She sighed at the crumpled pieces of parchment that littered her desk, all covered with terrible beginnings: Once upon a time there was a princess who wished to fall in love. Once upon a time there was a princess who thought marriage was a curse. Once upon a time there was a princess who dreamed of spiced cinnamon cake covered in candied oranges.

The last one was particularly mortifying. It read like a menu. Not that she'd mind if a serving girl showed up with a tea tray laden with spiced cinnamon cake to distract her. Guin sighed, setting down her quill and stretching the tension from her back.

The problem was, she couldn't think of anything important or interesting to say. All she could think was how indulgent she was acting while her kingdom was being torn apart by King Yurien and his men. A knock sounded on the door, and Guin looked up to find a page boy standing there with a tray, which sadly contained zero refreshments.

"Er, a letter came for you, Your Highness," he said with a bow.

Guin frowned. A letter? For her?

She held out her hand, and the boy gave it to her. *Guinevere Merlin* was scrawled across the front of the parchment in a copperplate hand that looked familiar. She turned it over, but there was no stamp in the wax seal. The letter was worn, as if it had traveled a great distance. "Where did this come from?" she demanded.

The page was staring curiously at the crumpled papers on her desk, biting his cheek as he scanned the menu one. "By messenger," he said, with a bow. "Er, if that's all . . ."

Guin waved him away, lifting the seal on the parchment. And then her heart leapt as she read the first line: *To my dearest sister . . .*

"Oh, thank goodness!" she said, hugging it to her chest. So her brother was alive and well. She had hoped. Taking a deep breath to steady her nerves, she read his letter.

> *To my dearest sister,*
>
> *I hope you haven't worried too much, but knowing you, that's impossible. Mother and I have arrived safely in Andalusia. I write to you from the orange groves outside the palace, a place so beautiful that I wish we were visiting under better circumstances.*
>
> *I am trying to be strong for Mother, who is beside herself with grief, and for Cameliard. As well as the mighty responsibility that now rests upon my shoulders. God gives me strength, but he also gives me doubt. I have never wanted to be king, and reclaiming Father's throne in Cameliard feels like an impossible task . . . one I don't have the strength or knowledge to begin. I suspect you might, for you have always been more capable than me in matters of politics and persuasion. If I loved God less, I might like the idea of becoming king more. In truth, I'm relieved to be in exile, where I can devote myself to spiritual*

pursuits, though I know that's a terrible thing to admit. Which is why I write to you with the hope that you will find ways to help our people that I cannot. Cameliard would be lucky to have you as its champion, and protector. If your heart leads you down that path, follow it, and be well.

Your loving brother,
Gott

Guin frowned at the letter, reading it through twice. Her brother and mother were safe. That part was a relief. But her brother's ramblings about not wanting to be king . . . it almost sounded as if he wanted her to take the throne. But surely not. Their father had never believed she had a head for politics, and Guin had always assumed her brother felt the same. Yet his letter, with his urgings that she help their people . . .

Urgings she couldn't dismiss, because she'd been having the same thoughts. Only she'd tried to tell herself it was nonsense. That she was a princess whom her father had intended to trade in marriage to help her people, not to lead them.

But if she *could* help in this time of crisis, of course she would. She didn't need to ride off to battle or put herself or the baby in danger. There was plenty she could do from right here.

Plenty she *should* be doing, she decided, pushing back her chair. After all, Arthur had given her a place on his personal council. True, that had been just the one meeting, right after King Uther had died, but still, it counted. And if her memory was correct, the council was meeting right now.

◑ ◑ ◑

"I hope I'm not interrupting," Guin said sweetly, even though it was clear that she was.

"Princess." Lord Agravaine frowned at her from the head of the table. "Are you lost?"

"Not at all," Guin said, lifting her chin and taking one of the empty chairs. "Forgive me for not knowing the protocol of where I should sit. I assume here is fine."

Everyone was staring at her. Sir Ban, Lord Howell, Lord Agravaine, General Timias, Sir Tor, and a half dozen others she didn't know by name. Apart from Sir Tor, they were all men, and all decades older than she. And here she was, seventeen and pregnant, a princess in a silk gown with rosebuds embroidered on her satin slippers. But she refused to be intimidated. She had just as much right to be at that table as any of them.

"Er, Your Highness, this is a council meeting," General Timias said gently, as if she had mistaken it for a tea party.

"Yes, I'm aware." Guin smiled prettily at him. "I'm only sorry I haven't made the time to attend one sooner. After all, I am a member of the king's personal council. Isn't that right, Lord Agravaine?"

The man looked as if he'd tasted something sour. "It is."

"Of course, I wouldn't dream of overstepping on matters pertaining to Camelot," Guin went on, "but I expect you'll welcome my insight concerning Cameliard and the ongoing conflict with the usurper king."

Sir Tor grinned.

General Timias pushed to his feet, red in the face. "Listen here, lassie. This council is no place for women."

"I disagree," Guin replied evenly. "And I believe King Arthur does as well."

"Oh, let her stay, Timias," said Lord Howell. "I have a daughter her age. She'll tire of it after ten minutes."

Guin did not tire of it after ten minutes. In fact, as the meeting progressed, with ideas being debated about legislature and decisions on running the kingdom, Guin felt more alive than she had in a long time.

Finally, she was in the room where everything happened. And she had a seat at the table. Now all she needed was for them to take her ideas seriously.

She listened with great interest as the conversation moved from petition to petition, some sparking debate, others inviting flat refusal. After a long while, the discussion turned to Cameliard, and news of the soldiers who were causing havoc there. A few of the villages near the southern border were requesting refuge for their women and children in Camelot until the attacks died down.

"If we agree, the towns that take them in will need the crown's resources," said Sir Ban, looking at sheaves of ledgers. "That comes out of the royal coffers."

"We can't foist an onslaught of refugees on Camelot's villages simply because they lie near the border," protested Lord Howell.

"We must," said Sir Tor. "It's the honorable thing to do."

"Where will they stay?" Lord Howell inquired. "In the village barns, in the cold?"

He had a point. And then a thought occurred to Guin. "They will stay with the lords who sent men to aid Cameliard," she proclaimed.

Everyone turned to stare at her.

"Respectfully, princess, I doubt that will go over well," said the general.

Sir Tor glared at the general. "Let her speak her piece. Your Highness, what did you have in mind?"

"You're not seriously—" began the general.

"I am," said Sir Tor. "And it would behoove you to remember that Princess Guinevere was nearly your queen, had she not refused Arthur's hand in marriage."

The general grumbled but motioned for Guin to speak. Her heart thudded nervously as she explained, "You'd need to frame it as a reward, not a burden. The crown is sending skilled women to serve as housekeepers and governesses, to better staff noble households. As well as able-bodied children to learn trades and apprentice."

"That's a far cry better than saddling villagers with the responsibility of extra mouths to feed," said Sir Tor approvingly. "Gentlemen, I believe you'll agree."

There was a tense moment of silence, and then Sir Ban cleared his throat. "We could provide a stipend from the royal coffers to cover the wages for their new positions."

Guin smiled at the aging knight's suggestion.

"So the nobles we asked for help fighting King Yurien's army would feel indebted to us, when really they're doing us a service," mused Lord Agravaine.

"And any who refuse would be doing so at political risk and showing their lack of loyalty to the new king," Guin added. "If that sort of information would be of interest."

Lord Agravaine's expression turned shrewd. "It would," he said. "I—I thank you, princess, for your counsel."

Guin smiled sunnily. "You're very welcome."

When the meeting ended, Guin assured them that she would be on time for their next session, and then glided from the room, her heart racing with excitement. The baby kicked, and she pressed a hand against her stomach. "You liked that, didn't you?" she asked. "Listening to me take charge of things that men were making a mess of?"

The baby kicked again, as if in agreement. Guin felt invigorated. That was what she should have been doing all along. Finally, she'd found a way to help her people. To make a difference. To be listened to, instead of dismissed as a pretty face with an empty head.

She giggled, recalling how furious all those awful men had been that she'd actually had a good idea. She only wished Arthur had been there to witness it. Or Emmett. She couldn't wait to tell him.

When she got back to her apartments, she found Issie and Branjen sitting with their embroidery. The girls looked up eagerly at her entry. "Oh, no!" she said, realizing she'd invited them to stop by. "Have you been waiting long?"

Issie bit her lip, and Bran kicked her before she could say anything. "Not very," Branjen lied.

"I'm so sorry," Guin said. "But you won't believe where I've been."

She collapsed onto the sofa and kicked off her shoes, summoning a maid to bring them tea and cakes. While they waited, she explained about the meeting.

"I can't believe you did that," Issie said, her eyes shining with admiration.

"I *love* that you did that," said Bran.

"I believe I might have terrorized the entire royal council," Guin said, grinning.

"Serves them right if you did," said Issie. "I'm tired of a bunch of old men deciding everything."

"So am I," Bran agreed. "Please tell me you're going back."

"Of course," Guin promised.

"What does your husband think of all this?" Bran asked.

Guin frowned, unsure. She'd thought Emmett would be proud of her. But what if he wasn't? She'd promised him that she'd be content with whatever he could provide—with a quiet, small-town life together, at his cottage in Brocelande.

But that was before.

Before they'd both found themselves restless and frustrated on Avalon. Before Yurien had invaded Cameliard and shattered the fragile peace that she'd been counting on.

"What?" Issie prompted.

Guin sighed. "Politics wasn't something I'd ever pictured myself doing. I told Emmett I'd move to Brocelande . . . but I don't want to run away from my responsibilities to my people by using marriage and motherhood as an excuse."

Issie mulled this over a moment. "It's only running away if you don't know what you want. Otherwise it's running toward."

Guin realized her friend was right. Perhaps she'd known for a while that she didn't desire a quiet country life, only she hadn't dared to admit it, even to herself. "I suppose, if it were an option, I'd want to lead Cameliard."

"Why isn't it an option?" Bran insisted.

"Well, I have an older brother . . ." *Who wants to be a priest*, Guin thought but didn't say.

The problem was Emmett. Well, there were a lot of problems, but her chief concern was her husband. She'd promised that her love for him was worth more than servants and feasts. But it wasn't the privileges she would miss, it was the people. She missed living with her friends, seeing them at meals, always having exciting things happening around her. More than that, it was the ability to be helpful. To make sure people weren't suffering or unhappy, if she could do something about it.

Perhaps, if she explained, he would reconsider . . .

Not that it mattered so long as Yurien had control of Cameliard.

"It's never going to happen," Guin said. "But it's a nice fantasy."

◐ ◐ ◐

While Guin worked up the courage to tell Emmett about her change of plans, she attended two more council meetings. The royal advisors were, if not exactly open to her input, at least willing to hear her out.

But that was fine. She would prove her worth. And the chance to do so lit a fire in her. She was more than just a pretty princess to be auctioned off to the best-paying kingdom in exchange for alliance or goods. She had a sharp mind, and good ideas, and a newfound taste for power. And oh, she couldn't wait to show those arrogant men that they weren't the only ones who could run things.

After that morning's meeting ended, Guin decided she'd put off telling Emmett long enough. And so she marched up to the wizard's workshop to speak to her husband.

When she arrived, thoroughly out of breath and cursing whomever thought to invent spiral staircases, she laughed.

Emmett was covered in black powder, his wand gripped in his teeth as he mopped up a spilled potion.

"Guin!" he said, horrified. "I—er—no one was supposed to see this."

"What is 'this' exactly?" she asked, giggling.

"My pain tonic exploded," Emmett said with as much dignity as he could muster.

"You look like a chimney sweep," Guin informed him. She dug out her handkerchief. "Here."

He stared down at the small embroidered square in dismay, not seeming to understand Guin was teasing him. She rolled her eyes. "Use a cleaning spell."

"Can't," he said unhappily. "I've enchanted my clothing to be wrinkle proof, so it won't work."

He disappeared into a storeroom, then returned with a large sooty linen cloth, his face pink from being scrubbed. "Did you need something?" he asked sheepishly. "Or are you just here to laugh at me?"

"It can't be both?" Guin asked, taking a seat in one of the squashy armchairs by the fireplace. There was even a footstool, she saw with delight, kicking her feet up in a way that was entirely undignified for a princess. The ache in her back eased, and she sighed in contentment.

"You better not be overdoing things," Emmett warned.

"I'm not. I'm simply doing what needs to be done," Guin replied.

"That's right, how was your council meeting?" Emmett asked, dipping a rag into a washbasin and scrubbing the soot from his forearms. His sleeves were pushed up, and Guin took a moment to admire her handsome husband. Pity it was still so early in the day, though that had never stopped her before.

"Extremely satisfying," she replied. "Would you believe Sir Ban had the gall to refer to farming as 'men's work'?"

"Honestly, yes."

"My father's councillors are exactly the same," Guin went on. "So narrow-minded. When I'm—" She stopped, embarrassed. She'd almost given it away.

"When you're . . . ?" Emmett prompted, slouching back against the table.

Now or never, she thought.

"When I'm Queen," she finished, "I'm going to impose a mandatory retirement age on my advisors."

Emmett chuckled uneasily. "I hate to break it to you, but I don't think you're going to be the next Queen of Camelot."

"Of course I'm not," she said. "I meant Cameliard. After Arthur and Emry defeat King Yurien and win it back."

Emmett frowned. "Wouldn't your brother be king?"

Guin shook her head. "My brother doesn't want to rule Cameliard. But I do."

Emmett looked up at her in surprise. "You do?"

"Being Queen of Cameliard never seemed like an option before," Guin went on. "But Arthur respects me. He listens to me. And so do you. Which means there are others who would as well. I want the world to be better for our baby. I can either sit around making up stories about a world that doesn't exist, or I can start changing things in this one."

"If anyone can, it's you," said Emmett, smiling.

"Really?" Guin frowned. "Even if you'd have to live in Cameliard Keep?"

"If it will make you happy. And if you don't mind that I can't provide for our family."

"Of course you can," said Guin. "You'll be providing love and support. Our children will need their father, not just to teach them magic, but to make us a proper family."

"Children?" Emmett asked, raising an eyebrow.

"Why, do you object to having more than one?"

"Not at all," Emmett said.

"Good." Guinevere grinned.

"Then it's settled," said Emmett.

"You truly wouldn't be upset to be my . . . consort?" Guin asked.

Emmett laughed. "Not at all! I'd far rather be your consort than your court wizard! Do you really think I'd mind living in a castle with no responsibility?"

When he put it that way . . . "Still," Guin said, her voice small. "None of it will come to pass unless Arthur is able to defeat Yurien."

"He will," Emmett said with conviction. "Because he's got my sister helping him."

CHAPTER 41

Morgana watched her son run barefoot and screaming through the castle corridor, her eyes narrowed in annoyance. "Mordred," she warned. "Don't make me count to three."

"I don't care!" he shouted, whirling around, his face red, and his hands balled into fists. "I don't want to learn magic! You can't make me!"

Morgana took a steadying breath, trying not to lose her temper at the boy, even though he was testing the last of her patience. "And why not?" she demanded.

"Because magic is a service that others should do for kings! I won't dirty my hands with it!" he said, lifting his chin.

His words stabbed right into her heart. The way he was standing there, his tone, the reddish streaks lightening his hair. He was turning into his father. Into a brute of a man who craved the wrong kind of power.

She wished he was still small enough to fit in her arms, still a miracle of a new person, soft and sweet smelling and hers to mold. A do-over for the childhood she never had. But he had grown up faster than she'd thought possible. And now he was sneering at her.

No, not at her. At the idea of learning to wield his magic.

Something she would have given anything to learn when she was that age. But he'd come around. He had to. He was hers. A beautiful boy with magic that she could teach him to control, to wield, and to use to make his life better. A future king who wanted for nothing. Of course he was spoiled and acting out.

"Then today you shall have different lessons," she said. "What do you wish to learn instead?"

"How to kill a man in battle," he said, removing his knife from his belt and lunging at an imaginary opponent. The knife pulsed with a wicked enchantment, and Morgana frowned. She'd taken that knife from him before, knowing what it could do.

"Where did you get that?" she asked.

"Father returned it to me," he said smugly.

Morgana pressed back a shudder. "I'll see if the sword master has time for a lesson," she promised, holding out her hand. Some disciplined drills might do the lad good.

"I'm too old to hold hands with you." Mordred scowled.

"I want you to give me that knife," she said.

"No! It's mine! Father said!"

"You have no need of such a weapon."

"Yes, I do!" he shouted, stamping his feet. He reached into his jacket and withdrew his wand. *"Damnatio memoriae!"*

Morgana stiffened at the words. Thankfully, the memory-wipe spell didn't come.

"Who taught you that?" she demanded.

"Did it work?" he asked eagerly.

"No."

"Oh." He sounded disappointed. "I learned it from the lady who isn't you, but who wears your face."

"You should never, ever use a spell like that," said Morgana. She reached a hand to his shoulder, but he shrugged it away. "Promise me."

"No!" he said. "She told me I could use it on the servants if I was bad and they were going to tell."

"She was lying to you," said Morgana. "And you could get very hurt if you try it again."

"I don't believe you!" Mordred shouted, taking a step back, his eyes blazing with fury. "You don't like her because she borrows your body. But she gives me presents and she let me kill a man, and now all of the soldiers who used to tease me call me the Little Commander and give me *respect*!" Mordred's chest was heaving as he held the knife out in front of him, his hand trembling. And then he turned and ran.

"Mordred!" she called.

But he didn't stop. And she didn't know how to make him.

CHAPTER 42

"We'll never get there if you keep stopping to take plant clippings," Emry scolded as Arthur knelt to examine yet another unfamiliar bush.

"I want to ask the witch about these," Arthur said, tucking a spray of tiny, spiraled silver leaves into a handkerchief.

Her father hadn't been at the castle when they'd returned a few hours ago from killing the griffin. He'd left a note that he'd gone to Vivienne's cottage and had written out directions of where they could find him.

"She'll probably be too tired from sarding my dad to identify your plants," Emry retorted with a shudder.

Arthur looked up at her, his eyes dancing with mischief. "Just like how Sir Hafgan is totally sarding Princess Rhiannon?"

"Oh my *god*," Emry said, delighted at the opportunity to gossip about the annoying knight. "Her son is definitely his, right?"

"No question," Arthur agreed.

"Do you think he knows?" Emry asked, as they continued through the woods.

"He doesn't seem like the sharpest sword in the armory," Arthur said, "so let's go with no."

Emry batted a branch out of the way with a grimace. In the past few days, she'd had more than enough of hiking through the woods. She was tired, her arms were covered with scratches from branches and brambles, she was pretty sure there were leaves in her hair, and she was actually sweating from physical exertion.

Worst of all, their quest to the Four-Peaked Fortress promised to be yet more forest.

Arthur wiped a hand across his brow, and then squinted through the trees. "I think that's it," he said, pointing.

Emry could just make out the shape of a cottage, smoke curling from its stone chimney. As they got closer, she saw the cottage was more like a farm, with an enclosure for pigs, a chicken coop, goats grazing in the front yard, and a cat sunning itself on a fence post. The cottage itself was tidy and made of stone, with red shutters and a red door. A line of washing flapped in the breeze, hung with sheets and stockings.

There was a hand-painted sign on the gate that warned *Travelers, seek no refuge here.*

"Charming," Arthur said sarcastically.

"Oh, I don't know," Emry said. "If I were a woman living alone in the woods, I'd probably put up a sign, too."

Arthur suddenly had a loud coughing fit, and Emry looked at him curiously.

"Er, just trying to give them some warning," Arthur said.

"Not a visual I needed," Emry muttered, before knocking at the front door.

"No travelers!" a woman's voice called. "I don't care how tired you are."

"I'm looking for my father," Emry said.

"Not another one," the woman said, still not opening the door. "Try the pigsty! If he's not there, see if any of the goats have his eyes."

Emry frowned, thoroughly confused. "Um, my father is Willyt Merlin?"

The door flew open. "Why didn't you say so?" a woman asked peevishly. She was very beautiful, with bronze skin and long, tightly wound black curls that she'd tied back with a kerchief. She wore a simple blue dress under a stained leather apron. There was a smudge of yellow paint on her cheek. Her hands were covered in it, too. "He's in the library. Why don't you both come in?"

The cottage was much larger on the inside. It should have been a single room, judging from the exterior. But the space Emry found herself in had far too many windows, and far too many doors. In fact, there was an entire wall of nothing but different colored and sized doors.

The space they were standing in was an art studio, with canvases piled a dozen deep. A work in progress sat on an easel, depicting a familiar scene.

"Is that Lance?" Arthur asked, moving closer to see.

It *was* Lance, in the griffin's cave, the children behind him, his weapon raised against the young griffin.

"But that just happened this morning," Emry said wonderingly.

"I know," said the witch. "I've been working on it all afternoon." Given Emry's confused look, she explained, "My sister Nimue can see the future. I can see the past."

"That seems significantly less useful," Emry said, and just in case she was being rude, she added, "But still very nice?"

"There is something to be said for knowing the truth about things, and not having to rely on someone else's telling," said the witch.

Emry supposed she had a point. "Er, why did you think my father was a pig?" she asked.

Vivienne shrugged. "Travelers come here, and when they do, I'm compelled to offer them hospitality. If they wrong me, they're transformed in the night into beasts. Some become the creatures that terrorize the woods, like griffins and manticore. Others become harmless farm animals. Those I keep."

"And sometimes their families come looking for them," Emry finished.

"Their families are usually better off without them," said Vivienne. "But yes."

"If you get so many unwanted visitors, why don't you move?" Arthur asked.

Vivienne shook her head. "I can never leave this forest. It is part of my curse."

"Your curse?" Emry repeated.

"I must remain in the Silverwood Forest, and I can never seek out anyone's company," said Vivienne. "They must seek me."

"That sounds . . . lonely," Emry ventured.

Vivienne's eyes darkened, and she looked away for a moment, as if steadying herself. "Sometimes" was all she said. "Now. Let's find your father." She wiped her hands on her apron and opened a door that was painted bright green. "Willyt," she called. "Put down that book, and come to the kitchen."

"I'm busy," he replied tersely.

Emry could see what looked like a library behind that door, which couldn't be right. "No you're not," she told her father.

"Ah, Emry. So Arthur managed to slay the griffin?" he called.

"Actually, I did," she said. "But Arthur helped."

"I *told* you that," said Vivienne, sounding annoyed. "Kitchen. Now."

She slammed the door and opened the one next to it, which was tall, narrow, and painted purple.

They followed her into a cozy kitchen with herbs drying on a rack, and a vase of wildflowers set in the center of a round wooden table.

"You may hang Excalibur over there," she instructed, waving at a peg from which hung an assortment of colored aprons.

Arthur made a face but did as he was told.

There was only one door in the room, which briefly turned green. Merlin stepped through it, a book tucked under his arm. He shot Vivienne a look. "Happy?"

The sorceress shook her head in exasperation and got down four floral-patterned mugs from a cupboard.

"Is your magic fixed?" Emry asked.

Her father sighed. "It's not broken—"

"It's borrowed," the witch finished. "The stones must have taken it, which means he'll need to convince the stones to give it back."

Emry knew her father well enough to interpret what that meant. "So you're not coming with us," she said. "To the Four-Peaked Fortress."

"I'm not," he confirmed. "I have to go to the cave where I lost my magic. It's in the opposite direction, and a long journey from here."

Vivienne poured their tea, and Arthur sniffed his with interest. "Sweet mint," she told him. He looked unspeakably disappointed that it wasn't something more interesting.

Emry stared down into her mug, waiting for it to cool. Of course her father was doing his own thing instead of helping her. Why had she even expected otherwise?

"What can you tell us about the Four-Peaked Fortress?" Arthur asked Vivienne.

"Drink your tea before it gets cold," Vivienne chided. She took a sip from her own teacup, waiting for Arthur to do the same. When he did, she said, "Before you reach the fortress, you will come to a mound that rises out of the forest. You must wait there until a maiden on a white horse rides by. She will not stop, and you must not call to her. Follow her only at a distance. She will lead you the rest of the way to Sir Bran's castle."

"I can't just follow some woman through the woods!" Arthur protested, horrified. "That's creepy."

"It really is," Emry agreed.

"It is how it must be done. If you call to her, she will disappear," the witch cautioned. "She must not know that you are following her."

"This just gets worse," Arthur muttered. "Okay, so I stalk this maiden. What next?"

"Once you reach the fortress, you will meet a knight guarding the portcullis. To defeat him, you must strike only one blow. He will beg for more, but you must strike him only once. Any more, and he will defeat you."

"I don't have to kill him, do I?" Arthur asked uneasily.

"That is up to you," said Vivienne. "I have told you all I know of what awaits you on your quest."

She hadn't told them nearly enough. But it was a start, Emry thought. And a start was better than nothing. "Thank you," she said. "For helping us."

"It's the least I can do," said Vivienne, "since I'm responsible that Bellicent has access to your world."

Emry frowned, and so did Arthur. "I don't see how," he said.

Vivienne stirred her tea, staring into the depths of her mug as if reading her own tea leaves, though the cup was still full of liquid. "I sent your father to that cave, and told him how to defeat her. It was my plan that went wrong. My spell that twisted into a curse that put the entire world to sleep." She sighed. "It's for the best that I'm bound to solitude in these woods, for all the trouble I cause, seeing backward. Perhaps, if I hadn't interfered . . ."

"You mean if *I* hadn't agreed to a bargain I thought would save everyone, but instead became a curse," Merlin said, his voice full of anguish.

"Magic is the material from which curses are made," said Vivienne, sounding very much like the Lady of the Lake. "But the women of my family are uniquely cursed. We have too much fairy blood in our veins."

"I'm sorry," Emry said, "but did you say *fairy*?"

Vivienne nodded. "I did. Our magic is left over from the time when this world was ruled by the Fair Folk. It was used against humans, to enslave them. There has never been an age when man and magic have coexisted peacefully."

"Is Excalibur from the age of the Fair Folk?" Arthur asked, curious. Vivienne nodded. "But no one fears Excalibur," Arthur protested.

"Magical objects are less intimidating than magical beings," Vivienne told him. "They're more predictable. Though I've heard tell the villagers have become more fearful of any magic after Merlin's enchantment."

"They still don't know that was me," he said nervously.

"Us," Vivienne corrected. "The entire world fell asleep, and when they woke, no one could remember a thing. Crops had failed from neglect. Houses had collapsed from disrepair. Beasts like that griffin forgot to be afraid of men, and no longer kept their distance from villages. We were trying to help, but this world echoes with the ill effects of our help gone wrong."

"What we were trying to do was stop Bellicent," said Merlin.

"And we failed," said Vivienne. "But these two might yet succeed."

Emry hoped so. But she didn't see how. Not where so many others had tried without success.

"It's getting dark," said Vivienne. "You should head back."

Arthur went to fetch his sword.

"Are you going to be here when we return?" Emry asked her father. Before he said a word, she knew his answer.

"I have to restore my magic," he said. "And for that, I'll do whatever it takes."

"You're more than just your magic," Emry said.

He shook his head. "Perhaps I used to be, a long time ago. But I made my choices. I am only my magic. And without it, I'm not myself."

You're still my father, Emry wanted to remind him. *Magic or not.* But the expression he wore was so stubborn, and so determined, that she knew it would be no use. He had already decided what he would do. And it was beyond her to make him reconsider.

So she left him there, in Vivienne's cottage. In the world he had abandoned her for. And she wondered if he would ever choose the people who loved him, and how long it would be until she saw him again.

CHAPTER 43

Queen Bronwyn was as good as her word. In thanks for their slaying the griffin and rescuing the village children, she gave Arthur everything she'd promised and more. He and his friends left for the Four-Peaked Fortress the next morning on fine silver horses, their packs laden with provisions. Arthur rode in front, with Lance behind him, and Emry trailing behind.

Arthur didn't blame her for wanting some time to herself. He hadn't expected that Merlin would abandon them so quickly—that he truly had come only to recover his magic. But Emry had warned him her father cared only for himself. And he knew all too well what that was like.

So it was just the three of them, and Arthur found himself secretly pleased about the arrangement. It was rare that he got to spend much time alone in the company of his friends. Especially his best friend and his girlfriend.

"How did that ballad go again?" Lance mused. "Brave King Arthur swings his mighty sword . . ."

"And thus was the dread griffin gored," Emry finished. "Honestly, their bard is terrible."

"It's catchy, though," Lance said.

Arthur sighed. It *was* catchy. He had the chorus stuck in his head the rest of the way through the town.

When they reached the bridge, he saw two familiar figures waiting for them on horseback—Prince Tiernen and Sir Hafgan. They were dressed in their finest-spun tunics, with gold-plated armor and fashionable embroidered capes that flapped in the wind. Tiernen's arm was in a silk sling tied on over his armor.

"Are you here to see us off?" Arthur called, wondering why they were dressed as if for a fancy event.

"Of course not," said Tiernen. "We're coming with you."

Arthur hoped he didn't look as horrified as he felt. "Er, we have a map," he said, holding it up.

"A map is easily lost or confused," said Haf. "Besides, now that the griffin is no longer terrorizing the village, Prince Tiernen and I could use a vacation."

"We're not going to be sunning ourselves on the shore," Emry muttered, and Lance snorted.

"This is a quest, not a vacation," Arthur reminded them.

"It'll be great," Tiernen said enthusiastically. "You'll see."

Arthur's first clue that it would not, in fact, be great was when Tiernan and Haf insisted they stop for breakfast, and expected Emry to cook it, since, according to Tiernan, "women are suited to such domestic tasks."

Emry smiled sweetly at them, conjuring purple flames that danced up her arms. "If you're not used to food prepared by magic, it can wreak havoc on your stomach. So I hope you won't be too inconvenienced by explosive diarrhea."

Lance cackled, and Arthur pressed back a grin.

"Er, I think we'll just have some bread," said Prince Tiernen.

Arthur felt sorry for the prince. He certainly thought very highly of himself. But he seemed to be all bluster, without the skills to back it up.

After they'd finished their breakfast, Lance took care of their horses and Arthur gathered some berries he'd seen, which Haf assured him were edible. When he returned to the clearing with enough for everyone, Tiernen and Haf were engaged in a bout of swordplay. With

Tiernen's right arm in the sling, he clumsily wielded his weapon with his left.

Haf yawned into his fist as he parried, and Tiernen roared, lunging forward, unable to land a hit.

"This is horseshit!" the prince exclaimed, throwing down his weapon, and pouting like a child. "I can't even defend myself!"

"You could if you let me magic your arm better," Emry interjected. She was sitting under a tree, toasting a piece of bread against a magical purple flame that leapt from her palm.

"I'd prefer not to soil myself," Tiernen said, with as much dignity as he could manage.

◑ ◑ ◑

Arthur tried not to count the days that they rode, the time that slipped through his fingers until they would need to return home to face Yurien, either with the weapon they needed, or without.

He really hoped it wasn't going to be without.

After their third day, the forest started to turn colder, the trees stretched taller, and the mountains that had loomed so impossibly far in the distance were all around them.

"Nearly there," said Haf, which was good, since their supplies wouldn't hold out for much longer.

That evening, the forest gave way to a deep fog, and rising from the mist was a dark mountain. High upon it sat a shining castle with four peaks.

"The Four-Peaked Fortress," Lance said, grinning.

They had made it. Through the doorway to another world, and all the way to the place where the Lady of the Lake said they would find the one object that would help them defeat Yurien's army.

The fortress, or maybe the mountain itself, hummed with magic.

Arthur could feel it, could feel Excalibur pulsing at his side, as if dragging him the rest of the way.

"It's beautiful," said Emry. "Why is that somehow more terrifying than if it was hideous?"

Arthur rather agreed with her assessment. The place seemed to beckon to travelers, enticing him to ride there with haste. He turned to Prince Tiernan and Sir Hafgan. "You don't have to come with us."

"We weren't planning on it," assured the prince. "I just want to see it up close, then Haf and I are heading to the nearest village to get very drunk at a very nice inn."

Arthur rolled his eyes. As they rode, Lance drew his sword out of caution, but Arthur kept his sheathed. They continued toward the mountain that seemed to float in the mist. But the longer they walked, the more the mountain stayed firmly in the distance.

Arthur frowned, turning back to see if he could sight a familiar landmark, but he could see nothing beyond the mist. And when he turned forward, the mountain was just as far away as it had always been. "The mountain doesn't seem any closer," he said after half an hour.

"You're only realizing that now?" Emry said in frustration.

"I think we've passed that tree before," said Lance. "The one that sort of looks like a di—"

"Only one way to know for sure," interrupted Arthur, withdrawing his sword. Excalibur pulsed eagerly, and then sort of groaned when it realized what he had in mind. He slashed an X into the bark.

Ten minutes later, they passed the same tree again. It was beginning to grow dark.

"Sarding hell," Arthur swore.

"It's a ward," Emry pronounced. "That's what isn't letting us through. There's a ward around the fortress."

"The mound," Arthur said, remembering. "We can't get to the

fortress by ourselves. We have to be led, by the woman on the white horse."

"I bet you're right," said Emry.

And then Arthur thought of something else. "Vivienne warned me of my trials, but she didn't warn any of you. I think I'm supposed to do this on my own."

"Absolutely not," said Lance.

Emry frowned in thought. "Like when you got Excalibur."

"Exactly," Arthur said.

"We can wait in the village," the prince suggested. "Don't want the inn to run out of rooms."

Arthur sighed. Of course everyone else would get to sit around drinking ale and playing cards while he went off to procure some rare treasure through complicated trials.

"We'll save you a drink," Emry promised.

Arthur doubted he'd be back that evening, but he nodded anyway.

"Don't get into trouble," he told her.

"That's literally all I do," Emry pointed out.

"Well, don't get into a lot of it," Arthur amended.

They said their goodbyes, and then his company rode off in the direction of the town. He watched them grow smaller in the distance, and then he turned his horse toward the forest and went in search of the mound.

◐ ◐ ◐

The mound was there, just as the witch had said. Arthur tied up his horse, then sat upon the small hill, waiting. After an hour, he felt foolish and bored. He made a fire, toasted some bread for his supper, and laid out his bedroll. That night, he dreamed of monsters and mist, and when he woke in the gray dawn, his fire had gone out, and his shoulders were stiff.

Wait, the witch had said. And so he did. But still the maiden didn't come. Well, Vivienne didn't say he had to sit there doing nothing, he reasoned, so he took one of the books he'd brought out of his pack.

He was so engrossed in the story of the lovesick pirate captains that he almost missed the sound of hoofbeats.

He looked up just in time to see a beautiful flame-haired maiden seated upon a white horse ride past. It took everything in him not to call out to her. Instead, he mounted his own steed, and followed silently after her through the wood.

They rode for hours, and Arthur worried that perhaps she wouldn't take him to the fortress at all. It had looked like less than a half hour's journey from the mound. Perhaps he should call out to her, to make sure she was going to the fortress.

He raised a hand and was about to speak when his sword gave an insistent pulse and he came to his senses. Vivienne had told him to be quiet, and he had almost gotten it wrong.

Too much rested on his ability to get the horn. So he pushed on, that annoying ballad running through his head repeatedly, until finally, the fortress loomed ahead.

The woman rode closer and closer to the mountain upon which the castle sat, and Arthur wondered if she lived there. But at the last moment, she turned her horse back toward the woods.

Arthur saw a narrow path lined with vines that led up to the fortress. Well. He'd succeeded in the first part of the witch's instructions. He urged his horse up the hill, reaching a stone wall with a drawbridge that lay open across a foul-looking moat.

But a knight stood blocking the bridge.

No, not exactly a knight, for it was taller than any man by at least a head, and behind its visor there was no face, only darkness and glowing red eyes.

It was just an enchantment, he told himself. But that didn't do anything to extinguish his growing flicker of fear. He slid from his horse, reaching for his sword with a trembling hand. "I don't want to fight," Arthur said. "Will you let me pass?"

The enchanted knight raised its own blade. "I will not," it declared, its voice metallic and far too loud, as if coming from the armor itself. "You may not cross until I have been bested in combat."

Arthur nodded at the enchanted knight. "Very well. I will fight you. What are the terms?"

"Land a hit, and I step aside. Take a hit and keep going, as long as you can."

That sounded fair enough. Ominous, but fair. "Agreed," said Arthur.

"Good," said the knight. "Then pick up the sword leaning against that tree, and fight."

Arthur hoped he'd misheard. But when he looked at the tree the knight had indicated, he saw a rusted and ancient blade that looked as if it might snap in half if he landed a hit. He wondered if it was even sharp. "Can't I use my own sword?" he asked.

"You agreed to the terms. You did not ask which sword you would use."

Arthur supposed it was technically correct. So this was the trick of it. He grimly sheathed Excalibur and picked up the flimsy blade. "En garde."

He raised his weapon and moved cautiously forward, testing the knight's strengths and weaknesses. Before he could extend his arm for a hit, the knight bore its blade down, slamming him on the shoulder.

The pain was blinding. Arthur gasped, staggering back, somehow managing to keep his grip on his weapon.

He couldn't breathe. He could barely remain standing. The fight was unfair—he could see that now. The knight had far more reach with its longer sword arm and could land a hit far before Arthur's was in range to do the same. And its strength!

Arthur darted to the side, feinting a hit. The knight sidestepped, armor clanging. It was slow. Slow Arthur could use. Slow he could best.

He narrowed his focus until it was solely on the tip of his blade, on his footwork, on the breastplate of his opponent, and then the real fight began.

It wasn't easy. He took another hit to the shoulder that left him crying out in pain, and narrowly avoided a deadly hit to the chest. He stumbled back, lost his footing, and stared up at the knight from the ground, prone.

"Had enough?" the knight asked, raising its blade above its head with both hands.

"Not quite," said Arthur, pushing to his feet.

He could do this. He *would* do this.

He raised his blade again and darted forward quickly—but not quickly enough. The knight parried, blocking his blow and sending him reeling. When he regained his balance, the knight was on top of him, sword raised.

Desperate, Arthur raised his weapon as well, and then, at the last moment, brought it around counterclockwise.

Clang! It echoed off the knight's suit of armor.

He didn't breathe as he waited to see what would happen.

"You have landed a hit," said the knight. Its blade dropped to the ground, and its glowing eyes faded. "I am defeated. Finish me and claim your victory."

"You said all I needed to do was land a hit," said Arthur, sensing another trick.

"Please," begged the knight. "I am defeated. Let me have an honorable death in combat. If you do not, I will die here, of shame."

Arthur was pretty sure the knight was a bunch of magic in an enchanted suit of armor, and couldn't actually die, or have feelings, but it seemed rude to say so. "Perhaps you could take up a different profession?" he suggested. "There's a lovely maiden who rides through these woods, who I'm sure could use a brave knight to escort her."

The suit of armor actually appeared to consider it. "No," it said finally. "Just kill me."

Honestly, it was starting to sound like that horrible gargoyle.

"I refuse," Arthur said. For good measure, he threw down his blade.

The knight straightened. "You may pass," it said, and then it fell apart.

The helmet rolled to a stop at Arthur's feet. He stared down at it for a moment. Then he crossed the drawbridge on foot, entering the Four-Peaked Fortress.

CHAPTER 44

Lance pressed the tip of his sword to Haf's throat. He had won their sparring match, which he could scarcely believe. And he hadn't flinched once.

"I am beaten," declared Haf, dropping his blade.

"You made a worthy opponent," Lance assured him, offering a hand to help the knight up.

Haf took it, and clapped Lance on the back. "You show great skill. You and Arthur must be quite a hit with the ladies."

Emry fell all over herself laughing.

"What's funny?" Prince Tiernen asked. He'd sulked through the entire sword fight, clearly wishing he could challenge Lance himself.

Lance shot a warning look at Emry. He was fairly certain that these two lads wouldn't be as friendly if they knew he was courting a boy. He'd met plenty of their type before. The kind who laughed the loudest and told the raunchiest jokes and acted as though being emotionally vulnerable was a crime and being different was contagious.

"Arthur never notices when women throw themselves at him," Emry said instead. "I used to think he was doing it on purpose."

"He's actually that oblivious," Lance confirmed, relieved she'd steered the conversation so deftly away from his own love life. "And I did have a bit of a reputation as a flirt, but that's in the past. I'm courting someone now."

"I'd expect no less," said Tiernen. "King's champion *and* champion of the ladies."

"Er, sure," Lance said diplomatically.

"If you won't take your pleasure with our fair courtiers when we return to Pennard, then perhaps you'd want to train with us?" Haf suggested.

Lance brightened. "Truly?" he said. He'd watched the knights running drills in the bailey when his friends had gone off to the witch's cottage, and he'd never seen anything like it.

"We saw you watching us," Tiernen said. "Wasn't exactly subtle."

"Back home, knights train their squires individually," Lance explained. "We don't work as units—that's something the guard does. I'm curious about the strategy."

"Then learn it, and bring it home to your men," said Haf.

Lance frowned. "My men?"

"You said you're the king's champion. Surely you command his knights."

Lance supposed he did, technically. Not that he thought they'd listen if he tried to give orders. Between the older knights who sat on the royal council, and the general of Camelot's army calling the shots, it felt more like a courtesy title than part of his role. "I guess," he said.

"The king's champion," mused Sir Hafgan. "I wish we had such a title."

"If we did, it would go to your father," said Tiernen.

Haf sighed. "I believe you're right."

"That's why we call him Haf," Tiernen said to Emry and Lance.

"Because you already have a Sir Hafgan?" Emry asked.

"Because he's half as good as the one we already have," said Tiernen, his eyes dancing with mischief.

"Rescind that statement, sir, or face your justice at the end of my blade," said Haf.

"Can't," Tiernen said smugly. "I'm injured, it wouldn't be fair."

"Oh, I could take care of that," Emry offered. "I'll have you in fighting shape in two seconds. And it wouldn't hurt a bit."

Tiernen seemed to actually consider it. "I am rather sick of this sling," he mused.

"A moment?" Lance begged, and then dragged Emry aside. "You can't mend his arm," he whispered. "You don't have control of your magic here."

"Then I should probably practice on someone other than you and Arthur," Emry replied. "What if he returns injured? I'd rather Tiernen be my test subject, wouldn't you?"

Lance sighed, hating that he saw the logic in it. "Fine," he replied. "Just—don't turn his arm into a sword."

"That thought had never occurred to me, and now I don't know how to get rid of it, so if I do, it's your fault," Emry replied with a grin.

Lance shook his head. Honestly, between her and Arthur, he was practically babysitting. They both had the same annoying knack for never taking anything fully seriously, especially the things they should.

"Should be fine," Lance said, turning back to the two lads. "She's done it to me loads of times."

Tiernen still seemed torn, but Haf asked curiously, "You let a witch use magic on you?"

"Not a witch," Emry corrected tiredly. "A royal court wizard from another world. And you don't have to tell anyone I used magic. You can say you fell in an enchanted lake full of healing waters."

"Anyone would believe you fell in a lake," Haf said, and Tiernen glared at him. He hastily added, "While riding injured, and wielding your sword against a fierce assailant."

"We could make it more plausible and actually push you into a lake afterward," Emry suggested, not entirely joking. Lance's shoulders shook as he held back laughter.

"You forget yourself, witch. I am a prince of this realm," said Tiernen, raising his chin.

"And I can turn your nipples into bees," Emry replied. "Whenever I want. Without saying a word."

Tiernen paled.

"They would just randomly be bees," Emry went on, warming to the idea. "And I'd act like I didn't know anything about it."

"Tell him you're joking before he faints," Lance urged.

"Fine." Emry sighed. "I've never turned anyone's nipples into bees. Or anything else. Yet."

"I suppose regaining use of my arm is worth the diarrhea." Tiernen sniffed. Emry laughed, and Tiernen's eyes narrowed as he realized. "That was never a real thing, was it?"

"Nope." Emry grinned. "No side effects whatsoever."

Tiernen removed his sling. "Then you may heal me," he pronounced grandly.

Emry frowned, thinking. And then she took out her dagger and slashed a cut into her palm. Purple flames danced on top. "*Uruz,*" she said.

Lance had never heard her use that spell before. Not for healing. But he knew better than to question it. The flames leapt to Tiernen's arm, encircling it. Then they faded, and the prince grinned.

"I say, that's much better," he marveled.

Emry caught Lance's eye, and he nodded in encouragement. "All right there?" he asked.

"Fine," she said, grinning. "It was easy." Easy was good. Easy meant if anything happened to any of them, she could take care of it.

"Well, grab your sword," Tiernen told Lance. "Now we can spar."

"Another time," Lance said. He was fairly certain the prince was no great swordsman, and he didn't want to deal with the man being a sore loser.

"It's really healed?" Haf said, examining his friend's arm with interest.

Tiernen gave a lunge and a twist of his sword against an invisible assailant. "Really healed."

Haf turned to Emry. "What else can you do?"

"Loads of things," said Emry.

"She made suits of armor come to life to defend the castle when we were under attack," said Lance.

"From another sorceress?" Tiernen asked.

Lance shook his head. "From Arthur's uncle. He staged a siege on the day of the royal wedding."

"I did not realize your king was married," said Tiernen.

"Oh, he's not. His bride ran off with my brother," said Emry, and Tiernen choked.

"Dodged a blade with that one," said Lance. "Arranged marriages should be illegal."

"I disagree." Tiernen sniffed. "I love my wife deeply. It just . . . took some time for her to love me back. But now we couldn't be happier."

Haf looked as if he wanted to sink into the ground. "I hope that one day I find half the love and happiness that you have."

"Kiss enough frogs and you'll find your princess," Tiernen told him.

"Who said anything about a princess?" Haf replied, looking panicked.

"It's just an expression," said his friend, clapping him on the back obliviously as the others looked somewhere, anywhere else.

◐ ◐ ◐

Emry was surprised when Sir Hafgan sought her out after supper. The man was clearly deep into his cups and had lost enough rounds of cards that his mood had turned from jovial to melancholy.

"Ah, the wizardess from the other world," he said, easing himself down onto the tavern steps next to her. "What are you doing out here?"

"The constellations," Emry said. "They're different than back home."

Sir Hafgan frowned up at the sky. "You don't have the little dragon and great dragon?"

"We don't have any dragons at all," Emry said. She tilted her head, trying to figure out which stars in the bright scatter he was talking about. "Which are the dragons?"

Haf pointed. "Those. With the brightest stars at the tail."

"Huh," Emry said. "Never would've thought dragons. I'll have to tell Arthur."

Haf stared out into the darkness and sighed. "The way you two look at each other. Reminds me of how things used to be with the girl I loved, many years ago."

"You mean Princess Rhiannon?" Emry guessed.

The young knight looked stricken. "How did you—"

"It's obvious," Emry said. "You still look at each other like that."

"I try not to," said Haf, sounding miserable. "He's my best friend. She's his wife. And her little boy . . ." Haf trailed off, shaking his head.

"He's very, er, blond," Emry said.

"I know," Haf said. He put his head in his hands. "Tiernen is a fool not to see it."

"Or perhaps he's a loyal friend, who hopes you'll do the right thing," Emry suggested.

"I try." Haf hiccuped drunkenly. "But no matter how much I strengthen my sword arm, my heart remains weak."

Sard, he was practically spouting poetry. Emry gave him a reassuring pat on the shoulder. "You can't blame yourself. She's just as guilty as you are. Worse, since she's the one who's married."

"Not by her choice. They met on their wedding day." He stared up at the constellations, as if searching for an answer. "We both fell in love with her. But she was already his wife."

"The obvious solution here is that you marry someone else and get over her," said Emry. "Why haven't you?"

"Because even if I did marry, I would never get over her," he swore. And then he turned toward her, his eyes alight with excitement. "Unless . . . would you know a spell that would make me forget I ever loved her?"

Sard. That was an ask.

"Sir Hafgan—" Emry began.

"Please," he forged on. "I can't go on like this. None of us can. You could save us from this doomed love affair."

Emry shook her head. "I can't take your memory from you. Spells like that—they're no good. They're just as likely to snap back and take my memory instead."

Haf sighed. "It would be so much simpler if we could choose who we love and marry them if they feel the same."

Emry let out a hollow laugh. That was exactly how she felt about Arthur. "You'll be all right," she told him. "Just—keep your trousers on. And your eyes fixed elsewhere."

"I shall try," he promised.

CHAPTER 45

The Four-Peaked Fortress was eerily quiet. Arthur had expected guards, even of the enchanted variety, but there was no one.

The place gave the impression of being abandoned. Yet candles flickered in wall sconces, dripping wax into puddles on the floor. But there were cobwebs everywhere, the tapestries thick with dust, and the suits of armor rusted and in disrepair.

"Hello?" Arthur called, his voice echoing against the stone walls, then felt foolish. Perhaps he shouldn't have announced his presence, he thought, remembering the red-eyed knight. But no one answered, and he heard no footsteps of anyone coming to meet him. He wished Vivienne had given him more instructions.

He took out Excalibur just in case there were any more enchanted suits of armor lying in wait, the sword pulsing in his hand. When he crossed to a window, the sword's pulse grew fainter. He paused, frowning. Was the sword trying to guide him?

"By all means, lead the way," he told the blade.

It glowed ferociously in response, and practically tugged him up a staircase he hadn't seen before, which was a twisting, narrow thing made of bone-white marble.

Up he went, higher than he would have thought possible. Finally, he stumbled dizzily into a chamber occupied by a beautiful maiden. Her golden hair fell in waves down to her waist. She wore a simple white dress and matching slippers, and she seemed to be about sixteen. She sat upon a stool by the tower's only window, weaving a tapestry at a large loom. The tapestry was elaborate and skilled—

a portrait of herself in a small boat, floating down a river strewn with flowers. Propped at her side was a looking glass.

She did not turn when he entered. She wore a glazed expression, as if she did not weave from desire, but out of compulsion.

Arthur hesitated, not wanting to get too close, in case an enchantment might trap him as well. Finally he stepped forward. "Hello," he said politely. "Sorry to interrupt, but you're the first person I've found since I got here. I'm, er, looking for Bran Galed?"

The girl turned and stared. She seemed to come out of her trance all at once. She blushed and smiled demurely when she saw him. "Sorry, I cannot help you. But perhaps you can help me."

"How?" he asked.

"Set me free," begged the maiden.

"Are you a prisoner here?" Arthur frowned, hoping Bran Galed didn't keep teenage girls locked in towers. He didn't exactly want to ask a favor of a man like that.

"I am trapped," she said. "My father traded one of his treasures for my safety, and now I cannot leave."

"Is your father Bran Galed?" Arthur asked.

The maiden nodded. "He wished for me to keep my innocence, and so I know nothing of the world. I used to love to weave, but now my joy has become a misery, and my misery a prison. I may only set down my weaving and leave this place to go to my own wedding."

"Ah," Arthur said, taking a step back. "That's a shame."

"The spell has kept me a maiden at this age for a long time. You are the first brave knight to come in many years. The last was married and ancient. And he had a mole with a hair growing out of it. The kind that makes your fingers twitch with the urge to pluck it."

Arthur bit back a laugh. "I assume you didn't tell him of your problem."

"I pretended I could not speak," she said. "But you're handsome enough. And young, for a knight."

"I'm not a knight," said Arthur, annoyed that everyone thought he was.

"A prince, perhaps?" the girl said, perking up.

"I'm a librarian," Arthur lied.

"Oh. Books." She didn't seem enthused. "Maybe you could go off and tell a handsome knight to come instead. I prefer blonds."

Arthur rolled his eyes. She would. "I can do that," he said. "But I'm not leaving without one of your father's treasures. So perhaps we might help each other."

"Ugh, fine," the girl said, sounding far less fairy tale and far more like an annoying little sister. "That's the last time I try to hustle a *librarian.*"

Nettled, Arthur asked, "Where is your father?"

"In his lair, probably," said the girl. "Counting his gold coins or polishing his magic swords. Wait. You're not planning to steal the object you've come for? You're going to talk to him?"

"I'm no thief," Arthur said, offended. "I wouldn't take what isn't mine."

"Shame you're not a prince," the girl said. And then she told him where to find her father.

"Thank you!" Arthur called, backing out of the tower.

"Don't forget about my handsome blond knight!" called the maiden.

❶ ❶ ❶

Arthur's footsteps echoed through the empty castle until finally he came to the stone door the maiden had described. He pushed it open, stepping into a large banquet hall filled with cobwebs.

Hundreds of candles flickered on every available surface. Yet no pools or drips of wax marred any of the tables, and the candles stood tall, as if their wicks had just been lit. Enchanted, no doubt. At the center of the room was a long, rectangular table, and at the head of the table sat a weathered old man, a jeweled goblet in his hand.

He wore rings on every finger, and a fur cloak that fastened at one shoulder with a brooch made of diamonds. He was nearly bald, except for a few stray wisps of hair, and a long, thin beard. At first, Arthur thought the man was frozen, but then he lifted the cup and his gaze met Arthur's.

The man waited. Arthur stared, unsure what he was meant to do. And then he saw the bottle of wine on the table, and the pitcher of water.

"Pour a drink for an old man?" the man asked, his voice raspy from disuse.

Arthur reached for the wine, and then hesitated, unsure. He poured the water instead.

The old man lifted the cup to his lips and drank deeply.

"I know why you are here," he said. "You have come to steal my cauldron."

"I haven't come to steal anything. Certainly not a cauldron," Arthur said with a frown.

"My cloak, then."

"I already have a cloak," Arthur said, gesturing to his own, which wasn't looking so great after a few days riding through the forest.

"But not one that turns you invisible," said the old man.

Arthur was impressed. "You have a cloak that turns people invisible?"

"I have many treasures, as you well know, young knight."

"I'm not a knight," Arthur said patiently. "Or a thief. I'm sorry if those who have come before have been."

"You may apologize, but you are not sorry. You have come for your prize, like the others. And like them, you shall not have it."

"May I join you?"

"If you wish it," the old man grumbled.

Arthur sat. A feast had been laid a long time ago. Now it was bones and ash. Cobwebs and dust covered the plates. The silver was dull with tarnish.

"You do not seek my company," the old man observed shrewdly. "But you seek something I possess. You would not have followed the maiden or bested my knight if you did not."

"I don't just seek it, I need it," Arthur said. "I wouldn't have come if I wasn't desperate."

"Then you are not like most who have come before you, driven by greed," said Bran.

"I am not like any who have come before me," said Arthur.

"That I can tell from your sword." Bran nodded at the glowing blade hanging at Arthur's side. "For you already possess the greatest treasure, one that I have been seeking for a long time." The man leaned forward, his eyes glittering in the candlelight. "Anything I own is yours in trade, if you will give it to me."

Arthur's heart sank. "My sword?"

"No, boy!" said the knight, banging a fist upon the table. The plates rattled, and a goblet at the far end rolled onto the floor, disappearing beneath a tapestry. "Your scabbard!"

Arthur looked down. He wore a plain scabbard, as he always did, made of tooled leather with a steel buckle. It was entirely ordinary.

But Bran Galed didn't know that. He'd incorrectly assumed the scabbard Arthur wore was the one that had come with his blade, the one that rendered its wearer impossible to be killed. And Arthur's heart leapt at the man's error, because it gave him an idea.

"There is one thing I want," Arthur said.

"Name it."

"You have a magic horn that makes any who drink from it an ordinary mortal."

"That old thing?" The knight's bushy brows knit together. "Wouldn't you rather have my cauldron? That's the one everyone seems to want."

"Er, why is that?" Arthur asked, unable to help himself.

"Because it will bring back the dead."

Arthur choked. "I'm sorry—it does what now?"

"A man who is killed today and thrown in the cauldron will be restored to health by tomorrow, except he will not be able to speak. It is my greatest treasure."

Was it really? Arthur couldn't imagine what it must be like for dead men to come back to life, only to find they could not speak of what they had gone through.

"I would rather have the horn," said Arthur. "Do we have a deal?"

"We do," said the old knight, holding out a hand.

Arthur grasped hold of it, feeling Excalibur pulse nervously in his other hand.

Quiet, he thought.

"The scabbard first, boy," demanded the knight.

Arthur unbuckled his scabbard and held it out. The knight reached for it greedily, wrapping it around his own waist. "I shall be master of death," he declared, and then he frowned. "I don't sense any enchantment."

Arthur considered lying. But that wasn't fair. He didn't wish the old man any harm. "You wouldn't," he said. "It's not the scabbard that came with the sword. It's just a plain one."

All color drained from the old man's face. "You mean I agreed to trade my magic horn for an ordinary scabbard?"

Arthur shrugged. "It wasn't my idea. And you never asked."

"You've cheated me!" the man accused, jabbing a finger at Arthur's chest. "Thief! Liar!"

"You still owe me the horn," Arthur reminded him. "You promised."

The man's expression grew crafty. "Ah," he said. "I did. But I didn't say *when* I would give you the horn."

Arthur suddenly had a very bad feeling. "You wouldn't."

"Come back in twenty years," the knight snapped. "And then you shall have it."

Arthur didn't have twenty years. He doubted he had twenty days. "Surely I must have something else you would want," he said.

The old man stared pointedly at Excalibur.

"Not that," Arthur said quickly.

"You said you are not a knight," mused Bran Galed, "but your speech is fine, and your bearing noble. If you are no hero, then you must be a prince."

"I was," Arthur said. "Now, where I come from, I am king."

"Are you married?" Bran asked.

Arthur winced. "Er, no," he admitted.

"Then I shall give you my horn on the day you marry my daughter."

Arthur stared at the man in despair. "Marry your daughter?" he echoed.

"My Arden will make a good wife. And she will make a fine queen."

Arthur hesitated. He couldn't do it. His heart wouldn't allow him to say yes. The girl was a total stranger, and even worse, he would need to bring her back to his world, and there would be so many questions.

"To marry me would be a curse, not a gift," he said. "I am in love with another. And I live in a faraway kingdom that is currently at war.

If I took your daughter there, she would be in danger, and you would never see her again."

"I have a pair of boots that can step five leagues at a time," boasted the knight. "I can manage the distance."

"That won't help," said Arthur. "I've come here from another world."

"Another world?" The knight shook his head in awe. "I have heard of such places. Ones with too much magic, and ones with too little. Which is yours?"

"Too little," Arthur said.

The man shook his head again, as if this news disappointed him. "I cannot send my Arden to a world without magic, in a kingdom at war, to marry a man who loves another, so she might never see me again."

An idea occurred to Arthur. "I have a suggestion, Sir Bran. I am not a suitable husband, but I have met your daughter and I would like to help her."

"So she told you of her curse," Bran said. "I agreed to the terms to keep her safe. But I don't see how you can help."

"My companions and I are headed back to Castle Pennard, four days' journey from here."

"I know of it," said Bran.

"What if she came with us, where she might choose a husband for herself?"

"Choose a husband for herself," said the knight, brightening at the idea. And then he shook his head. "But it won't work. She may only leave this castle with the man who will marry her."

"Exactly," said Arthur. "With your permission, I will perform the ceremony, as is my right as king. I will 'marry' your daughter to the man she chooses."

After a moment's thought, the old man nodded. "Very well," agreed

Bran Galed, who seemed to appreciate Arthur's own craftiness. "She has ten days to find a husband. Marry them on the steps of the church in Pennard, and on their wedding day, I will give you my horn."

Arthur bowed. "It's a deal."

CHAPTER 46

Emry had resolved to go to the Four-Peaked Fortress herself if Arthur wasn't back in two days. By her second afternoon in the village, she was starting to grow impatient. The place was small and unimpressive, with little to do.

The boys had decided to spend the afternoon training, so she'd gone off to examine the goods in the market, not wanting to give them an audience for their bravado. Except the market wasn't nearly as interesting as she'd hoped. It reminded her of the small villages near where she had grown up, where the cleverest merchants hauled their wares to Brocelande's market instead of their own, knowing they'd fare better and could double the price. The theater troupe had traveled to such towns a few times, before learning that their custom was better earned elsewhere.

It was all so familiar, so mundane, that she could hardly believe they were in another world. A shepherd drove his woolly flock through the square. A red-cheeked woman with her hair beneath a scarf pumped well water into a bucket. Two children in homespun tunics ran barefoot, playing with toy swords as a dog barked at their ankles.

The only difference Emry could see was the thatch on their rooftops was black instead of the dun she was used to, and the sigil atop the church was a spoked wheel pierced through by an arrow. However, the market was just inside the town gates, which meant Emry spotted Arthur right away as his silver horse came through the gates.

"Are you buying that or not?" snapped the old woman selling necklace charms to ward off the evil eye.

"Not today," Emry said, putting down the one she was holding and rushing over to meet him. He didn't seem to be injured, which was a relief. But then he stopped his horse so another rider could pull up alongside him.

Emry stared at the beautiful girl on the cream-colored horse, who was gazing at the small town with its packed dirt roads and stone cottages and market carts as though she'd never seen anything more wonderful.

Arthur turned to her and said something. The girl beamed at him, blushing.

And Emry felt a flutter of jealousy. Who was this girl? Arthur was supposed to come back with a horn, not a . . . well, a maiden with golden hair and a heart-shaped face, who wore a traveling cloak of ivory-colored silk.

"Nice horn," Emry said, her voice dripping with sarcasm.

"Wh—Emry!" Arthur seemed glad to see her. He looked pleased. "Oh good, I was hoping we were in the right place. 'Aunt Matilda' led us here, but, well, it's a sword. So." Arthur shrugged.

That was when Emry noticed that his scabbard was gone, and he seemed to have wrapped Excalibur in a tea towel he'd tied to his belt. "What happened to—" she began.

"Not here," Arthur interrupted.

"Hello," said the maiden on the horse. "Are you one of the servants?"

Emry glared pointedly at Arthur. He tried to communicate something very long and confusing by opening his eyes wider, which Emry wasn't about to try deciphering.

"So this inn where everyone's staying," Arthur said. "Is it around here somewhere?"

"About a quarter of a league that way," Emry said pointing.

Arthur groaned. "Not leagues again."

"I love them. I'm referring to everything in fractions of leagues from now on, and no one can stop me," Emry proclaimed.

"Well, come on," Arthur said, offering her a hand. "Lead the way. I'll explain everything when we're with the others."

Emry swung up onto the horse behind him, wishing she was still wearing her trousers, since the dress she'd changed into made sitting astride difficult. But at least everyone in the village had stopped staring at her. Though they were certainly staring now. Silver horses tended to have that effect.

"Where do I hold on?" Emry asked.

"Me," Arthur said.

Emry wrapped her arms around his waist, and realized just how intimate it was, both of them straddling the same horse, her bodice pressed against his back, her hands clasped at his hips.

It was a short ride back to the inn, but Emry was keenly aware of every bump in the road, since she was jostled against Arthur.

When they got close, Emry spotted two figures shouting at each other down by the river that ran past the inn, and sighed. Lance appeared to be dueling Prince Tiernen.

"Um, I feel like we should go see about that?" she said.

"Probably a good idea." Arthur spurred his horse in their direction, unwrapping Excalibur from its tea towel. The sword lit up, its glow distracting the men from their duel.

"What's going on?" Arthur called.

"Best two out of three!" Tiernen called cheerfully. "Do you want to challenge the winner?"

So it wasn't anything serious. Emry was relieved. And Arthur seemed to be as well.

"Your arm is healed," he called, sliding from his horse.

"Your wizard fixed me up," said Tiernen, and Arthur looked shocked. "I suppose magic isn't all bad."

Emry grinned. "I've made a convert out of him."

Tiernen shrugged. "My judgment was misplaced," he agreed. "Magic is like a weapon. Neither good nor evil on its own."

"A wise belief," Arthur said.

"Who's that?" Lance asked, nodding his chin at the maiden who was still seated atop her ivory horse.

"Funny story," Arthur hedged. "And long. I'll tell you both later."

"Did you get the horn?" Emry asked him.

"Not yet," Arthur said tightly. "But I will. There's just one condition."

"He has to marry me," the girl said, sliding gracefully from her horse to join them.

Emry was certain she hadn't heard the girl correctly. "Excuse me?" she said, not at all amused. Surely Arthur wouldn't agree to something like that, especially after their last fight. The girl was beautiful, but she couldn't be older than sixteen. And Arthur was nineteen. And from a different world.

"Arden," Arthur said, his voice low with warning.

"Ugh, *fiiiiine*," the girl whined. "He has to perform the marriage ceremony to whichever painfully attractive knight or prince falls desperately in love with me."

Well, that was a completely different thing. Emry folded her arms across her chest. "Explain," she said.

Arthur ran a hand through his hair and told the most absurd story about fighting a suit of armor, and trading his plain old scabbard for a treasure, and still getting swindled. When he got to the part about breaking the girl's curse, Prince Tiernen took the girl's hand in his.

"I'm sorry you were cursed, fair maiden," he said, raising her hand to his lips. "But rest assured, my companions and I will do all we can to assist you."

Lance coughed, and Arthur rolled his eyes. Emry arched an eyebrow at the pompous prince. He'd actually called them his companions. *His*. He didn't even rank as a top-three member of their company, yet he was acting as if it was his own.

Royals. Honestly.

While Tiernen kissed the girl's hand, she giggled and blushed.

"He's married," Lance informed her. "He has a kid."

Arden scrunched her nose, noticeably less enthused. And then she turned to Lance. "You wouldn't happen to be either a prince or a knight, would you?"

"I'm a lowly servant," Lance said, bowing obsequiously to Arthur, who glared at him.

"Wait a minute," said Tiernen. "You're not a servant, you're a—"

"Bees," Emry threatened. Tiernen went pale and clamped his lips shut.

Just then, Sir Hafgan waded out of the river, shirtless, wearing only his wet, clinging trousers. He slicked back his golden hair with one hand. Water droplets actually glistened on his well-defined chest.

Emry stared. Lance stared. Hell, even Arthur stared.

Arden gasped. And then she let out a high-pitched giggle as Haf came over to join them.

"Hey, you're back," he said. "Got the horn?"

"No, but she has," Lance replied, nodding at Arden. Emry whacked him.

Arden eyed Haf appreciatively. "You didn't tell me you were traveling with such handsome companions," she coyly accused Arthur.

"I mean, it would be weird if I had?" said Arthur.

Haf stopped finger-combing his wet hair long enough to take in their new companion. "And who might this lovely young maiden be?"

The girl giggled again, lowering her eyes and dropping into a curtsey, but doing that thing with her elbows where the curtsey was really just an excuse to display her bosom. Some innocent maiden indeed.

"I am Lady Arden of the Four-Peaked Fortress, daughter of Sir Bran Galed," she said grandly. "I was trapped there under a curse, but now it is broken, so long as I find a suitable husband."

"Sir Hafgan the Younger," said Haf, with a bow.

The girl's eyes lit up. "You're a knight?"

"I am," he confirmed, reaching for her hand and lifting it to his lips. She squealed. "It tickles," she said.

"I'm growing a quest beard," he told her, scratching at his stubble. "They're very popular. But, er, I could shave it, if you prefer?"

"I'm not sure," Arden demurred. "Kiss my hand again, so I may form an opinion."

He did, his lips remaining on her skin so long this time that even Tiernen sensed something was up.

"Well?" Haf asked, his eyes locking with the maiden's. "What is your pronouncement, my lady?"

"You may grow your quest beard," she declared. "But only so long as it doesn't come in patchy."

Haf nodded gravely at her proclamation. "You said you've been under a curse?"

"I was trapped in a castle with nothing to do except clean. Which, I'm sorry, but no thanks. Oh, and my only entertainment was weaving tapestries," she said. "I have seen nothing of the world."

"Then I shall show you the world," Haf declared, offering his arm. "How about a tour of this village to start?"

"Yes, please!" said Arden, eagerly taking his arm.

"Aren't you forgetting something?" Emry asked.

Haf frowned, wondering what that might be. Emry snapped her fingers, and the cloth tunic he'd discarded beneath a nearby tree took flight, slapping him in the chest. "Your shirt."

◐ ◐ ◐

"I can't believe they're still not back," Tiernen said, lounging in their booth.

They were seated in the great room of the inn, eating rabbit stew and some sort of bread that came in braided loaves studded with seeds. It was delicious, but a seed was stuck in Tiernen's teeth, and no one quite had the heart to tell him.

"It's a good thing, right?" Lance said. "Quest complete, horn gained."

Arthur drummed his fingers against the table, thinking. "I'm not sure," he said. "Would Haf marry her? It doesn't sound as if he's interested in marriage."

Tiernen shrugged. "I don't see why not. He's my best friend, and he deserves to be happy. Besides, I've seen the way he looks at my wife . . ."

Arthur stiffened.

"As though he wishes he had a wife of his own," Tiernen finished.

Arthur breathed a sigh of relief. "Right. Yeah."

Either Tiernen was truly ignorant of what was happening between his best friend and his wife, or he was in denial. But Sir Hafgan the Younger was exactly what they needed right now.

"I believe I have seeds in my teeth," Tiernen announced petulantly, examining his reflection in a metal spoon. "Were none of you going to tell me?"

Everyone shrugged guiltily, and Lance muttered something incoherent.

"Honestly," the prince snapped, stalking off.

Once he was gone, Arthur sighed.

"You all right?" Emry asked.

"Fine," he said. "I just hate that the fate of our kingdom is in the hands of a himbo knight who can't stay away from his best friend's wife, and hinging on whether he'll marry a sixteen-year-old girl who spends her time weaving portraits of herself."

Emry burst out laughing. "When you put it that way."

Lance took out a deck of cards and shuffled them with a snap. "Anyone up for a distraction?" he inquired.

Arthur grinned. "I thought you'd never ask."

Tiernen returned when they were through their second round of cards, and by the time Haf and Arden arrived, red faced and grinning as though they had a secret, everyone was drunk and laughing and having a fantastic time.

"Sarding hell, what's all that?" Lance asked as Haf set down an armload of packages.

"I haven't been shopping *ever*," Arden said, as though this was a crime. "Surely if I'm to secure a husband, I can't frump around in an awful, shapeless gown."

Emry exchanged a look with Arthur. This girl was a handful. And she acted more like a princess than an actual princess.

She sat down with a sigh. "What is there to eat? Back home, we have a magic cauldron that is always full of the most delicious things."

"Here, we have stew," Arthur told her.

She pouted.

"But I could ask the innkeeper to prepare something else, if you'd like?" Sir Hafgan said hastily.

She brightened. "Could you? I'd like roast chicken and carrots glazed with honey, and for dessert, an apple-and-brambleberry pie."

Haf looked horrified. But he put on a brave face. "I'll go check."

When he returned, it was with a bowl of stew and a gorgeous-looking slice of berry pie sprinkled with sugar. "Best I could do," he said.

Arden beamed. "It's wonderful, Haffy!"

"Haffy?" Lance whispered. Emry elbowed him.

"You got *pie*?" Tiernen asked, scandalized. "How?"

Sir Hafgan went red. "Said it was for my pregnant wife, who had a craving."

Emry elbowed Arthur. "Go and do the same. I'll split it with you."

"Unfair," Tiernen complained.

Arthur disappeared, and then returned with an entire pie, looking smug. "Said it was my wife's birthday and I'd forgotten."

"I will murder you if you sing 'Happy Birthday,'" Emry told him.

They sang it anyway. She put her face in her hands as some of the drunker patrons of the establishment joined in. But after one bite of pie, she had to admit it was worth it.

Arden took a sip of ale, her eyes going wide. "Is there alcohol in this?" she asked excitedly.

"Very much," Emry told her. "So be careful."

The girl drank down her glass eagerly, and then reached for another. "I take it back about saying you were the most storybook maiden I'd ever met," Arthur murmured into Emry's ear.

A fiddler from the village turned up, taking his place in a corner and sawing away merrily at his instrument. Many got up to dance, and Arden, on her third drink, did as well, her cheeks flushed.

"Oh, come on!" she begged, tugging at Emry's arm.

"Not for all the ale in the village," Emry returned. The last thing she was going to do was put on a show for the drunken men who populated this tavern.

"I'll dance with you," Sir Hafgan said, leading the girl into the merriment and giving her a spin.

Within minutes, Arden was dancing with half the lads in the village, her hips swaying, her loose cream-colored gown having fallen from one shoulder, leaving it bare. Her hair twirled around her shoulders, and she giggled at all the attention.

For a girl who'd spent decades under a curse, she sure could drink. And dance.

"We could join them," Arthur suggested quietly.

They did. The dancing wasn't stuffy, like it was at court, with set steps and people watching if you made a mistake. It was wild and carefree. Arthur was adorably awkward and laughed at himself when he realized he had no idea what he was supposed to be doing.

"Oh my god, you're hopeless," Emry scolded. "You have to move your hips."

"I am," Arthur insisted.

"Not like that!" Emry put her hands on his waist to show him, and suddenly they were standing very close, in each other's arms, in a crowded tavern. Emry's heart was beating way too fast, but she didn't take her hands off his hips.

They danced. Not to any pattern, but to the beat of the music, and to how it felt to be young and off on an adventure with unexpected pie.

"I have a room key," Emry murmured when they stopped to catch their breath.

"Do you?" Arthur looked extremely interested.

"But I'm pretty sure I'm supposed to play chaperone to that annoying maiden you brought back instead of a horn."

Arthur shrugged. "Who needs chaperones on a quest?"

Emry reached for his hand and pulled him off the dance floor. "That," she said, "is an excellent point."

CHAPTER 47

They left early the next morning, traveling with the rising sun. Emry had changed back into her trousers and tried to pretend she didn't notice Arden staring at her. She also pretended not to notice that the girl had changed into a frilly peach dress with ribboned sleeves, and dabbed tinted salve onto her lips.

She was wearing makeup. For riding a horse through the woods.

But as Sir Hafgan drew his horse alongside the girl's and regaled her with tales of his derring-do and bravery, Emry realized that perhaps Arden wasn't dressed for their quest, but for her own. As silly as the girl was, she had absolutely captivated the eligible young knight. Emry doubted Sir Hafgan would give much attention to Princess Rhiannon upon his return. Perhaps that meant everything would be all right between the prince and his best knight.

Emry couldn't believe she'd actually grown to care about them in such a short amount of time. But she had the strangest feeling that, so long as everything worked out for Tiernen and Hafgan, it might do the same for them as well.

They stopped for lunch by a stream with cool running water, letting the horses graze, and having a contest of skipping stones. Emry cheated, making her stones dance in intricate patterns across the top of the river, and Tiernen sulked about it.

"Ohhhhh, look at the bunny," Arden cooed, crouching down and holding out her hand. "Hello, little bunny-wunny. Who's a pretty little baby?"

The creature hissed, baring sharp little teeth.

"What's wrong, little bunny? Are you hungry?" Arden went on, getting closer.

"That's not a bunny, it's a questing beast!" said Tiernen, flinging himself behind a tree.

"A questing beast?" Haf repeated, stepping back into the clearing and adjusting his trousers in a way that made it clear he'd just done his business in the woods. "Oh, hell!" He darted behind a tree as well, pressing his back to it and breathing hard.

"Am I missing something?" Lance said, frowning at the small fuzzy creature, and at the two men hiding behind trees in terror.

"It looks quite harmless," Arthur added.

"That's what it wants you to think," Tiernen said, gripping his sword so hard that his hand was shaking.

Emry remembered what the Lady of the Lake had told her about such a creature, a long time ago. "Its blood can bring someone back from a freshly dug grave, but its bite is a pain worse than any mortal wound," she recited.

"Arden," Arthur called. "Get back! The creature isn't safe!"

"Of course it is. Aren't you, little sweetie?" she crooned. "Do you want to be my very special pet?"

"It's mesmerized her!" Tiernen said in horror. "They get in your head and draw you near. Quick, think of something else so it doesn't get you, too."

"Like what?" Lance asked.

"Ninety-nine casks of ale at the inn, ninety-nine casks of ale . . ." Tiernen started to sing, loudly and off-key. Lance gave a shrug and joined in as all the while Arden inched closer to the creature, her expression blank.

Arthur drew his sword and stepped forward. But Haf knocked him out of the way, rushing past him with his own blade raised.

"I'll save you, fair maiden!" he cried, stepping in front of her and brandishing his sword at the creature.

It hissed again, rearing back, displaying teeth that had lengthened into wicked fangs. It no longer looked cute or innocent. It looked savage.

Please don't harm him, Emry thought. The creature swiveled in her direction.

You, it replied in her head, its voice high-pitched and lilting. *You rescued my brother when he was stuck in the other world.*

Then repay me by leaving my friends alone, Emry thought.

The questing beast closed its mouth and sat back, blinking at Hafgan. And then it bounded away.

"There," Haf said, helping Arden to her feet. "Scared it off."

"You can stop singing now," Lance told Tiernen, who had reached ninety-two casks of ale, to no one's delight.

Arden frowned. "What happened?"

"You were mesmerized by a terrible beast, but Sir Hafgan saved you," said Tiernen.

Arden gasped and threw her arms around Haf. "My brave knight!" she proclaimed. "You saved my life!"

"I did." Haf puffed out his chest. "Because rescuing fair maidens is what I do."

Arthur made a disgusted noise and sheathed his sword in his tea towel with as much dignity as he could muster.

Arden was beaming at Sir Hafgan, and he was beaming back, and the rest of the way back to Pennard, the two of them were revoltingly inseparable.

◐ ◐ ◐

Four days later, they reached the bridge that led toward the now-familiar village. The sun was setting in the distance, painting the river in shades of gold. The guards only gave a passing glance at their weapons before hurrying them through with respectful salutes.

"Ugh," Prince Tiernen complained. "Is that all? I was hoping for fanfare."

"There's still a chance when we reach the castle," Haf said consolingly. Tiernen perked up at that.

The town felt different this time, Emry noticed. The people seemed happier. Less afraid. But then, they weren't being terrorized by a magical beast any longer, and the children it had taken had returned home unharmed.

"How wonderful," Arden said, staring wide-eyed at the children playing in the streets, the sellers hawking their wares, and a young couple wrapped in an amorous embrace around the back of the inn.

"It's home," said Haf.

The villagers waved merrily at them, some bowing when they noticed Prince Tiernen, and the returning party all waved and smiled back.

"You know," Arthur said, pulling his horse alongside Emry's as they rode up the steep lane to the castle gates, "I believe we actually helped these people."

"Of course we did," Emry said. "We literally saved the village. Or have you forgotten the words to our ballad?"

"I'm begging you not to—"

"King Arthur rode out on a fine silver steed," Emry began.

"Stop!" Arthur insisted. "The song is ridiculously inaccurate. We set out on foot."

"I guess the bard thought it sounded more poetic for you to have a silver steed," Emry said.

"The details don't matter," Lance said, joining them. "The point is, the three of us helped people, like in an adventure story. The clever king, his brave knight, and his talented wizard."

"That's right," Arthur said, sounding surprised. "I didn't need my advisors to help me through it or tell me not to bring you along. I just followed my instincts, and with the two of you at my side, I knew what to do."

"Does this mean when we get back, you're going to dissolve the royal council?" Emry asked hopefully.

Arthur shrugged. "We'll see."

But he couldn't get the thought out of his head that, if he could do all this with just a sword, his wits, and his friends, then perhaps Sir Tor wasn't wrong—perhaps he could defeat Yurien and be the king his people needed.

◐ ◐ ◐

Tiernen got his fanfare when they approached the castle. As the portcullis raised, trumpets sounded, announcing his arrival. His family gathered on the steps to greet him, and so did an unexpected yet familiar figure.

"Father!" Emry said, sliding from her horse and rushing into his arms. "I thought you'd already left."

"I meant to," he said. "But I couldn't. Not without making sure you were all right. So I waited for you to come back."

It was the best thing he'd ever said. Emry hugged him even tighter. "I'm so glad you did," she told him. "But how did you know we were coming back today?"

"Vivienne," he said.

Emry bit back a smile. "And how is the Witch of Silverwood Forest?"

Her father looked entirely too pleased with himself as he said, "She seems to have enjoyed my visit."

Emry just bet she had.

They recounted the tale of their quest over supper, where Sir Hafgan sat next to Arden, the two of them never taking their eyes off each other.

Princess Rhiannon seemed relieved to see Haf so besotted, but even so, Emry saw the woman was anxiously twisting the fabric of her skirts beneath the table. No doubt she was desperate to slip away with Haf and discuss this unexpected development.

Thankfully, Prince Tiernen seemed to notice none of the tension. He kissed his wife and swung his young son around in his arms while the boy giggled and shrieked, and the queen, when she met Emry's gaze, nodded in approval.

When the minstrels began to play, they started with "The Ballad of King Arthur and the Griffin," which made Arthur put his head in his hands and blush while Emry and Lance gleefully shouted the chorus. There were dancing and tiny cakes filled with jam and dusted with sugar, and upon Tiernen's urging to show his son some magic, Emry enchanted a dish of whipped cream to float across the table to whomever called for it.

After a while, Emry noticed that her father had quietly left the table.

"He's in the study," said Princess Rhiannon.

"Thanks," said Emry, who went off to find him.

The study was cast in dim light, the candles burning low, and the fire in the grate little more than embers. Merlin sat hunched over a chessboard, a glass of wine at his elbow. He looked up when Emry entered, as though he'd been expecting her.

"Come, sit. Tell me what move you would make, in my position," he said, gesturing toward the chessboard.

Emry pulled up a chair next to him, accidentally knocking into the table. One of the pieces that was out of play, a black pawn, rolled out of sight.

"*Raidho*," she mumbled, tracing the rune with her hand. The fallen chess piece obligingly flew into her palm, and she set it back on the table. "Is it far?" she asked. "The cave where you lost your magic?"

Her father shrugged. "Three days' ride. Do you have to form the rune as well as speak its name for your spells to work here?"

Emry was taken aback by the question. "I'm not sure," she said.

"Try one just with the command, and another just with the motion," her father said, dropping a captured chess piece to the floor. A white knight.

Emry stared down at the carved figure. "*Raidho*," she said, holding out her hand. The chess piece leapt into her palm.

"Again," said her father, this time dropping a scattering of pawns to the floor. "Silently, this time."

Emry traced the three lines of the rune, concentrating on the closest pawn. It floated up and landed gently in her palm. "Should I try the others all at once, in the same way?" she asked.

"Not yet," said her father, steepling his fingers. He looked far more interested than she'd seen him in a while. "Tell me what was different when you cast the rune rather than commanding it."

Emry frowned. Had something been different? "I'm not sure."

"Speed," her father said. "Your accuracy remained, but the magic responded much slower."

She thought back. "You're right," she said. "It was slower."

"So if you need your magic to act quickly, you know which spellcasting to choose. And if you need to perform a spell without anyone knowing, you know what to do."

Emry grinned. Her father had never spoken to her like this. To her brother, sure. But she couldn't remember the last time he'd given her magic lessons. Just her. Not lessons meant for her brother, that she was grudgingly allowed to join. Her heart ached with how wonderful it was to be sitting there with him, in the dim library, experimenting with magic.

"Do you think if I practice, I might be able to speed up my silent spellcasting?" she asked.

Her father drummed his fingers on the table, considering. "It's worth a try," he said. "I don't believe I've ever asked you this, but what's your limit?"

Emry felt tears prick at the corners of her eyes at the question. It was one Master Ambrosius had asked her on her very first day at Castle Camelot, back when he'd thought she was her brother. Back when she'd wanted to learn magic more than anything, and had thought she'd never be given the chance.

A tear spilled down her cheek, and she wiped it away.

"Oh, sweetheart," her father said, reaching his hand across the table and placing it over her own. "What's wrong?"

"It's silly." Emry sniffled, shaking her head. "It's just—the last time someone asked me that question, it was Master Ambrosius."

"He taught you well," Merlin said.

"Thank you," Emry said, surprised by the compliment.

"He meant for you to be his successor," Merlin went on. It wasn't a question.

Emry nodded. "That very first day, in the workshop, he knew I wasn't my brother. But he taught me anyway. Alongside Arthur."

"Arthur was learning magic?" Her father's brows lifted in surprise.

"Herbs," Emry corrected. "Tonics, curatives, that sort of thing. Master Ambrosius taught us both the medicinal preparations and taught me the potions."

"I never knew that." Merlin leaned back in his chair with a considering look.

"Arthur and I were lab partners," Emry went on. "Then companions on a quest to Avalon, while he still thought I was a boy. Then he stabbed me and found out the truth. But nearly as soon as he did, I saved his life with a poison antidote."

Merlin grimaced. "I had imagined it differently," he said, "how you got to be so close."

"You imagined we got drunk and I threw myself into his bed," she said dryly.

"Emry!" Her father was aghast.

"You did," she said with a shrug. "You never even asked. You just assumed I'd made an embarrassment of myself at court. And to answer your question, I haven't found my limit. I think I'm magic all the way down."

"You may be right about that," said her father, picking up his wineglass and draining it.

He reached for the bottle, only to discover it empty as well. He sighed. "I suppose if I got another bottle . . ." He raised an eyebrow.

"Then you could bring a glass for me as well," Emry confirmed. She studied the chess set while he was gone. It was a complicated game, one where both sides obviously knew what they were doing. Her father played the white set, and since it was his move, she came up with a strategy to back their opponent into a corner. She imagined it in her head, and then moved his bishop, just to make sure she had it right.

To her surprise, the black castle shot forward, taking one of her pawns. It was a move she'd anticipated, but she hadn't expected the board to move on its own.

"Fine, but I'm getting one of yours in exchange," she warned, taking her father's seat and capturing one of the black pawns with her knight. "Check."

She was so engrossed in the game that she hardly noticed her father's return.

"Queen's sacrifice," he suggested, peering at the board.

"Shhh," Emry said, flapping a hand at him. "What if the board can hear you?"

"It can't anymore," her father said fondly. "I took that enchantment off it after King Arawen caught it eavesdropping."

"A shame. An eavesdropping chessboard sounds useful," Emry deadpanned.

Her father laughed. "I said the same thing." He studied her the same way she had studied the chess set. "It's getting late. Shall I let you finish your game?"

She hated the idea of him leaving. Of this moment between them ending for good. "And deny me your judgmental commentary?" she asked, in mock affront. "Pour some wine and have at me."

Her father did. After Emry had won the game against her invisible opponent, her father yawned and stretched. "That's a night for me," he said.

She figured she had nothing to lose by asking: "I was hoping you could teach me some magic tomorrow."

"What kind of magic?" her father asked.

"The kind I'll need when I accompany Arthur to fight King Yurien's army."

His lips thinned. She half expected him to refuse. To say a battlefield was no place for his daughter, or for any woman. To try and talk her out of it. Or to say he didn't plan on sticking around past dawn.

But he did none of those things. Instead, he said, "Meet me in the bailey tomorrow morning."

CHAPTER 48

"Focus," Merlin warned as Emry gritted her teeth, struggling to maintain the ward.

They were in the gardens behind the stables. Emry closed her eyes, smelling the hay and horses, and feeling the heat of the late-morning sun. Listening to the birds in the trees, the stamp of horses, her father's breathing, and her own. And convincing herself that the ward was a part of it. That the hum of magic belonged here, just as much as the leaves on the trees, or the dirt under her feet.

The hum quieted to a whisper, and Emry felt the ward flicker. She concentrated, and the hum grew louder, the ward steadying. She breathed a sigh of relief, opening her eyes.

"Good," said her father. "Now I'm going to try and distract you to see if you can still hold it."

"Please tell me you're going to sing bawdy drinking ballads," Emry said, not entirely joking.

Her father sighed. "I couldn't have been blessed with a daughter whose words are as pretty as a sunset?"

"You could have," Emry said, "but what would be the fun in that?"

"Fine, then." Merlin bent down to scoop up a handful of fallen nuts from a nearby tree. "But don't say you weren't asking for it!"

"Asking for wh—*ow*!" Emry shrieked as her father threw a large brown nut at her.

"Hold the ward," he warned, lobbing another one.

Emry dodged out of the way. "This is assault," she insisted as the chestnut smacked her on the arm. The ward's buzz dipped again to a low hum.

"Concentrate!" her father snapped. "Are you a wizard, or aren't you? Defend yourself while holding the ward!"

Ah. So that's what he was doing. Emry grinned, raising her wand. "*Ignis*," she insisted, and the next nut burst into flames before dropping to the ground at her feet, smelling deliciously roasted. Her ward held steady.

"Good," her father said, tossing two nuts in quick succession.

When Emry's spell hit the second, the ward wobbled.

"Watch it," Merlin warned.

"I am," Emry snapped, splitting her attention between the ward and the flying nuts.

Arthur wandered into the bailey, sword in hand. He was frowning.

"Hi?" Emry said, wondering what he was doing there.

"Hi," Arthur said, seeming surprised to see her. "Oh, it's you. Excalibur was being weird, so I wanted to see what was going on."

"Being weird how?" Emry asked curiously.

"It's hard to explain," Arthur said, raising the tip of his sword to the boundary where she'd set her ward. "I couldn't see it before, but now there's a sort of net of magic, right here."

"That's my ward!" Emry said.

"You can see her enchantment?" Merlin said excitedly.

"Is it not supposed to be visible?" Arthur bit his lip. He tossed Excalibur to the ground. "Ah, right, it's gone now."

"Clever Aunt Matilda," Emry said fondly. "The sword was showing you my magic."

"I wonder if it would show me if an object is enchanted," Arthur mused, retrieving his blade. "You wouldn't be willing to enchant something for me, would you, wizard?"

"How about your nip—" Emry started to suggest.

"Use this," her father said, holding out the branch he'd been using as a staff.

Emry waved a hand at the staff, casting a *kenaz* rune.

Her father nodded. "Go on, lad."

Arthur peered at the staff and shook his head. "Nothing," he said, disappointed. "Unless . . ." He laid the sword against the staff, and his eyes widened. "Sard. If the sword is touching magic, it lets me know."

"Magic, or enchantment?" Emry asked.

"An important distinction," her father said approvingly.

"One way to find out." Arthur brought the sword down on her shoulder, gently, as he would if bestowing her a knighthood.

He was standing so close, his eyes a deep, yearning brown. They locked on hers, and she swallowed, unable to look away. He smelled of spiced soap and familiar leather, like the most important bit of home she could imagine. She blushed at his closeness, and how intently he was staring at her.

"Going to knight me?" she teased, her voice soft.

"If you earn it," Arthur returned, grinning.

"What would you have me do?" Emry asked.

Arthur's grin stretched wider. "What's on offer, wizard?"

Emry's imagination helpfully supplied the image of her mouth against the soft curve of his throat.

And then the ward dropped. She cursed. "You made me lose my concentration."

"Then try again. This is important." Arthur turned to her father. "How can I help?"

Merlin held out a handful of chestnuts.

"Oh no," Emry said, realizing what was about to happen.

Arthur beamed. "Oh yes."

◑ ◑ ◑

Lance crossed the castle courtyard toward the training yard, trying to push away his nerves. But it was no use. His chest was so tight with worry that he could hardly breathe. He hung back behind a stone pillar, watching the knights train from a distance. Instead of working individually, as the knights did back home, they worked together, as a unit.

A man of perhaps fifty, with bright blond hair threaded with gray and a tanned face full of freckles, was in command. Sir Hafgan the Elder, Lance supposed. The resemblance was startling. The knight split them into two groups, simulating a battle.

"You lot, guard the fort," he told one group. He pointed to the other. "And you attack."

Lance watched with interest as they formed strategies and faced one another in formation, working as a unit. And then he sneezed. A few of the men looked over, Prince Tiernen and Sir Haf among them. They gave Lance a cheerful wave.

"There you are!" said Tiernen. "We were worried you wouldn't join us."

"*He* was worried," said Haf. "*I* told him you'd show. Come, meet my father."

Lance's heart thudded with panic. What if he lost his nerve in the middle of their fake fight, recalling the battle where he'd nearly been killed? What if he embarrassed himself? His thoughts and his heartbeat raced as he met the elder Sir Hafgan, who looked him over critically.

"King's champion, eh?" he said. "And where is this king of yours now?"

"Honestly, I'd go with the library," Lance said as Tiernen snickered.

"I saw him behind the stables with your wizard earlier," said Haf.

Lance had a choking fit. Surely they were more discreet than that.

"That's right," said Tiernen. "He had his sword out, and I believe he was hitting her with his nuts."

They have to be doing this on purpose, Lance thought. But looking between them, he realized they really were that dim. Lovable, but dim.

"Hitting her with his nuts?" Lance repeated, unable to make sense of what the lads were saying.

"It looked quite painful," Haf mused. "I wonder why he was doing it."

"Some sort of training exercise, no doubt," Tiernen said with authority. "Merlin the Elder seemed to be overseeing it."

"Forget this, I think I'll go watch that instead," Lance said, not entirely kidding.

"Or you could show us what you're made of, Sir Lancelot," said Sir Hafgan, and Lance startled at the title.

It still didn't sound as if it belonged to him. It felt surreal that he had earned his knighthood. Not only that, but his place by Arthur's side, as his knight champion. He picked up a sword and a shield, joining Tiernen and Haf's group, which was defending the fort. There were seven of them in total, and they stood together in a line.

"Advance," Tiernen called, leading the maneuver from the center with his pike extended.

Lance was on the left end, his shoulder pressed against a young ginger lad who looked more like a stork than a soldier. The men advanced, one step at a time, with painful slowness, their shields held together in an interlocked formation.

"Again," called Tiernen, and they took another step.

Lance, who was used to the fast pace of the joust, felt his jaw tighten with impatience.

"Hold," Tiernen called when they were barely more than a pike's length from their opponents.

Lance saw that the opposing group kept a similar formation, their shields together in front, forming a wall between them. His stomach twisted with nerves at the sight. At the wall of enemies, ready to strike. He felt trapped in the formation, fearful of what might happen if they didn't attack first. They were waiting. Why were they waiting? His heart pounded, and then he saw his opening. The lad mirroring him had a careless gap between his shield and face.

He lunged forward with his blade, catching him on the top of his breastplate.

"Sir Lancelot!" Sir Hafgan barked, sounding displeased. "Why did you break formation?"

Lance frowned. "I had an opening," he said.

"You left your men exposed from your absence," he said. "Your formation is your shield. You move as one under your leader's command, or not at all. Is that clear?"

"Yes, sir." Lance bowed and returned to the formation.

At first it was difficult to hold his position and wait for instruction, to fight as part of a unit rather than as an individual. But after a few clumsy attempts, something happened.

They stepped forward, shields interlocked, shoulders pressed together, responding to their leader's commands as one. And Lance realized that Sir Hafgan was right. He didn't worry he was open to attack. He did as he was told along with the others, linked together by more than just the arrangement of their shields and shoulders.

And he found that, moving as part of a unit, he knew that others had his back, just as he had theirs. That knowledge, that relief, emboldened him to stop worrying, and to focus on what needed to be done.

He did not flinch away from the fight but instead welcomed it. The memories of what had happened on that battlefield were still there, but he could push them down, where they didn't bother him. For the first time in a long while, his confidence didn't waver, and he felt like his old self again.

◐ ◐ ◐

"You look happy," Arthur observed at supper that evening. "Please tell me it isn't the kitchen lad."

Lance rolled his eyes. "Of course not. I love my boyfriend."

"Just checking." Arthur grinned.

"What's this I hear about you tormenting Emry with your enormous nuts?" Lance inquired, and Arthur choked on a mouthful of lamb. "Haf and Tiernen told me, so I'm only repeating what they've said."

Arthur's face was crimson. "Merlin was teaching her how to hold a defensive ward. I was merely assisting them—"

"—with your nuts," Emry finished gleefully.

Arthur looked as if he wanted to bang his forehead against the table in frustration. "Well then, where were you today?" he asked Lance.

"Training with Tiernen and Haf in the courtyard."

Arthur turned to him with interest. "Truly?"

"I *am* a knight," Lance reminded him. "Training in the courtyard is what we do."

"Well, how was it?" Arthur asked.

"They all fight together, in a style we don't use back home. It's fascinating."

"How so?" Arthur asked curiously.

Lance took a sip of his mead before launching into a detailed explanation. Arthur was as interested as Lance had hoped he'd be, eagerly asking questions. Emry, meanwhile, had folded her linen hand cloth into the shape of a swan, and enchanted it so it floated above her plate.

"Well," Arthur said, after Lance's goblet of mead was well drained. "There's only one thing to it. You're joining them again tomorrow, I assume?"

"I am," Lance confirmed.

"Then I'm coming with you."

CHAPTER 49

G awain strolled through the castle gardens alongside the King of Flanders, wishing he didn't look quite so travel worn. His coat was actually wrinkled, and one of his boots had a noticeable scuff.

Next to him, the king clutched his hands behind his back as he walked, considering his every word before he spoke. He was a quiet, imposing man, nothing at all like his effervescent and rambling son. Their only resemblance was in the rosy pink of their cheeks and the pale blond of their hair.

Gawain and Hugo's ship had arrived just hours ago, a royal emissary waiting for them at the docks with not one, but two gilded carriages, an extravagance that had impressed Gawain considerably. Prince Hugo's mother had rushed tearfully from one of the carriages to wrap her son in her arms. From the intensity of her embrace, it was clear she'd never expected to see her son alive again.

"I'm fine, Mother," Hugo had said, annoyed. "As you can see."

But she'd still stared at him nervously on the way to the castle, pressing the back of her hand against his forehead to check for fever and asking after his appetite.

Hugo had rolled his eyes in Gawain's direction more than once, and now he was rushing ahead of them in the gardens, running after two sleek hunting dogs whose tongues lolled with pleasure. Hugo picked up a stick and tossed it, the dogs giving chase.

"I'm not convinced that getting involved is a smart idea," said the king. "Lothia is nothing to us. A faraway place run by a madman who gives us no thought. Why should we remind him of our riches and our political leanings?"

Why indeed? Gawain walked silently, trying to think. He watched as one of the dogs came running back with the stick and leapt up, placing his front paws on Hugo's chest, and accidentally knocking the lad to the ground.

The king gasped. But Hugo only laughed, rolling around with the animal as if he'd grown up in the kennels himself.

"Because Flanders owes Camelot a great debt," said Gawain. "You doubted your son would live to see another year. But his condition is much improved, thanks to our intervention. And so is the status of your kingdom, now that he's engaged to the French princess."

"True enough," said the king, "But to repay that debt in kind, I would offer you one of my daughters' hands in marriage, not a fleet of warships."

"I believe marriage to me would be a punishment for anyone's daughter," Gawain said with a self-deprecating grin.

They came to a rose garden, and the king reached for one blood-red bloom, examining it. "My wife has a great love of these," he said. "They're a temperamental flower. One night of bad weather can ruin the entire garden. But we cannot control the weather."

"No, we can't," said Gawain.

"Every season, my wife insists we plant them anyway, knowing they might wither on the vine. But they are flowers, not people. I have worked too hard to cultivate balance in my kingdom to knowingly lead it into war."

Gawain sighed, knowing what he had to do. He only wished it hadn't come to this. To the blackmail that he'd memorized, the horrible facts he'd tucked away to get what he wanted by force, just as his father had trained him. "If you don't help us, then I'll have no choice but to inform the King of France that his daughter's betrothed is not only disinterested in women, but in worryingly weak health besides. And that you were aware of both concerns."

The king sucked in a sharp breath. "You wouldn't."

"There are few things I wouldn't do, to secure your aid," said Gawain. "Including informing King Louis of the truth you so cleverly hid while sending your son to the French court to try his suit."

"But I never sent—" the king spluttered.

"The King of France is not a man of reason," Gawain went on. "He would consider your actions at best an insult and at worst an attack."

The king grimaced. "I see you're moving pieces around a giant chessboard, lad. I hope you know what you're doing."

"My strategy is without flaw," promised Gawain. "Once Camelot is victorious, and King Arthur reigns over all of England, your son will confess his change of heart to the King of France. He will claim that he has recently realized his disinterest in women. But that his younger brother, who is closer in age to Princess Anne, will happily uphold the betrothal, as a sign of friendship between your two kingdoms."

The king nodded in understanding. "If I help Camelot, Flanders profits. If I refuse, we are damned."

Gawain raised an eyebrow. "Then I suppose you had better not refuse."

CHAPTER 50

Arden and Hafgan's wedding took place on the steps of the church, much to the annoyance of the priest once he'd learned he wouldn't be performing the ceremony, but only a blessing at the end.

The steps were hung with garlands of pink and yellow flowers, and Bran Galed came, wearing a pair of enormous purple boots painted with shimmering golden runes, which he thankfully changed out of before the ceremony.

He pinned a flower to his jacket and walked his daughter toward her waiting groom, beaming with pride. She wore a white gown with trailing sleeves and flowers woven in her hair, which hung in waves down her back.

Both of them were grinning so widely during the ceremony that Emry felt herself smiling as well, even though she'd never really cared for weddings. All the dusty Latin was boring, and the ones in her town always seemed like a union of two people who were in love with the idea of having a safe life together in a place they had always known and would never leave.

The last wedding she had attended had been Arthur's. Seeing him standing there now, on the church steps, a sprig of herbs pinned to his jacket, one lock of hair dangling over his eye, wearing his hastily polished boots and his sword, but no crown . . . he looked perfect.

Like the version of himself that they both wished he could be, instead of the king he'd been forced to become.

If she had a wedding, she'd want something like this, Emry thought. Something casual and small, without a priest or a church altar. Perhaps in the evening, with enchanted candles floating all around them. She'd make Lance and Percival strut down the aisle tossing flower petals out of dainty little baskets, to lighten the mood.

And then she was horrified she'd had that thought at all.

She'd never seen the point of promising in front of an audience and a priest what they could easily promise each other in private. But Arthur wasn't a boy she could promise to be with in private. He needed someone who would stand by his side as he ruled Camelot, taking on the responsibilities and role of his queen.

She didn't want to lose him. But she hated the thought of losing herself in a role she'd never wanted and wasn't suited to. She wished there was a third choice. A way to choose Arthur, and only Arthur. But if there was, she hadn't found it. So she dragged her attention back to the wedding, just in time for Arthur's eyes to meet hers.

"We are gathered here today to celebrate the union of two people who are deeply in love, and who wish to pledge themselves to one another," said Arthur, his gaze never straying from her own.

Emry swallowed nervously. They weren't the traditional words. And she was certain that he wasn't talking about Hafgan and Arden. That he was being infuriatingly clever, and annoyingly Arthur, and letting her know what he wanted.

And she wanted it, too. At least, she thought she did. Just, not for a while. But Arthur didn't have the luxury of time, and they both knew that.

Emry watched as the couple had their hands bound together by a length of ribbon. As they pledged their love, exchanged rings, and kissed to loud cheers.

◑ ◑ ◑

Arthur stood at the edge of the crowd, nodding his head to the music and watching as everyone danced. Lance spun Emry, who was laughing. He should cut in, he knew. But he so rarely had the chance to observe without being needed or watched, and he was enjoying it.

He hadn't known what they'd find, traveling to a different world. But things here were much the same as they were back home, even with the addition of magic curses and monsters. Knights still trained in swordplay, and townsfolk still gathered at taverns, and people still fell in love.

He had come here thinking only of what he needed to attain to defeat King Yurien. But along the way, he had saved the people who were dancing here tonight, and that accomplishment felt just as valuable as any treasure. Sir Tor had been right to tell him to believe in himself. He only wished he'd realized what he was capable of sooner.

When the song ended, he began to make his way onto the dance floor, but before he reached his friends, Bran Galed stepped into his path.

"I have something for you, young king. Something better exchanged in private."

The horn. The reason he had come here in the first place. Arthur nodded and followed the man away from all the merriment.

The old knight held out a smooth brown horn that lightened to cream at its tip. It was banded with hammered gold and had a golden bauble at the tip. Golden feet like a bird's or a reptile's, with sharp talons on the end, jutted out from the horn, so it could stand upright. It was beautiful and strange, and as Arthur took it, it seemed to pulse in his hand with power.

"Thank you, Sir Bran," Arthur said, threading it through his belt, where it hung alongside Excalibur. The sword hummed happily.

"It is a dragon's horn," explained Sir Bran. "A source of ancient magic. And the word of command for it to fill with its elixir is 'κέρας.'"

"κέρας," Arthur repeated. It was fitting—the Greek word for *horn*.

Truly, the horn was a treasure. And now that he had it, his quest was complete. He felt a little disappointed at the thought. Now there was nothing left to do but return to Camelot and march his remaining soldiers back to face King Yurien's men, and hope the Lady of the Lake had steered him true.

"I believe you were meant to have it," Sir Bran confessed, staring out at the distant dancing, where his daughter and her new husband twirled and laughed. "I had no greater purpose when I acquired the horn. I sought riches for the sake of being rich. And I believed that all others would do the same."

"You give me too much credit," Arthur protested.

"I think you give yourself too little. When this is all over, and your battle is won—you should do something entirely for you, and not for your kingdom."

Arthur sighed. "I'm not sure I know how."

"Of course you do," said the old knight. "What is it you dream about, but think you can never have? Start there."

Arthur's gaze found Emry on the dance floor once again. She was still dancing with Lance, the two of them looking delighted as they made a mess of the steps. Someone had given her a crown of flowers for her hair, and Lance plucked one out, tucking it behind his ear.

"I believe I will," said Arthur, and then he went to join his friends.

"Your crown, sire," Emry joked as he approached, lifting the garland of flowers out of her hair and placing it on his.

"How do I look?" he teased.

"Very regal," Emry said, her lips twitching as she held back a laugh. "What was—oh!" She nodded at his belt. "You have the horn."

Arthur grimaced. "Why does that sound like slang for something entirely undignified?"

"*We've* got the horn," Lance proclaimed, and then made a face. "Oof, you're right, it does sound terrible."

"I don't care how it sounds," Arthur said with a grin. "We actually have a chance at defeating Yurien's army."

Emry folded her arms across her chest. "Nope," she said. "None of this 'save our kingdom' nonsense now. We're at a wedding, the wine is free, and the bard is about to sing your favorite song."

Arthur paled. "Surely not."

"*King Arthur rode out on a f*—" Lance belted, before Arthur clapped a hand over his mouth.

"I'm revoking your knighthood," Arthur threatened.

Lance rolled his eyes. "Go right ahead. I'll just teach the lyrics to every other knight in Camelot in my abundant free time."

Arthur groaned.

"Dancing," Emry insisted, grabbing at his hands.

Her eyes were shining with mischief, her cheeks pink from exertion. And she was right. They were at a celebration. There was dancing and merriment. Jugglers dressed in bold patterns, musicians with painted faces, and wine that tasted sweet like honey.

"If you insist," he said, taking her hand and giving her a twirl. She wore a dress in the style of what the ladies wore in Argatnell, with long, trailing sleeves and ribbon wrapped around her waist, her hair loose. She looked wonderful.

"Why do I suddenly feel like a third wheel?" Lance grumbled.

"Oh, go and dance with some maiden and make her night," Emry said, flapping her hands to shoo him away. A new song started, and all around them, couples pressed their right hands together, their left hands behind their backs. She smiled at Arthur. "Do you know the steps?"

Arthur watched the other couples for a moment, how they bowed to each other and circled, then clapped.

"I don't," he confessed, his heart sinking.

"Me neither," said Emry. "So we'll just have to make up our own."

Arthur balked. Surely they couldn't do that. What would people think if the king refused to follow the steps? And then he laughed, realizing he had no such responsibility.

"I shall put my hand here," he said with a grin, pressing one against her lower back. Emry blushed. Good. "And I shall require your hand in mine," he finished, drawing her toward him. It felt impossibly intimate, the two of them there, in each other's arms, in full view of anyone who might see them.

"And I shall step on your feet, as is the custom," she said, trying to make light of it.

But for once, Arthur didn't want to make light of things. "I won't mind. It would be a privilege to have my feet trodden on by you," he returned, taking her hand that was clasped in his own and pressing it to his lips.

"Careful what you wish for," Emry warned.

"That isn't what I wish for," Arthur murmured in her ear. "But if you're curious, I could show you?"

He let his hand slide from her back to her waist, over the soft fabric of her gown. She shivered. "You're never this forward," she observed. And then her eyes narrowed in understanding. "This is our last night here, isn't it?"

"Now that we have the horn . . ."

"There's no reason to stay," Emry finished.

"So are you going to dance with me some more?" Arthur asked.

"Absolutely not," Emry said, pulling away from him.

Arthur frowned, unsure what he'd gotten wrong.

"Why waste tonight dancing?" She gave him a wicked grin.

"Your room or mine?" Arthur asked.

"Yours," Emry replied. "But there's one thing I have to do first."

◖ ◖ ◖

"Father?" Emry asked, pausing in the doorway to the library. Merlin was hunched over a stack of books in dim light. His candle had almost burned down completely. She hadn't seen him at the dancing or the feast, and she wondered how long he'd been there, and if he even knew it was dark out.

Merlin startled. "Oh, sweetheart, come in," he said, gesturing for her to join him.

He reached back and stretched his arms, twisting the stiffness from his neck, a gesture Emry recognized from her childhood.

"We're leaving tomorrow," she said, pulling out the chair across from him. The flickering candlelight caught in his eyes, making them look weary. Even though his face hadn't aged in the nine years he was gone, she could tell something within him had. "We have Bran Galed's horn, so we should get back."

"To save Camelot," he said, with a note of pride.

"You could come with us," she said. "And forget about trying to restore your magic to what it was. You could just . . . be my father. And pretend that's enough."

Her father gave her a sad smile and put his hand on top of hers. "I could," he said, which wasn't a promise that he would.

"But you won't," Emry finished with a sigh.

"You don't need me. I'd only get in the way."

"That's not true."

Her father shook his head. He stared off into the distance for a moment, as if his thoughts were very far away. "The Lady of the Lake warned me I might make a sacrifice from which I could never recover, a very long time ago. I thought she spoke of trapping myself here to imprison Bellicent."

"The Lady of the Lake speaks in riddles," said Emry.

"She does. But she is on our side, and that is no small thing," said Merlin. "If you are ever in need of anything, go to her."

"There's nothing I can say to make you come back with us, is there?"

Her father shook his head. "If there's a chance to regain my magic, I have to take it."

"But you—you were teaching me how to make wards in the garden." Emry pushed back her chair and surged to her feet. "You could keep teaching me and Emmett. And it wouldn't matter how much magic you could do, because we'd be together."

"It would matter to me," he said. "All I know is magic. It's all I am. I was never a father to you. Never a mentor or a teacher. Arthur was right to name you his court wizard. Together, the things you will accomplish are the stuff of legend. If I don't regain my magic, my time will have passed. And the Lady of the Lake promised that Vivienne could help me. Once she does, I'll have the strength to open the portal and return home."

She didn't want to say goodbye. To leave him here. Even though she knew it was what he wanted. She had lost him once, and she wasn't ready for him to slip away again. For him to choose magic over family.

Her impossibly selfish father.

"You don't need me," he said. "But I need this."

"You *want* this," Emry argued. "That's entirely different."

"I have to see this through. And when I have, I'll return home."

Emry bit her lip. "What if you can't?"

Her father didn't say anything.

"How about this," Emry bargained. "In six months, I'll come back. If you haven't regained your magic by then, come home with me."

Merlin nodded. "Six months," he promised. "Perhaps it won't take that long, and I'll rejoin you myself in a week." Emry knew neither of them believed that.

She shook her head, her eyes welling with tears. She hated

goodbyes. She had wanted so badly for her father to be different. But he wasn't going to change. And she needed to accept that fact. He wasn't going to be there for her, not when he could be there for himself.

❍ ❍ ❍

When she reached Arthur's chambers, she no longer felt like the giddy girl who'd twirled on the dance floor. She felt unspeakably disappointed that the people she most wanted to keep close were the hardest to hold on to. Arthur opened the door in his rumpled tunic and hose, still wearing her flower crown. She could see a stack of books by his bed in the candlelight and neat rows of herb clippings drying on a table.

He looked entirely like the boy she had met in the library all those months ago. The boy she'd tried to stay away from, because princes didn't choose girls like her. But that wasn't true. He had chosen her, and she was done being afraid of what that meant, for tonight at least.

So she threw her arms around him. He hugged her back, holding her, and when their mouths found each other, she melted into the soft, sweet pressure of his lips. He kissed her as eagerly and seductively as he had danced with her, nipping at her bottom lip, then sliding his mouth to the sensitive hollow of her throat.

Oh, how she wanted this. And there was no reason to deny themselves a final night pretending that the future wasn't rushing toward them, full of obligations that might ruin everything.

He guided her toward the bed and onto his lap, until she was straddling him. He stared up at her, the desire in his gaze so intense that she shivered.

"Can we?" he asked.

Emry nodded, guiding his hands to the laces at the front of her dress, and eagerly reaching for the ties of his tunic. The dress slipped from her shoulders, and Arthur smiled wickedly before lowering his mouth to her breasts. Her eyes fluttered closed, and she lost herself in the sensation of his soft lips, and his arms around her.

It wasn't enough. And Arthur seemed to feel the same way. He tugged off his tunic, then reached for the ties of his trousers.

"Let me," Emry said, removing herself from his lap. She stepped out of her dress, enjoying the way Arthur watched everything she did as if she was performing magic just by being here with him.

He groaned when her fingers undid the knot at the front of his too-tight trousers. "It was very clever of me to bring my girlfriend along on a quest," he announced, kicking off the offending garment.

"Technically, I brought you," Emry corrected, pushing him back on the bed. He lay there in nothing but her flower crown, staring up at her. "Just like how I've saved your life more than you've saved mine."

He arched an eyebrow. "Is that so?" he asked, drawing her down on top of him.

"When are you going to admit, wizard, that I've saved your life more than you've saved mine?"

"You have not," Emry said. "If anything, we're even."

"Yes, but each time I save yours, it's worth more, because I'm royal," Arthur said, innocently trailing his fingers from her shoulders to her hips.

"I hate you," Emry insisted, shivering as his clever fingers circled her hips.

"If you did, you wouldn't let me do this," Arthur said. He kissed her again, deeply, with all the assurance of a king who was returning home victorious from a quest, and all the charm of the boy from the library. He kissed her until kissing wasn't enough.

Emry surrendered into it . . . into the two of them, this quiet room with its locked door, and the knowledge that he was right, she didn't hate him. She never could. Not after all they'd been through. Being with him felt more natural than anything, like she didn't have to try. Like, for once, she could just let herself be.

So she let herself drown in being with him, until she wasn't thinking about her father, and the war that was coming.

Until she wasn't thinking about anything at all.

CHAPTER 51

Willyt Merlin was used to being alone, he just wasn't used to feeling lonely. And somehow, as he rode back through the Silverwood after seeing his daughter, King Arthur, and Sir Lancelot safely returned to their world, the feeling finally found him. Loneliness gnawed at him from within his chest. He wasn't expecting it.

"Well, they've gone," he told the brown mare, who was plodding methodically through the trees, leading the way for the three silver horses that followed without riders. The horse couldn't have cared less.

"And I'm going to regain my magic," Merlin promised, even though Vivienne had warned him that the chance of it happening was small. What was it she'd said? Ah, yes. *The stones have their own reasons for the choices they make, and very rarely listen to the pleas of man.*

But it was *his* magic. Surely that had to count for something.

It was late when he arrived at Vivienne's cottage, the Silverwood chirping and chittering with the movement of nocturnal beasts. He put his wand back into his jacket, not wanting her to know how fearful he'd been after the sun had set. But he suspected she knew that sort of thing even without his saying.

When Vivienne came to the door, she was wearing an apron over her dress, and she held a finger to her lips. "I have a visitor," she warned.

Merlin groaned. *Not again.* What was it with men seeking shelter at the witch's cottage, and feeling it was their right to steal away in the night with her possessions? Or worse, to try and take what she didn't wish to give? In a world full of monsters, it only made sense that men who acted like beasts were turned into them.

The young man seated at the witch's kitchen table seemed to be on his third bowl of stew. He was thin and wiry, with a hungry look to him that Merlin doubted could be satisfied by a loaf of bread. His shoulders slumped when Merlin entered.

"Oh," he said to Vivienne. "I thought you lived here alone."

"The wizard is merely visiting," she said, taking down two more bowls and serving them both their supper.

"Wizard?" The lad looked frightened.

"That's right," said Merlin. "I'm the most powerful wizard in this world and any other, and should you overstep the lady's hospitality, I can assure you that the consequences will not be pleasant."

The lad gulped nervously and stared down at his bowl of stew as if he'd lost his appetite. "I could do the dishes?" he offered. "After you've eaten?"

Vivienne actually smiled. When she did, her whole face transformed from merely pretty to something extraordinary. Merlin wished once again that they were alone in her cottage, and that they had more time.

"And after the dishes?" Vivienne asked.

"I could muck out the pigsty in the morning, before I'm on my way," the lad said. "As payment for the lodging and the food."

"Good lad," Merlin said with a nod. He snapped his fingers, and one of the candelabra flew into his outstretched hand, and the lad paled. "I'll be in the study."

"I'll join you," said Vivienne, spooning up the last of her stew. Her apron untied itself from her waist and flew onto the peg with the others.

Once they were settled in the study, Merlin watched as Vivienne moved her knight on the chess set.

"That game is shaping up nicely," he commented. "Any idea who you're playing?"

"I believe it's Princess Rhiannon again. She always protects her queen and sacrifices her knights."

Merlin thought back to the game Emry had taken over at the castle. To all the things he hadn't told her. Unimportant ones, like the true nature of the enchantment on the chess set. And ones of great consequence.

"I'm leaving for the crystal cave tomorrow," said Merlin. "I was wondering if I might have—"

"I've already packed you a bundle of sandwiches and a sleeping roll," said Vivienne.

"Some advice," Merlin finished.

Vivienne's eyebrows rose in surprise. "The great wizard Merlin wishes for *my* advice on what he should do?"

"I'm not *that* pigheaded," he protested.

"Oh yes, you are," she said. "But something's changed." She stared at him intently, and Merlin shivered from the pressure of her gaze. "You have seen your legacy," she declared. "And it wasn't what you expected."

Merlin sighed. "No," he agreed. "It wasn't."

He had never thought his daughter would be the one to take over his position as court wizard. Even seeing it for himself, he had repeatedly insisted it was a mistake. But he'd been wrong.

She had brought them here to the Otherworld, killed a magic beast at the king's side, and ridden off on a quest, only to return victorious, even rescuing a cursed maiden besides.

She was everything he had been, and more. And he now knew it was no mere infatuation or courtly strategy that had driven her into Arthur's arms. She loved the king, and he loved her back. She would ride off to war at his side, not because it was expected of whomever held the position of court wizard, but because she wanted to protect everyone she cared about most in the world.

He hadn't wanted to see it, because he had a son, and he thought he knew best what that son should be. Except Emmett didn't want any of it. He wanted a wife and a family, as well as friends to drag out to the tavern and divest of their gold in a game of cards. He didn't want danger, adventure, or the responsibility of saving their kingdom. And he wasn't suited to that kind of life.

They had told him, and he hadn't listened, and now it was too late. He'd chosen himself, and his magic—magic that he might never regain. And they knew that about him because they weren't children anymore. They saw him clearly, when he had only seen what he'd wanted.

And Emry was right—there was a life for him back in Camelot. His child was the king's court wizard, and she could use some more training. And he was about to become a grandfather. His mother didn't have much time left, either.

"I have to get back to my family," said Merlin resolutely. "Which is why I can't fail my quest."

"It's not up to you, what the stones choose," said Vivienne.

He knew that. "But the stones gave Emry back *her* magic," he said, remembering the story she'd told him.

"Because she didn't give it freely," said Vivienne. "Stolen magic is corrupt. Whether it's taken from a wizard, an enchanted object, or a place of great magic."

"So I just have to hope magic is on my side?" he said glumly.

"You just have to hope the stones see what's in your heart," she said, moving her queen across the chessboard. "Checkmate," she said softly. "That poor girl really doesn't know what she's doing."

CHAPTER 52

Morgana drew her shawl tighter around her shoulders as she descended the rough-hewn stone steps to the castle dungeon. The lantern she held was lit by magic, its flame a bright, sickly green that cast twisted shadows against the walls.

She hated coming down here. Hated that Bellicent had ordered her things moved to this dank cave beneath the castle, instead of claiming one of the airy gilt rooms or conical towers for a workshop. But at least she'd have her privacy here.

Morgana hung the lantern on a peg and snapped her fingers at the candelabra, the candles flickering eagerly, each with a pale purple flame.

She missed Lothian Keep, with the hidden door in her bedroom that had led to her private study, with its golden chairs and shelves of books and tapestries covering the stone walls. She missed her gardens there, with marble sculptures dotting the paths and the wooden swing that hung from one of the oak trees where she used to push her son when he was small, watching his little legs kick out with glee.

She felt like a stranger in this castle. An interloper. Because that's what she was. And though the maids curtseyed in the hall when she passed, they watched her with fearful eyes. Their obedience and loyalty were not freely given, but taken by threat, and she hated that.

The books she'd sent for were stacked on a rickety old table. She ran a hand over the stack, and her palm came away covered in dust. But what use did she have for research on Anwen, or magic spells her son didn't wish to learn?

What use did she have for being queen, in this castle that wasn't hers, with a husband who didn't want her?

She picked up one of the books and hurled it against the stone wall with a scream. She threw another book, and another.

When the stack ran out, she was breathing hard, and her heart was pounding, and her magic seemed to pulse with the urge to get out. And why shouldn't she let it?

She flicked her wrist, sending a brass-bottomed cauldron flying.

Bellicent had upended her life. Made the court see Morgana as a madwoman and her husband lose interest. Turned her son into a little devil and taken her away from her home. It had been weeks since Bellicent had shoved her out of her body to wear her skin. And with every passing day that the sorceress lay dormant, Morgana's panic grew. She didn't know what Bellicent was planning. And she hated being toyed with.

"What are you waiting for?" she howled. "Why are you doing this?" She wished she had never gone to Anwen.

You seem upset, a voice crooned inside her head. *Did you miss me?*

"I thought you'd gone," said Morgana.

No, you'd hoped I'd gone, Bellicent replied. *But you weren't sure.*

Morgana didn't answer. But she didn't have to.

The truth is, I no longer have need of you, said Bellicent. *Your magic is weak. Your husband bores me. Your son is pathetic. I would rather wait until one of the wizards in your world opens a doorway into mine. I've set a trap, so I'll know when it happens. And when it does, I'm coming back with them. As myself.*

"Then you'll leave me alone for good?" Morgana asked, hardly daring to hope.

I will, confirmed Bellicent. *I've found another way into your world. One where I can be my true self, in my own body.*

No, Morgana thought. It wasn't possible.

Oh, it's very possible, hissed Bellicent. *Goodbye, my desperate little queen.*

Morgana gasped, suddenly dizzy. She reached for the table to steady herself and saw that her hands were shaking.

She was gone! Bellicent wouldn't possess her again. Wouldn't shove her down into the darkness, where her screams went unheard, and Bellicent wore her skin and did as she pleased.

She was finally free of the sorceress's grasp. She could stop worrying that she'd awaken standing on the edge of the roof, or choking underwater in the bath.

The nightmare was over. At long last.

She looked around the smashed-up workshop and laughed. And then she went to tell her husband the good news.

"What is it?" Yurien snapped, looking up from sheaves of ledgers.

"Bellicent is gone!" Morgana said, unable to hold back her grin. "I'm finally free of her."

Morgana watched her husband set down his papers and push to his feet, his expression unreadable. She thought he was coming to hug her. To comfort her now that the ordeal was done.

"She's gone?" he said, as if he didn't believe it.

"For good!" Morgana said, beaming.

She wasn't expecting him to hit her. When his fist connected with her cheek, she stumbled back, crashing into a table and chair. She gasped from the pain and the shock of it, locking eyes with him. But he didn't look horrified at what he had done. Instead, he looked angry. He moved toward her, his hand still in a fist, his expression cold and impassive.

"You did this on purpose!" he accused. "Because she was helping me, and you can't stand when someone else is more powerful than you."

Morgana lifted a hand to her cheek, her eyes stinging with tears. She blinked them away because she wouldn't give him the satisfaction of letting him see that he'd made her cry.

"I didn't do anything," said Morgana. "But I'm glad she's gone. She humiliated me and tortured me and poisoned my son against me. And you just watched! You did nothing to help me."

He stared at her with a haughty expression. "Why would I, when I preferred her?"

Morgana lunged at him with a scream, swiping at him with her sharp nails. He grabbed hold of her wrists, a darkness coming over his expression. His grip was tighter than it needed to be, and she wasn't sure he would let go. She could see the part of him that wanted to squeeze and squeeze until her wrists broke, that wouldn't calm until he had won.

"Let go of me," she said, her voice low. "Now."

"Not until I see that you're afraid of me," he hissed. "And I know that you'll never displease me again."

Morgana's heart pounded, and she felt dizzy. This man didn't love her. Maybe he had once, but what joy had been between them was long gone. She was a prize he no longer cared for, an object he wished he could tuck away on a back shelf in a spare room, unwanted and unloved.

She had come back to him, and he was *angry* about it.

"Mother? Father?" Mordred said.

No. Morgana twisted around as best she could and saw her son standing in the open doorway.

"What are you doing?" he asked curiously.

"Teaching your mother a lesson," said Yurien.

"Oh," Mordred said, disinterested. "Can I have a second slice of lemon cake before supper? My nurse said I had to ask, because she thought you'd say no. So you have to say yes, or else she'll think she's in charge."

"Fine," said Yurien, sounding bored.

"When the other lady comes back, tell her I want a magic sword," said Mordred. "The fencing master won't let me practice with my knife."

"The sorceress isn't coming back," Yurien sneered. "Your mother saw to that."

Mordred's face turned into a storm of emotions. He stared at his mother, her wrists caught in his father's hands, and it didn't even register that something was wrong, that his father was treating her in a way he shouldn't. "I hate you!" he screamed. "You're the worst mother ever, and I wish you never came back!" He turned and fled down the corridor.

Yurien grinned. "You're crying," he said with satisfaction.

He let go of her wrists, and Morgana rubbed at the red marks he'd left behind. "Don't you ever do that again," she said.

"I'll do whatever I want," said her husband, pulling himself up to his full height. "Once I'm High King."

CHAPTER 53

Emry had never seen London in the spring before. As they rode through the city gates, returning from their Otherworld quest, the streets seemed vibrant and full of life. Flowers bloomed in riots of color from window boxes. People had taken off their heavy woolen cloaks and sat in the sunshine, enjoying the spoils of the city markets and in no hurry to get inside.

The market wares had never looked so appealing. Airy lace fabrics and plump, juicy berries and mugs of frothing ale. A musician strummed his lute, his tights a lurid shade of green, a feather in his cap bouncing as he sang of a hero defeating a dragon to a crowd of wide-eyed children.

"We're home," Arthur said with a smile.

"Feels good," said Lance.

"Feels *amazing*," said Emry.

The villagers caught sight of them and sank into bows and curtseys where they stood. "It's the king!" they whispered amongst themselves.

Arthur sighed but bore it with good cheer. Emry performed a clothes-cleaning spell without his having to ask, and Lance sat up straighter in his saddle.

"They want to see Excalibur," he called.

He was right. Arthur drew his glowing blade, and his people cheered. Their king had returned home with Excalibur in hand.

"Sir Lancelot!" some of the younger boys called, running alongside their horses with wooden practice blades. "Is it true you won the king's tournament as a squire?" one asked.

"It is," Lance said, and the boys seemed suitably awed.

The ladies looked to Emry with pride, seeing a girl from Camelot, of no title or wealth, riding with their king, not as his servant, but as his equal.

"Are you a princess?" a little girl called to Emry, her eyes wide, clutching a poppet that dragged in the dirt.

"I'm not. I'm a wizard," Emry replied.

The little girl frowned and tugged at her mother's hand. "Mama, I thought only boys could be wizards!"

"She's better at magic than all the boys," Arthur called, winking at the child. And then he turned to his friends. "What do you say we stop here a moment, for snacks?"

Emry frowned, wondering what Arthur was doing. They weren't in the Otherworld anymore. Usually, when he was recognized, he was mortified, and insisted on hurrying back to the castle.

"I never turn down snacks," Lance declared, dismounting his horse.

They visited the market, buying food and drink. Arthur overpaid for everything waving away his change. He spoke with the merchants, asking how their businesses were faring, how their harvests were, how far they had traveled to sell their wares.

Emry and Lance exchanged a look. This was . . . different. In a good way. They bought far more than they could eat, offering pies and cool drinks to the curious children who trailed after them, the women who soothed crying babies, and the old men who grinned with missing teeth. Emry helped heal a young woman in a maid's uniform who struggled to carry her market basket with her arm in a sling. After she did, others approached Emry with their ailments, curious if magic might help.

Lance took up a stick and ran drills with a couple of young boys and one young girl who wore wooden toy swords at their belts.

And Arthur spoke with his people, hearing what they needed, and promising to do his best.

When they climbed back onto their horses, the crowd cheered as they left. Arthur blushed but lifted a hand in farewell. Emry and Lance did the same.

We're going to save them, Emry thought. *We're going to save Camelot and bring peace to all of England.*

When they arrived at the castle gates, Saf didn't notice them at first. He was bent over his sketchbook, his halberd leaning against the wall.

"Not even a hello, Saf?" said Lance, shaking his head. "Brutal."

Saf looked up and let out a swear. "I—my apologies, Your Majesty," he said sheepishly. "Welcome back!"

Arthur shook his head at the lad and rode into the courtyard. Fanfare sounded as they crossed the outer courtyard, and when they arrived at the steps of the castle, a crowd had gathered, waiting for them.

Lord Agravaine stood at the front, relief plain on his face. "Welcome home, sire," he said with a bow. "I trust your journey went well?"

"Extremely," Arthur said. "But I must confess, it's good to be back."

For once, Emry thought he actually meant it.

Guin rushed forward, wrapping Emry in a hug the moment she slid from her horse. "I knew you were all right," she said.

"I'm always all right," Emry assured her. And then she got a look at the princess. Something was different. Guin's hair was twisted up in an elaborate set of braids, and topped with a delicate golden crown. Rubies hung from her ears, and her lips were painted to match. She wore an impressive silk gown embroidered with crimson flowers, which swelled over her enormous baby bump. "Look at you!"

"I know, I'm the size of a small kingdom," Guin said, pressing back a smile.

"Well, yes," Emry said. "But I was going to say, you look like a queen."

Guin's grin came out in full force. "I've been busy while you've been away. Scheming."

Emry's brows knit together in curiosity. "And I intend to hear all about it over the largest mug of coffee and slice of cake possible," she promised.

"There's coffee?" Arthur said hopefully, joining them.

"It's *your* castle, of course there's coffee," Emry told him.

Arthur raised an eyebrow at Guin. "Why am I very afraid of what you've been up to?"

Guin shrugged regally.

Emmett rushed toward them, frowning. He was holding a balled-up leather apron, his sleeves were rolled, and he smelled of the metallic, spiced scent that only came from potion making. "Where's Father?" he asked.

Emry and Arthur exchanged a very weighted look. "He's fine," Emry said quickly, pulling her brother aside.

"But he stayed there," Emmett finished, shaking his head in disappointment. "I can't believe he's still pulling this shit."

"Me neither," Emry said.

"Did you even try to convince him to come back?" Emmett demanded.

"Of course I did!" Emry burst out. "But he wants to restore his lost magic, and until he has, nothing else and no one else matters. If I could change that, I'd be capable of performing miracles, and you know it."

Emmett sighed, his shoulders slumping in defeat. "It's not fair."

"It really isn't," Emry agreed. "I did make him promise that he'd let me drag him back in six months, if he hasn't found his magic by then."

"Good," Emmett said. They walked up the steps of the castle, and when they reached the top, Emmett asked, "Did Guin tell you she's joined the royal council?"

"She *has*?"

"It's brilliant," Emmett enthused. "She just showed up one day and started bossing everyone around."

"Good for her." Emry grinned. That sounded exactly like something Guin would do.

"Once we defeat King Yurien, Cameliard's going to need a queen. Guin has decided to take on the task. And bend the knee to Arthur as High King, of course."

Emry shook her head, taking it all in. "What happened to her brother?"

"He's holed up inside a monastery in Andalusia and begged Guin to handle things." Emmett shrugged. "Guin said I'll get to be her consort."

Emry laughed. "Literally the one job you're suited for."

Emmett beamed. And then he frowned. "Wait. I can't tell if you're insulting me."

"That," Emry said, "was exactly my plan."

○ ○ ○

Arthur studied his reflection in his bedroom mirror, then pushed back his crown, wishing it didn't give him a headache.

"You look ridiculous like that," Emry told him. She was leaning against the door, tapping one foot impatiently. They were going to be late to the council meeting, but that was part of his strategy.

"It's heavy," Arthur complained. "Can't you, I don't know, magic it lighter?"

Emry raised an eyebrow. "You want me to *magic the crown jewels lighter*?"

"Well, not when you put it that way." Arthur made a face. Heavy would have to do. He straightened his jacket and reached for his scrolls. He'd thought he would be nervous, but strangely, he wasn't.

Lance, who was waiting for them in the corridor, had gotten sucked into a game of cards with Tristan and the other guards. "Sorry, gentlemen, I'm needed elsewhere," he said, throwing down his hand. The guards booed.

"Don't look so upset, he would have trounced all of you," Emry told them.

Lance grinned. "Really?"

Emry shrugged. And Arthur realized something. "You said you didn't cheat at cards," he accused.

"That hardly counts," she protested. "I wasn't even playing." But her cheeks were pink.

It was strange being back, Arthur thought, as maids bobbed curtseys in the corridor when he passed. The castle hadn't changed at all. Yet he had.

When they arrived outside the council chambers, a page scrambled to open the door and announce them. "King Arthur, Sir Lancelot, and the wizard Merlin," the lad said, looking unsure. Arthur nodded his approval.

The members of his council stood for their king's entrance. Guinevere and Sir Tor clapped, and a few of the men shot them annoyed looks before halfheartedly joining in.

"Is this everyone, sire?" Lord Agravaine asked with a frown.

And Arthur realized what the man meant. "Master Merlin will be away on royal business for the next six months," he said. "So it's a good thing I have more than one court wizard."

General Timias grumbled at the news.

"Unfortunately, we don't have enough chairs," Lord Howell pointed out.

Emry grinned. "*Congemino*," she commanded.

Lord Howell squawked as his chair split in half, then regrew its missing pieces. Next to it, a perfect copy appeared and did the same.

"Fixed it," Emry said smugly, as Sir Tor cackled over the spectacle.

Arthur grinned. He was going to enjoy this.

Lord Agravaine went over what had happened while they'd been away, and Arthur stopped him when necessary, asking questions and demanding clarifications. Sometimes, he turned to the other members of his council for more details.

After he'd finished, General Timias spoke up. "In terms of our ongoing conflict with King Yurien," he said, "we'll need a new plan of attack. I've devised some ideas and—"

"As it happens, I have a plan of my own," Arthur cut in. Many of his advisors exchanged nervous looks, radiating disapproval.

"You do?" The general sounded skeptical.

"I do," said Arthur. "You'll remember that's why I went to the Otherworld in the first place."

"The Otherworld is nothing but a children's story," General Timias protested.

"Strange, then, how I seem to have brought back its treasures, which will help us defeat Yurien's army," Arthur said, placing Bran Galed's horn upon the table.

His advisors peered at it curiously.

"It's very pretty," Guin said tentatively. "Er, what is it?"

"Dragon horn," Lance said, giving her his best grin. "With a fairy enchantment."

General Timias's lips disappeared into a thin line.

"I vowed I'd find a way to defeat Yurien's soldiers, and I have," said Arthur. "When Yurien arrives at Joyous Gard, we won't be waiting. We'll have barricaded ourselves inside the fort as though we're afraid to fight in the open."

"But—" the general started to protest.

"I'm not finished. And I'm not taking questions until the end," said Arthur. "Yurien's men will make camp. They'll have assumed we would be camped as well, and now they'll think they'll need to attack a fort, instead of meeting our forces in the open. It will take time for them to develop a new strategy. And the river will be right there."

"But there is no river in that valley, sire," ventured Lord Howell.

"There will be," said Emry. "I'm going to divert it with magic. And cast a ward over the valley to make the weather unseasonably warm."

"You can do that?" Lord Howell said, aghast.

"Easily," said Emry. "I can spoil the soldiers' rations as well, and turn their ale to vinegar, so they have no choice but to drink the river water."

"To what end?" asked Lord Agravaine. "Poison?"

"Poison is a coward's strategy," protested General Timias.

"Oh, I agree entirely," said Arthur, "which is why I did say no questions until the end."

Lord Agravaine's expression went sour.

"This horn has a very peculiar magical property," said Arthur, holding up Bran Galed's horn. His advisors regarded it with confusion. "It pours a drink that changes any who consume it into ordinary mortals, no matter what powers they have, or what enchantments they might bear."

His advisors gaped at him.

"I'm going to pour it into the river," Arthur explained. "Once Yurien's men drink, their enchantments will be gone, but they won't know it. Our army will arrive in the morning, and the men stationed in the fort will ride out to join them. The battle will be at our advantage, both in terms of defensive strategy, and in fighting an opponent who overestimates their own strength."

"Just to be clear," said Lord Howell, "Yurien's soldiers won't be unkillable?"

"And they won't know it until it's too late," Arthur confirmed.

General Timias nodded in approval. "A bold plan, lad," he said.

"I appreciate the vote of confidence," said Arthur, "but in the future, I'd prefer to be addressed by my name or by an appropriate honorific, and not as 'lad' or 'boy.'"

The general inclined his head in respect. "As you wish, Your Majesty."

"If you have any further questions about the magical aspects of this plan, feel free to consult with my court wizard," Arthur said, gesturing to Emry.

She gave the general her best smile. "I believe you know the way to the wizard's workshop," she told him, and he nodded unhappily.

"And there's one more thing," Arthur went on. "My knight champion will be assembling our castle guards, our knights, and our squires in the courtyard tomorrow morning for instruction in a new style of defensive fighting."

Sir Tor grinned. "I look forward to it, Sir Lancelot," said the knight.

"Well." Arthur regarded his stunned council members. "I suppose that covers it? Unless, Princess Guinevere, do you have anything to add?"

"I'm sorry," she burst out, "but did Lance say there are *dragons*?"

◐ ◐ ◐

"I can't believe this is my castle," Lance said, shaking his head at the crumbling fortress, which was missing half its roof, and had crows roosting in the battlements.

"No need to thank me," Arthur joked, riding alongside him.

"Believe me, he wasn't going to," Emry murmured.

At their backs rode the first wave of Arthur's forces. Knights and squires, along with guards and common soldiers, too. Thankfully, they had arrived before Yurien's forces, just as they'd planned.

Lance's lessons in combat by unit had been a success, and soon even General Timias had joined the training sessions back at Castle Camelot, demanding that his military commanders do the same.

Emry had watched out the window of the wizard's workshop with pride as Lance commanded the drills, no longer just Arthur's champion in name.

And Arthur. Emry fought back a grin as she rode at his side, wearing her favorite pair of trousers. He'd been different since they'd returned from Anwen. More assured. Less afraid of what others might think. And less mortified when people addressed him as their king and called him by his title. He had even made certain to keep his promises from that day in the market square, sending some of his guards to help erect a covering so the vendors could sell their wares in the rain, and having one of the city gates open earlier and close later than the others to allow merchants through.

The royal table at supper had all but been disbanded. Arthur joined his courtiers at their tables, so they no longer felt desperate to accost him for an audience after the meal.

It would have been perfect, if only her father were there.

Five months and thirteen days, Emry reminded herself. *And if he hasn't returned by then, you can go after him.*

"Well, wizard," Arthur said, turning to her with a smile. "I suppose we're up."

He adjusted the horn he'd fixed to his chest with a leather strap. And then he directed his horse to break from their company. Emry did the same. They rode out across Camlann Field, away from the fortress, and toward the looming forest.

"Where's this river I'm supposed to move again?" Emry asked.

"Er, I have a map," Arthur said, unfolding a piece of parchment. He held it with one direction up, then flipped it.

"Hold, sire!" someone called, riding toward them.

Arthur groaned, then pasted on his best royal grin. "General Timias. How good of you to join us."

"I figured you could use someone who knows this terrain," said the general. He eyed Emry doubtfully. "How long will it take, lass, to divert the river?"

"Oh, probably not more than a week," she said.

"A week!" the general spluttered.

"She's joking," Arthur assured him.

Emry batted her eyes at the man. He glowered.

The river was a ways into the forest, and thankfully, the general rode ahead, showing them the way, or else they truly might not have found it.

It was twice as wide as Emry had expected, with a gentle current and large rocks that formed a haphazard path across. She slid down from her horse and examined the water, jumping across the stones once, and then twice. Her heart was pounding with nerves, and for a moment, she wondered if she could truly do this.

But then she saw Arthur watching her from atop his white horse, with all the confidence in the world that she would pull this off. She looked to the general, whose expression was full of doubt, and a fire lit within her.

Just watch me, she thought.

She rolled up her sleeves, then knelt at the riverbank, pressing a hand to the water's surface. With her magic, she felt for the bottom of the river. She could sense the dark silt, the current, the fish that swam in its depths, and the plants that grew beneath the surface.

And then she reached for her magic.

"*Transmigro omnia!*" she demanded.

The surface of the river bubbled and churned as General Timias gasped.

"Go on, lead it where you want it," she told him. And then she turned her attention back to the river. "Er, follow him, please."

The general spurred his horse and galloped off in the direction they'd come.

With a roar and a crash, the river followed him.

"Sarding hell, Em," Arthur said, once the river had settled down in the valley, just where the general wanted it.

Emry grinned. "Not bad, huh?"

"It'll do," Arthur told her, unstrapping his horn. *"κέρας!"*

At the word, the horn filled with liquid. He poured it into the river. The horn refilled, and he poured again, then again.

Finally, after the tenth pour, the horn did not refill.

"I think it's done," Arthur said. He looked to Emry. "Go on, enchant someone, so we can test it."

The general looked between them with horror. Emry grinned.

"Oh no," he said, backing away.

"It's so difficult to choose which ailment to afflict you with," Emry mused before she was struck by an idea.

For a moment, she wasn't sure her spell had worked. Then the general got a sour look on his face and burped.

A honeybee flew out of his mouth, buzzing indignantly. The general blanched. And then it happened again. "Make it stop!" he shouted, his face a worrying shade of red. "Please, make it stop!"

"The river's right there," said Emry.

The general rushed to its bank, then cupped his hands in the water and drank deeply.

Emry stared at him, waiting. The general was tense, waiting as well. And then, when a minute had passed with no more bees emerging, he sighed with relief.

"Guess it works," Emry said with a grin.

"Guess so," said Arthur. "Although I'm extremely disappointed, wizard. You really missed an opportunity to do the nipples thing."

CHAPTER 54

Morgana couldn't believe her husband had insisted on letting their nine-year-old son ride with him to battle. Yet she hadn't been able to talk sense into him.

"The lad will be safe. Let him see his father become High King," Yurien had boasted.

So Morgana had come along, riding at her husband's side as though nothing was amiss between them. As though he still saw her as his queen.

But she knew better. Just as she knew that helping him conquer other kingdoms had been a mistake. She hadn't seen it before, because she had been so fixated on causing King Uther to suffer. To fall. To realize that he had been beaten by the little girl he had thrown away and forgotten years ago, returned to exact her revenge.

Except Uther was dead. The Duke of Cornwall had seen to that, driven by his own greed for a throne. And Arthur, her half brother, was nothing to her. She had almost killed him once, yet when he'd held a blade to her throat, he had shown mercy. And concern for that little witch of his. He wasn't his father. If anything, he was too much like their mother. She took no joy in the death of his soldiers, or the bloodying of a battlefield.

This wasn't what she had wanted. But now it was too late.

From Cameliard, the journey wasn't long to Joyous Gard. Three days on foot. But the soldiers were unruly, their ranks having shrunk considerably. Giving angry young men invulnerability had been a terrible idea—nearly three hundred had deserted, and four hundred more punished for their unspeakable crimes against the people of Cameliard.

Still, the men were strong, their spirits high. They marched through the woods bragging of the victory they would claim. When they emerged, it was into a large valley, which was perfect for a camp. A river ran through it, sparkling and clean, and just waist deep.

"This is it," said one of Yurien's commanders. "The hill of Camlann is just there, beyond the valley."

Yurien grinned. "Perfect," he said. "We'll set up camp here and send a scout up the hill to see what lies ahead."

As the men began to erect their camp, Morgana couldn't shake the sense that something was wrong. She paced outside her tent, trying to put together what was causing her unease. The weather was unseasonably warm, and already the soldiers had shed their tunics and mail.

The scout returned, and Morgana made an excuse to ask her husband some inane question, so she might overhear what was being said.

"Well?" Yurien demanded, not giving the man a moment to catch his breath.

"They're sequestered in an old fort," the lad reported nervously, hands on his knees, his brow shining with sweat. "It's little more than a ruin. We could take it, with proper strategy."

"I'll decide what we will and will not do," Yurien snapped. But his eyes glittered with greed. "You're certain they're all in this fort?"

The man nodded.

"Cowards," Yurien said with relish.

He disappeared into a tent with his commanders and his seneschal, and Morgana could hear the men arguing. One of the standard-bearers, a lad of perhaps sixteen, had taken a liking to Mordred and was running drills with the boy, who swung a wooden sword with glee. She watched them, tensing every time the standard-bearer lunged forward, but Mordred parried expertly.

Men went to bathe and fill their flasks in the river, and she turned away from the sight of them stripping off their clothes. The last thing she needed was for her husband to accuse her of straying. She made her way into the woods, wandering wherever she pleased. After a minute of walking, she frowned. The weather was much cooler here. And she didn't believe it was the tree cover.

The feeling of wrongness came over her again, tracing a shiver down her spine. She headed back to the camp, feeling for her magic and throwing it in front of her like a wall. When she stepped into the valley, her magic shimmered and dropped away. *A ward.* The valley where they'd made camp was warded by magic. And the enchantment felt fresh. So it hadn't all been in her imagination.

She marched to her husband's tent and pushed her way inside, past his protesting guards.

"Get out of here," he growled.

"No!" Morgana said. "King Arthur is taking you for a fool. His wizard has tampered with this valley."

The seneschal raised his eyebrows in disbelief. "Tampered how?"

"I don't know," Morgana said. "But the heat isn't natural."

"The weather?" her husband said, advancing toward her. "You interrupted us because you're concerned that a little girl has changed the weather?"

Morgana winced. When he put it like that . . . "I know how it sounds."

"Do you?" His voice was low. Dangerous. "And what do you expect me to do? Call off my unbeatable soldiers because it's warm out?"

"You underestimate them!" Morgana cried. "Something is wrong, and you're not listening!"

"The only thing that's wrong is my bitch wife refusing to get out of my tent!" Yurien accused, raising his hand. Morgana didn't cringe away. She stood there, daring him to do it. He shook his head in disgust, lowering his hand back to his side. "Go, and don't bother us again."

Morgana stumbled from the tent, burning with rage.

And then she saw the fight between her son and the standard-bearer. They no longer used wooden swords, but real ones. Soldiers crowded them, cheering like it was a sport. The older lad lunged forward, landing a hit on Mordred's arm that welled red with blood. The soldiers shouted in amusement. Her son cried out, dropping to one knee.

"Yield!" taunted his opponent.

"Never," Mordred swore. "I'll make you regret that!" He rose to his feet, darting forward in attack. Morgana didn't see the second blade her son held until it was too late, and he was plunging the enchanted dagger into the other lad's leg.

The standard-bearer fell to his knees, his face ashen. The soldiers jeered. Mordred stood there, his shoulders heaving, his mouth tipped up in an expectant grin.

Morgana watched in horror as the other boy slumped to the ground, dead. No. Her son couldn't have done this. Not her little boy, who had spent the afternoon waving around a wooden sword with berry juice staining his face. He was becoming a monster. And she didn't know how to stop it.

"*Mordred!*" the soldiers cried raucously. "*Mor-dred! Mor-dred!*"

Something made Morgana turn, and when she did, she saw her husband watching from just outside his tent, his expression proud. "That's my boy," he said with a smirk when he saw Morgana watching.

And that was the moment she realized something she had known for a long time but hadn't wanted to believe: If there was one person she wanted to see defeated, it wasn't her half brother. It was her awful, vile husband.

CHAPTER 55

The morning dawned reluctantly, as if even the sun didn't wish to drag itself to the battle but preferred to stay out of things entirely.

Arthur could relate. He stared out the window of the tower he'd claimed as his bedchamber, looking down at the soldiers' encampment.

"Do you think it worked?" Lance asked from the doorway. He was already dressed for battle, armor over his mail, a sword at his waist, and a shield at his back.

Arthur was still in his tunic, a mug of coffee in hand. "I don't know. And I hate not knowing."

"I suppose we'll know soon enough," said Lance, picking up a piece of Arthur's padding. "You should get dressed."

"To go to war," Arthur said with a sigh.

"To end this thing with King Yurien once and for all," said Lance. "So we can actually enjoy your being King of Camelot."

"Wouldn't that be something," Arthur said.

"I might even settle down," Lance said, fastening Arthur's padding with expert precision. "Perce has been wanting to adopt a dog." Lance reached for Arthur's mail, and it felt like a hundred lifetimes ago that Lance had played squire for him at the sword-fighting tournament, helping him into his armor in a tent.

"You're not dressed?" Emry said from the doorway. She was wearing suede leggings and a tunic of mail, her black cloak swirling around her ankles. Her hair was in a braid, and there were deep purple smudges under her eyes from maintaining the wards on the valley. She clutched a mug of coffee that couldn't have been her first.

"I'm getting there," Arthur said. He nodded at her chainmail tunic. "Planning on fighting?"

"More like hoping no one's planning on stabbing me," she said.

"You should have a sword," Arthur said, noticing that she didn't carry one. He looked around. "Do we have any spares?"

"I'm not actually your squire," Lance said, annoyed. "You do remember that I'm the king's champion, and a full knight?"

"Exactly what a squire who didn't want to go look for a spare sword would say," Arthur returned.

Lance sighed. He opened a trunk and dug through the contents. "This one should do." He held up a light rapier. "I'm hoping you know how to use it?"

"Poke them with the stabby end," Emry said confidently, tucking the sword into her belt as Lance choked.

"The stabby end," Arthur repeated, incredulous.

"I know how to stage fight," Emry said. "How different can it be?"

Arthur and Lance exchanged a look. "Stick to magic, and once this is over, I'll train you myself," Arthur promised.

"In sword fighting?" Emry said, beaming.

"That should be fun," Lance muttered.

And then Lord Agravaine entered. "It's almost time, Your Majesty. A soldier has ridden ahead with news that the rest of our forces will arrive within the hour."

Arthur nodded. "I'll be a minute," he said, gesturing at the last plates of his armor, which hadn't yet been fastened.

Lord Agravaine left, and Arthur looked at his two friends, suddenly struck by the horrible thought that this might be the last time the three of them were together.

No. Better not to think like that. Better to remember what he was fighting for. The new Camelot that they would build together.

Lance finished buckling Arthur's armor and held out his sword on both palms.

Excalibur glowed faintly, and when Arthur wrapped his hand around the hilt, his sword gave a reassuring pulse.

There was nothing left to do here but join his soldiers. Arthur put a hand to Emry's cheek. "I hope we know what we're doing," he said.

"What *are* we doing?" she asked.

Arthur shrugged. "Building a better world?" he suggested.

"Oh, right. That." Emry grinned. "So I guess we'd better win this battle, then."

"I guess so," Arthur agreed.

Emry looked at him with so many words Arthur knew she was holding back, because he was doing the same. She stepped forward and pressed her lips to his. His helmet and armor got in the way, but they didn't care. Their kiss was many things. It was grief and love, fear and hope, it was luck . . . and goodbye, just in case luck wasn't on their side.

◑ ◑ ◑

Arthur's lips still tingled from their kiss as he paced the courtyard of the old fortress, his soldiers waiting for his command.

They were ready to fight, but more than that, they were ready to fight together. Arthur walked down the lines, acknowledging all of them. When he returned to the front, they stared at him expectantly, and he realized he was meant to make a speech.

He didn't have anything prepared, so he said what he would have wanted to hear in their position. "Today, Camelot needs us," he began. "Today, we come together to defend our kingdom, not just from an invading army, but from a man who craves power, and doesn't care who he harms to get it. We will not let him take Camelot from us! We will not let him win!"

The soldiers cheered.

"We've faced him before and tasted defeat," acknowledged Arthur. "But we were not prepared. Today, we are. I journeyed to a different world to acquire the weapon that will bring his unbeatable soldiers to their knees." Arthur held up the horn. "I have made certain that their magic will fail." The men cheered once again. "So raise up your swords, for Camelot!"

"For Camelot!" the men echoed.

Arthur raised Excalibur into the air, its glow blinding. The men raised their own swords.

They were ready. There was only one thing left to do.

Saf and Tristan raised the portcullis, and Arthur rode out across the bridge to meet King Yurien.

The Lothian king rode forward, dressed in golden armor. His thinning reddish hair was slicked back from his face, which appeared even ruddier in complexion from the heat. His eyes were flat, dark, and calculating. The sword at his belt had a wicked curve to its blade, and he wore his crown, as if he needed such ornamentation in battle.

Arthur felt plain in comparison, dressed the same as his knights, in well-fitted plate armor, and a crimson cloak. He wore no crown or circlet. Just Excalibur, in an ordinary sheath.

And his heart was pounding so loudly that he wondered if anyone else could hear it.

"Yurien Vortigen," he said. "Unrightful King of Lothia."

"Arthur Pendragon, the boy who calls himself High King of England," Yurien replied with a sneer.

"It's not too late to call this off," said Arthur. "Give back Cameliard to its rightful ruling family. Remove your men from Northumbria. Sign an accord of peace with all the kingdoms of England, and we will not hold grudges for your designs at an empire."

"There it is," said Yurien. "The presumption of youth. Of a boy who has never spent a day without a crown on his head. You don't want peace. You want power."

"I want my men to go home to their families," said Arthur.

"Give me Camelot, and they can," said Yurien. "Let them watch their king die a martyr, on his knees, right here, and yours will be the only blood I shed on this day." His smile was an awful thing. "Will you sacrifice yourself for them?"

"You have an army that cannot be killed," Arthur said, wondering what the man was trying to prove.

"Exactly," said Yurien. "I'm not the villain you make me out to be. You're the one who would send your people to fight a losing battle, not me. You're the one who claims to be High King, yet who takes no action to seize that title. What are you so afraid of? Everyone seeing you for the failure you are? I offer you a noble death. Sacrifice yourself."

"You'd give me your word that you would call off this battle?"

"Do you trust me so little?" Yurien inquired with a sharp smile.

Yes, Arthur thought. The bargain made no sense. Yurien still believed his army to be unbeatable. He knew Arthur would never agree to such terms.

"I trust you as much as you have given me reason to trust," replied Arthur. "If I refuse?"

"Then you may return to your men and watch them suffer. Watch them die. And know that you are responsible. Their blood will be on your hands, and your crown will be on my head."

So it was an intimidation tactic, Arthur thought. Yurien meant to unsettle him in these final moments before the battle. But it wasn't going to work.

"I believe you know my answer," said Arthur. "I am the rightful heir to Camelot, and the future king of all England. You may believe you can change your fate, but you cannot change mine. The only blood on my hands will be that of your soldiers."

"A pretty speech for a scared boy who needs a magic sword in order to fight," sneered Yurien.

"Said by a king-killer who needed to make a bargain with a sorceress so his soldiers would have the advantage."

Yurien grinned. "This battlefield will be your tomb."

Arthur stared coolly back. "We shall see."

CHAPTER 56

Lance's heart pounded and his focus narrowed as he rushed forward, leading the first wave of the attack. He had volunteered for this, had wanted this, but now that the honor was upon him, it seemed more like a curse.

So many men rode at his back, following him into battle. He was the king's champion, and for the first time, the weight of what that truly meant pressed down on his shoulders.

The Lothian archers loaded their bows and fired, a volley of arrows flying toward them. Lance forced himself to keep his eyes forward, not to look up at the approaching assault. Emry's magic would protect them. He saw the first arrows hit her ward and bounce back as if they had encountered a tightly stretched sail.

"It's working!" some of the men cried in relief, as if they had doubted it.

"Bows out!" Lance shouted. "Aim! And fire!"

The arrows his own men shot arced overhead and rained down on the Lothian forces. Many were blocked, bouncing off shields, but some of the soldiers fell.

And did not get back up.

He watched, waiting. Hardly daring to believe it. Yet still they did not rise.

Lance felt a small spark of hope flicker within him.

Arthur had done it. The horn had taken away the protection that had made Yurien's soldiers unkillable.

His soldiers fired arrows again and again as they rode toward their enemy. More of Yurien's men fell. Lance's heart was pounding as they rode closer still, yet his hands did not shake. He felt fear, yes, but more than that, he felt determined as he called out, "Bows away, swords out! And *charge*!"

◐ ◐ ◐

"Why are my soldiers dying?" Yurien bellowed, his face a deep shade of puce. He held back in the last lines of the battle, watching in disbelief as his soldiers fell by arrow and sword, ordinary mortals once again.

"I don't know, sire," stammered one of his commanders.

"Then find out!" Yurien snapped.

"I already told you," Morgana called. Her husband glared at her, but she forged on. "I told you their wizard had done something, but you didn't listen!"

Yurien gritted his teeth in annoyance. "You told me she'd changed the weather!"

"I would have told you that probably wasn't all she'd done, but you kicked me out of your tent before I could," Morgana reminded him.

His eyes flashed with anger, and he raised a hand as if to strike her again.

"*Confuto*," Morgana drawled, as if bored. She stared at her husband's metal gauntlet, frozen in midair.

His face turned red as he realized what she'd done.

She waved a hand, releasing the spell and stepping neatly out of the way. Her husband lost his balance, stumbling forward. "I don't suppose you'll try that again," she said coolly.

He glared, the fight having gone out of him as he proclaimed, "It isn't possible for the girl to be as powerful as you claim."

"She is! I've told you from the beginning, but you never listen to me! And now it's too late. You didn't want my help, so watch what happens now that you no longer have it!" Morgana whirled around, hurrying away before he could see the smile on her face.

Yurien had made it clear he didn't care about her. He had bargained gleefully with Bellicent, and laughed as he urged his son down a terrible path, and made her feel alone, when the thing she needed most in the world was a partner.

So she was done. She only wished that being right tasted sweeter. She'd known her half brother wouldn't have agreed to face an immortal army without some powerful magic of his own. He was too set on peace, too much like their mother. He cared about his people, and he'd never subject them to a second round of slaughter.

Morgana should have guessed Arthur had more up his sleeve than a couple of paltry wards. Meeting at Camlann at an appointed date and time was a strategy, yet her husband had only seen weakness. And now Morgana knew the rest of the strategy: her brother had found a way to beat Bellicent's magic.

Whatever Arthur had, Morgana wanted it.

So she went off in search of Arthur Pendragon, son of her most hated antagonist, whom she had once tried to kill, to learn whatever trick he had used to defeat Bellicent's control.

CHAPTER 57

Arthur galloped across the battlefield, his crimson cloak snapping in the wind. Again and again he sliced at soldiers with his sword, felling them in sprays of blood and gore. He felt sick from the count of it, and sicker when he stopped counting.

All around him, the battle raged. Yet most of the bodies that decorated the battlefield wore black cloaks instead of crimson. Everything was a blur of steel and blood, of mud and shouting, of his heartbeat thundering in his ears, and his grip on Excalibur, and the fatal strike of his blade, again and again.

It wasn't fair. War wasn't fair. There was no glory or honor in this, in blacksmiths slaughtering bakers, in men of the same island fighting for different kings, because of some arbitrary lines on a map they'd had no hand in drawing.

An arrow caught his horse in the flank, and she reared back with a high-pitched whinny. Another arrow struck, and Arthur dismounted in a hurry, knowing better than to keep his seat. He winced as soldiers struck at his horse, an innocent creature who knew nothing of kings, until she, too, lay fallen in battle.

He dropped into a fighter's crouch, gripping his sword, and steeling himself for a crush of Lothian soldiers to attack. But his common armor had done the trick. As had Excalibur's grudging agreement to dim its glow. On the ground, he appeared no different from any other soldier.

The fighting felt more monstrous to walk through, however. Arthur choked back bile as he stumbled over a beheaded body in Camelot's crimson. A wounded soldier's hand shot out and caught him around the ankle, and he realized with horror that it was Safir, the young castle guard who never quite did his job.

"Sire," the lad choked.

Arthur bent down and grasped his hand. Sard, he was young. Eighteen, if that. His face was tight with pain. The wound in his side was bad, blood gushing from between his ribs. A trickle of it ran from a corner of his mouth. That, Arthur knew, meant his internal injuries were too severe. He wouldn't make it. His time was nearly up.

Arthur wished he could do something more for the lad. But the field of Camlann was covered with lads like Safir. With idealistic young fighters who had eagerly volunteered, thinking themselves heroes and wishing themselves immortal.

Saf coughed, and more blood darkened his lips. "Did we win?" the lad asked weakly.

"We will," Arthur promised. And then he had a thought. "Hold this."

He wrapped the young guard's hand around Excalibur's hilt, over his own. Saf closed his eyes. Sighed. "It doesn't hurt anymore," he whispered in wonder.

And then he went still.

Arthur blinked away tears as Saf's hand dropped lifelessly to his side.

And then he clenched his jaw, hefted his sword, and kept fighting.

○ ○ ○

Emry stared down at the chaos of the battlefield, her sword at her waist, her wand in hand. She was in one of the lookout towers of the old fort, where she might survey the field, yet be clear of it. The ward she'd placed over the soldiers was the biggest one she'd ever cast. Her father had trained her well, back in Anwen.

Not a single arrow had gone through. Taking the ward down momentarily so their own archers could shoot had been difficult. But she had enjoyed the challenge. Now there was no challenge to be had, other than holding the wards steady, and watching the gruesome battle play out. There was little for her to do except keep her enchantments going and wait. And she hated waiting.

"Well, well, if it isn't the little witch," a voice said. "I hoped I'd find you lurking around here somewhere."

Emry looked down and saw a black stallion, its rider dressed in a midnight cloak and skirts. The woman put back her hood, and Morgana glared up at her. Emry flinched, but then she realized it was truly Morgana. Not Bellicent. She pointed her wand at the sorceress. "What do you want?"

"To talk," Morgana said. "Can you come down?"

Emry deliberated. What if it was a tactic?

"If I wished to harm you, I would have simply snuck up and flung you from the tower," Morgana pointed out.

Emry sighed, hating that she saw Morgana's logic. "Fine, I'm coming down."

The fight was at a distance on Camlann Field, but still, Emry's shoulders were tense as she faced her one-time opponent. Morgana swung down from her horse. She looked awful. There were dark circles under her eyes, and her skin was mottled pink from old burns.

Burns Emry had caused. She winced, remembering.

"I know you spoke with her," Morgana said. "With Bellicent."

"And what if I did?" Emry replied. "I didn't promise her anything."

"Then you're the only one." Morgana sighed.

"How could you bring her back here?" Emry accused.

"I didn't know!" Morgana said, her expression fierce. "I thought I was escaping, not playing into her hands. And then it was too late. You don't know what it's taken to wrestle back control."

Emry didn't care. She had no time for Morgana's sob story.

"You tried to kill me. And Arthur," she said. "You struck a bargain with the high sorceress of Anwen. You did this to yourself."

"It was never about me. She wanted you!"

Emry frowned. "Me?"

"You're the one who can open a doorway between worlds. That's what I've come to tell you. She let me go. She said she'd found a way to come into our world as herself. Who else could she mean but you? I'm not asking for your help. I'm giving you a warning."

Emry folded her arms across her chest. "Why should I believe a word you say?"

Morgana gave Emry a searching look, as if trying to determine how much to confess. And then she admitted, "My husband let Bellicent torture me. He knew she was controlling me like a puppet, and instead of trying to save me, he made a deal with her. He let her corrupt my son! Do you think I care at all about his selfish war?"

Emry swallowed thickly. "He let Bellicent torture you," she repeated, horrified. "He knew."

"He knew," Morgana said darkly. "As I said, this isn't my war. All I care about is what happens to me. To my son. To the witch who tried to lock me away in the darkness of my own mind and wear my skin."

Emry shivered at the description. "Then prove it," she said. "Prove that you're not here to, I don't know, kill me or offer me up to that horrible sorceress."

"How?" Morgana demanded.

"Figure it out!" Emry snapped.

Morgana looked around. Far off, on the battlefield, Yurien's men shot flaming projectiles from two trebuchets. She closed her eyes, breathed deeply, and murmured something under her breath. Emry watched as one of the catapults collapsed, its wood splintering.

"There," Morgana said. "Believe me yet?"

Strangely, Emry did. "Bellicent really said she'd found another way into this world?"

"Yes! And if it's true, it's us against her, so we either have to stop her or figure out what that looks like before it's too late," said Morgana.

Emry hated that she agreed. "Would you speak with Arthur and me, after the fighting is over?" she asked. "Maybe together, we can figure out what to do."

"I will," Morgana promised. She climbed back onto her horse. As she raised her hood she said, "By the way, what did you do to our soldiers?"

"Removed their enchantment," said Emry. "You might know a little something about that."

Morgana scowled at the accusation. "Was it the ward?"

"The river," Emry said, and Morgana nodded, impressed. "We only wanted a fair fight," Emry explained. "Your husband's the one who started this war."

"War is the game of men who have no power within them."

"Or who mistake strength for power," Emry returned.

"You didn't have to listen to me," Morgana said.

"I know," Emry replied. "So don't make me regret it."

CHAPTER 58

Arthur wiped the blood from his blade on a dead soldier's tunic, hating himself for it.

He couldn't tell if they were winning or losing. Yurien's men were skilled soldiers, even without the enchantment, and many of his own were barely more than boys holding blades they'd never used.

In the distance, one of Yurien's trebuchets collapsed, and Arthur half expected the man to have another wheeled out from the forest to take its place. He hadn't anticipated the catapults, the cannons—weapons that had demolished the walls of their fort, targeting their best archers.

The battlefield was littered with too many bodies. They were going to kill each other until there was no one left. Until a dozen survivors stood amidst a blood-soaked valley and declared one side's victory, though it wouldn't be a victory at all.

This was going to be his legacy. The thought made him sick. He never should have let it get this far. If he had died in that cave beneath St. Paul's Cathedral, none of this would have happened.

His fault. His fault. His fault. His mouth was metallic with the taste of it.

A soldier in Lothian black rushed at him, and he barely registered raising his sword, driving Excalibur's blade through the man's stomach, watching him fall.

Arthur shook his head in despair, and then he noticed a strange shadow cresting the hill. Not a shadow—soldiers. Their footsteps stamped like thunder as they marched in orderly lines. There were thousands of them.

His heart sank. Yurien had called for reinforcements. He had even more soldiers who hadn't drunk from the river laced with the elixir. Thousands of soldiers who couldn't be killed, marching their way to the battlefield, while his own men would be none the wiser.

It was over. Done. Camelot had lost. Perhaps the fight had never been his to win.

But when the soldiers got closer, Arthur saw they were dressed in gold tunics with a black sigil.

And riding at the front was a young man atop a black horse, his brown skin contrasting against the silver of his mail and armor. A red cape flowed from his back, and behind him flew a banner that Arthur knew well . . . *his own*.

Gawain raised his sword, shouting at the men. They plunged into battle, and it was immediately obvious that Lothia's forces were out-numbered. Then Arthur realized where he knew their sigil from.

Flanders had come to their aid!

"Over here!" Arthur called, waving to his cousin.

Gawain rode across the field, pulling his horse to a stop at Arthur's side. "Sorry I'm late. I just had to blackmail the King of Flanders into sending us aid."

"Actually, you're just in time," Arthur said. "Honestly, you might just have saved us all."

"God, I hope not." Gawain made a face. "I'd hate to be good at war."

They watched the fighting for a moment, together. Yurien's men were in trouble. And Camelot's spirits were high at the arrival of their reinforcements. They fought with renewed vigor, driving back the Lo-thian soldiers. Arthur's chest squeezed with hope. If this kept up—if he didn't have to lose more of his men—truly, Gawain couldn't have arrived at a better moment.

"Where's your wizard?" Gawain asked.

"Oh, she's around here somewhere," Arthur said.

"So you came to your senses." Gawain grimaced. "A part of me hoped that you wouldn't."

"I almost lost her," Arthur said. "I almost lost sight of the king I wanted to be."

"And I almost ran away to France with the most incredible girl I've ever met, but then she chose you."

Arthur couldn't help but grin. "She did, didn't she?"

"Stop gloating," Gawain snapped. "Or I'll tell my army to switch sides."

"To fight for Yurien?" Arthur asked, deliberately misunderstanding.

"To fight for—oh, forget it," Gawain said. "You know I don't want that kind of responsibility. After this is over, I intend to take a chest of gold and a case of wine and board the fastest ship I can find to somewhere interesting."

That actually didn't sound like the worst plan. "Room for a few more on that ship?" Arthur asked.

"Survive this battle first, and we'll talk," said Gawain.

"Done," Arthur declared. "And there better be room on this ship for my books."

Gawain winced. "No promises."

◐ ◐ ◐

Arthur waited on the field of Camlann, pacing nervously. Lord Agravaine stood at his side, holding the treaty that King Yurien would sign, relinquishing his hold on Cameliard and declaring the victory at Camlann to be Camelot's.

Yurien and his men rode up, and Arthur saw with surprise that Yurien's young son, Mordred, was at his side, dressed in boy's chainmail with a small sword at his belt. Morgana trailed behind them, smiling as though she had a secret.

Arthur tried to imagine his father taking him along to a battle, letting him witness the atrocities of war at such a young age. It would have given him nightmares for months. Yet Mordred looked delighted by all that was going on and gazed adoringly at his father.

"You've called me here, Arthur Pendragon?" King Yurien boomed.

"I offer peace," said Arthur, dispensing with any pretenses. "Enough blood has been spilled in this competition to wear the crown. Keep yours and rule over Lothia. Relinquish your claim on all other lands. And bow to me as High King."

"Is that all?" Yurien said nastily.

"That's more than fair," said Arthur. "You will still be king of your own kingdom. I will take only what you wish to give in tribute and will not intervene in your rule, so long as your laws and treatment of your people are fair. Your son can rule as king after you, provided he is just. I've had my advisors draw up a treaty. All you have to do is sign."

"And if I refuse?" Yurien asked mildly.

"You will not receive such an offer again," said Arthur. "Bow to me, sign the treaty, and we will ride into the field at each other's sides and call off the fighting. Your men will thank you for your mercy. Your people will still have you as their king."

Yurien frowned, and Arthur had no idea what the man might do.

And then Morgana rode forward. "Sign the treaty, husband," she urged. "Let us return to our castle. Let our son become a king."

After a long moment, Yurien dismounted his horse, and then, with rage in his eyes, he bent the knee. "High King," he said, his head bowed, his voice a dangerous whisper.

"I accept your fealty, Yurien Vortigen," Arthur replied.

"Give me a quill," Yurien snarled. "Let's get this over with."

Lord Agravaine stepped forward and presented the document with a flourish. Yurien read through it and nodded. "All is as you say," he replied. A table was laid, and the document stretched across it.

Lord Agravaine unfurled a second copy. "So you may each have one," he said.

Arthur watched in disbelief, hardly daring to breathe as King Yurien dipped his quill into the inkpot and stared down at the scroll, at the line that would end their fighting. After an interminable pause, he scrawled his signature on the first parchment, and then the next.

And then he threw down the quill. Arthur seized it and signed his own name.

"It is done," Lord Agravaine pronounced.

Arthur called forward a herald and motioned for King Yurien to mount his horse. "We will ride out and break the news that the war is ended. Bring your family with you, so your people can see that I have left them unharmed."

Emry nudged her horse forward. "I'm coming, too," she said. "You should have someone by your side."

"Very well, wizard," Arthur said. His eyes met hers, and she, too, seemed as happy as he felt in that moment. They had done it. All was well.

And so they rode out onto the field, the herald riding ahead and trumpeting for the fighting to cease. "Lay down your swords. Stay your blades!" the man called.

"We have reached an agreement," Arthur proclaimed, "to end this war for good." He slid from his horse and unfurled the treaty from his belt, holding it up.

Yurien dismounted and stood there, his chin raised. "I, Yurien Vortigen, King of Lothia, sovereign of Northumbria and Cameliard, have been asked to bend the knee to Arthur Pendragon, King of Camelot."

He withdrew his sword to toss it to the ground, as was the custom for surrendering. Instead of letting go, Yurien held his sword high as he announced, "But I refuse."

Before Arthur knew what was happening, Yurien lunged at him, sword in hand. Arthur had no time to reach for Excalibur. The blade thrust deep, finding the opening in his mail and piercing through him.

He gasped, staggering back at the blinding burst of pain in his stomach.

Yurien had betrayed him.

The scroll of their peace accord fell from his hand, rolling across the blood-soaked battlefield. Arthur gritted his teeth and scrambled for Excalibur. The moment he gripped the sword, his pain abated. The wound dripped blood, but he could no longer feel it. All he felt was the pulsing sword in his grip and a roaring sense of injustice.

"How dare you?" Arthur demanded, advancing on Yurien.

The king paled. He clearly had not expected Arthur to survive such an attack.

"This man signed a peace accord," Arthur said, raising his voice. He felt strangely cold and shaky, which wasn't painful but was something else entirely. Like he was disconnecting from his body. "He bent the knee to me as High King. We rode out here to announce an end to the fighting. Let it be known throughout England that Yurien Vortigen is a liar without honor."

"Say that again, boy," Yurien sneered, raising his blade.

"This is your final chance," Arthur said. "Stay your sword. Or I won't hold back."

"Do your worst," Yurien said, a smug expression on his face as he settled into a fighter's crouch.

Arthur's blade flashed bright as he lunged forward, steel meeting steel in a clash of blades. The battlefield watched in horror. Dimly, Arthur knew he was wounded, badly. He also knew that, so long as he wielded Excalibur, he could not lose. So he held on to the sword for all that he was worth, parrying and thrusting against the insistent, spineless Lothian king.

Arthur's blade caught the man's shoulder, and Yurien shouted in pain, lashing out with his own blade.

A miss. Arthur pressed his advantage again, his movements lightning fast, the blade moving practically of its own accord. He caught Yurien on the opposite shoulder, and then on the leg, and finally the man stumbled and slowed.

Arthur approached. There could be no mercy. The time for showing kindness was past. Yurien had shown him only violence.

Yurien fell back, staring up at Arthur in horror.

Arthur didn't hesitate as he raised his blade and plunged Excalibur into Yurien's chest.

The blade stuck fast, and for a moment Arthur was reminded of another blade he had once pulled free, in a similar position. The sword in the stone.

The sword whose legacy and legend had led him here—to this blood-soaked battlefield, a killer who wielded a magic sword, staring down at a dying king.

"You'll regret this," Yurien swore.

"I won't," Arthur said. "I offered you peace. I offered you a kingdom. Your death is on your own hands."

"It should have been you lying here," Yurien spat.

Arthur knew how close he had come to that fate. He didn't want this. Any of it. He felt faint as he watched the life drain from Yurien's eyes.

And then he remembered the wound in his stomach. He grimaced, clapping a hand to the bleeding gash and staring down at the man he had just defeated.

"No!" a voice shouted, high and clear and young.

Arthur looked up and saw Yurien's son standing by the body, his expression a mixture of horror and pain. He was so young. Perhaps eight years old. He stared at his father's body, and Arthur winced.

"You killed him!" Mordred accused. "You killed my father!"

And then he launched himself at Arthur.

Arthur didn't see the dagger, but he felt it drive into his side. Felt the hot, angry tears the boy was crying. Felt the fury of his small fists banging the mail on Arthur's chest.

"He couldn't die! He wasn't supposed to die!" the boy wailed. "I hate you!"

Arthur fell to his knees, the boy hanging on him still. Searing pain shot through his side, getting worse by the moment. His vision swam. He nearly passed out from the pain. He heard shouting, and dimly realized that was him.

And then Morgana was there, pulling her son off of him, looking terrified. "Mordred!" she shouted. "What have you done?"

"He killed Father!" the boy screamed.

Arthur waited for Morgana to finish it. A dagger to the throat was all it would take. He doubted he could even lift a hand to fight back. He lay staring up at the clouds, waiting for his death. They reminded him of the mists of Avalon, of the magic he had found there, falling in the lost king's tomb, facing his fears, the sword growing heavy in his hand. Yet he didn't have the sword anymore. And even if he did, he doubted it would help. It wasn't pain so much as his body knowing what awaited it. He didn't want to die. He had known there was a possibility that he would, but now, all he could think about was how much he still had left to do. How little he had lived.

And then Emry was there, crying, clasping his hand in hers. His wizard. He was a great king, and she was by his side, and perhaps the brief time they'd been together was all they had. Perhaps it was all history now.

"Hold on," she told him.

But he was so cold, and everything was collapsing into mist. He shivered, he couldn't stop shivering. The clouds were fog, he was on a boat, sailing away. Or maybe he was still on the battlefield at Camlann, the dagger still in his side that had almost been his death once before.

He doubted he'd be lucky enough to escape that fate again.

CHAPTER 59

Emry squeezed Arthur's hand in hers, hating how cold it felt.

She wasn't going to be able to save him. He was so far gone. But she had to try. She wiped the tears from her eyes and reached for her magic, commanding it harder than she ever had before.

"*Angsumnes,*" she cried. *"Angsumnes!"*

But the damage was too complex. He had been stabbed with a dagger and sword, and there was so much blood, even foaming at the corner of his mouth.

She didn't know what she was fixing, and when she reached out to feel for his injuries, they didn't make any sense. All around the knife wound was a cloying darkness that made her head spin. Still, she tried again.

Magic surged from her and left her gasping, but Arthur's body just seemed to drain it. She tried to heal him again and again, until her teeth were chattering and her vision swam. She tried the rune magic she'd used in Anwen, but that only made her dizzier.

Nothing was working.

And then she felt a hand on her shoulder.

She looked up into Lance's heartbroken face. He shook his head. "It's too much, isn't it."

It wasn't a question so much as a statement.

"He's going to be okay," Emry said dully. But they both knew it wasn't true.

She couldn't imagine a world without Arthur. Couldn't imagine him dying here like this, betrayed by a man who had agreed to peace, and finished off by a furious child whose attack he hadn't even thought to block.

"Here," Lance said, holding out Excalibur. "Maybe this will help."

Emry gently eased the sword into Arthur's hand. His eyes opened, glassy with pain. She helped him to sit up, just a little. He coughed wetly, his chest rattling.

She held him in her arms, her shoulders shaking with despair. She had seen him like this before, but somehow, this time felt different.

Morgana picked up the scroll that Arthur had dropped. She held it overhead, addressing the stunned and silent battlefield, who was still gathered to witness the peace accord. "My husband spoke false," she said. "I saw him bend the knee and sign this treaty. We are at peace. As Queen of Lothia, I accept Arthur Pendragon as High King." She curtseyed to Arthur's prone form. "Your Majesty."

Emry frowned. "What are you doing?"

"Preventing these men from murdering each other, and us along with them," she said.

If Emry still had doubts that Morgana was truly their ally, as she'd claimed, this proved it. Morgana turned back to the soldiers. "Hail, King Arthur," she cried. "High King of England!"

Slowly, the entire battlefield dropped to their knees. "Hail, King Arthur," they cried. "High King of England!"

Emry blinked back tears. And she saw that Arthur was doing the same.

CHAPTER 60

Emry held Bran Galed's horn to Arthur's chapped lips, her heart thrumming with hope that it might work.

Please, she thought. *Please let this save him.*

"Drink," she urged, brushing his hair from his damp brow.

He swallowed weakly, liquid dripping down his chin. His eyes closed, and he took a ragged, heartbreaking breath.

"Did it work?" Lance asked, still pacing the length of the bedchamber.

"I don't know," Emry said. She peered down at Arthur, who looked so pale and so weak laid out on top of the covers in the first bedchamber they'd been able to find in Joyous Gard.

"It's—not—getting—any worse," Arthur whispered.

Emry reached for her magic again, trying a healing spell. But that awful darkness pushed back, resisting. The darkness was larger now, taking up more of his stomach and chest. She waited a moment, then cast her Anwen healing spell. The darkness drank it in, and she shivered at the sensation.

Whatever that awful dagger had done, Bran Galed's horn hadn't fixed it. But it did seem to have stopped it from spreading even more.

"That's a start," Emry told him. "You should rest." She handed the horn to Lance. "Have him drink more of this. It can't hurt."

Lance frowned. "Where are you going?"

"To find Morgana."

◖ ◖ ◖

The sorceress was pacing the courtyard, her expression tense. She looked up at Emry, genuine worry on her face as she asked, "How is he?"

"Alive," Emry said with a ragged sigh. She shook her head. "But I can't heal him."

"Then there's no time to waste," said Morgana. "We should get him to Avalon immediately."

"Avalon?" Emry repeated, taken aback.

"It's the only place that might save him. Or have you never heard of its healing waters?"

Of course she had. The sorceress was right. And Emry wished she'd been the one to think of it. "I'll take him," Emry promised.

"You mean *we'll* take him," Morgana corrected. "It's my fault my son had that dagger. He got it from Bellicent. She put a horrible enchantment on it."

The enchantment that was preventing Arthur from recovering. Even with Excalibur. Even with Bran Galed's horn. Even with all the healing spells Emry had tried.

"He can't die," Emry said fiercely. "I won't allow it."

"Neither will I," Morgana agreed. "Besides my son, Arthur is all the family I have left in this world. He could have killed me when he had the chance. Instead, he spared my life. He offered my husband mercy, and my son a crown. I cannot keep blaming him for the circumstances of his birth. He is my half brother, and we are not enemies. We have only wanted different things."

It was strange to see this side of Morgana. The woman who Merlin had chosen as his pupil, and who had the same mother as Arthur. Before, Emry hadn't understood how those things were possible. But now the sorceress before her was no archvillain, just a woman who had suffered, and raged, and fought all the ill fortune that fate had given her, and refused to allow fate to have this victory, too.

"If you're coming with us, we'll need a horse and cart," Emry said. "A carriage will attract too much attention."

"I'll get one from our camp," Morgana promised. "Have him ready to travel within the hour."

Morgana was as good as her word. Emry made Arthur as comfortable as possible in the back of the cart, covered with his cloak. But still, his face was pale, his skin stretched too tightly over his bones. Still, he winced and gasped at every movement, even with Excalibur in his hand.

Emry felt hollow seeing him like this, like his pain was leeching away her own life as well. Morgana took up the reins, and Emry nodded. They jolted off.

"Wait!" a voice cried.

Emry turned and saw Lance riding after them on a brown horse.

"Stop the cart," Emry said.

Morgana sighed. "This isn't a passenger wagon."

Lance pulled his horse alongside them, and Emry saw he had packed provisions, and was dressed not in his armor but in plain, sturdy clothing. "I'm coming with you," he said.

"We don't need your help, knight," Morgana sneered.

"Maybe not, but Arthur would want me by his side," Lance said, lifting his chin. "As he was by mine when I faced a similar fate."

"Lance is right," said Emry. She gave Arthur's hand a squeeze, and he nodded. "Arthur would want him to come."

"Er, about that, where are we going?" Lance asked.

"Avalon," said Emry.

Lance shook his head. "Somehow, it's always Avalon."

It took them two days to reach the isle. Two days of begging sleeping arrangements in barns, paying off farmers and grooms handsomely so they might sneak Arthur inside unnoticed. Two days of tense, horrible suppers and sending Lance to trade their horses at inns, and keeping awkward, silent company.

"What really happened?" Emry asked Morgana on the second day. "In Anwen?"

Grudgingly, Morgana told the tale of the frozen world, the beasts that had been immune to the curse, of Bellicent wearing the skin of the dead and burrowing into her mind, twisting her words until they had a meaning Morgana never would have agreed to.

And Emry found herself believing that Morgana had truly undergone a change of heart in her quest for power and would not make the same decisions again.

When the mists of Avalon came into view, Arthur stirred. He'd grown weaker by the hour, and anyone could see his time was nearly spent. The darkness still consumed him. Every time Emry felt for it, it was the same, and she didn't know how much longer he could last like this. She was existing in a perpetual twilight of horror, worried they wouldn't make it in time.

Yet they had.

"We're here," she told him.

He nodded tightly. "Good," he murmured, but it was so soft that he might not have said anything at all, that perhaps he had merely sighed and Emry had imagined it.

And then Emry saw the boat, and her heart sank. It was too small. A rickety thing, barely large enough for two people to squish in, with their knees touching. And she doubted Arthur could sit upright.

It would never work.

"*Amplius*," she commanded.

The boat stayed the same size.

Please, she thought. *We need more space.*

The boat didn't change.

They couldn't have come all this way only to be felled by a boat. It was laughable. Emry sat down on the shore, put her head in her hands, and promptly burst into tears. Now that the tears had started, they flowed freely.

A hand rested on her shoulder. She looked up to find Lance staring down at her.

"The boat," Emry moaned.

"We'll make it work," he assured her. "If you can't make the boat bigger, what if you made Arthur tinier?"

Arthur let out a weak but indignant cough.

"I'm not shrinking the King of Camelot so he fits in my pocket," Emry protested.

"I was thinking more the size of a cat," said Lance.

She didn't think Arthur would be able to withstand such a transformation.

And then she felt a voice reach out to her.

Morgana will not be joining you. Help your king into the boat, wizard of Camelot.

It was strange to have the Lady of the Lake's voice in her head when she wasn't on Avalon. She hadn't realized Nimue could manage it.

Morgana had an odd expression on her face, and Emry realized the Lady had not spoken to her alone, but to them both. "Better do what she says," said Morgana.

Lance and Emry helped Arthur into the boat, and to Emry's astonishment the vessel grew to allow him to lie down on the bottom.

"I'm not getting left behind," Lance said, climbing aboard and taking up Arthur's hand in his.

Emry turned to Morgana. "Thank you," she said. "For everything."

"Don't let him die, wizard," Morgana snapped.

When Emry stepped into the boat, it shot out from the dock, gliding across the pristine surface of the lake and into the mists of Avalon.

❶ ❶ ❶

The Lady of the Lake was waiting for them on the shore, still as stone, a lantern raised against the mist.

Lance carried Arthur from the boat, Excalibur trailing limply from his hand. His breath was shallow, and Emry had never seen him so pale.

"I have been expecting you," said Nimue.

"Please, my Lady," Emry said. "You have to help him. He's dying."

"What would you have me do, wizard of Camelot?" the Lady asked.

Emry frowned at the change. The Lady had always called her "child of Merlin" before. "Whatever will restore his health. I'll give anything."

The Lady gestured to a stone slab that rose from the sand, where Lance gently laid his friend. Nimue closed her eyes, and raised her hands above Arthur's chest.

Emry's breath hitched at the otherworldly sight. He looked like a corpse, laid out like that. Like an effigy of a former king. Like a monument to someone she had already lost. His chest rose slowly, painfully, though not by much. But she took comfort in that fact.

He's still here, she told herself. *You did it. You brought him to Avalon. If there's anything that can save him, it's this place.*

The Lady of the Lake stepped back, shaking her head. "His time grows short."

"What about the healing waters?" Emry asked.

"There will be a price," the Lady warned.

"I will gladly pay it," said Emry.

"As will I," said Lancelot.

"The waters may not help him," she cautioned.

"We'll try them anyway," Lance insisted stubbornly. "We came all this way to save him."

"Then bear your king to the sacred waters."

She waved her hand, and a stretcher appeared beneath Arthur, with poles so they might carry him. Emry took up one end, Lance the other. When they reached the cloister, dozens of girls peered at them with dark, worried eyes, the white of their gowns suggesting mourning.

They bore him to the dark pool that Emry had visited once before, and gently lowered him into the healing waters.

Arthur's eyes closed. He sighed. Emry's heart leapt at the sound. He was going to be all right!

And then his body rose into the air, hovering above the water, before being gently deposited on the stone floor. He was soaked, but he didn't look healed.

"What happened?" Emry demanded.

Nimue shook her head. "The waters cannot save him. Magic does not work on magic."

Emry had thought her heart was already broken, yet she felt it shatter into even more pieces. For a moment, she had hoped . . . but now there was no hope left in her. Arthur was beyond even the Lady of the Lake's help.

"So that's it?" she said. "Arthur's just . . . going to die?"

"Walk with me," said the Lady.

CHAPTER 61

"Do you understand what I have told you?" asked the Lady, her expression grim in the moonlight that lit the cloister.

Emry nodded, tears threatening to spill out. "Arthur must die," she said. The words tasted bitter on her tongue, like ash, and she nearly choked on them.

The Lady of the Lake nodded. "It was foretold," said the Lady. "But death does not need to be his ending."

"How is death not an ending?" Lance demanded.

The Lady of the Lake met his eye. "You have brushed close to the veil yourself. You know what it is to touch death."

Lance shook his head, his voice hollow as he muttered, "I'd rather forget."

"You came here once," the Lady said to Emry, "and defied me, opening a doorway to the Otherworld so a lost creature might find its way home."

Emry frowned. "The questing beast?" she said, remembering the soft, fox-like animal who had called to her in her sleep. She hadn't known it was dangerous. She had only wanted to help it.

She thought of Prince Tiernen's and Sir Hafgan's reactions when they'd encountered such a beast on their quest, and her chest squeezed at the memory of riding back from the Four-Peaked Fortress that day in victory, believing all would be well.

"Do you remember what I told you of its powers?" the Lady asked.

Emry did. "Its blood can bring someone back from a freshly dug grave, but its bite is a pain worse than any mortal wound." Her eyes went wide as she pieced together what the Lady was saying. "So Arthur has to die, but he doesn't have to . . . stay dead?"

Nimue nodded.

"His return is up to you. A questing beast favored you once. Perhaps it will do so again. Its blood will revive him, but should the creature refuse you, you will suffer beyond measure. The pain will be so great that you will beg for the escape of death."

Emry didn't doubt that the Lady of the Lake meant what she said. Still. If it was the only way to save Arthur . . . she would pay any price.

Emry looked to Lance, whose expression was determined.

"So we're doing this?" he asked.

Emry squared her shoulders. "We're doing this."

◑ ◑ ◑

That night, Emry and Lance kept vigil by Arthur's bedside. His breathing was shallow, his sleep fitful. Emry ached to help him. To cure what ailed him.

Arthur must die. It was foretold.

The Lady's words echoed through her head, mocking her. She might have told them that at any point. But no, she'd kept the knowledge to herself.

Emry stared down at the book in her lap, realizing she hadn't read a single page. She'd selected it from the library so she might read it to Arthur, but when she'd opened it to try, her voice had been too rough, her throat too choked with tears.

Lance sat with his head bowed, his expression one of pure anguish. The candles dripped wax and burned low, and the night felt impossibly long. The shadows on the walls flickered and lengthened, and in the gloom, Arthur's body stretched out like a pale effigy. Excalibur's glow was so dim that it barely gave off any light at all.

Suddenly, Emry couldn't stand it anymore. "I can't just sit here wait-ing for the questing beast," she said, closing the book and rising to her feet. "I'm going to find it."

"I'm coming with you," said Lance.

Emry shook her head. "You should stay here, with Arthur. In case he needs you."

Lance's lips flattened into a line at the implication. But he didn't protest. "You're really going to do this alone?"

"I have to," Emry told him, with more bravery than she felt. "Re-member what Nimue said. A questing beast favored me once."

"It was probably a bunny, and you got mixed up," Lance joked.

Neither of them cracked a smile. Emry nodded at Lance, and he nodded back, his expression solemn. And then, by the light of her wand, she reached for her cloak and slipped into the cool darkness of the cloister.

The woods were unsafe, and the creature was dangerous, and she didn't have a plan. Just her magic and her nerve. She hoped that would be enough.

Above, the moon shone full and bright, casting a blue tint on the cloister's pale stone. The forest, however, was a strange, sickly green, swirling with mist that let off an unearthly glow. Emry held her wand high, and her fear close.

The brush underfoot was dry and brittle, and snapped with each step she took. The noise would attract every predator in these woods. One twig snapped so loudly that Emry gasped, startled by the sound. She had no doubt that the Lady of the Lake heard it and knew what she was doing.

Branches snarled overhead, scraping at her cloak with their rough edges. A nearby owl hooted, and in the distance, something shrieked, perhaps a small animal, or perhaps the woods themselves. The trees grew wider and more ancient the deeper she went. Their branches blocked out the sky, and Emry couldn't help but think that the forest was trapping her. Her heart pounded in her chest. She was truly alone. Not just here, in these woods, but in the deepest part of her soul. And she couldn't take it. She had to save Arthur, to help him. She couldn't lose him like this, couldn't have gone to all this trouble for nothing. *I have to find the questing beast.*

Almost as if the forest heard her thoughts, a whisper of an idea formed in her head of which direction she should go. She didn't question it. She followed her instinct, venturing deeper, until she came upon a dark cave. Something was drawing her inside, a feeling she couldn't explain. She held her wand in front of her, and the glow brightened, which was either a very good sign or a very bad one. Not that she could tell.

The cave was enormous. Crystal formations hung from the ceiling, glittering like many faceted daggers in her wand light.

"Hello?" Emry called, and then instantly felt foolish.

But there was something here. She could feel it.

Something ancient and magic and, most of all, *important.*

She came to a room that seemed to have been carved out of rock itself, all except for a strange tomb that sat at its center. Emry frowned, remembering the story Arthur had told her of his adventures on Avalon the first time they had visited.

The Lady of the Lake had brought him to a strange cave and made him lie down in a creepy tomb, where he'd faced his fears and gained Excalibur.

Perhaps the same thing would work for her.

Will it? she thought.

But the cave didn't answer.

She was already here, so she might as well try it.

She peered inside the raised tomb, hoping there wasn't already a body inside. She was met with only darkness and dust and cobwebs. So many cobwebs.

Here goes nothing, she thought, maneuvering herself onto the edge of the stone tomb. She climbed inside, lying down against the cool stone. She held her wand at her chest and closed her eyes. She didn't know what she was waiting for, but nothing happened.

Immediately, she felt foolish. She was no royal. No prophesied king of all England. No immortal sorceress had led her here to claim her destiny. She was just a girl with a great deal of magic and a great deal of heartbreak, lying in someone else's grave.

And then a thought occurred to her. Perhaps the Lady of the Lake had said something, an incantation or a spell, that had activated whatever happened to Arthur. When she had opened the door in the stones, she had needed to speak. She had needed blood as well, but she figured she'd try that only as a last resort.

"Δείξε μου," she said, the Greek low and lovely on her tongue.

Show me.

Nothing happened.

And then she was falling.

She fell a very great distance, through nothingness, or perhaps no distance at all. It was as if the world was rearranging itself, creating forms and plates, bringing the places to her that she most needed to visit.

She was in the woods, behind the cottage she had grown up in, crouched in a tree, watching as her father led her brother out to a clearing, and showed him a spell to levitate a fallen leaf. Emmett chewed his lip and repeated the spell, but nothing happened. He tried again and again, and Emry felt enormously impatient. Why couldn't he do it? The spell was such a simple thing. From where she watched in the tree, she dug her own wand out of her apron skirt, raised it, and whispered the word her father had shown her brother. A leaf rose into the air, swirling in a magical gust of wind. Her father grinned, pleased.

"Emmett, you clever lad! You've done it!" he cried.

Emmett twisted around, finding Emry perched in the tree, and glared. But all he said was "Yes, Father."

"We'll come back here tomorrow," their father promised, "and I'll show you so much more. I'll show you all the magic I know. And one day you'll grow up to be the greatest wizard that Camelot has ever known."

Emry burned with resentment. She wanted to scream and cry out, "What about me? You wouldn't even show me the spell!"

At supper that evening, she asked her father if he would teach her some magic.

"What do you need with magic, sweetheart?" asked her father. "You should leave such things to the men of this family. I'm sure your grand-mother doesn't need her helper running off to cast magic spells when there's so much work to be done here."

Emry remembered how she hadn't protested. Hadn't fought back against his narrow worldview. But this time, she did.

"You're wrong," Emry said, pushing back her chair. "And if you won't teach me, that won't make me less of a wizard. It will just make you less of a father."

The scene collapsed into mist, and once again Emry had the curious sensation of falling. Then she was in Arthur's tent, at the sword-fighting tournament from months ago, disguised as her brother. Arthur lunged for her with Excalibur in hand. She felt the weight of his formerly en-chanted scabbard at her belt, and the sharp strike of his sword against her side, cutting open her flesh.

Her knees buckled, and Arthur was at her side, helping her into a chair.

"Sard, Emmett, why did you flinch?" he asked.

He pulled her tunic over her head, and there she was, her chest bound, her deception laid bare.

He frowned at her. "You're not Emmett Merlin."

"I'm his twin sister, Emry. The *other* Merlin."

She felt Arthur's disbelief, his pain. She had lied to him. Betrayed him with her false identity. His eyes narrowed. "You played me false! Guards!"

But that wasn't how it had happened! Emry's heart pounded in fear, and her side ached from the wound. "No!" she pleaded, reaching for his hand. "Don't! Please."

"Why shouldn't I have you thrown in the dungeons for deceiving me?" he asked in this horribly twisted memory, the way she'd worried he would.

"Because I love you," Emry confessed. "I risked myself to protect you, and I'd do it again. I'm meant to be by your side, and not in some grand metaphorical way, but in all of the ways that matter."

The scene changed.

Emry sat at Arthur's bedside. He was dying. He moaned, staring up at her, reaching weakly for her hand. He was so pale, his lips chapped as he whispered, "Don't let me die. You have to save me."

"I'm trying," Emry promised.

"I need you," said Arthur. "I've always needed you."

Once, Emry had been afraid of this. Of mattering too much to the boy who would never choose her. But now she knew he'd chosen her in every way that she had let him. She needed to save him. Not just for the future of Camelot, but for their future. Together.

"I need you, too," Emry confessed. "If there was anything of my-self that I could give, anything I could trade to save you, I would."

"Would you give up your magic?" Arthur asked shrewdly.

Emry frowned. "My magic?" And then she saw a strange shadow

behind Arthur's eyes. She realized she was no longer talking to Arthur, but Bellicent.

"Make a deal with me, child," Bellicent said, her voice spilling from his chapped lips. "I will save him. I will save you both. Your magic is a small price to pay for a miracle."

"What would you do with it?" Emry asked.

Bellicent's laughter was high and clear. "Whatever I choose," crooned the sorceress. "Do we have a deal or not?"

Emry ached to say yes. To save Arthur. But somehow, she knew he wouldn't want this.

"No," Emry said, "we don't."

Abruptly, the chamber fell away, and Emry was back in the mist. Flashes of moments danced before her eyes, tantalizing glimpses of things she could only partially make out, scenes she was desperate to study.

She and Arthur at the prow of a boat. A baby in a cradle. A jail cell. A golden cup. The gateway between worlds crashing down, crumbling at her feet into so much sand.

She was falling, through snatches of time and memory, of past and future. And then suddenly she was back in the tomb, staring up at the crystals on the ceiling of the cave. She sat up, her heart pounding.

And then she saw the creature sitting on the floor of the cave, staring at her with its wide, strange eyes.

Emry froze at the sight of the questing beast.

"Please," she whispered. "I need your help."

She didn't know if the creature understood. It blinked at her, its fluffy, catlike tail wrapped around its feet.

"I really need your help," she repeated.

The creature tilted its head and stared at her. *I do not know you*, it said, the words forming in her head much like Bellicent's.

She saw now that it was not the same creature she had rescued. This one was smaller and pure white, and its tail was much shorter.

I am alone and lost, said the creature. *But I do not desire the company of a human.*

"Perhaps we can help each other," Emry proposed.

How?

"I met another questing beast once," she said. "It wanted to go home, through the stones. I helped it."

We were together, said the creature. *Now I am alone.*

"But you don't have to be," said Emry. She took a careful step toward the creature, and when it did not run away, she took another. "I can help you rejoin the one you have lost. But first, I'll need a favor."

Name your price, and if it is fair, I will consider it.

Emry bit her lip. This was it. Either the creature would agree, or it wouldn't.

"The man I love is dying. The only thing that can help him is some of your blood."

How much? the creature asked coyly.

That was a very good question.

"How much will bring someone back from a freshly dug grave?" Emry asked.

Its eyes narrowed into slits. *I do not know.*

"This much?" Emry bargained, holding up the stoppered glass container she'd slipped into her cloak.

The questing beast nodded. *That much you may take, but not a drop more.*

"Then we have an agreement," Emry said, relieved.

She drew her dagger. The creature stayed where it was, staring at her with a trusting expression. Emry hoped she could trust the animal in return.

Its bite is a pain worse than any mortal wound.

She reached gingerly for the beast's paw, and lifted it, making a neat slice with her knife. Blood bubbled to the surface, staining its snow-white fur a deep red as it bloomed. Emry let the blood drip into the glass bottle. The creature hissed in pain but remained still until the vial was full.

Emry stoppered it and put it into her pocket. "Thank you," she said.

Now give me what you have promised, the questing beast demanded.

Emry nodded. "Follow me," she said.

When they reached the doorway to Anwen, Emry stopped short, staring at the stone arches. She hadn't realized they'd bring up such memories in her, of her father, of the way he had abandoned her. Of being at Arthur's side on an adventure, trying to do what was right with no idea of what would happen next. They had been so naive, so sure that they would succeed. So convinced that there would be no ill consequences. She was far wiser now.

Emry reached for her dagger again, slicing a shallow cut on the palm of her hand. She placed it on the altar, mumbled the words that would open the gateway, and waited.

Mist swirled between the stones, and gradually took the shape of a forest, with ink-black trees, silvery leaves, and berries red as blood. The creature tossed her a grateful glance and leapt through without a word.

It stared at Emry from the other side, its nose twitching, and then it bounded off into the forest. Into the world where her father was without her, through the door that only she could open.

She closed the portal and stared at the stones a moment, her cut hand throbbing. And then she patted the bottle in her pocket and headed back to the cloister.

◑ ◑ ◑

"How on earth did you get this?" Lance asked, staring down at the bottle.

After she explained about the tomb, and the questing beast, and the door to Anwen, Lance shook his head and said, "You didn't need me at all, did you?"

"Of course we do," she said. "It's Arthur. He always needs you. For moral support."

"I suppose," Lance said, unconvinced.

"Besides who else is going to threaten to slay his nipple?" she asked as they walked into his chamber, where the Lady of the Lake sat at his bedside in the gloom.

"I heard that," Arthur said, his voice so faint that it was as though he hadn't spoken at all.

"We have a plan," Emry said, holding up the bottle.

The Lady of the Lake rose, looking pleased. "I see you have accomplished the impossible," she said.

"The first part, at least," Emry said.

"What plan?" Arthur asked.

"Right." Emry sat down at his side. He looked so fragile. So wounded. "You're going to die. And then we're going to use the questing beast's blood to bring you back to life. Easy peasy!"

Arthur winced. "Any other options?"

"We let Bellicent heal you at whatever price she demands," Emry said without pause.

"Pass." Arthur was silent a moment. "I've nearly died before," he said.

"So have I," added Lance. "It isn't so bad, really. The hard part is the nightmares afterward."

"I won't mind those," Arthur said. He nodded slightly, and then coughed. "Okay. Let's do it."

Lance rested a hand on Arthur's shoulder. "It's going to work," he promised.

"Course it is," Arthur whispered.

"Come, knight of Camelot, walk with me," said the Lady of the Lake.

And then they were gone, and Emry and Arthur were alone.

"You'll stay with me?" he asked.

"Until the end," she promised, swallowing back a sob.

"Not much longer, then," he said weakly. He let go of Excalibur, and his face tightened with pain. "Take the sword," he whispered.

Emry took up Excalibur, which glowed once and then calmed itself, pulsing weakly in her grip.

And then Excalibur vanished from her grasp.

One moment it was there, and the next, it wasn't.

"It's gone," Emry said wonderingly.

"Must not—need it anymore," Arthur gasped.

Emry knew what that meant. They both did.

She bent down and pressed her lips to Arthur's. His were so cold, and the kiss was mostly ruined by her tears and his shivering, but they both pretended it wasn't. Emry thought of the boy in the library, dressed as plainly as a librarian, and letting her think that's what he was. Of Arthur, bent over his mortar and pestle in the morning sunlight, smelling of coffee and smiling at her jokes. Of his arms around her, dancing. Of the evening they'd watched the sun set over the Paris rooftops from the tallest tower of Notre Dame. Of the way his hair ruffled in the sea breeze, and how earnestly he'd promised that he would choose her forever, in the dark water of Madame Becou's bathhouse, the night before his wedding.

It wasn't enough. They hadn't had enough time. She could feel him slipping away, leaving her behind, to the one place she couldn't yet follow.

"I love you," she whispered. "You're going to come back to me."

And then his eyes closed and his hand slipped from hers, and there was nothing left to do but sob helplessly over his lifeless body.

CHAPTER 62

Emry didn't know how she found the strength to dig his grave. Lancelot worked silently at her side, stopping only to wipe tears from his eyes. The Lady of the Lake watched, stoic and silent in the mist.

When it was done, when they stared down at the rectangular space they'd carved from the loamy soil, it suddenly felt even more real. "Has anyone ever done this before?" Emry asked Nimue.

The Lady gave her a long look. "You would be the first."

So it might not work. It was only a fairy tale, a guess, a shot in the dark. Somehow, she had expected that. Had known it all along but hadn't wanted to acknowledge the dark shadow of it, lest that shadow grow larger and more powerful.

She felt dull and detached, like she wasn't really here. Like she couldn't be here, digging Arthur's grave with Lancelot mourning by her side. The world had been jolted out of alignment. Nothing made sense.

The Lady motioned, and in the growing darkness, a young priestess stepped out of the woods in her white gown, clutching a candle.

Behind her was another girl, and another.

They all came to stand in a circle around the grave.

Behind them came the older girls, carrying the narrow wooden box that contained Arthur's body. It was plain, and not at all how one buried a king, but Emry suspected that didn't matter. She saw as they got closer that the girls weren't carrying the box at all. That it was floating, and they merely accompanied it.

The Lady of the Lake made a gesture, and the coffin lowered itself into the grave.

Emry stared down at it, feeling ill. Her vision blurred with tears, her throat went tight, and she reached for Lance's hand, needing something to hold to anchor herself here, to this horrible moment in this strange place, so she didn't split apart entirely, fractured by her grief.

"Today a man is buried here who died too soon," said the Lady of the Lake. "He was a just and fair king who gave his life in the service of his people. A life that shall be returned to him, for King Arthur Pendragon will rise again. He was king once, and he will be king once more," said the Lady of the Lake. "Today we bury Arthur Pendragon, the once and future king."

"Arthur Pendragon, the once and future king," everyone echoed.

The Lady turned to Emry and Lance. "You must do this properly," she said. "Take up the shovel and finish this grave."

Emry reached for the shovel with trembling hands, and picked up a mound of dirt, pouring it on top of the coffin. It landed with a thud that made her shudder.

She passed the shovel to Lance, who did the same.

Silently, the girls filed back into the woods. The Lady of the Lake remained, standing like a statue in the purpling twilight. Together, they buried their king. Their friend. The boy who they both loved, in different ways.

Once it was done, Emry stared down at the grave, choking back tears.

"Will this work?" she asked the Lady of the Lake.

Nimue shook her head. "I cannot see his future," she said. "It is well shadowed by the veil of death. But yours leads you away from Camelot."

Away from Camelot? Surely that couldn't be true.

"Walk back with me, knight of Camelot," said the Lady of the Lake.

Lance gave Emry a nervous look before departing with the Lady.

Emry was alone, staring down at Arthur's grave. She took a steadying breath, picked up the shovel, and began to undo what they had just done. She dug until her shovel hit the wood of his coffin, and then she lowered herself into the grave and brushed away the last of the dirt. With a trembling wave of her hand, and a choked spell, she loosened the lid of his coffin and peered inside at Arthur's lifeless body.

He was beautiful in death. A marble statue, pale and still. Emry wiped tears from her cheeks with her sleeve. She hadn't even realized she was crying, but tears came so easily these days that she wasn't surprised. It was like they were constantly beneath the surface, waiting, just like her magic.

"This is going to work," she whispered, withdrawing the stoppered bottle. And then she paused, unsure what she was supposed to do.

Did he need to drink it? That seemed foul, not to mention impossible. The way to create a monster, not to bring back the boy she loved.

She lifted his tunic, finding the soured, ragged wounds that lay beneath. She didn't even flinch at the sight of them. Not after all that she had seen of war and violence and death.

This is the theater, she told herself. They were in a play, onstage, acting out a scene about doomed, star-crossed lovers. She had brought the magic elixir to his tomb, and he would awaken in her arms.

She imagined it, *willed* it to happen.

She took her blade to his cut from Mordred, opening it. And then she poured the questing beast's blood upon his wound.

The thick liquid bubbled the moment it hit his skin. Encouraged, she poured more on Yurien's traitorous gash. Then she sat back and watched with hungry eyes and a heart full of hope.

Slowly, so slowly that it made her want to scream, his wounds began to heal. The edges turned red, then pink, forming jagged, puckered scars.

Yet Arthur lay still, his chest unmoving, his eyes closed.

Emry sat there and waited, her hope slowly draining away as the minutes, then hours ticked by.

She held his hand, cold and pulseless. Held it in her own. "Come back," she whispered. "Please, come back to me."

But he didn't.

She waited, her despair growing, until at last the Lady of the Lake returned with Lance stone faced at her side.

"Well?" the Lady asked.

"It didn't work," Emry said, her voice small.

Lance bit his lip and turned, rushing away in anguish.

"The questing beast's blood healed his wounds, but that's all," said Emry.

"Then that is all there is," said the Lady. "Come, child. It does not do to linger too long with the dead. We must leave them behind, in order to move on."

But Emry didn't want to leave him. And she certainly didn't want to move on. "I'm going to stay a little longer," she said, lifting her chin in defiance.

"It is your life. Spend it as you will," said the Lady, disappearing back into the woods.

"I'm right here," Emry told Arthur's lifeless body. "I'm by your side." She raised her eyes to the forest, addressing it. "Isn't that the prophesy? That he'll be a great king with me by his side? Well, here I am, so make him king again!"

The branches stirred, and she wondered if it was the forest laughing at her.

And then, impossibly, it started to rain.

Emry let out a hollow, defeated laugh as the first hard drops splashed onto her face. She stood and put up her hood. And then she reached for her dagger. "*Algiz*," she whispered, pricking her thumb.

The magic bubbled up, and a small ward settled over his grave, protecting it from the rain. It was the last thing she could offer him.

She did not close the lid of his coffin, even though she knew she should. There was no reason to hope, but she couldn't help it.

The rain soaked through her cloak instantly, but she hardly noticed. It was time to return to the cloister. To try and do as the Lady had told her, and accept that Arthur had sacrificed himself, that he was lost to her, and that somehow, impossibly, she had to keep going.

Even though that was the last thing she felt like doing. Each footstep was heavy and fraught. She wiped away tears, or perhaps rain, or maybe a mixture, following the footsteps the girls had left in their procession to and from the cloister.

She could cast a spell to find her way, but the thought of more magic made her sick. What good was magic if it stopped short of doing what she needed? If it couldn't give her back those she had loved and lost.

So she walked on, in the pouring rain, not a powerful wizard, but just a girl who had buried the boy she'd hoped to spend her life with.

CHAPTER 63

The pressure in his chest was agony. Arthur opened his eyes, staring up at what was surely an impossible sight. Rain, sliding off an invisible barrier above his head.

His mouth was dry, his throat so parched that it felt as if he had swallowed sand. His arms, when he tried to move them, felt clumsy and heavy. In one hand, he clutched a bottle of blood. And he was lying in a box that looked suspiciously like a coffin.

He sat up slowly, wincing in pain. His heart was pounding like he'd just run a marathon, and his thoughts were sluggish, his head full of fog, and there was an ugly collection of scars on his stomach that he didn't remember.

There were a lot of things he didn't remember.

He had been on the battlefield at Camlann, so convinced he had brought peace to England, uniting its kingdoms. Then he had been betrayed and wounded. He had killed King Yurien. And Mordred had rushed at him with a dagger.

After that, it was just snatches. The knowledge that he was dying. Emry by his side. Some sort of boat. Was he . . . on Avalon? Or somewhere else, even farther from the world he knew?

He pushed to his feet, his vision swimming and threatening to go dark. All around him were woods. They looked magic, but they didn't look like the trees in the Otherworld.

It was harder than he'd anticipated to climb from the grave. When he had, he stared down at it, at the golden glow that rose up around it, that had protected him from the rain.

The ward was Emry's work. He would know it anywhere. *Emry.* His heart squeezed at the thought of her.

Had she buried him? Did she think him dead?

He tilted his head up toward the sky, letting the rain pound against his cheeks and drip through his hair.

He was alive! Very much alive. And he didn't understand how that had happened.

But there was one thing of which he was absolutely certain: Somehow, impossibly, Emry had saved him. Again.

◐ ◐ ◐

Emry pushed around the food on her plate at supper, saying nothing and eating even less. Across the table, Lance was shredding a piece of bread to sawdust in his lap, seeming a million miles away.

She couldn't take it anymore. This grief they were both drowning in, this silence that shouted in her ears. She stood, making her excuses. Lance merely nodded.

And then, instead of going back to her room, she slipped out of the cloister. She needed to—someone needed to—she couldn't even think the phrase . . .

Bury him properly.

She had left Arthur's open coffin at the bottom of a grave, in the rain, protected by a ward that wouldn't last forever.

And if she didn't go back to do it right, she didn't know who would. So she conjured some light at the tip of her wand, put up her hood, and made her way through the forest. Tears slipped from the corners of her eyes. She had been crying for so long that it amazed her she still had tears left, when she felt so hollow. She didn't bother to brush them away as they trickled down her cheeks. There was no point. No reason to dry them.

And then she heard footsteps behind her. She spun around, her wand raised.

But it was only Lance.

"What are you doing here?" she asked, sounding angrier than she felt. Or perhaps she was angry, but not at him. Angry at the world.

"Same as you," he said. And then he paused before asking, "Isn't it going to be wet?"

"I put up a ward," Emry said. "To protect him from the rain."

"Clever," Lance said, but the praise rang hollow.

"Don't," Emry whispered. "Please."

"I loved him, too," Lance said quietly.

She knew he had. Lance had loved Arthur as fiercely as if they had truly been brothers. She could feel their shared loss drawing them together, stitching their friendship into one that would last a lifetime. They had both lost him, and with him, crucial parts of themselves.

Emry reached for his hand and squeezed, and he squeezed back, smiling sadly.

The rain had tapered, leaving behind a world that seemed to be too raw to wipe away its own tears. They walked in silence toward the place where they had laid Arthur to rest.

And when they reached it, Emry gasped and Lance cried out.

The grave was empty.

◐ ◐ ◐

"It wasn't like this when I left it," Emry said.

"I'd expect not," said Lance. He frowned, then turned to Emry and asked, "Do you think it worked?"

She shook her head, staring down at her muddy shoes. "It didn't," she whispered. "I'm certain of it."

"Don't doubt your own magic, wizard," a familiar voice said.

Emry looked up and found Arthur standing at the forest edge, smiling at her. His clothes were muddy and damp, and his hair a mess, but it was truly him. *Alive.*

She pressed a hand to her mouth, her eyes clouding with tears of joy. By her side, Lance let out a colorful swear.

"It worked," she said in disbelief.

"It did." Arthur nodded at Lance. "You look like you've seen a ghost."

Lance rushed at him, tackling him to the ground. Emry watched as the two of them rolled, Arthur laughing and Lance crying, until they came to a stop with Lance on top, staring down at his best friend.

"Don't you ever do that to me again," Lance scolded.

"Let you have the upper hand?" Arthur said. "No promises."

Emry stood over them, scowling. "Honestly," she said. "Did you have to tackle him? He was just dead!"

"There, you heard the wizard. I'm delicate," said Arthur. "Now, get off me so I can kiss her properly."

Lance obliged, and Arthur climbed to his feet, brushing the mud from his clothing with a grimace.

Emry stared at him. Their eyes locked, and something in her that had broken, that she'd thought was a burden too heavy for her to bear, seemed to melt away, replaced by a giddy, impossible lightness.

Arthur was alive. She had brought him back.

"I thought you were really gone," she said.

"Good thing I have a court wizard who knows some pretty impressive magic," he said.

"Stop flattering me and get over here," Emry said.

He did. Their kiss was everything she'd thought she'd lost and would never find again. It was a future that was possible, even after she'd mourned it. It was sweet and perfect and wonderful, and she never wanted it to end.

But then Lance cleared his throat, loudly. "Plenty of time for that later," he said. "But we should probably, uh, let the Lady of the Lake know that you're alive."

Arthur sighed. "I hate it when you're right."

"You do not," Lance said.

"Er," Arthur said, looking down at his belt. "Where's Excalibur?"

"It vanished," Emry said, surprised he didn't remember. "Right before you . . ." She trailed off, not wanting to say the rest of it.

"Ah." Arthur nodded. "It left when it was no longer needed. I was wondering when that was going to happen. Well, come on, you can tell me everything on the way back to the cloister."

CHAPTER 64

Willyt Merlin pressed his bleeding palm against the ancient stone of the cave.

"I have come to reclaim my magic," he announced.

Having heard him, the stones buzzed beneath his hand, and he felt the pulse of their magic course through him, rattling his teeth and rushing through his veins.

What would you do with it, if it was given back to you? the stones asked.

"I would return home, restored to what I once was."

Not good enough, whispered the stones.

Merlin groaned in frustration. Vivienne had been right. The stones wouldn't just return his magic because he'd asked. "What do you want from me?"

The truth.

Well. If that was all. Merlin sighed and confessed, "I'm not ready to stop being the most powerful wizard in my kingdom. There's so much more I have to do. I can't be done yet. I can't."

Yes, you can, replied the stones. *Your arrogance betrays you. You treasure your magic as if it is the most valuable part of you. But you have changed since we last met, wizard. If you regain your magic, you will forget all you have learned. You will betray all you care about. You will be remembered throughout history as a lonely old man with magic and nothing else. Do you truly want this?*

Merlin hesitated. He had chosen wrong in the past, and he knew this was a moment where he might correct that course and choose differently. But his magic was right there, pulsing in the stones. He had journeyed so far, and he couldn't leave with nothing. He *wouldn't* leave with nothing. His fists clenched. He wouldn't leave without his magic.

"I do," he said. "Give me back my magic."

The stone went icy beneath his palm.

And then he heard footsteps behind him.

Bellicent swept into the cave, lowering the hood of her green cloak, her grin sharp and dangerous. "Am I late?" she purred.

Merlin's stomach twisted. He had not thought he would face her again. Especially like this, practically powerless. *Come on*, he thought, pressing his palm more deeply against the stones. *Give it back*. But the magic still churned beneath the surface, just out of reach.

"Bellicent. I wasn't expecting you," he said, his voice tight with worry.

"Then you're a fool," she snapped. "Did you think I wouldn't sense it the moment that doorway opened between our worlds?"

"Doorway?" Merlin frowned. "I entered weeks ago. Months."

"Interesting," Bellicent purred. "So it wasn't you. But yours is the only magic of its kind I can sense in Anwen."

So she had followed him here. He swallowed nervously. He'd hoped she hadn't noticed. That she was still distracted by whatever game she was playing with the Lothian king. Clearly he had underestimated her. He had done so once before, and it hadn't gone well.

"You know why I am here," Bellicent went on. "What I want."

"I'll never open a doorway for you into my world," Merlin warned.

Bellicent shrugged. "That is no matter. I don't need you. All I need is your magic. And fortunately, it is up for the taking."

She plucked a dagger from her waist and struck it across her palm. With a wolfish grin, she pressed her palm to the stones.

Merlin felt the pulse of his lost magic change course, flowing away from him.

"No!" he cried out in anguish, but the stone sucked at his hand, trapping him in place, powerless to do anything but watch.

His magic. He'd been so close to regaining it. He struggled, unable to break free, forced to watch as Bellicent stole what was his. She tipped her head back, her eyes closed as if slaking her thirst, a triumphant grin upon her lips.

Finally, the stone released him. He stumbled back, losing his balance. When he regained it, Bellicent was watching him. He had the impression of facing a predator. Of standing too close to something ancient and evil that knew it had won, and was merely playing with its prey.

"Your magic is mine now," Bellicent told him. She shivered with pleasure, examining her hands where the veins pulsed bright and silver.

Two broad-shouldered men in tattered guard's uniforms stepped into the cave, their expressions vague and empty.

"Bring him with us," Bellicent ordered.

The men, who were hollow and unfeeling, and whom Merlin suspected were no longer men at all, grabbed him by the shoulders.

"Don't do this!" he protested. "There is nothing for you in my world!"

"Yes, there is," Bellicent replied. "A new start. A world ripe for the taking."

"A world with little magic," Merlin countered.

"Then mine will seem even more impressive," said Bellicent. "This world is rotten to me. The people whisper my name in fear. Mothers terrify their children with tales of what I might do to them. But your world is fresh. They would worship me as a goddess."

"They won't!" Merlin snapped. "They'll know you for the monster you are!"

One of the guards twisted his arm, and he gasped at the pain. He recognized it as a warning that the guard could do even worse, and so he remained grudgingly silent the rest of the way.

The stone arch rose tall and pale in the forest, and Bellicent stroked a loving finger down the altar while Merlin watched in disgust.

"I do love an audience," she said. She slashed her palm again, making a fist and holding it above the altar. Her blood dripped onto the stones, and she licked her lips.

"If you're going to kill me, do it," Merlin said tightly.

"Kill you?" Bellicent sounded amused. "No, you're coming with me. You tried to defeat me, and you failed. Now you can watch as I claim your world for my own."

And then she spoke the words that opened the doorway.

◖ ◖ ◖

Emry woke with a gasp as the Lady of the Lake threw open the door to her room. It was dark outside, not yet dawn, and the Lady held up a lantern, her expression tense in its weak glow.

"Get dressed and come with me," she said. "Both of you."

Arthur, who was burrowed under the covers, groaned. Emry kicked him.

"Yes, my Lady," she said.

Something was wrong. Emry knew that much. She and Arthur dressed in tense silence, then joined the Lady in the corridor.

"What's going on?" Arthur asked.

"Perhaps nothing, perhaps something," said the Lady, in that infuriating way she had of speaking in riddles.

And then a door at the other end of the corridor opened and Lance stepped out, fully dressed, buckling a scabbard around his waist.

"I did not summon you, knight," said the Lady.

"There was banging and talking in the corridor," he said. "Once a guard, always a guard." He yawned. "Anyway, I'm here now, so wherever you're going, you're not going without me." He tossed Arthur a shirt of mail and Bran Galed's horn. "Put these on. I've watched you die enough times."

Arthur rolled his eyes but shrugged into the tunic and strapped the horn and a sword to his belt.

"What about me?" Emry asked.

Lance shrugged. "You can take care of yourself."

"Enough chatter," said the Lady. "We must go."

Their walk through the dark forest was tense and silent. Emry and Arthur kept exchanging nervous glances but didn't dare to speak. The trees seemed to rustle in fear, and it wasn't until they reached the familiar clearing that Emry realized where the Lady had taken them.

The stone arch looked as it always did. Crumbling and lost to time, as if there was no longer any use for it. As if it wanted to be forgotten.

Emry was about to ask a question, but the Lady held up a hand. "Wait" was all she said.

A moment later, the stones shimmered. A scene grew clearer between them—a woman and Emry's father. The woman pulled him through the stones.

Emry stiffened in recognition. Even though she had never seen the woman before, she knew Bellicent on sight. She shuddered as the sorceress stepped through the stones, dragging Merlin after her. He looked shaken from the journey, but other than a shallow cut on his cheek, he seemed fine. Emry took in the cloaked woman with silver hair, whose tawny skin seemed stretched too taut across her bones, whose smile was sharp and eyes were hungry.

Emry shivered. This was bad. Catastrophic.

Judging from Arthur's grim expression, he very much agreed.

"Aren't you going to greet me, sister?" Bellicent asked, tilting her head at Nimue, and watching the Lady of the Lake as a fox would watch a wounded bird.

"You are not welcome here," Nimue said harshly.

Bellicent merely laughed. "Yet you have come to welcome me. And you've brought a brave knight, a merciful king, and a little witch."

"I prefer the term *wizard*," Emry said stubbornly.

"Look at all that fire in you," Bellicent crooned, stepping forward and taking Emry's chin in her hands. Emry tried to twist away, but the woman's grip was strong. At such close range, the emptiness in her eyes was terrifying. Emry had never seen anyone consumed by so much of their own darkness.

And this creature had been inside Morgana's head, controlling her body as if she pulled invisible strings? Emry fought a wave of sickness at the thought.

"What have you done to my father?" Emry demanded, turning her head until she twisted it free of Bellicent's grasp.

Bellicent tutted. "Nothing you need to worry about," she said. "The stones gave me his magic. I want him to watch what I do with it."

The stones gave Bellicent his magic? No. Surely that couldn't be true. Yet seeing her father cringing there, looking unwell while Bellicent's palms were crusted with blood, Emry knew the sorceress wasn't lying.

"Father?" she said questioningly.

"I'm okay, sweetheart," Merlin promised, though he sagged back against a tree. "Don't—"

Whatever he was about to warn her not to do, he never got the chance to say. Bellicent held up a hand and squeezed it around nothing—around the air—and her father choked. His eyes bulged, and his face turned red.

"Much better," Bellicent said.

"Stop it!" Emry demanded.

"Stop what?" Bellicent frowned. "I'm merely testing my new magic. Seeing how it works. After all, I plan to be here for a while."

"This world isn't for you, sister," said Nimue, stepping forward. "You must leave."

"Is that a threat?" Bellicent asked lazily.

"You have no fate here," said Nimue. "At least, none that I can see. Go back to your own world and forget this place."

"I could do that," Bellicent said. "Or I could be treated as a goddess in a world where magic is rare and my story isn't told to frighten children when they've been bad."

"I can't let you do that," said Nimue.

Bellicent laughed. She flicked her hand, and vines shot out from the forest, wrapping themselves around Nimue's arms and legs. Her lantern rolled to the ground and flickered out. The vines pulled and stretched, until she was strung between the trees. She glared at Bellicent, her eyes going full white.

"And how will you stop me, dear sister?" Bellicent asked.

Vines studded with sharp thorns shot out and wrapped themselves around Nimue's head. The vines squeezed tight, poking out her eyes as she screamed.

Emry winced, looking away.

"Oh god." Lance moaned, as if he was about to be sick.

The forest seemed to echo Nimue's scream, or perhaps it screamed back in protest.

Blood trickled down the Lady of the Lake's blinded face, dripping onto the soil below her. She hung from the vines limply. It hurt Emry to see the legendary oracle so helpless.

But if they didn't stop Bellicent, Emry knew far more people would get hurt. She looked to Arthur, who had drawn his blade.

"Let her go," Arthur commanded, his voice ringing through the clearing.

Bellicent laughed. "What's this? A king who wishes to defend a sorceress?"

"Wouldn't be the first time," Arthur said tightly.

"You cannot defeat me with an ordinary blade," she said, her voice mocking.

That was right. Emry had forgotten he no longer carried Excalibur. What a time for the sword to desert them. Unless it knew something they didn't. "I'll find a way," Arthur insisted.

Bellicent considered him and grinned, as if taking his vow as a challenge. She raised a hand, magic crackling at her fingertips.

Emry didn't think she could bear to see what the sorceress would do to him. "Wait," she cried desperately. She tried to think. She looked at Lance, who gripped the sword he had drawn as if unsure whether to use it. At Arthur, with his mail tunic and the horn hanging from his belt. And suddenly she had an idea.

"I want to join you," Emry said. "To rule this pathetic world together. I'm done taking orders from men who use my power for themselves, and have no magic of their own."

"No!" Lance cried out. "Emry, you can't!"

Emry tensed.

"I suspected this might happen," Arthur said gravely. "If the witch is to betray me, I won't beg her to reconsider." Arthur never called her a witch—he knew she hated it.

Emry glared at him, keeping up the lie and glad that he was playing along without knowing her plan. "A pity, I'd love to see you beg," she said to him. She turned to Bellicent. "So? Will you have me?"

"You would join me even after I have taken your father's magic?" Bellicent asked.

"My father was the first man to abandon me, lie to me, reject me. He refused to teach me magic because I was a girl, and he's ashamed of what I can do. What do I care if you've harmed him? He probably deserved it," Emry said with a shrug. "You asked me to join you once, to save him, and I refused. But only because I didn't care for what you were offering."

"Interesting," Bellicent said, her eyes glittering with curiosity. "So you will make a bargain with me?"

"I will join you to save myself from living in his shadow, when I'm more powerful than he'll ever be," Emry said carefully. She could feel Lance's frown and Arthur's questioning gaze, and she hoped they wouldn't intervene.

Bellicent considered her. "You'll bow to me?" she asked.

"I will serve you as a trusted advisor who has valuable knowledge of this world," Emry said. "We are the only two people with the power to walk between worlds. It only makes sense that we should be allies and control them together."

Bellicent's smile was bright with greed. "Then promise me your loyalty," she demanded.

Emry fought back a shiver. Her eyes met Arthur's, and he shook his head in warning.

Trust me, she thought.

"*Veni omnia!*" she called.

Arthur's blade flew from his grasp and into her outstretched hand. Lance's sword did the same.

"I've always preferred actions to promises," Emry said.

Bellicent looked pleased.

Emry held out her hand to Arthur. "Give me your drinking horn."

Arthur frowned but unclasped it from his belt.

Emry threw down the swords and took it, her heart pounding with the weight of what she was about to do. She crossed to the narrow stream that trickled through the woods, so narrow here that she could stand with one foot on either side.

"κέρας," she whispered.

She knelt, pretending to dip the horn, though it already bore the liquid she needed. And when she straightened, she made sure to prick her finger on the knife she wore at her belt.

Bellicent watched with narrowed eyes.

"I only wish it were wine," Emry said sadly. And then she raised the horn in toast. "To the women with the power to walk between worlds, and who will finally rule them."

She brought the horn to her lips and took a mouthful of its elixir, mentally tracing the rune *isaz*, and feeling Anwen's magic rise to the command and the liquid turn to ice on her tongue.

And then, with a smile, she handed the horn to the high witch of Anwen.

Bellicent sniffed the liquid, then took a sip. "Very well," she said. "Now will you make your bargain with me?"

"I don't think she will!" Arthur said. He'd retrieved his sword, and with it, he lunged forward, plunging it through Bellicent's chest.

She stared down at the blade and laughed. "You fool," she said. "Your sword cannot harm me."

Emry held up a finger and spat. A cube of frozen liquid fell to the ground. "Are you sure about that?" she asked Bellicent.

Blood darkened the pale fabric of the sorceress's dress. Bellicent stared down at it in disbelief, watching as the stain spread. She stumbled, reaching for a tree to steady herself. "How?" she demanded, her voice weak and raspy.

"You became mortal when you drank from Bran Galed's horn," Arthur explained smugly.

"You tricked me, you little witch," Bellicent slurred.

"For the last time," said Emry, "I prefer the term *wizard*."

Bellicent trembled, her face pale and drawn. Her once-powerful hands fluttered at the sword still stuck through her chest, and she groaned.

"I told you that you had no fate here," said Nimue.

"Fate is for the powerless," Bellicent retorted. Blood trickled from her mouth. Her knees buckled, and she slid to the forest floor, coughing wetly, the dark stain at her stomach turning into a pool of blood.

Emry wanted to look away, yet she forced herself to watch as the high sorceress of Anwen breathed her last breath, then closed her eyes for a final time.

"No!" Merlin cried, one hand outstretched to Bellicent's lifeless body. "My magic!"

"Your magic is gone," the Lady of the Lake told him as the vines restraining her loosened and she floated softly to the ground. "It died with my sister."

Nimue flicked her hand, and both Bellicent and the blade disappeared.

"But your eyes," Emry said helplessly.

The Lady of the Lake merely tore a piece of fabric from the trailing sleeve of her dress and tied it over her injury. "I can still see what's important," she said. "England's future is secure. You have brought us into a golden age, young wizard. And you as well, King Arthur."

Arthur bowed, then seemed to realize the Lady might not know he had and said, "Er, thank you."

Lance gave a soft cough.

"And you, Sir Lancelot, were clever to bring that horn," said the Lady.

Lance blushed. "I, uh, grabbed it by accident in the dark," he admitted. "I thought it was a blade."

Emry and Arthur exchanged a look and burst out laughing. They were still laughing as the new day dawned. Because Bellicent was truly defeated, and because they had survived, and because, impossibly, they had won.

CHAPTER 65

Every morning, Morgana checked whether the boat was waiting for her at the dock. Until, finally, on the ninth day, it was. She hadn't thought she would see Avalon again. The isle had banned her from returning on her last visit, but when she'd helped her half brother into the boat, the Lady of the Lake had spoken to her in her head, urging her to wait.

So wait she had.

And now she was gliding across the mist-choked lake in a boat that needed no oars or sails. She grinned, standing at the prow and savoring the feel of the wind on her face.

When the air begun to taste of magic, the Isle of the Blessed came into view.

And waiting for her on the shore was Nimue herself. Except something was wrong. The priestess wore a strip of white linen around her eyes, like a blindfold.

"You sent for me?" Morgana asked, climbing from the boat.

"I did." The Lady nodded. "I did not expect I would, the last time we met, but you have proven yourself capable of change, child of Igraine."

Morgana flinched at the name but knew better than to issue a correction. "How fares King Arthur?" she asked.

"He died some days ago," said Nimue.

Morgana's heart sank at the news. She'd thought—she'd hoped—but it didn't matter. "I see," she said quietly. "I should like to visit his grave, at least, while I'm here."

"Such a visit would serve no purpose," said the Lady.

Morgana fought back anger at such a callous response. "He was my half brother! I acknowledged him as High King. I wished to save his life, not to end it! If I have missed his funeral, I will not ignore his grave."

"Trust me, it's not that impressive," Arthur said dryly, stepping out from the forest. "But I appreciate the thought."

He wore all white, in the style of the cloister, his clothing loose and unadorned. There wasn't a scratch on him.

Morgana gasped, stumbling back as if she had seen a ghost. "You're supposed to be dead."

"I was," he said. "I just didn't stay dead."

Morgana looked accusingly at Nimue, who faced the lake, wearing that strange blindfold.

Not a blindfold, Morgana realized. The Lady of the Lake had lost her eyes.

"I believe I owe you my gratitude," Arthur went on. "For helping Emry and Lance to get me here in time for, well, everything."

That cryptic thank-you was the last straw. Morgana folded her arms across her chest.

"Someone better start explaining," she said. "Now."

Arthur did, as they walked toward the cloister. About the questing beast, and then about Bellicent.

"She's truly gone?" Morgana asked, hardly able to believe it.

"She's truly gone," Arthur confirmed.

"It is the dawn of a new age," said the Lady of the Lake. "One that has many possible paths."

Arthur made a face. "On that note, I suspect I'm meant to leave the two of you to talk."

Once he had gone, the Lady of the Lake laid a hand on Morgana's shoulder. "You have done well. I would reward you."

With magic? A flicker of hope sparked inside Morgana. But then she remembered the Lady's tricks. "With what?"

"A purpose."

That sounded like the opposite of a reward. But Morgana knew better than to say so.

"This island has been a prison to me," Nimue went on. "It was a lighthouse between worlds, that I might give a warning if yours was threatened. But my services are no longer needed, and I wish to be done here. To go home."

"To Anwen," Morgana said.

The Lady of the Lake nodded. "On my parting, I can ensure that our worlds will remain separate, as they should have been all along. I can destroy the doors in Anwen, and over time, Avalon will become less an isle apart. Its magic will fade. Perhaps all magic in this world will do the same."

"But what about the girls? And this island?"

"I would entrust it and them to you," said the Lady.

"To me?" Morgana said in surprise. "But why?"

"Because you know what it is to be unwanted, and to be a young girl who doesn't know her place in the world. You could help them. And the magic of this island would acknowledge you as its Lady. You would have access to power beyond what you have ever known."

Morgana felt a hunger within her at the thought of such power. But then she realized what sacrifice would be required for such a gain.

"Except I could not leave this place," Morgana finished.

"No," said Nimue. "Not until someone else replaced you."

It was an interesting offer, one that Morgana ached to accept.

"I can't," she said. "I won't abandon my son. He needs me, especially now. I—I'm sorry."

The Lady of the Lake said nothing. Morgana had the sense that she'd disappointed her.

"Perhaps there is another way," said a familiar voice.

Master Merlin stepped from the woods, his daughter behind him.

They both wore the white linen garments of the cloister, and Emry held a wand that glowed purple at its tip. She nodded at Morgana in acknowledgment.

"We saved him."

"I already know that," Morgana said, annoyed. "Well, what's this suggestion you have, Willyt?"

"More of a proposal," said the wizard. "If Nimue is looking for someone to take stewardship over Avalon, I'd like to volunteer."

"Impossible," said the Lady. And then she added, "But not impossible together."

Morgana frowned. "Both of us? How would that work?"

"I have an idea," said Emry. "Instead of taking travelers' unwanted daughters, why don't you make this place a refuge for children who are magic? Their parents can send them here for instruction. That way your son could join you and be around other children his age as well."

Morgana hated that she hadn't come up with the idea first. It was perfect. Being Queen of Lothia no longer appealed to her. She had no interest in politics and widowhood, of raising her son amongst scheming courtiers. He needed to be around other children. To learn discipline and humility and magic.

"Interesting," Morgana mused. "I'm not opposed to the idea."

Merlin smiled at his daughter. "How did you get so wise?"

Emry snorted. "Trust me, I'm not. I'm just really creeped out by the soap thing. Besides, you're a good teacher. And Castle Camelot can't have two court wizards."

There was something else they weren't saying, Morgana realized. She could barely sense Merlin's magic. It was gone. Lost, she suspected, in defeating Bellicent. He was just as hungry for this island's magic as she was.

"Then this island shall house all who come here with a talent for magic, and teach them of its uses," said Morgana. "Willyt and I will make sure of it."

"A wise choice," said the Lady, turning to Emry. "And you, wizard of Camelot. What will you do?"

That was a very good question.

And Emry wished she had an answer.

CHAPTER 66

On the journey home from Avalon, Arthur chose not to stay at travelers' inns, as he had always done, keeping his hood raised so he wouldn't be recognized as their king.

Instead, he rode to grand manor houses and spoke with the lords and ladies there, securing their loyalty and making certain his nobles acted with chivalry and duty toward their people.

His most faithful knight rode at his side, only making fun of him where no one could overhear. His court wizard, or maybe she was his girlfriend, or both, if that was allowed, rode slightly behind, cursing her horse, and making fun of both her companions where everyone could overhear.

They drank in the taverns with the villagers, listened to their stories, and helped when aid was needed. They healed the wounded, restored poor crops, fixed broken mills, and promised to send teachers and healers and magistrates to places where there were none.

Word of King Arthur's return trailed him in whispers, and when he arrived at Castle Camelot, he was not greeted as a ghost returned from the grave, but welcomed as their beloved king, returned in triumph from uniting all of England.

Queen Guinevere of Cameliard was the first to swear fealty. She did not take a knee, as she was holding her infant daughter in her arms, but merely kissed the king on both cheeks, promising love and friendship between their kingdoms and expressing her gratitude for all Camelot had done. At her side stood her court wizard, or maybe he was her consort, or both, if that was allowed, with a leather sling across his chest so he could carry his daughter and have his hands free for getting into trouble.

Arthur stared down at the child, whom they had named Avalon, and wondered who she would grow up to become. The girl was a princess, and most likely a wizard. But she didn't know any of that yet. Nor anything else of the world but her doting parents.

Arthur wasn't ready for that yet. And that was okay. He was nineteen years old, and he had time. He couldn't picture studying at a university anymore. Maybe that had been his chosen path, once, but too much had happened for him to find his way back to that eighteen-year-old lad he'd been, a spare to the throne, with a head full of dreams of potential futures.

When Guin and Emmett left for Cameliard, he watched them go with an ache in his chest because he would miss them, and because he would miss the rare time when they had all been young and foolish and lived in a castle together pretending no one was sarding anyone else's fiancée in the hedge maze.

He thought of his journey to the Four-Peaked Fortress, the debauchery of Gawain's house party in France, the tavern where he and Emry had danced, the terrible play with the wonderful special effects he'd seen in Brocelande, and Lance threatening to slay his nipple as they tested Excalibur on their quest to Avalon.

And then he thought of the council meetings that awaited him, the endless protocol and bowing, the courtiers who whispered that he was still unmarried, and the guards who fell asleep waiting for him outside the doors to the library.

And he knew what he would do. He would travel.

He couldn't stop being the King of England, but he could visit places beyond the borders of his kingdom, places where he was just a traveler. He thought of that day in Paris that he'd stolen with Emry, where they had explored the city without care, wandering the street markets and watching the sun set over the rooftops.

That was what he wanted. To be a part of the world. To experience life on his own terms, instead of everyone else's. And he hoped his wizard would feel the same.

◐ ◐ ◐

Emry lay in a magnificently warm bathtub, her eyes closed, pleased with her cleverness. She'd figured out how to enchant the water so blasts of air bubbled below the surface, kneading at the sore spots on her back. She'd spent the afternoon training in swordplay with Lance and Percival, and it turned out sparring was one thing she didn't have a talent for.

But she would improve, even if it took a lot of work. Because she wanted to become even more fearsome. A girl with magic was one thing. A girl with magic and a sword was quite another.

Besides, weapons training was a good excuse to wear trousers. Not that she cared what people thought as she walked the castle corridors. Okay, perhaps she cared a *little*.

When a knock sounded at her door, she sighed. Issie had promised to come by to return a book, and the girl's timing was terrible.

"I'm not dressed," she called. "Can you slip it under the door?"

"Er, is that a sex metaphor?" Arthur called back, amused.

Emry rolled her eyes and stepped from the bath, snapping her fingers to summon her dressing gown. "How would that be a sex metaphor?" she demanded, belting her gown closed and throwing open the door.

Arthur shrugged. "I could show you?"

He was leaning against the wall of the corridor, looking pleased with himself. Emry stuck her head out and was surprised to find it empty of guards. "Impressive," she said.

"I told them I was going to visit Lance and Percival."

"Solid lie."

"I know." Arthur followed her inside. "I should have thought of it ages ago. Then we could have done this all the time."

He reached a hand to her cheek and tilted her face up to his, kissing her as though he meant to do far more than just kissing. Emry shivered, not hating the idea. But then Arthur pulled away, his eyes dancing with mischief.

"What was that for?" she asked.

He shrugged. "Can't a king just kiss his court wizard because he feels like it?"

"I believe King Louis and Master Flamel would strongly disagree."

"Funny you should mention them," Arthur said, sitting down at the edge of her bed. He looked nervous, Emry realized. The kind of nervous that meant he had something to ask her.

"Oh god," Emry said, hoping it wasn't anything important. After all, she was in her dressing gown.

"I've been thinking."

"Never advisable. But go on."

"I'm leaving," Arthur said, biting his lip.

"You're leaving?" That was the last thing she'd expected him to say.

"I've spent my entire life trapped in this castle, and if I don't leave now, I'll never have the chance," he said.

"Where will you go?" she asked.

"Anywhere. Everywhere. Across the continent, and back again. It doesn't matter," he said. And then he reached for her hand. "The important part is, I want you to come with me."

"Come with you," Emry repeated, making sure she had it right. "Across the continent and back again?"

He nodded. "We can just be Arthur and Emry, and nothing else," he promised. "No courtiers, no gossip, no responsibilities."

It sounded perfect. Like the sort of thing they'd dream about doing one day when they were on their second pitcher of ale in a tavern, and everything felt fuzzy and hilarious, instead of depressing.

"Aren't you needed here?" she asked, leaning back against her wardrobe and twisting her damp hair into a braid.

Arthur shrugged, which was a yes. "I don't mean to leave forever. Just as a sort of . . . extended vacation."

"You can't go on a vacation from being king," Emry protested. "At least, I don't think you can?"

"That's why I'm going to call it something else," Arthur said, beaming at her.

"Not a honeymoon," Emry said, her stomach twisting with nerves.

"Don't worry. When I ask you to marry me, you'll know it," he assured her.

"Who says you're the one who's going to do the asking?" Emry returned.

Arthur choked. And then his lips hitched into a smirk. "Are you planning on asking me to marry you, wizard?"

Was she? She'd certainly never thought of it before that moment. But she found she didn't hate the idea. At least that way it would be on her terms, how she chose to spend her future. And with whom.

She shrugged, trying to defuse the seriousness of the moment. "One day, perhaps, if you don't mess things up," she said.

Arthur's cheeks were pink, and he was fidgeting with his jacket. "I'd like that," he managed. And then he cleared his throat. "So, what do you say, wizard? Are you coming with me?"

◐ ◐ ◐

"Leaving?" Lord Agravaine looked as if he might faint. "But . . . what am I to tell the people?"

Arthur shrugged. "Say I've gone off in search of the Holy Grail."

"The Holy Grail," Lord Agravaine repeated, stunned. "The most sacred relic in the Western world, which most definitely does not exist, and if it did, has been lost for centuries."

"Oh good, you know it," Emry said helpfully.

"I already pulled the sword from the stone and recovered Excalibur," Arthur reminded him. "A grail quest sounds like something I might do."

Emry tried not to laugh. Lord Agravaine glowered at her, clearly having decided this was her fault.

"And what will you really be doing?" asked Lord Agravaine, looking back and forth between the two of them.

Arthur grinned. "Going off to see the world. Together."

Lord Agravaine sighed. "Are you sure that's wise?"

"Probably not, but if there was ever a time to make a foolish decision, this is it. I'll return when Camelot needs their king once more. But I'm going. And so is my wizard."

"Percival and I are coming, too," Lance interjected from the doorway. Arthur hadn't realized he was there.

"For the last time, we don't need chaperones," Emry said, rolling her eyes.

Lance grimaced at the joke. "If you're telling everyone you're off in search of the Holy Grail, you'll need knights to come with you, to make it plausible."

Arthur considered this and nodded. "Clever," he said.

"Actually," Emry added, "it's the perfect excuse for any who wish to take their leave of court."

She's right, Arthur realized. He wasn't the only one who felt stifled by life in this castle. If he was going, he might as well make sure his friends had the same opportunity.

"Then I shall let it be known that any knights who wish to take on a grail quest will be given permission to do so," Arthur proclaimed.

Lord Agravaine looked horrified.

"Don't worry," Arthur told him. "For all I know, one of us really will return with a magical object. It's happened before."

"How hard can a Holy Grail be to fake?" Emry wondered aloud as Lord Agravaine's eyes bulged.

"There, you see?" said Arthur. "Emry's got it covered."

"You're not actually going to fake the Holy Grail as an excuse for a vacation, are you?" Lord Agravaine asked nervously.

"Of course not." Emry grinned.

◑ ◑ ◑

Two days later, a small collection of knights waited in the castle court-yard, clad in armor and crimson cloaks. They rode fine horses and wore shields painted with their house sigils. Some were of noble birth and some not, but all were of noble heart.

The King of Camelot joined them, dressed as plainly as any librar-ian. He carried a satchel laden with books, a collection of herbs, and a drinking horn that pulsed with magic. Around his waist was an ordi-nary sword in a plain scabbard. He was nineteen years old, and in love.

At his side rode a girl in her brother's clothing, her dark hair in a braid, a velvet cloak embroidered with stars flowing from her shoul-ders. She had a wand up her sleeve, a dagger at her waist, and a smirk on her lips.

"Ready?" she asked.

"It's not a race," Lance admonished.

"Last one to find the grail wins?" Arthur suggested.

Percival laughed. "Oh, that's much better."

"Only because if it were a race, I'd win," proclaimed Gawain.

"It's not too late to revoke his knighthood," said Tristan.

"Don't tempt me," said Arthur. He took one last look back at the castle, and then motioned for the guards to step aside.

"Camelot will be waiting," Emry promised.

"That's what I'm afraid of," Arthur said with a sigh.

And then, together, they rode through the castle gates, in search of their next adventure.

The End

Acknowledgments

If you're reading this, stop and get a pen. I'll wait. Do you have one—yes?—perfect. Now fill in your name on the line below:

I'd like to thank my readers, especially_____,
because this book wouldn't exist without you. I'm not kidding—I was writing an entirely different book when I got the call that my publisher wanted to buy Merlin 3. Never mind that the second book in the series wasn't out yet, that I hadn't pitched an idea, or written a single word. My incredible readers had spoken—loudly, all over the internet—and had willed this story you've just read into existence.

So thank you, truly, for your part in manifesting my dreams. Not every author gets to finish a series, and I'm honored that so many of you championed this one and made sure I could.

Thank you also to my wonderful editor, Jenny Bak, for your invaluable wisdom. And to my fearless agent, Barbara Poelle, for snatching my query out of the slush pile and expertly steering a half-finished manuscript into a three-book series. And of course, thank you to everyone at Penguin Teen for your dedication and enthusiasm.

I also owe an enormous debt of gratitude to the booksellers, the librarians, the educators, the loudmouths—you know who you are—who so fiercely shouted from the rooftops about my silly little Arthurian retelling and so kindly looked past the first cover. For those of you that roasted it instead, fair. I likely have you to thank for our gorgeous new cover direction, amongst so many other things.

To my daughter, who should be here just before this book is published, and who kept me company from beneath my laptop while I wrote it, I hope your bookshelf is always filled with stories about strong girls saving the world and finding love and friendship along the way.

Lastly, to Booktok, Booktube, and Bookstagram—I wished with all of my heart that you would find these books, and YOU DID, and it has been WONDERFUL. I hope you're just as in love with whatever I write next.

Speaking of, since this book series is over, and we can't make plans to meet up here in the acknowledgments again, I'm on Instagram if you'd like to follow my next adventures and add those stories to your shelves, too.